BRIGHT HORIZON

HJ WELCH

Bright Horizon
Pine Cove Book Four

Copyright © 2019 by HJ Welch

This book is a work of fiction. Names, places, and incidents are either products of the author's imagination or are used fictitiously. Any resemblance to actual events, locales, or persons, living or dead, is entirely coincidental.

All rights reserved. No part of this book may be used or reproduced in any manner whatsoever without written permission, except in the case of brief quotations embodied in critical articles and reviews.

1

BEN

It was a Tuesday morning when Ben Turner burned his favorite spiced apple muffins.

It was also the day he discovered he'd become a millionaire, but the muffin thing annoyed him first.

"Oh, fuck you *and* the bike you rode in on," Ben cried in dismay. It was his own fault. He'd completely forgotten to set his timer. Really, though, it wasn't the end of the world. He could make more. He just hated seeing anything go to waste, let alone delicious treats like that.

"Language, Benjamin." The owner, Lars Jansen, grumbled good-naturedly from where he was moving a tray of freshly baked rolls out front. The store had only just opened, but they still had a few customers hanging around, waiting to be served on their way to work or heading back home after an early workout.

Ben blushed, hoping no one had heard him. The music was playing softly in the background and a few people who were awake enough to be having conversations, so there was a chance he'd been lucky. He was the cute one in the store who the little old ladies liked to fuss over. It wouldn't do much good for the bakery's branding if they caught him swearing like a sailor.

"Sorry, Lars." Ben wafted a dish towel, trying to disperse the burned smell that was doing its best to override the bakery's usual aroma of rich coffee and warm bread. He tipped the ruined muffins out upside down onto a cooling rack, poking the bases. Those parts were fine – perfect even. If he sliced the blackened tops off, perhaps he could still salvage the bottom halves.

He could mull that over while he served the increasing crowd who were patiently waiting for Rise and Shine to start officially serving. So he took a deep breath and found his smile. He loved greeting their customers almost as much as the baking itself. He was lucky really. He might live a simple life, but at twenty-three he was pleased to say he was already on a path that made him happy.

Most days.

As he stepped from out the back, he immediately spied the tall, dour looking man in the somber brown tweed suit near the rear of the small crowd. He had to be from The Happy Baker Inc.

Those corporate asshats had gotten wind that Lars was coming up to retirement, and as much as the bakery seemed to be doing well on the surface, the reality was it was barely keeping above water. But the thought of selling Rise and Shine off to some faceless chain was heartbreaking to Ben, Lars, and everyone else who worked there.

Such a miserable-looking stiff had to be calling to pester from Happy Baker again. When Lars caught sight of the suit, his eyes widened in fear. Ben squeezed his shoulder. "It's okay. I'll deal with him. We're still not selling, right?"

"Right," Lars said. This was his life's work. Ben didn't want to see it pawned off to some soulless corporation that would change everything about it. So as much as he didn't want to speak to the goon either, he'd do this for Lars.

People always underestimated Ben. It really got under his skin, because in a way, they had a point. He knew he wasn't as self-assured as he wanted to be due to his petit stature. It was difficult to be taken seriously a lot of the time, being a short, slim guy. But for Lars and the bakery he puffed his chest out and pooled together all the feistiness he possessed.

"Thank you, Benjamin," Lars said. "Just send him away."

"I will," Ben promised.

To hell with it. The suit was behind several other people, so Ben would bide some time and serve them first, building up his confidence as he did. As it was morning, he was mostly handing out pastries for breakfast and uncut loaves for people to make their own sandwiches later. "Thank you, come again!" he said cheerfully several times before he looked up from the antique cash register...

...and his stomach dropped.

This was ridiculous. He couldn't keep almost having a heart attack every time he saw this guy. But it was *him*. Ben's beautiful man.

All thoughts of The Happy Baker Inc. and the burned muffins flew out of the window as Ben felt that usual goofy smile creep over his face. "Oh, hi," he said breathlessly as his man stepped closer.

Ben would have guessed he was in his mid to late-thirties, with soft brown hair and forest-green eyes. He had a medium height and build, but that still made him bigger than Ben. It was harder to see now fall was settling in and he was more inclined to wear a jacket, but Ben could usually make out toned muscles under the neatly ironed shirts he wore.

Ben imagined he worked in some sort of management position, maybe for an IT or tech company, or maybe he was the boss of some business here in Pine Cove or a neighboring town. He looked like he had a great job and didn't worry about money all the time, unlike Ben.

But none of that really mattered.

What mattered was the way his eyes lit up whenever he saw Ben.

Ben was sure he wasn't imagining it. They would just get that tiny bit wider and a smile would transform his face, showing a few lovely laughter lines around his mouth and eyes.

It was just a stupid crush, but it brightened Ben's days whenever he came in. "How's it going?" Ben asked, proud of himself for managing not to stutter.

Sure enough, the man smiled as he leaned his hands on the glass counter that was displaying all the bakery's goodies. No wedding ring. That didn't necessarily mean anything at all, but it gave Ben a little thrill of silly hope all the same.

"Yeah, pretty great," the man said happily. "Today's a cheat day, so I thought I'd get something naughty for breakfast."

I'd give you something naughty, Ben thought, all manner of sinful things flashing through his mind. Of course, someone so sophisticated would never be interested in a dumb twink like him, but it didn't hurt to dream.

Or fantasize. Quite vividly.

"Excuse me?" the tweed suit from the back growled impatiently.

Ben smiled but his eyes didn't leave his man's gaze. "Someone will be with you in just one moment, sir." As much as Ben loved customer facing, not everyone was a pleasure to deal with. This guy probably thought because he had money, he could skip the line. Whether it was to buy a cupcake or the whole damn store.

Ben's man chuckled, making Ben wonder if he knew he was plastering on a smile for the rude jerk.

"What can I get you today?" Ben asked him, forgetting about the tweed Happy Baker guy.

His man licked his lips and Ben tried not to groan. He looked so delectable in his well-fitted black suit and crisp white shirt. The top button was undone and he wasn't wearing a tie, so the dip at the base of his neck was showing along with a wisp of chest hair.

Ben tried not to imagine licking that sweet spot, and failed.

"I was hoping for a muffin?" Ben's man said as his eyes trailed over the display case.

Ben sighed. "Unfortunately, the muffins had a little accident this morning."

"Excuse me, sir?"

"I'm just with a customer, *sir*," Ben shot back.

His man definitely laughed that time. "Oh, that's a shame. What would you recommend instead?"

"Hmm," said Ben, not wanting this conversation to end. He loved the days where he and his man shared more than just a polite hello. "Maybe the cherry-almond Danishes?"

"Pardon me. Sincere apologies. Sorry, ma'am." Ben realized with increasing annoyance that the tweed suit was using his broad shoulders to barrel his way in front of the other customers. He was also speaking with an English accent. A fancy one, at that.

Ordinarily, Ben might have been excited. He wasn't sure he'd ever met a British person, and his mind immediately wanted to daydream about all his favorite books set in England. But this guy didn't look like any of his childhood heroes. In fact, he looked like he could be the villain of a modern-day Dickensian novel.

"Sir, there's a line," said Ben through gritted teeth. He'd be upset by this kind of behavior anyway, but it was interrupting the precious couple of minutes he had with his fantasy man. "If you'd just-"

"Mr. Turner," Mr. Tweed snapped, slapping a large white envelope on top of the display counter and huffing. "I simply must speak with you."

A chilly sensation washed through Ben. He glanced from his man, to the other customers, to Mr. Tweed, giving him a steely glare. "How did you know my name?" Happy Baker Inc knew who Lars was, not him.

"Because I am not here to purchase a *croissant*," Mr. Tweed said with a sneer. He straightened his brown-and-cream-striped tie and pushed the envelope toward Ben before clasping both hands over the handle of his expensive-looking, shiny leather briefcase. "My name is Mr. Cabot, and I am here on behalf of Aldridge Harding Carmichael."

"AHC?" Ben's man said with obvious interest. "What's one of London's top law firms doing in a small Pacific Northwest town, Mr. Cabot?" Whoa, how did he know that so fast? And…was Ben crazy, or had his man moved a little to put himself between Ben and Mr. Cabot?

"A-am I in trouble?" Ben was aware everyone was looking at him. "Is that…a subpoena?"

Mercifully, Lars seemed to have sensed there was an issue and stepped out from the back. "Okay, who's next? How can I help?" he asked, moving the small crowd over to the left, while Ben shifted to the right.

Mr. Cabot and Ben's man moved with him.

"It is not a subpoena." Mr. Cabot used a single finger to slide the envelope along the top of the counter, sniffed, then whipped a handkerchief from his inside jacket pocket to dab his nose. "I have however been tasked with delivering these documents to Mr. Turner in person," he said in a clipped voice, not even bothering to look at Ben's man even though he was clearly addressing him. "If you'll excuse us, Mr…?"

Ben's man raised his eyebrows. "Mr. Turner is entitled to have his own lawyer present when faced with a representative from the Magic Circle. That's an elite group of London lawyers," he explained to Ben with a wink, then looked back at Mr. Cabot. "Everyone in the world knows what you folks can be like."

Ben had a feeling that was an insult to Mr. Cabot, but he was too caught up with what was unfolding before him to worry about it either way.

"If Mr. Turner *has* legal representation-" Mr. Cabot began.

"Ben," his man asked, ignoring Mr. Cabot's splutter of indignation and turning toward Ben. "Do you have a dollar?"

"A dollar?" Ben repeated in confusion. But he retrieved one from his pocket anyway. "Sure, but why-?"

His man pinched the bill between his fingers and raised his eyes at Ben. "May I?" he asked softly, sending lustful shivers down Ben's spine. *Jesus*, it wasn't hard to imagine him asking Ben that same question in far more intimate circumstances.

That was ridiculous. *Get a grip*, Ben urged himself.

He nodded, letting his man take the dollar. Then his man broke into a dazzling smile. He folded the bill up, slipped it into his pocket, then thrust his hand forward at Mr. Cabot. "He does have legal representation! Elias Solomon of Pine Cove Legal Services. Pleased to make your acquaintance."

Ben almost choked on his own spit. His secret, silly crush was a *lawyer*. And he was jumping in to defend Ben without even being asked to. Ben knew he should be asking many serious questions as to what was going on right now, but all he could think was how fucking *hot* that was. He knew his man – Elias – was impressive. But a *lawyer*? That was awesome. Ben's dick got a little hard just thinking about it.

But he wasn't allowed to dwell on it long. Mr. Cabot gave

Elias's hand one quick squeeze, looking like he'd been forced to suck a lemon, then turned back to Ben. "Mr. Turner," he said, his voice ice-cold and silky. "I am here on behalf of the late Anne Grimaldi de Loutherbergh, CBE. Aldridge Harding Carmichael are handling the enactment of her last will and testament." He pursed his lips. "And the contesting thereof."

Ben blinked and waved his hands, trying to work out all the terms he'd just used. "Wait, what?" He could feel a panicked lump rising in his throat. "Who are you talking about? I don't know anybody called Anne...whatever you said. Last will? Do you mean I have an inheritance?"

Mr. Cabot's eyes were calculating as he dabbed the end of his nose with his handkerchief again. It was as if the homely bakery and its aroma were offending him.

"Everything is detailed in the documents I have provided," Mr. Cabot sneered. "However, as you have so eloquently pointed out, you were completely unaware of your great-grandmother. Her surviving family were equally ignorant of your existence. Therefore, they are already in the process of contesting the will. Your presence is not required in London nor Wiltshire, where the family estate resides. I was tasked to come and make the situation clear to you, and impress that your attendance of this matter need not be in person."

Elias blinked. "You came all this way to tell Ben that face-to-face," he said with his brow creased, "only to insist that he *doesn't* follow it up. Is that a threat, Mr. Cabot?"

Mr. Cabot gave Elias a sickly, wicked-looking smile. "Did I say it was a threat, Mr. Solomon?"

Ben got a chill down his back. Not only was Mr. Cabot tall and broad, but there was something dark about his slightly bloodshot eyes that sent a chill down Ben's spine. His heart was racing in confusion. He had some relative who had left him something, but her family didn't want him to have it?

Hang on a minute – her family would be *his* family as well, wouldn't it? He had more family he didn't know about? "How exactly is she related to me?"

Mr. Cabot sniffed and turned his cold eyes back to Ben. "She was your grandfather's mother. He was her oldest son. Your father's father."

"Gramps?" Ben clarified, emotion immediately making his voice thick as he snatched up the envelope. Grandpa Thomas had passed when Ben was only seven, but he'd taught Ben to make his very first Victoria sponge. He'd almost forgotten Dad had said he'd moved from England. Dad, and therefore Ben, never really known why Gramps had come to America.

Elias shifted fractionally again, very definitely aligning himself with Ben to look at Mr. Cabot. "If Mr. Turner is Mrs. Grimaldi de Loutherbergh's lawful great-grandson, why is anyone contesting the will?"

Mr. Cabot's nostrils flared. "I am not at liberty to discuss any further with regards to the family's – *my clients'* – legal matters, Mr. Solomon. However, the fact that your client was unaware of her very existence until five minutes ago speaks for itself, wouldn't you say? The Grimaldi de Loutherberghs will not have their estate divvied up piecemeal and given to some...*baker.*" He rolled his wide shoulders as Ben stared at him, his skin crawling.

There was something threatening about him, and not just his hostile language. Ben was glad he wasn't facing him alone, grateful again for Elias's good timing being in the bakery at just the right time this morning.

However intimidating Mr. Cabot was, though, indignation rose in Ben. How dare he talk to Ben like that? Ben mustered up some of that courage he'd been building when he offered to speak on behalf of Lars, and looked squarely at Mr. Cabot.

"Look," Ben said firmly. "I didn't ask for any will or inheritance or whatever, so I'd appreciate you treating me with a little more respect."

Mr. Cabot laughed. It didn't reach his eyes. "I've said all I have to say on behalf of the firm and of the Grimaldi de Loutherberghs, Mr. Turner. My plane leaves in two hours. The matter is settled. We are legally required to inform you of your inclusion in the will, but you are not to set foot in Wiltshire, or any other part of England for that matter. Is that understood?"

"I suppose that's not a threat either, Mr. Cabot?" said Elias with a raised eyebrow and a twitch of a smile that had no warmth to it. Mr. Cabot simply glowered at him, then Ben, then turned on his heel.

People hurried to jump out of his way like the parting of the Red Sea. There was a hush to the bakery as the crowd watched him march back out onto Pine Cove's boardwalk and into the chilly fall morning air. After the bell above the door tinkled and he strode out of sight, chatter gradually began to bubble up again. Lars made a big show of getting another co-worker to serve the next customer.

Fuck. What the hell had just happened? Why was Ben reeling like he'd just been accosted? He supposed he had, in a way. Why had Mr. Cabot hated him so much? How could Ben have a great-grandmother he'd never heard of? And why had she left him something in her will? Why didn't other members of her – *his* – family want him to have it?

Ben didn't realize he was shaking until he felt Lars's strong arm slip around his shoulder. Ben was holding the thick envelope with one hand, so Lars pressed a cup of sugary coffee into the other with a sympathetic look on his face. "We're good here, Ben. You go take a look at your letter, okay?"

Ben glanced at the other remaining customers who were looking at him with a mixture of curiosity and sympathy.

All except his man, Elias, who leaned over the counter to get closer to Ben.

Despite all his shock, Ben smelled his freshly applied aftershave that made him think of the ocean, and his cock throbbed.

Down, boy!

"I'm so sorry for interfering like that," Elias said, blinking his forest-green eyes. "I've just seen a lot of lawyers and legal assistants try and bully people, and he just set off all my alarm bells."

Ben spluttered, moving to the end of the counter to come out into the front café part of the store. "Please, don't be sorry" he said incredulously. "You were great! Um, are you really...?"

"A lawyer?" Elias chuckled as he led Ben to sit at one of the empty tables. Luckily, at this time of day, most people didn't stick around to enjoy their purchases, so there was one free. "Yes, absolutely. I worked for over a decade at Mansell and Collier in Seattle. Now I practice here in town." As Ben sat down with his coffee, Elias stopped and raised his hands. "Sorry, I'm assuming you might want some help looking over those documents, but if you need a moment-"

"N-no, please," Ben spluttered. *Jeez*, it would be nice to get a clean word out in front of this guy. "I'd *love* some professional advice. I...oh..." He watched dumbfounded as Lars placed another coffee and two cherry-almond Danishes on the table in front of them.

"Mr. Solomon will look after you, Ben," Lars said with deep sincerity, before rushing back to his customers.

Ben felt like his eyebrows were in his curly bangs. Could this morning get any weirder? He'd had a rude Brit accost him, and now he was having a business breakfast with the guy he'd been crushing on for months.

Well, it was probably best to just roll with it.

"I helped Lars out with something a little while back," Elias said bashfully as he sat and took a sip of his coffee, gesturing to the pastries. Ben had no idea why he'd be shy about admitting that. From Lars's attitude offering them the free Danishes, Ben had to guess that Elias had done a good job.

Ben watched Elias rub the lid of his coffee cup with his thumb and tried not to think what that might feel like on his nipple. Fucking hell, he was sex obsessed. Normally that didn't bother him, but this was an adult situation and he needed to focus.

Lars must know how Elias took his coffee as well, because he beamed as he took another sip. Ben was aware that Elias liked no sugar with low-fat milk. Ben had three sugars and full cream, because he was apparently a child who wanted all his teeth to fall out.

"I really have never heard of this great-grandmother," he said weakly.

Elias chuckled. He did that a lot, Ben realized. It was a comforting, easy sound. "Clearly. And your family here in town never mentioned her?"

Ben shook his head, fiddling with the corner of the envelope. "Both my parents were only children, and the grandparents who were still alive when I was born all passed before I turned ten." He smiled sadly. "I'm an only child, too. I always dreamed of a big secret family, waiting out there for me. But as I grew up, I forgot about that daydream." *Until now.*

"Well," said Elias, leaning his elbows on the small table between them. "Maybe it's not a daydream after all? Mrs.

Grimaldi de Loutherbergh obviously knew about you. Do you want to open that letter and see what it says?"

Ben licked his lips and thought about it. He wasn't sure he really wanted to know now, seeing as Mr. Cabot had told him his estranged family was angry about it and already contesting what it said. It was so strange. Ben was used to it just being him and his folks...did he have great aunts or uncles? Second cousins? Who else was out there he could call kin that he'd never even known existed?

Damn. All those holidays when he'd felt ungrateful for being so lonely, he'd had more relatives after all. He'd always tried to be content that it was just him and his parents. How many gay kids were disowned by their families? But it was difficult not to feel jealous when he saw families on the TV with dozens of members all together for Thanksgiving and Christmas, and when his Facebook feed showed the same thing from his friends throughout the holidays. Was all that about to change?

It didn't matter if they already hated him as much as Mr. Cabot seemed to imply, but curiosity was winning out. What *had* his great-grandmother left him? Who were all these people he hadn't heard of until now?

Only one way to find out.

He nodded at Elias, then carefully ripped open the top of the envelope. He half expected it to have a wax seal, but it was a pretty ordinary-looking white envelope with what looked like the fancy London law firm's logo embossed in the paper.

There were several sheets inside along with a return envelope. Ben tried to skim through and pick up the important points, but the words didn't seem to make sense. There was so much legal jargon and it looked like it had all been photocopied twenty damn times it was so blurry. He bit his lip, the confusing language swimming in front of his eyes. It might as well have been written in Elvish.

Humiliation was bubbling up inside him. He'd never had to deal with anything like this before and he wasn't sure what he was supposed to do. College-educated kids would have dealt with hundreds of forms, but Ben was completely lost.

"I-I don't..." he said, keeping up his stammering tradition. "It's all – uh – I can't..."

Elias squeezed his wrist. Ben looked up from the papers in surprise to see Elias giving him a kind smile. His hand was deliciously warm against Ben's skin, but of course he removed it when he'd gotten Ben's attention.

"Do you want me to take a look?" He wasn't pushy. Ben felt assured handing over the various documents. Ben pulled flakes of pastry off his Danish as he watched Elias's green eyes dart over the pages.

They got bigger. And bigger.

"Ben?" he said slowly. Ben noted how tingly it made him feel to hear Elias say his name. But mostly he was preoccupied with what the hell that will was telling them.

"Elias?"

Elias shook his head and rubbed the side of his nose, his eyes still like saucers. "Do you understand what this is saying?"

"Not one bit," Ben said seriously.

Elias licked his lips again. "It says that your great-grandmother has left you *her entire estate.* The family house, the grounds, and the hard cider business they have been running for several decades."

A wave of shock washed over Ben and he gripped the edge of the small table. He wished he hadn't drunk any coffee now, as it felt like it started to curdle in his stomach. "What?" he whispered. "T-that sounds like a lot?"

Elias held his gaze, not flinching. "I'm converting from

British sterling off the top of my head here," he said. "But Ben…you are, as of this moment…worth approximately *sixty-five million dollars."*

Ben stared.

Then he laughed.

Then he fell off his chair, smashed into the wooden floor, and completely blacked out.

2

ELIAS

ONE THING WAS FOR SURE, THIS WAS *NOT* HOW ELIAS HAD expected his morning to go.

He always looked forward to his Rise and Shine visits. Of course they did excellent pastries, but there was always a chance that his adorable young man might be working. He seemed to be there most days, but Elias was always irrationally disappointed when he wasn't serving, or if he got caught with another customer.

Ben, his employee badge read. Elias tried not to use his name, because that seemed a little creepy. Like he had an unfair advantage when Ben had no clue as to Elias's name.

They seemed to be past that now.

"Ben, can you hear me?" Elias asked, trying not to panic.

The second Ben had fainted – understandably from the shock of suddenly discovering he was a potential millionaire – Elias had also dropped to the floor and implemented his first aid training. Luckily, Ben didn't appear to have hit his head. Elias had him lying on his back with his feet propped up on Elias's thigh. Absurdly, Elias thought the way he was down on one knee could almost look like a proposal.

Crazy.

Ben blinked his eyes open. "Wha-?"

Elias sighed in relief, nodding to the bakery owner, Lars, who was hovering anxiously, as well as the other concerned customers. They'd gotten quite the show from Ben this morning between Mr. Cabot demanding to speak to him and then the fainting.

"Whoa, take it easy," Elias said as Ben attempted to sit back up. "Just give the blood another minute to get to your head. You passed clean out."

Ben allowed Elias to gently push his shoulder so he lay back down. It was impossible for Elias's body to ignore the way touching Ben after all this time was making him react. He was being a creep, though. This guy had to be twenty years younger than him and he was in a crisis. This was no time for Elias's dumb puppy crush.

If only his cock would get that memo.

"I feel ridiculous," Ben mumbled as he clasped his hands on his belly and glanced around the bakery.

Elias grinned. "Well, you look ridiculous, so at least you match."

Ben groaned. "Asshole," he said playfully.

Were they flirting? Urgh, Elias needed to get a grip. They couldn't be flirting, because Ben was a baby. Just because he acted mature didn't mean Elias could let this flight of fancy he'd been nurturing get away from him.

Elias had moved back home to Pine Cove several years ago after city life had begun to lose its appeal. He'd always been a regular at Rise and Shine, so he'd noticed right away when the beautiful young man with the honey-blond curls and hazel eyes had started working at the bakery about a year and a half ago. There was just something about him that made Elias's stupid heart flip.

Enough. This was inappropriate, no matter the circumstances, but especially considering Ben's recent news.

"I think we can probably get you up now," Elias said, "if you feel able."

Ben nodded, swinging his legs down from Elias's thigh and sitting up on the wooden floor of the bakery. It was so quaint in there, which was why Elias and most of Pine Cove adored it. Burlap bags printed with faded grain names lined the high shelves. Flowers grew from tin watering cans and the menus were written on chalkboards. Outside, there was a vintage bicycle with more gorgeous flowers growing from the front basket, even at this time of year.

Elias always got a sense of home when he came in here.

Ben looked dazed, his forehead creasing. "Did you just say what I thought you said?" he asked in a small voice. "About the sixty-five...um..." *Million dollars.* Unsurprisingly, he seemed overwhelmed.

"Well, the will says fifty million pounds. I checked the exchange rate recently, though. So, yeah..." Elias nodded sympathetically. "Hey, do you think your boss would let you take a bit of personal time? I'd like to help you look through these documents a little further."

Ben's eyes widened. "I can't afford a lawyer," he stammered.

Elias couldn't help it. He snorted. "I think you can," he said, hoping he wasn't pushing Ben too far. Luckily, he got the joke and rolled his eyes with a chuckle. But Elias knew this was complicated. "Seriously, though. Don't worry about that. My firm takes on a percentage of pro bono work, and I don't have any on my caseload right now. What do you say? Do you think Lars can spare you for a little while?"

"Go, go!" They looked over to see Lars already waving them away from behind the counter. "The others are here," he said in what Elias had discovered long ago to be a soft Dutch accent. "We'll be fine. This is very important."

It was.

Elias smiled at Ben as he helped him to his feet. "Would you be betrayed if I suggested we go to Sunny's? We can get a booth for some breakfast and have a little space as well as privacy to talk this through."

The relief on Ben's face made Elias's stupid heart dance. Ben was just grateful for the help. This wasn't like some breakfast date. Elias needed to be professional.

"That sounds great," Ben said. "I'll just grab my things."

A few minutes later, they were strolling down the boardwalk in the bright November sunshine. Halloween had just gone, so the stores and arcade were getting geared up for Thanksgiving. There was a chill in the air, but with their coats and gloves on, it was very pleasant.

"I'll warn you now," Elias said as they strolled toward the diner. "I'm an American lawyer. UK law is different. There might only be so much I can advise you."

Ben snorted. "My legal expertise extends to that TV show with the two hot guys and one of them is only *pretending* to be a lawyer."

He glanced over at Elias, who suddenly felt he was being tested. Except it didn't feel like an exam in the slightest.

It felt like a gift.

Ben had just freely admitted he was into men.

"Damn, those guys had great chemistry," Elias said, shaking his head. "I liked the girlfriend well enough, but I always just wanted to gently push her out of their way."

This time, Ben's relief wasn't as obvious, but it was just as welcome. "I always wanted to set her up with the sassy PA lady, myself."

It felt so easy and natural chatting with Ben about TV legal dramas as they approached Sunny Side Up. Elias gave up wrestling with himself and conceded there wasn't anything wrong that they were doing. He could enjoy good conversation with a handsome young man.

In fact, he was starting to suspect Ben wasn't as young as Elias might have first thought. Yes, he was petit, but there was a sharpness to his eyes that made him seem older.

Elias absolutely didn't miss the way Tyee Perkins's eyes darted between him and Ben as they walked into Sunny's, inhaling the delicious smell of fried potatoes and steaming coffee. Elias loved both the husbands who ran the diner, especially the more friendly Tyee who was almost always out front, greeting customers. But Elias really hoped he wouldn't say anything awkward to them in that moment.

Luckily, Ben was still clutching his official-looking white envelope, a slightly dazed look on his face. Tyee was nothing but courteous. "A booth, for breakfast and work?" he asked, picking up a couple of menus for them from the stand.

Elias smiled gratefully. "Thanks very much."

As they walked through the busy diner, Elias caught sight of Tyee's youngest son, Micha, happily serving a table full of moms with strollers. He didn't see Elias looking, but that was okay. Elias knew his boyfriend, Swift, and liked to think he'd had a little something to do with encouraging them getting together. It was so heartwarming to see people finding someone special.

Even if it did cause him the smallest, *tiniest* pang of sadness.

He mentally shook himself. He had no right to be jealous of happy couples. He was the master of his own destiny. Maybe the stars would align and he'd finally meet his own special guy. For now, he had work to do.

He'd already shot his boss a quick text to explain he'd be late as he was with an unexpected client. Elias knew he was a model employee, so he didn't feel too guilty. Thankfully his boss agreed, telling him not to hurry in.

So after he and Ben placed their orders with Tyee's perky granddaughter, Rona, they had all the time they needed.

"So…I'm a millionaire?" Ben asked quietly over their coffee and orange juice.

He'd tipped three heaped spoons of sugar into his mug, and was now stirring it absently as he stared at the will he'd opened out in front of him. Elias knew he shouldn't even really have coffee at all because of his health, but he hadn't drunk that last one and he'd stick to green tea for the rest of the day. He envied Ben's carefree attitude toward his food.

Elias sipped his own drink and licked his lips. "It certainly looked that way."

Ben rubbed his temples. "This is crazy, though. How can some lady in England who I've never even heard of leave me all of this? *Why* would she do that? No wonder her family is pissed."

Elias tilted his head. "Be that as it may, they call it a last will for a reason. If this is what she wanted, they should honor that."

"But what if I don't want it?" Ben asked earnestly. Elias's heart went out to him. He knew he was being a sap, but it was refreshing to see such pureness. How many people would be knocking others out the way for this opportunity?

"You don't want sixty-five million dollars?" Elias asked gently.

A wry smile twitched at Ben's mouth. "I didn't say *that,*" he conceded, making Elias chuckle. "It's just, well, it feels like I'm taking this house from its rightful owners, as well as the business. No wonder they hate me and don't want me anywhere near them. What do I know about orchards? Let alone making cider? I read that in Europe that means hard cider, the alcoholic kind. I've only been able to drink for two years!"

So he was twenty-three. Definitely older than Elias had presumed, but still too young for him at thirty-nine.

Still, he couldn't seem to help himself from leaning over and placing his hand over Ben's hand and rubbing his thumb against his warm skin. "It's a lot of responsibility. But well…"

"What?" Ben asked, his eyebrows rising.

Elias shrugged. "Just something I feel I need to say after all the cases I've seen. This could be some sort of scam."

Ben frowned. "How?"

"Honestly, I'm not sure," Elias said. "But experience has taught me to be vigilant when things seem too good to be true. This is like something out of a film."

"You're telling me," Ben scoffed. "I feel like Harry Potter getting that letter from Hogwarts."

Despite his best efforts, Elias's heart fluttered. He adored Harry Potter, even though he'd read it as an adult.

He gave Ben a sympathetic smile. "This very well could all be exactly as it seems. The London firm is certainly real. But then that leaves you open for a different kind of abuse."

Ben's eyes narrowed. "From the rest of the family. It's kind of fishy that they really don't want me to go over there and stop them contesting this Anne's wishes." Elias couldn't but feel a small spark of pride. Ben was pretty smart.

"Agreed," he said as their food arrived. Steaming, thick oatmeal for him, and a stack of glistening, sweet-smelling banana pancakes for Ben. The diner was full of chatter around them and the sounds of other customers clinking their cutlery, but Elias felt like he and Ben were in their own little world. "And if that's the case – if Mrs. Grimaldi de Loutherbergh really did want you to have all of this – what right do they have to meddle with that?"

"Mr. Cabot was pretty clear," Ben said in a small, slightly

trembling voice. Elias prickled. He loathed bullies, and Mr. Cabot had reeked of intimidation tactics. Elias wondered if he was even a lawyer, or simply hired muscle.

"He doesn't have a leg to stand on," said Elias firmly. "It's tough if they don't want you to come over and defend your position. You're perfectly entitled to do so."

Ben groaned and poked at his sticky pancakes. "It feels like I'm being greedy. And why should I even accept it? She's been alive all this time, and I never knew. Gramps passed fifteen years ago. Why didn't she reach out to me when she was alive?"

Elias frowned and shook his head. "If this inheritance is rightfully yours, you should damned well fight for it. For whatever reason, your great-grandmother wanted this to be yours. So why shouldn't it be?"

Ben appeared to think that over for a minute. "I don't know. Maybe." He didn't sound all that convinced. "But what can I do, anyway? I'll just have to sit here in Pine Cove and wait and see if they can argue against me. I mean, maybe I could hire a lawyer over there?"

"You could and you should," Elias agreed. "But would you consider flying over there?"

Ben barked out a laugh. "Last-minute flights to London? How much would that set me back? I don't actually have any of the money yet and I'd be a fool to gamble thousands on credit cards if I never got the chance to pay it off again. I might not get a cent."

"Very sensible," Elias agreed, meaning it.

But this was Ben's whole life – this could change everything for him. Was it really fair to let strangers argue against what Ben's great-grandmother had wanted for him?

The words were out of his mouth before he could even double-check himself.

Because the thing about being thirty-nine was it meant

that Elias was almost forty. And forty scared the ever-loving shit out of him. In the past several months, he'd been anxious that he hadn't been doing everything he'd wanted with his life, letting past mistakes hold him back. There was a prevailing sense that he needed to make up for lost time.

He thought of Harry Potter and all the other books he'd read before that as a child. His mid-life crisis had reawakened the sense of adventure he'd felt so strongly as a boy.

So in that split-second, his suggestion seemed like the obvious solution.

Until he actually said it.

"I have an *obscene* amount of air miles."

Ben paused with a chunk of syrupy pancake halfway to his mouth, staring at Elias. "Huh?"

'Huh' was right.

"I mean, uh," Elias bumbled, shaking his head. "Forget it, that's insane."

Ben lowered his fork and frowned. "Yeah, no. I couldn't take your air miles."

But Elias chewed his lip. *Was* it so insane? "The thing is," he said slowly. "The reason I have so many is that I literally never use them. I fly all the time internally for work, but if I take vacation time, I just spend it here in town with friends. They're honestly going to waste."

Ben was giving him a really serious look. "You don't know me, but you'd be willing to do this?"

Elias licked his lips. Yeah, when he put it like that, it did seem nuts. "Sorry," Elias mumbled. "I probably sound so weird right now. I just like to solve problems."

To his surprise, Ben laughed. "No, you sound incredibly generous. Elias, if you're serious, that would be so unbelievably kind. I...I don't know what to say."

Maybe this wasn't creepy or insane.

Maybe this was the adventure Elias had been looking for.

"I could book flights for you," he said. "That would be absolutely no issue. But…" he huffed. If he was going to jump in, he might as well do it with both feet. "I could accompany you so you don't have to face these people alone. Unless – sorry, that's ridiculous. You probably have a boyfriend or a parent you'd want support from."

Ben raised his eyebrows and scoffed. "Definitely no boyfriend. And my folks are…well, they don't really travel. They're a bit old, but they're also completely out of their depth the second they leave town. I can't remember the last time they left the state, let alone the country. Their outlook on life is generally 'don't rock the boat.'"

"Oh," Elias said, trying not to get his hopes up. Now he'd suggested this crazy plan, he was kind of keen to just do it. When was the last time he'd done something this spontaneous? "Well, a friend then. I don't want you to think I'm offering these miles assuming I'd get a jaunt to England."

Ben gave him a funny look. "I didn't think that," he said, sounding fairly sincere. "I mean, I have some friends. But… okay, *I'm* the one who's going to sound nuts now. But I personally think I'd be a moron to turn down someone who actually knows what they're doing. I know you said British law is different, but you're still a lawyer here. There must be some overlap? Or at least you might be able to tell if I'm being screwed over better than lil' old small-town me."

Elias wasn't sure he was still breathing. Was this really happening?

Well, if it was, it was basically business. At the most friends. It wasn't like Ben was inviting him on vacation to a country he'd always dreamed of going to.

Because he had. Elias had wanted to go to England his whole life. He had to be careful he wasn't just using Ben to get his wish. But he didn't think so. It was just a happy coincidence.

"I *would* be able to help you," Elias said, toying with his oatmeal. It had gone cold and he'd hardly even taken a bite. "And there are plenty of alarm bells going off about this whole situation. I'd worry about you facing this family alone."

Ben chuckled and looked at Elias through long, golden lashes, making Elias's stomach flip. "Have we both lost our minds? I don't think we've spoken more than a hundred words to each other before today. But...I kind of love this plan. If my life is going to turn completely upside down – why not jump in with both feet?"

Elias rubbed his temple and shook his head. "That's exactly what I just thought."

Ben set his cutlery down and pushed his mostly full plate aside. "I don't want you to feel obliged. This would only be if you'd like to go to England. It's a hell of a long way to go."

Elias's insides twisted as he smiled, trying not to get tearful. After so many years unable to fly internationally, he couldn't think of anything he wanted more. "I've dreamed of going to England since I was a child and read The Lion, the Witch and the Wardrobe."

"Oh my god, me too! I *love* that book!" Ben exclaimed, grinning.

Elias's heart skipped a beat. He wouldn't have expected Ben to have read The Chronicles of Narnia, but why not? Elias was starting to think he'd grossly underestimated Ben as a pretty maker of cupcakes. He had more depth to him than that, evidently. And he wanted to travel to England as well? Most young guys wanted to head to big cities or party resorts, not the idyllic countryside of Great Britain.

For a second, they just stared at each other. Something

bloomed in Elias's chest that he wasn't sure how to describe. Hope? Excitement?

Ben sat back in his seat, looking stunned. Then half a smile crept onto his face. "So, really," he said, a glint in his eye, "if I let you come along, I'd be doing *you* a favor?"

Elias's laugh was so loud he felt people turn and look, but he didn't pay them any mind. It was probably relief, exhilaration, nerves, and incredulity, all rolled into one.

"We can both help each other out. How does that sound?"

Ben grinned. It was a wicked, delicious thing that made Elias's insides squirm with desire. Of course nothing of that nature was going to happen between them. However, he couldn't help but feel elated all the same.

Ben thrust his hand out. "I think it sounds like we're going on an adventure."

Elias didn't know if he was purposefully quoting from The Hobbit, but it seemed incredibly appropriate. All he knew was that he reached out and shook Ben's hand, his skin warm and his grip firm.

They were indeed going on an adventure. And Elias was surprised by how much he couldn't wait to leap headfirst into the unknown with Ben.

3

BEN

WAS BEN OUT OF HIS MIND? WAS HE GOING TO FIND HIMSELF strangled to death and thrown in the River Thames? Who in their right mind would accept an offer from a near stranger to fly across the Atlantic Ocean, meet their long-lost family, and involve them in some serious legal issues?

Ben, apparently. Because as crazy as he was aware this sounded on paper, inside he knew that was exactly what was going to happen.

And it had *nothing* to do with his silly little crush.

If Elias had turned out to be an insurance broker or IT engineer or a manager at Pine Cove First and National Bank, there was no way Ben would have indulged in this farfetched scheme. But the fact of the matter was that Elias had a solid legal background – even if it wasn't in British law – and the air miles to enable them both to travel for free. Otherwise, Ben was powerless to these people who, rightly or wrongly, had decided he wasn't owed this inheritance.

It probably *didn't* hurt that his surprise lawyer was super-hot. Would Ben have accepted this offer from anyone else? If one of the bakery's regulars was a greasy sixty-something guy, or a mom with two kids who just happened to be a lawyer too, would Ben be preparing to hop on a plane with them right now?

He knew full well he almost certainly wouldn't, but what did that actually matter? He could feel guilty that his crush had turned out to be on someone who could genuinely help him in this crazy mess, or throw away the opportunity of legal aid when he really needed it.

However, no matter how many times he told himself all of this, the thought of telling his parents everything made him want to black out again.

It was utterly preposterous. Outrageous. *Absurd.* Ben was no more a millionaire than he was a bodybuilder. He had been talked into going away with an older man who he was besotted with, and therefore clearly vulnerable to being manipulated by. He was being reckless and stupid.

So then he should surely decline the offer to fly to London and forget he ever saw that will. Right?

That option, somehow, seemed even more unbelievable.

He was distracted all of the rest of the day. Lars did his best to be sympathetic, bless him. However, in the end even he lost his patience and banished Ben out back to cleaning duty.

Ben had trouble concentrating at the best of times, unless he got hyper focused. As pissed as he was at being told off like a child, he knew that Lars knew this, too. He was fully aware how soothing Ben found repetitive tasks, even though in theory he preferred creative ones. That was how he found himself getting through a mound of dirty dishes without even knowing he'd done it, switching his brain off in an almost meditative state.

Taking his mind off the problem helped ease his stress for a while, but Ben knew that as soon as he was left to chew over it all by himself again, he was going to be right back where he started. He needed to talk it through, but not with his parents. He needed to know where he stood before he faced them. As much as he loved them, they were never good at big changes, making decisions, or doing anything that might appear even remotely reckless.

He had to be ready with a plan to present to them.

Then who could he confide in?

Not Elias. They'd already talked enough and agreed they were going to jump in with both feet. If Ben texted him now, it might feel like he was backtracking, even though he absolutely wasn't. He just needed to vocalize this crazy plan a bit more and convince himself it was as good an idea as it had felt in Sunny Side Up that morning.

The fact that he even *could* text Elias was kind of unbelievable. After over a year of pining, Ben would never have thought the two of them would swap numbers. He kept looking at his phone, like it was somehow a trick. But the test hellos they'd sent each other at the diner confirmed it wasn't.

It was stupid because this was the most they'd ever spoken, but Ben had felt so reassured hashing all this out with Elias. Possibly because Elias was a proper grown-up, the kind Ben hoped to be one day, with his shit apparently together. It meant that Ben really trusted him despite not actually knowing him at all. It was only once they'd parted ways had Ben's doubts started creeping in. Was he being gullible? It didn't feel like it, but he was quite aware of how little real-world experience he had.

He needed to talk to someone who had at least some, if not a lot more.

Ben had friends at work and a few from his high school days, as well as several online buddies he was probably closer to than anyone thanks to their anonymity. Sometimes, it was easier to share your deepest secrets with people you'd never met, whose real faces you hadn't ever seen.

However, the thought of trying to explain everything that was going on to any of those people seemed too daunting. It was too random. As Ben left the bakery that afternoon, he felt restless, convinced the answer was just within his grasp. Who would believe him that, yes, it really did look as if some crazy old relative had left him an estate worth millions, but there was some kind of mysterious family drama going on, and that he was considering jetting across the world to secure his fortune with an older man who Ben was completely infatuated with-

Oh, right.

There was only one person in the entire town who led an even crazier life than that.

Ben just hoped he was *in* town, and not scuba diving in the Seychelles or appearing in a Below Zero music video or something equally ridiculous.

"Darling!" Emery Klein cried after the third ring on his cell. "I'm just having my hedgehog's nails manicured. How are you?"

That wasn't ridiculous at all.

Ben was sitting on one of the benches overlooking the lake that Pine Cove was built around. The water glinted in what was left of the afternoon sun and the wind coming off the rippling surface was bitingly cold, cutting through Ben's coat and making him shiver. He took a deep breath and screwed up his eyes. "I just became a millionaire and I'm thinking of flying to London with a complete stranger."

Emery squealed. Ben had to hold the phone away from his ear for a second. "Oh em gee, this is *everything!* I want to hear it all. No! Wait! How soon can you get to Aquarium? She'll have a porn star martini and something colorful to shoot. Preferably something we can light on fire. See you in half an hour. Love you! Mwah!"

Ben wouldn't say he was best friends with the lavish

social media influencer, but they'd become quite close over the last couple of years. They'd met through the high school's LGBT club alumni, attending many events together and eventually becoming friends outside of the group. Then there had been that one time where Emery had been given free tickets to promote something or other for his work, so had whisked Ben off to Vegas not long after Ben's twenty-first birthday. That kind of experience went a long way to bonding people.

In fact, if Elias hadn't have made his mad-cap suggestion, Emery might have been a good person to ask to go with Ben to England for moral support. He traveled extensively and had money of his own. Not exactly millions, but enough that he never let Ben pay for dinner or drinks or even the movies. He probably would have come to the UK in a heartbeat to meet these estranged relatives.

But he wasn't Elias.

Because Elias was a *lawyer.* No other reason.

When Emery said half an hour, he really meant an *hour* and a half. So Ben knew he had time to head back home, where he lived with his folks, have a quick shower, change his clothes, then grab an Uber over to the town's only gay bar. His parents never really pressed him on his comings and goings, so he was able to fend them off with a simple 'fine' when they asked how his day was. He'd explain it all to them later...once he could fully explain it to himself.

Aquarium might have been Pine Cove's only queer bar, but that was because they didn't need another. It had fabulous decor, great music, and was fiercely inclusive of all the LGBT community, unlike some bars Ben had been to in other towns which just catered to gay men. Some nights were country and some nights were rock and some were even completely sober. They hosted drag acts and poetry readings and had even done still life classes and tarot readings before.

Having Aquarium had made growing up gay in this small town so much easier. It was always difficult to be different from most people around you, but knowing there was a place he could find others like him had always made Ben feel less alone. Having the bar and also Sunny Side Up, which was also run by a gay couple, meant he'd never felt so different that he couldn't cope.

It was the perfect place to come in his state of turmoil, and not just because of the excellent cocktails they made. Sitting surrounded by the glittery blue wallpaper and all the gorgeous under-the-sea paraphernalia made him feel calmer.

Whatever was going on, he could get through it.

To paraphrase his favorite playwright: Ben might have been small, but he was fierce.

He took little sips of one of the two porn star martini drinks while he waited for Emery to arrive in a cloud of glitter. He spent a few minutes scrolling through his Facebook. Everyone seemed to be having pretty normal days.

The thought of trying to convey what he was feeling right now in a few written sentences was laughable. If he posted an update saying he was suddenly some sort of English aristocrat, absolutely no one would believe him.

He didn't believe it himself.

"Now, the important question is," Emery said as he materialized through the crowd of Tuesday night drinkers, "whether or not this is flammable."

He dropped into the opposite side of the small booth Ben had managed to grab for them, pointing at the green shots next to their cocktails. Ben had very strict instructions on what they should do with them if they ever wanted to be allowed in the bar again.

He wasn't worried, though. Emery knew what he was doing.

Ben's fabulous friend was wearing thigh-high black boots, denim shorts that were basically briefs, and a flowy peasant top. Ben might have felt underdressed, but Emery never made you feel like that. He always just wanted you to be your most *you*. For Ben, that was a pretty simple pair of jeans and T-shirt. So far, he hadn't really mastered dressing like an adult.

But then there was the jock-strap under his jeans that no one else needed to know about, and he felt appropriately dressed after all.

He sighed in relief and nudged one of the shots toward Emery. "The bartender said it's absinthe. So, yes, flammable."

Emery gasped and clutched at his top. His highlighter shimmered under the disco lights. "Absinthe? On a *school night*." Then he laughed. Some might have described it as maniacal. "This is why I love you, beautiful. Look! Mama has a lighter!"

Ben wasn't convinced this was the best idea, but after the day he'd had, he needed something to shake a few brain cells loose. For once, he wasn't working at the bakery the next day, so no harsh early morning start for him.

He followed Emery's lead as they lit the alcohol on fire, slammed their palms over the shot glasses to suffocate the flame, inhaled the fumes, then knocked the absinthe back in one.

Jesus fucking Christ. That would put hairs on your chest. Both Ben and Emery coughed and spluttered, and Ben was grateful he'd also thought to get ice water for them both. Holy fuck, why had he thought that was a good idea?

"You maniac," Emery said with tears in his black-lined eyes. "Let's never do that again."

Ben gave it three weeks, for Emery at least. He'd probably need a few months.

Or years.

"So," Emery said once they'd calmed down and finished their waters. The absinthe had been like fire down Ben's throat and he could already feel it swimming inside his veins. He enjoyed drinking, but he'd have to see how he did sipping more of his porn star martini.

"So," Ben parroted, looking pointedly at Emery.

Emery slid a lip gloss from his pocket and considered Ben through his dark lashes as he applied it. "You weren't kidding, were you?" he said in all seriousness. "You've come into some money."

He wasn't sure why he was nervous. He'd already told Emery the basics. But he was still glad that there was no one else around to overhear them aside from the fish in the tanks next to their booth. It was still so ridiculous to say out loud. However, the alcohol was thrumming through his blood, and he was starting to feel like maybe it wasn't quite as crazy as he'd thought. Other people led thrilling lives. Just because Ben's had been uneventful until now didn't mean he wasn't due his fair share of excitement.

"So apparently, my great-grandmother passed away."

Emery placed a hand on Ben's arm and gave him a sincere look. "I'm sorry, gorgeous."

Ben shook his head. "I don't like the idea of anyone dying, but I never met her. I had no idea she existed. But she's left me *everything*. Her whole estate in England."

"And what's that worth?" Emery asked.

Ben told him.

"I'll get more shots," Emery said, jumping to his feet.

"No, no!" Ben pulled Emery back into his seat and pushed his cocktail closer in front of him. "Let's finish these first, and I'll try and explain."

So he did.

"And this guy Elias just *happens* to have all these air miles and is all geared up for a jaunt to Europe?" Emery asked incredulously. "I mean, it's something I would do in a heartbeat, but most people aren't me."

"I know, I know," Ben mumbled, stirring what was left of his ice cubes with his paper straw. "When I say it out loud it sounds totally nuts. But how else am I going to get to the UK and find the truth? Why have I never heard of this family? Why did this Anne woman leave me everything? But also… what if it was legally all mine and I let it slip away? I just think…I think Elias can help with all that. He's a real grown-up, not just a lawyer."

"I'm a real grown-up," Emery grumbled, fiddling with his My Little Pony ring.

Ben chuckled and rubbed Emery's hand. "You're my other option, if I'm honest."

"Oh dear baby Jesus!" Emery squawked. "No, Ben! Are you insane? Take the clever lawyer man, not me! So long as you don't think he'll try any funny business." Emery softened immediately and cupped the side of Ben's face. "You are devastatingly cute."

Ben leaned into the sweet touch. He knew it was just between friends, but it was nice. Ben had enjoyed a lot of sex, but he'd never really had a boyfriend. Someone to hold him and tell him everything would be okay might be nice for time to time. Emery was always generous with his touch.

"Elias *so* isn't like that," Ben said firmly. A warmth flurried over him, picturing Elias's gorgeous smile and thinking of the assuring way he'd immediately taken charge of Ben's surprise situation. "He's sweet and kind and respectful. I feel totally safe with him."

Emery pulled his hand away and gave Ben a shrewd look before catching the eye of one of the servers who was passing. "Oliver, darling," Emery said while batting his eyelashes. "Could we possibly have the same again if we ask *very* nicely."

Oliver winked back at him. "No. But you can if you *tip* nicely."

Emery gasped. "Rude!" he cried, while brandishing a twenty he'd pulled from god knew where.

Oliver plucked the note from between his fingers. "Coming right up, hot stuff."

Unfortunately, once it was just the two of them again, Emery's discerning look returned. "This Elias," he said, practically purring. "I've met him. He's very handsome and unquestionably gay."

Ben shifted in his seat, realizing just how tipsy he was. "Maybe we should have ordered some food..." he said with a frown.

Emery waved his hand impatiently. "We'll get fries and whatever else you want when the lovely Oliver returns. Focus, darling. Mama needs her tea. Elias is a hot daddy, yes?"

Ben wrinkled his nose. "I'm not into the daddy thing," he said unsurely. "No offense to anyone who is."

Emery chuckled and licked his glossy lips. "You're not denying that Elias the Lawyer is hot as fuck, though?"

"I guess," Ben mumbled as their drinks arrived. As promised, Emery asked Oliver for several snacks, and then they were alone again. "That's not it, though. He's nice."

"Oh, *very* nice," Emery agreed, lighting their next round of absinthe on fire.

Shit. Should Ben do another? Oh, to hell with it. This was unlike any day he'd ever had in his whole life. He and Emery followed the ritual again, knocking the shots back and spluttering at the ferocity of the liquor, which was just as bad second time around.

"Honey," Emery said once he'd brushed the alcohol induced tears from his eyes, "It's *okay*. You're allowed to be whisked away on vacation by a hot guy! It's exciting!"

"No," Ben spluttered indignantly. "It's not like that! I'm his client. Like I said, he's looking out for me."

"With all his many British law degrees." Emery flicked his eyebrows wickedly as he sipped his cocktail.

"It's better than my zero law degrees from anywhere." It was only after Ben had spoken did he realize he'd snapped. He took a big gulp of his fresh glass of water. "Sorry," he mumbled, immediately ashamed. "It's been a very weird day and I'm fully aware how nuts this sounds."

To his surprise, Emery laughed. *"Babe,"* he said, throwing up his hands. "You just won the lottery! You want to run off into the horizon with some *gorgeous* more mature man, I say tally-ho!" He put on an appalling upper-class English accent for that last word and twirled his fingers.

Ben couldn't help but laugh. However he was also shaking his head. "You're actually *supporting* this hair-brained scheme?"

For a second, Emery just stared at him. "Yes, I am," he said like he was speaking to a dummy. "Because life is too short and you never know what it's going to throw at you. So when it throws you *millions of actual dollars* and a *yummy*, experienced man, you take that and you see where that leads you, okay? You follow that *all* the way to the end of the rainbow."

"And what if I don't find a pot of gold when I get there?" Ben asked. "And I don't just mean the money, not even a bit. What if I'm taken advantage of? By Elias *or* this so-called family of mine. I'm...I'm not very worldly."

"Sugar," Emery said, taking Ben's hand in his own slender one. "You don't let them, you hear me? This family of yours has told you not to come? Fantastic. You need to get over there even faster and show them who's the boss of you. I'll give you a hint: it's *you*. And no matter what happens, you can always just come home, where people will always love and accept you. But will you really be satisfied if you don't go and see what this might bring?"

Even through the liquor haze, Ben could see that made sense. He hummed in agreement. "And Elias? Not-!" he added hastily, "that there's anything going on there!"

"Of course not," said Emery slyly, taking his time to sip his drink while he regarded Ben. "But just so you know, if something *did* happen, that would be okay, too. Life is *also* too short to turn away a stud like that. Just keep an open mind, okay, beautiful?"

Ben snorted and shook his head. Elias would never be interested in an immature guy like him. Ben might have been experienced with guys, but not with life. What would he have to offer a smart, accomplished man like Elias?

Emery nudged his sneaker with the pointed toe of his boot. "Promise me, babe?"

Ben laughed and rolled his eyes. "Yeah, all right," he said, mostly to placate his friend.

Mercifully, their many deep-fried bar snacks arrived to sober them up a bit. Ben crunched on an onion ring as he thought everything through. It wasn't right to say 'what did he have to lose?' because the answer was possibly a shit ton of money.

And also his heart, if he wasn't careful. Traveling internationally with his crush was going to be a thousand times more intense than trading hellos in the bakery. There was a very real chance he was going to get hurt.

But Emery was right. How could he *not* go for this? He had to see where this path might take him. If nothing else, he'd have a story to tell and life experiences he'd never otherwise get. He couldn't very well lament never doing anything interesting and worldly if he was going to run away from the first exciting opportunity that came his way.

The next (several) rounds of cocktails helped strengthen his resolve. Yes, this was a crazy plan. But life was boring if you played it safe all the time.

He had to at least try. And if he happened to have a gorgeous man by his side, one with a beautiful smile who believed in Ben…well, that wouldn't exactly harm, would it?

4

ELIAS

On a scale of one to ten, how horrendous was this idea, really?

"What do you think, buddy?" Elias asked, looking down at his faithful Irish Red Setter. Rosie lolled her tongue and panted, wagging her tail. "Yeah, you're biased," Elias said with a chuckle. "You think everything I do is a good idea, especially if you think it'll somehow get you fed."

Rosie barked and chased her tail once in a circle. Then she ran off to the entrance hall to fetch her leash for Elias.

Yeah, she was no fool. She knew what was going on.

"Is this your way of saying 'get a life, Daddy'? Or perhaps, 'get out of the damned house, Daddy, it's been years'?"

Rosie barked again, jumping around her leash that she'd dropped at Elias's feet.

"Okay, all right," Elias grumbled. "You don't need to rub it in."

It was too late now, anyway. The flights were booked, his bags were packed, and he had officially started his two weeks off work. All there was left to do was take Rosie to where she'd be staying the next couple of weeks.

But in doing so, Elias knew he'd really have to face the music.

When his dear friend Darcy Lott (once Decker) opened her front door, she folded her arms and narrowed her eyes up at Elias from her wheelchair. "What was Elias's locker combination at school? Who's the president? What year is it?"

Her husband, Leon, chuckled from behind her. "You're checking for an evil twin, not amnesia."

"It could be both," said Darcy, leaning forward, resting her elbows on her knees. "Or it could be one of those rubber masks they wear in those spy films."

Elias waved his hands at her while Rosie barked. "Yeah, yeah. I've been abducted by aliens. The *real* Elias would never do anything like this. Can I come in now? It's chilly out here."

Darcy arched an eyebrow at him as she rolled back enough to let them pass. "I'm watching you, mister," she said, clearly amused by her hilarious schtick.

Leon shook his head and Elias's hand as Elias wiped his shoes on the mat. "Are you *sure* you're okay to watch over Rosie for a couple of weeks?" Elias asked as they shut the front door. There were still Halloween decorations up and the sound of kids' voices drifted down from upstairs.

Leon scoffed and peered at Elias over his gold-rimmed glasses. "Are you kidding? Pepper and Charles haven't talked about anything else for two whole days. We're going to be blaming you when we end up at the animal shelter before Christmas."

"I think they're old enough for a dog now, babe," Darcy said comfortingly as she rolled toward the kitchen in their large house. "I hope you don't mind, Elias, but we invited a couple more people over?"

"Swift! Micha!" Elias cried in delight as they entered the kitchen to find the boyfriends deep in conversation over glasses of cola. Elias wouldn't necessarily mind if his friendship group became a little more drink orientated, but he had to say it was a relief that neither Swift nor Micha WAS particularly keen on alcohol. It made his life easier.

Plus, they were lovely guys. Elias was genuinely thrilled they'd worked out their differences and gotten together. Micha was Darcy's younger brother, and since he'd decided to stay in town, she'd mentioned they'd been hanging out more.

Swift was Elias's personal trainer, and Elias would be forever grateful to him for helping him get his six-pack back at almost forty. He'd never been in better shape, even when he'd been fitness obsessed in his twenties.

Maybe he should blame *Swift* for his sudden sense of adventure?

Deep down, Elias knew that wouldn't fly. This had been years in the making, and he knew it. He wasn't going to regret taking an opportunity that came knocking on his door, but he wanted to make sure he was going about it the right way. The last thing he wanted was for Ben to get hurt.

Why would he get hurt, though? Elias was just going as a friend. As informal legal counsel. There was nothing to worry about.

Or was there?

"Elias!" Swift cried happily, rising to shake his hand. "How are things?"

"We're considering ordering him a CAT scan," Leon answered on his behalf with a wink.

"Now, now," Darcy said with a huff as she parked herself at the table where there was an open space. "I'm the only one who's allowed to tease him."

"No, you're right," Elias agreed with a sigh as he took a seat himself at the sleek white wooden table. He ran his hand along the decorative edge while Rosie lay at his feet, looking up at him with big brown eyes. "This is easily the craziest thing I've ever done."

"I think it's romantic," Swift said. Then he hastily threw his hands up. "Not that," he spluttered. "Uh, Darcy explained you're not a couple or anything. I just mean the situation. Dropping everything to go to London to help a friend. It's like an adventure book."

"It seems a *bit* romantic," Leon grumbled as he worked at the kitchen counter, tenderizing some meat.

"Ben is a nice guy," Elias said, repeating what he'd been telling himself the past few days. "We've been speaking for like a year and a half."

Darcy arched an eyebrow at him. "Saying hello and giving you change for your coffee doesn't count as conversation. Come on. You've never even been on vacation with *us!* Admit it, this is pretty out there."

Elias knew she was only teasing, but it struck a small nerve. He was doing his very best to keep this whole thing professional and forget about his dumb crush. "I know that," he said patiently. "But aren't you the ones that have been telling me for a while now that life is too short, and that I should seize more opportunities without being so scared all the time. This is an adventure! I'm being spontaneous!"

Swift reached over and squeezed Elias's arm. "Good for you, dude."

"You're right, you're right," Darcy conceded, waving her hands. "I just thought you might join Grindr or try salsa dancing before making a snap decision to fly on an international escapade with a twenty-something."

"Ben is...different," Elias said, trying not to let the mushy feeling in his chest betray him to the others. "More mature than I thought. I genuinely think this is a chance to become actual friends." He sipped the cherry cola Micha had poured him. "But that's secondary, honestly. I'm genuinely concerned he might get taken advantage of by these people. So why not use my air miles and go help him?"

"How are you worried they'll take advantage?" Leon asked over his shoulder from where he was tending to their dinner. "I thought Ben was the one with the money now?"

"And from the legal representative they sent over to scare Ben into keeping away, I'm worried what lengths they'll go to in order to get it back." Elias shook his head determinedly. "I'm *not* going to let that happen."

Everyone was looking at him and he tried not to squirm in his seat.

"Yeah, totally," Darcy said eventually. Leon was starting to cook the beef he'd been preparing, filling the kitchen with the comforting smell of sizzling meat and seasoning. "It makes sense."

"But?" Elias could tell there was a 'but' coming.

Darcy threw up her hands. "I just think that, well, if there was a *little* romance involved, that wouldn't be a bad thing."

Elias huffed. "Darcy-"

"Elias." She folded her arms. "I know you think you were being subtle, but it's not like you haven't mentioned this guy Ben before."

Elias could feel heat rising in his cheeks and he tried desperately to will it away. He would be *mortified* if he'd let slip about his silly crush.

"Because he's a nice guy and I like that bakery," he said, trying not to sound defensive.

"Oh, Rise and Shine is great!" Swift agreed, looking between Darcy and Leon for support.

Leon snorted. "Yeah, but we go in for the cupcakes."

Darcy patted Elias's hand. "You might have mentioned...once or twice...how sweet and nice Ben is. And how cute his curly hair is."

"And his hazel eyes," Leon muttered with a smirk while he was stirring the pan.

Elias looked helplessly between them. To be fair, Darcy and Leon might have had pretty determined expressions, but Swift and Micha looked hopeful and excited. Rosie wagged her tail, making it thump on the tiles. She seemed torn between wanting to support Elias and going over to investigate the beef cooking in Leon's pan.

"Guys," Elias said weakly. "He's twenty-three. Don't make this weird."

Swift bit his lip and looked remorseful, but Darcy leaned forward. "Hon, no one wants to make you uncomfortable. But I have known you for far too long, so I'm going to be your friend and tell you that a bit of an age gap is no big deal, whatsoever. I know I just cracked a joke about him being in his twenties, but that's because I'm a dick."

"She is," Leon agreed sagely, nodding his head. Darcy flipped him the bird.

Swift perked up and lifted up Micha's hand, their fingers entwined. "Hey, though, Darcy's right. There's seven years between Micha and me, and we're perfect together."

Micha smiled bashfully at his enthusiasm. They really did adore each other. Leon pretended to make a gagging noise at them, then winked to show he was only kidding.

What did Elias do? Admit they were right? The cat seemed to be out of the bag, anyway. He sighed. "There's a bit of a difference between seven years and sixteen. I just like him. But it's never going to be anything more than that, otherwise I'd be taking advantage."

"Whoa, hey, no." Leon dropped the wooden spoon in the pan and crossed his arms, giving Elias a stern look. "He's an adult, fully capable of making his own decisions. If he's interested in you, then no one is doing anything wrong."

Micha nodded. "Especially queer couples," he said,

looking around the table as if he was a little nervous about voicing an opinion. But Swift squeezed his hand and he continued. "I've known a lot of LGBT people in relationships with several years between them. When there are fewer people to choose from in a partner, what's the point in getting caught up about age? Especially when a whole generation of gay men...well, you know..."

He bit his lip, but Elias didn't mind him bringing that up. There had been such unspeakable losses to the gay community due to the AIDS crisis. He knew full well that went a long way to dispelling prejudices against large age gaps that other sections of society held.

"You're right," he said kindly to Micha, not wanting him to feel like he'd put his foot in it. But he still bit his lip in apprehension. He had expected to be given a hard time for his super spontaneous travel plans. He hadn't been prepared to defend himself over his dumb crush. "I honestly don't think Ben feels like that, though. I promise that's not why I offered to go to England with him."

"Oh, god, no," Darcy said in alarm. "That would be creepy!"

"*But*," Swift said. "If something just happens to develop between you guys in the beautiful English countryside, while you're on this amazing adventure, *that* would be pretty romantic."

"And we'd all support you," Leon added firmly.

Darcy smiled warmly. "You deserve to meet someone nice, hon."

"And it wasn't long ago," said Swift, glancing at Micha then back at Elias, "that you told me life is too short and to just go for it."

"That was different," Elias grumbled.

To his surprise, Swift quirked an eyebrow and gave him a

devilish smile. "Yes. Because now the shoe is on the other foot."

Elias huffed. The trouble was, he'd truly meant it when he'd said to Swift about life being too short. It was a philosophy he was trying to live by more and more, because he knew how easy it could be to let a good thing pass you by.

So should he follow his own advice?

"You're really telling me you're all okay with me hopping on a plane and seeing what happens?" He was met by a chorus of nods. He chewed on his lip. "Okay...and...if there was a chance Ben might be interested in me...you're saying that wouldn't be a massive scandal?"

"Definitely not," said Swift earnestly.

"Hon," said Darcy. "I would throw a parade. We've been saying for years that you need to get back on the horse. You're a catch! Any guy would be lucky to have you. So long as he's nice and treats you good, we'll love him."

Elias rubbed his thumb along the rim of his tumbler.

Something akin to excitement fluttered through his chest. "My priority is helping Ben with this inheritance claim," he said firmly. "But...he *is* kind of gorgeous."

Darcy whooped. "Go get 'em, tiger."

Elias still was mostly convinced nothing was going to happen and Ben didn't think of him like that. He also felt strongly he wouldn't want to do anything that might make Ben feel obligated. Elias was more or less acting as his lawyer, so there would be a power imbalance.

But even just admitting to his friends that he had any kind of crush was more than he'd done in years. It was oddly freeing.

However, reality then hit. So what that Elias liked a cute young guy? Never in a million years was Ben going to like him back in the same way. Elias was old enough to be Ben's *father*, for crying out loud. What would Ben see in him? Some sad man who liked old musicals and even older books. Who hadn't done anything much more exciting than adopt a dog in the past ten years.

So he allowed his friends to be cheerful for him and drop little teasing hints about him wooing the younger man, but it was hard for Elias to really believe anything could come from it. He almost wished he'd lied and said he didn't feel anything for Ben, because surely everything he was feeling was just in his imagination. You couldn't fall for someone you hardly knew.

Luckily, he was given a rest from his interrogation as the sound of several feet thundering down the stairs filled the house. Before the children could emerge, though, a ginger cat shot into the kitchen, his tail swishing as he looked around at the humans who had all leaped back or shoved their chairs away.

"Don't move," Darcy whispered, her eyes wide and locked on the cat.

Swift laughed nervously, his arm protectively in front of Micha. "Oh, he's mostly harmless these days." He swallowed and glanced at his boyfriend. "Mostly."

Elias had already suffered a couple of run-ins with this particular cat, however, and maintained his distance. Even Rosie whimpered and scooted backward until she was partially hidden by Darcy's chair.

"Oh, Butter!" Swift's daughter, Imogen, cried as she skipped into the kitchen. "Are you being silly again?"

Leon looked down at the cat, his spatula raised in case the cat wanted to try anything. "'Silly,' yeah," he said weakly.

Imogen picked the furball up and there was a collective sigh, like she'd just defused a bomb. Elias was very fond of the little girl, despite her hellcat companion. "Hey, kiddo. How's it been?"

Imogen shrugged and glanced out toward the den where

it sounded like Darcy and Leon's two kids had started up a video game. "Good. Oh! Daddy said you were going to England. Is that true?"

"It is." Elias allowed himself to feel a flurry of excitement again. Despite all his worries, he was still finally visiting a country he had wanted to see for most of his life.

"Wow," Imogen said, dragging out the word as she pushed her sparkly glasses up her nose. "Will you meet the queen?"

Elias smiled down at where she was rocking the purring ginger beast in her arms. "Probably not, sweetie. But maybe I'll see Buckingham Palace."

She nodded thoughtfully. "How about pirates? They have pirates in England, right?"

Elias and the rest of the adults laughed. "Sure," Elias told her. "I bet they still have a few lurking around."

She seemed happy with that answer. "Well, if you see any, please say hello from Imogen Dillard, age five and a quarter. I'm going to go play with Pepper and Charles now. Bye, Daddy! Bye, everyone!" And with that, she marched happily out of the kitchen toward the den.

Having broken up the inquisition into Elias's speculative love life, the conversation flowed more naturally around several different topics as dinner was served. They discussed work and the upcoming holidays, then before he left, Elias went through his instructions for looking after Rosie.

His friends kept smiling at him encouragingly, like they were all in on a fun secret. But Elias would never put Ben in that position. He vowed to himself that he would be nothing short of gentlemanly throughout their trip, doing his best to shield Ben from any nastiness his estranged family might throw his way.

Elias wished someone had shielded him when he was Ben's age. The least he could do would be to spare another vulnerable young man from any similar kind of hardship.

So he played along with his friends' well-intended banter. It *did* feel kind of nice to entertain the idea that he could have a crush on a guy. He'd been so afraid to even have that much for a long time. Maybe one day, he would join Grindr and meet someone his own age who he felt a spark with. But in the meantime, he'd take his role as Ben's protector very seriously.

Except when he went to bed that night in anticipation of their long journey the next day, loneliness crawled into Elias's veins. He'd been single for so many years, pushing anyone away in his terror of being intimate again. He knew that these days there was no real danger, but it was difficult to convince his heart of that when it had been broken so thoroughly.

Especially when he'd been the one to break it.

For just a second, he gave in and wondered what it might be like to hold Ben in his arms. To kiss him softly on the lips. To feel his bright smile directed solely at him. But then guilt overrode the fantasy, making him push it savagely away. After that, he felt even more hollow than before.

It was a long while before he was finally able to drift off to sleep.

5

BEN

"So, London, huh?"

Ben shifted in the back of the blue Ford Mustang, meeting the driver's gaze as he glanced in the rearview mirror. They were taking a cab all the way to SeaTac airport, and Ben had hoped to catch up on his social media during the journey. But apparently the Uber driver Emery had recommended liked to chat.

"Have you noticed that London is the city they like to destroy in films these days," the driver – a guy called Kamran – said, shaking his head. "It's like Hollywood got tired of blowing up the White House and the Empire State building, so now it's all Big Ben and Tower Bridge. That's what everyone calls London Bridge, did you know? But it's not. The famous one that splits in half for the boats is *Tower* Bridge." He winked and saluted at Ben, who wasn't sure what to say.

"Yeah, London Bridge is just a regular old bridge," said Elias, coming to Ben's rescue.

Kamran's eyebrows shot up. He had copper skin, a short beard, and hipster glasses. Although he was obviously handsome, objectively speaking, Ben got the sense he was probably a handful to be around. Ben wasn't exactly sure how he and Emery had met, but Emery had given him Kamran's card a couple of months ago and made him promise that he should always try him for a cab first before booking any old Uber.

"Oh! You've been before?" Kamran asked excitedly.

A hint of sadness flashed across Elias's face. He was sitting in the back seat next to Ben. If Ben wanted, he could reach over and hold his hand, but of course he didn't.

"No," said Elias. "I've always wanted to see the city, but I doubt we'll get the chance this trip. We're going straight to Wiltshire once we land. Not much opportunity for sight-seeing."

"Ah," said Kamran, waving his hand dismissively as he casually changed lanes on the freeway. He was going like a bat out of hell, but Ben had to say he seemed like a very capable driver. That didn't stop him from gripping onto the side of his door, though. "I bet you'll find some time. You can't fly all that way and miss the sights! I always wanted to see the London Dungeons. It's part museum, part live experience. It shows how they had crazy cool ways of killing folks, you know? Really twisted shit."

Kamran cackled but Ben's stomach flipped at the mere thought of anything that awful. He swooned as the blood rushed from his head. He took a deep breath to try and steady himself.

To his absolute shock, Elias reached over and squeezed his hand, like Ben had been imagining. It only lasted for a second, if that, but it made Ben's heart flip. Elias was probably just being supportive so Ben wouldn't throw up in the car, but it was still appreciated.

Elias smiled bashfully at Ben, then turned to Kamran. "It's

more of a business trip. But if we get the chance, we'll be sure and take some pictures of the capital."

"Sweet," Kamran said, nodding and fiddling with the music player. Ben gasped as a car braked ahead, but Kamran didn't even seem to flinch as he expertly maneuvered out of the way. "So, Emery said you were seeing family." He waggled his eyebrows at them both in the rearview mirror. "Who's meeting whose parents, huh?"

"What?" spluttered Ben in horror. He was going to kill Emery. Had he said something?

"Oh, no," said Elias equally as quickly, shaking his head. "We're just friends. I'm kind of Ben's legal counsel."

"Yeah, it's this bizarre series of events," Ben added, feeling like his face was on fire. "I didn't – I don't know why Emery would think – uh…"

Kamran raised an eyebrow at him in the mirror. "My mistake," he said, the corner of his mouth twitching. "I must have misunderstood."

Ben hummed. He stared determinedly out of the window for several minutes until he felt less like a human beetroot. Damn Emery. Ben hadn't meant to blab about his stupid crush, but the absinthe had gotten the better of him.

No, Emery would never betray him like that. Kamran probably had just read between the lines and made assumptions. Just because those assumptions were secretly sort of *true* didn't mean anything.

When Ben risked glancing at Elias again, he was absorbed with something on his phone. But just as Ben was going to turn away, Elias glanced over at Ben for a second with a smile, making him feel a little less awkward. Only a little, though. Crap, he needed to shake off this weird mood. He'd made up his mind that this trip was not only happening but also a good idea and that he was going to keep his feelings for Elias neatly zipped up.

Elias made things easier by not reaching over again during the rest of the drive, but all the way to the airport Ben's hand tingled where they'd touched so briefly. What he wouldn't give to just hold hands in the back seat like a couple. He was being stupid and childish. Elias was sophisticated and not interested in him like that. But still, it had been nice, if only for a moment.

Everything about this situation was so alien to Ben, making him feel even more out of his depth and inexperienced than usual. The airport was manic when they arrived. Ben stood on the sidewalk and craned his neck, slowly turning on the spot to take it all in, inhaling the pungent aviation fumes that were drifting through the chilly afternoon air. He hadn't even realized Kamran had pulled their suitcases from the car until the sound of the trunk slamming shut caught Ben's attention.

"All right, then," Kamran said as Elias handed over several twenties without batting an eyelid. "You crazy kids have fun. I'll be here to pick you up in a couple of weeks. Just text if there's any change in the flights."

With a salute, he hopped back into his car, revving the engine so loud that several passers-by stopped what they were doing to stare, and then he sped off out of sight.

Then it was just Ben and Elias.

Of course there were hundreds of people all around them, but it was finally sinking in for Ben that over the next couple of weeks he and Elias were going to be in each other's pockets. He hoped they hadn't made a gigantic mistake. When Ben had traveled with Emery, there was no chance to worry. Emery was a constant blur of glittery energy. But Ben and Elias were both kind of quiet souls. Ben hoped they could shake off the slight awkwardness of the cab ride.

He didn't have to wait long for something eventful to happen, though, offering up some distraction.

"Oh, *shit*," he muttered to himself as he crouched down at the check-in desk, frantically searching his carry-on luggage. The clerk had just asked for their passports, and Ben knew full well he'd almost forgotten his on the way out of the door earlier. His mom had one hundred percent handed it to him, but now he couldn't for the life of him remember where he'd put it.

His cheeks burned in humiliation, feeling Elias watching him. He would not cry. He *wouldn't*. But where could it be?

"Hey," Elias said as he touched Ben's shoulder. His eyebrows were raised but he didn't look mad as Ben glanced up. "Did you check your coat pockets?"

Relief washed through Ben. Elias was totally right. The second he said it, Ben remembered that he'd put his passport in his inside breast pocket. Thank fuck. "Sorry, sir," he said sheepishly to the clerk as he handed it over. He then set about putting his carry-on luggage back together.

Ben expected Elias to be annoyed at him, but he gave him a dorky thumbs-up when Ben got back to his feet, dispelling some of the tension that had built up in his chest.

"Thanks," Ben said.

"No problem," said Elias with a shrug. "I'm here to look after you."

Ben wasn't sure if it was better or worse to take that comment in a chaperone kind of context. He sighed internally, admitting that he really would have preferred it in a boyfriend context, but he was being ridiculous.

They made it through security without much incident. Ben had forgotten to take a bottle of water out of his bag when it went through the X-ray machine, but they just tipped the contents away before giving the empty bottle back to him.

"Wow, I really suck at this," he said with a self-deprecating chuckle. Elias shrugged again, though, and didn't seem annoyed. In fact, he grinned down at Ben.

"You're lucky," he said. "It'll get boring real quick the more you do it, I promise. It's nice to be traveling *with* someone for a change. It shakes things up."

Ben was sure he imagined it, but the look they shared set a shiver down his spine. Elias just meant that he was less bored than on his usual work trips with a bit of company, that was all. It had nothing to do with Ben in particular.

Right?

Ben shook it off. It was easy to find other things to think about now they were in the belly of the airport. It was so busy, like a beehive.

As their flight was transatlantic, they'd had to arrive extra early and therefore had some time to kill before boarding. Ben didn't want to hang around Elias like some lovestruck puppy when he was wrapping up the last of his work emails on his laptop. So Ben went for a wander, looking absently at the shops, then buying them both a coffee to take on the plane. He might have been doing his best not to fawn over Elias, but Ben still got a thrill at Elias's delight when he realized Ben knew his coffee order by heart.

Elias had explained at the diner that he'd flown internally a lot for work. That was how he'd amassed so many air miles. One of his firm's clients had their head office in Salt Lake City, another in Sacramento, and his own firm attended conferences frequently in Vegas and Portland. Ben had only flown that one time Emery had dragged him to Vegas, and that definitely hadn't been for a conference. They'd flown premier economy then, but Ben still wasn't prepared as they finally stepped onto the plane and found himself in business class.

"Holy shit," he whispered as he took in his individual little luxury cubby with a welcome pack of free gifts, pillows, proper headphones, and so much leg room he could practically swing his feet. Ben gasped and dropped into his seat, tearing open the goodies like a kid on Christmas morning. "Elias, this is amazing!"

Elias looked bashful as he settled himself in the seat across the narrow aisle. "It's a long flight. I thought we should have a little comfort."

Ben tried not to let it get to him. Of course Elias wouldn't want to fly in economy. Ben was just lucky that they were traveling together and that meant Ben got an upgrade too. It wasn't like Elias had done this as a gift for him or anything. But he felt like a prince as he excitedly rummaged through his goody bag filled with an eye mask, socks, single-serving toothbrush and paste, earplugs, and other cute, novelty things.

"Champagne, sir?" Ben looked up at the smiling flight attendant with an actual glass flute of bubbly in her hands.

"Uhh…" he croaked, suddenly unsure.

But Elias winked at him. "It's complimentary," he said softly. Ben might have been ashamed that the reason for his hesitation was that obvious, but there was a sparkle in Elias's eyes. "All the food and drink is. Knock yourself out."

"Oh, wow, thank you, ma'am," Ben said breathlessly to the attendant as he accepted the glass.

"None for me, thank you," Elias said. Ben frowned.

"Aren't you going to celebrate? This is the start of our adventure!"

Elias looked embarrassed and Ben cursed himself. He'd obviously put his foot in it for some reason. "I don't really drink," Elias explained, "but I'll certainly celebrate with you."

Ben felt terrible, the glass suddenly heavy in his hand. "I'm so sorry. That was thoughtless." He hated when people tried to pressure others into drinking.

But Elias waved his hand. "No, please, I don't mind. I'd

actually love a glass. It's for health reasons, you see. But...
well, I guess I could go wild and have a mimosa."

Ben shook his head. Damn, there was that awkwardness
between them again. "Please don't feel you have to," he said.
Jeez, was this what the trip was going to be like? Him
constantly saying dumb things?

However, Elias grinned. "No, we *are* celebrating, and I can
relax from time to time. Nothing bad will happen unless I go
crazy and start doing shots."

Ben recalled his and Emery's absinthe night and his
stomach rolled. "No, no shots," he agreed emphatically.

It was funny how they kept lurching from uncomfortable
to relaxed. Ben would rather they skipped the awkward bits,
but he kind of loved how good Elias was at bouncing the
conversation back again. Maybe with a bit of practice, Ben
would get better at not saying the wrong thing so often.

The attendant kindly brought Elias his Champagne and
orange juice, then he held the glass out for them to toast. "To
our adventure," he said hesitantly, but there was a smile
playing on his lips telling Ben that he was just as excited as
he was.

"To our adventure," Ben agreed enthusiastically as they
clinked glasses. The liquid sloshed a little over their fingers,
making them both laugh, and Ben felt himself relax again,
just a fraction.

This was going to be magical, no matter what. As the
wheels left the tarmac, there was no denying this was really
happening. He was going to England to chase his fortune,
with a gorgeous guy by his side.

It was so nearly perfect.

He knew he shouldn't pry, but Ben couldn't help but
worry what Elias meant by 'medical issues.' Hopefully it
wasn't anything serious. Maybe he was just on antibiotics.
Elias hadn't appeared particularly distressed when he'd

mentioned it after all, and he'd said something about having medication packed in his carry-on.

But there was a part of Ben that felt strangely protective toward the older man, which was ridiculous as he could certainly take care of himself. However, now they were getting to know one another, Ben would be upset if his health issue turned out to be anything really troubling. Hopefully, it was nothing to worry about.

In the meantime, he sipped his drink and flicked through the movies as soon as the in-flight entertainment became available. Elias was engrossed in a big, heavy-looking book that appeared to have something to do with UK inheritance law. Ben tried not to let his heart flip that Elias was doing extra research on his behalf, but it was difficult not to.

The air-crew kept them fed and watered with a non-stop parade of surprisingly good food and more bubbly. Ben had declined at first, but Elias had insisted he have fun. "You're making up for all those vacations I never went on," he said earnestly with another wink. "So long as you don't start singing, I'd say have as much as you like."

But Ben didn't want to get foolish in front of Elias. He might get loose-lipped like he had at Aquarium with Emery and confess something embarrassing. Like how soft Elias's hair looked or how it glowed amber when the setting sunlight hit it through the window at forty thousand feet. Or how much it meant to Ben that Elias was here with him, on his side to face his estranged family.

So he had a few glasses of Champagne, then snuggled up with an historical drama and a packet of peanuts to pass the time .

After a time, the crew dimmed the lights and Ben pulled out his complimentary blanket and pillow. His heart skipped a beat when he realized that Elias was already snuggled up sound asleep, clutching his pillow like a teddy bear with his eye mask on. He looked so vulnerable that Ben's instinct to take care of him intensified. But he was just being silly. Elias didn't need that.

He must have dozed off himself eventually, because the next thing he knew the nine hours had flown by. The lights came back up and the pilot made several announcements as they descended into London Heathrow. Ben had his nose practically pressed up against the glass as they touched down, only bumping a little on the tarmac.

"Oh my god," he breathed, fogging up the oval glass. "We're really here!" He didn't care that the weather that morning was dreary and gray, or that it felt like it took forever for them to taxi to their gate. He was in *another country*. He felt like that was something he could finally cross off his bucket list.

He became aware he was practically bouncing in his chair against the seat belt, but when he glanced over at Elias, he was grinning at him. Rather than looking like he thought Ben was being childish, it felt like they were in on a secret together.

Eventually, the plane came to a final halt and the seat belt lights went off. The first thing Ben noticed that Elias did was get his small case down from the overhead bin, take his medication box out, then skim the instructions for it with a frown.

"Everything okay?" Ben couldn't help but ask as he gathered up his own stuff.

Elias blinked and looked up. "Yes," he said with a smile, but there was a hint of anxiety there that Ben noticed. Ben didn't want to pry, but a selfish part of him wanted Elias to confide in him. "I normally take this every morning. Just deciding how much of an issue the time difference will be. Oh, your passport."

Ben quickly forgot about Elias's pills as his stomach

dropped with a sickening lurch. He looked where Elias had pointed, and sure enough, he'd shoved his passport and paper tickets into the pouch in front of his seat after showing them to the flight attendant at the door. He'd almost left them behind.

"Jesus. Thank you." He clutched them to his chest. "Honestly, what would I do without you?"

There it was again. That little spark as they shared a look. But the other passengers were starting to push their way down the aisle, so Ben pulled himself together and hauled his carry-on case down and followed them. Even though he was glad to be stretching his legs, he was almost sad to leave his little cubby. The next time he'd see one would be on the return trip.

Who knew what was going to happen between now and then?

It felt like it took forever to navigate their way through passport control at Heathrow. It was a pretty huge airport. As much as the flight might not have totally sucked, Ben was very glad to be breathing un-recycled air again, even if the weather beyond the airport's floor-to-ceiling windows looked horrendous. Dark clouds, rain, and wind. Hardly a great first impression of a country. Ben was still skipping along as they pulled their suitcases through Arrivals toward the airport's exit, though. He was in *England.*

"Is it everything you imagined?" he asked Elias enthusiastically. He wished he had ten more pairs of eyes to take everything in, like Harry Potter when he got to Diagon Alley. Even just seeing the prices on things as pound signs instead of dollars was tickling him silly. Some stores he recognized, like the coffee chains, others were brand-new novelties.

Elias hummed. "I mean, as exciting as the airport is, I think I'll be more excited when we get out of it. We're going to be taking the train into London, then the underground, then another train from Paddington station. Like Paddington Bear." He winked at Ben. "So at least we can escape the rain as we won't have to go outside for a while. What?" He laughed nervously.

Ben hadn't realized they'd stopped walking, but they had. For a second they stared at one another and Ben's heart stuttered. He was aware he was probably giving Elias a goofy look, but he couldn't seem to help it. "Nothing," he said bashfully. "It's just that I know you talked about our onward journey to Wiltshire before, but I'd forgotten everything. I was just going to double-check it once we got here. Yet you know it all off the top of your head."

Elias had a strange expression on his face, but something told Ben it wasn't a bad thing. It was almost fond. Did he like that Ben was impressed with how organized he was?

"Like I said," Elias murmured, giving Ben a shy smile. "It's my job to look after you."

These signals were driving Ben insane. He really wanted to believe that Elias was being sweet toward him, but it had to just be in a friendly way. He was a nice guy, after all! There was nothing more behind it. There couldn't be.

Elias broke the moment when he shook his head and blinked, looking over Ben's shoulder in confusion. "Uhh... that guy has a sign with your name on it. I don't suppose there's a chance there's someone else here with your name?"

Sure enough, Ben turned to look. They'd paused just as they'd walked through Arrivals where people were congregated to greet loved ones. But there was also an older man with graying hair in a ponytail, and a pot belly. He was wearing a black suit under a bomber jacket, holding up a sign with Ben's name on it.

Ben frowned. Mr. Cabot had been very clear that Ben's extended, estranged family didn't want him to come to

England. So even though the idea of arriving unannounced made him nervous, Ben had decided against contacting any of the phone numbers or email addresses attached to the will to let anyone know he and Elias were coming.

So how in the world could there be someone waiting for him right now at the time their plane had landed? A chill ran down his spine, but when the man saw Ben reading his name and look up at him, he broke into a big grin.

"Oh, you ain't Mr. Turner, are you?" he asked with a rough cockney accent.

"I am," Ben confirmed as he and Elias stepped closer.

The man stuffed his sign under his arm and thrust his hand toward Ben. "A pleasure to meet you, my son. A pleasure. I'm Gary Decker, but you can call me Gazza, everyone does. I trust you had a good flight?"

Ben glanced at Elias in confusion. "We did," he said slowly, "but we weren't expecting a car. In fact, we didn't tell anyone here we were going to come."

Gazza was a pretty grizzly-looking man, but at Ben's words he looked sheepish. "Ahh, yes. I'm sorry, sir. We didn't mean to snoop, but we were hoping you *would* in fact come. When you said on your Insta-whachamacallsit photo thing that you were flying in first class, we worked out it must be this flight." He beamed at Ben. "I *had* to be here to meet you! Miss Nancy wouldn't have had it any other way, I can assure you." He glanced upward. "God rest her soul."

Ben could have kicked himself for posting on social media. What had he been thinking? He looked guiltily at Elias, but Elias was focused on Gazza.

"Miss Nancy?" he repeated. "Do you mean Anne Grimaldi de Loutherbergh? Ben's great-grandmother?"

Gazza nodded solemnly. "I do indeed. What a lady she was. She'll always be Miss Nancy to us." He thrust his hand out at Elias. "I'm sorry. I wasn't expecting Mr. Turner to have company. Are you a friend?"

"And informal legal counsel," Elias said, shaking Gazza's hand. "Elias Solomon. Pleased to meet you."

"So," Ben said anxiously as people weaved their way around their little trio standing in the middle of Arrivals. "I take it Mr. Cabot didn't send you? Or someone from the family?"

Gazza lowered his head and clasped his hands in front of him. "Ah, no. Sorry, sir. They are aware of your trip, however, and are in fact quite *furious* that you've come over."

He laughed and rocked on his heels as Ben's stomach dropped. However, Elias squeezed his shoulder, sending electricity flying through his body. Ben met his gaze, just for a second, but it was enough to give him strength.

"They shouldn't be furious," Ben said firmly, jutting his chin up. "I didn't ask to be left an inheritance, but I have every right to find out what's going on and defend what's mine."

Gazza regarded Ben thoughtfully, then nodded with a sad sigh. "Oh...I wish Miss Nancy could be here to see this. She would have loved to have met you, I reckon. Her Tom felt it best not to, but when it came to her passing, Miss Nancy decided enough was enough. She was going to set things right." Gazza wagged his finger, then clasped his hands again. "Good old Miss Nancy."

Ben felt a lump rise in his throat at the mention of his gramps, several emotions swirling through him. He thought he'd known his grandfather pretty well, but it seemed he had this whole secret life he'd left behind. Why had Gramps left his home and his family behind? Again, Ben found himself wondering if there was something hidden there that might explain why his great-grandmother – Nancy – had left him everything in her will.

"I wish I could have known her, too," Ben said sadly.

Gazza nodded, a slight wetness to his eyes. He cleared his throat. "Well, yes, I dare say there's a fair amount of regret going around. But you're here now, and that's all that matters. How about I take your luggage, sirs? The car is this way, and we can talk more as we go."

"Oh, no," Ben said as Gazza reached for their suitcases. "We can manage."

Gazza looked scandalized. "It's my job, sir. Don't you worry about a thing. You just follow me now, and I'll get you chaps sorted good and proper."

Before they could reply, he grabbed both the suitcase handles, and began marching their bags away. Ben and Elias quickly fell into step to follow him.

"You can take us to our bed-and-breakfast?" Ben asked.

Gazza glanced over at him. "Oh, no, sir. Now the family are aware you're in the country, I'd advise you to make your introduction as soon as possible. Am I right your UK legal representation has been in touch?"

Gazza seemed to know everything. Ben nodded, trying not to let his panic well up. He wasn't prepared to meet any of these estranged relatives yet, especially not right after a long-haul overnight flight.

"I've been dealing with the solicitors," Elias confirmed. He'd explained to Ben that was what lawyers were called in the UK. Barristers were the ones that stood up in court. "They've been in contact with Aldridge Harding Carmichael."

"Great stuff," said Gazza pleasantly. He skirted around a group of school children with matching backpacks speaking what sounded like Italian. It looked like they were following the signs to the short stay car park. "Then, if you'd like my advice, you'll be wanting to speak as soon as you can with Mr. Grimaldi de Loutherbergh. That's your great-uncle, Kenneth."

"Right," said Ben, feeling sick. "And he doesn't like me, does he?"

Gazza's mouth pressed into a thin line. "I wouldn't like to speak for Mr. Grimaldi de Loutherbergh, sir."

That was a no, then.

"Mr. Grimaldi de Loutherbergh is Miss Nancy's youngest son," Gazza continued. "Your grandfather's younger brother. He runs the family estate."

"That's good to know," Elias said politely, shooting Ben a sympathetic look.

It seemed like there was no getting out of it, so Ben just nodded. He was meeting his estranged family now, and that was that. At least he could look forward to escaping to the cute bed-and-breakfast he and Elias had booked later.

"So, people called my great-grandmother Nancy?" he asked, changing the subject.

"We always called her Miss Nancy," Gazza said as they approached the exit. "Ever since she was a girl. Formally, she was Anne or Mrs. Grimaldi de Loutherbergh, and the family called her Aunt Annie. But to those who really knew her, it was always Miss Nancy. Oh, mind how you go. It's just this way, sirs."

He led Ben and Elias outside and over a crossing, briefly plowing through the rain before heading under the cover of the multi-story parking garage. Ben was wearing his coat, but he still gasped at the cold, dashing out of the deluge that quickly seeped into his clothes. The air was chilly and thick with car and aviation fumes.

"Miss Nancy told us," Gazza continued. "She said 'You look after that boy. Lord knows *they* won't. You see he's welcomed.' I figured that meant to have the car waiting for you lads." He stopped abruptly by a sleek black BMW. Although it was shiny, Ben guessed it was at least fifteen years old. "It's nice to see you're not traveling alone, sir."

Gazza nodded and popped the trunk with a key fob. "You guys mates, then?"

"Mates?" Ben replied, immediately thinking of animals on nature documentaries bonding for life. Not to mention the act of *mating* itself. He felt the tips of his ears get hot and his spine tingled. Gazza seemed friendly enough, but Ben had no idea what his views were on being gay. A working-class man of that generation might have deep prejudices. Then he realized (feeling a little stupid) that Gazza had meant 'buddies.'

But Ben didn't have anything to be ashamed about, and the truth was that he and Elias *were* just friends. It was irrelevant that they were both also gay.

"Oh, right, yes," he said confidently. Because if he couldn't say they were friends now, after all this, he probably never could. "Elias is also a lawyer."

"Oh, nice," said Gazza. Having loaded the suitcases into the trunk, he slammed it down, making the car bounce. "Yeah, the house has been full of solicitors lately, all huffing and puffing. Glad you've got someone who knows what they're talking about. Right then. In you hop."

He opened one of the back doors and Elias extended his arm, inviting Ben to seat himself before him. As he got inside the car, he noticed firstly that the steering wheel was on the wrong side. Then secondly, he realized that the passenger seat was occupied by an enormous silver tabby cat with icy blue eyes who swished their tail as Ben froze.

"Cat!" he squeaked, immediately feeling ridiculous for pointing out the obvious. But that had been the last thing he'd been expecting to see.

"Oh, don't mind her," Gazza said with a chuckle as he dropped into the driver's seat. "She's a law unto herself, that one. Cheeky madam goes wherever she likes. Luna, meet Mr. Turner and Mr. Solomon."

Luna's only response was to yawn widely, showing off all her teeth. She really was humongous.

"That's a pretty name," said Elias as he closed his door and they all buckled up. "Is she yours?"

Gazza laughed as he started up the car and reversed out of the space. "I don't think she could ever belong to anyone, that cat. But she does seem to like me from time to time. Not sure if anyone calls her anything else. I just think she looks like the moon. She's almost the same size as it now."

Gazza laughed at his own joke, navigating them out to a big intersection with a circular island in the center. Ben believed it was called a roundabout. It all seemed incredibly confusing as cars rushed around it in the pouring rain on the wrong side of the road, but they managed it without incident.

According to Gazza, it would take a couple of hours to get to the estate of Whittingar Abbey, which was located on the outskirts of a small town called Horncaster, situated midway between the bigger towns of Swindon and Bristol. Ben was a bag of nerves. His and Elias's plan had been to get settled, talk more with the UK solicitors representing Ben, then set up a meeting via them with whoever was in charge of contesting Nancy's will. This was all very sudden. Ben hadn't even brushed his teeth.

He felt like he was in a Jane Austen novel, introducing himself to the new neighbors who already hated him. It was a quite surreal.

The thing was, though, this was all very much like a regency novel. In theory, he had the power to evict everybody from the estate now. It was his property according to the will. Therefore, in fairness, the Grimaldi de Loutherbergh family had every right to distrust him and want him out of the picture. He was a stranger who could remove them from their home. He had no intention of doing that, so maybe it was a good idea to see them in person as soon as possible. He wanted to tell them that, and what better way than face-to-face?

As they drove down the highway through rolling fields under dark clouds, Ben felt an overwhelming sense of otherness. He was in a foreign land. Even if his family didn't want him there, it was still all very exciting.

He looked over to see Elias watching him. He blushed. "What?" he asked quietly. Gazza was listening to some sort of sporting commentary on the radio, so probably couldn't hear them.

Elias smiled. "You've got this look of wonder on your face. I was just appreciating your enthusiasm. A lot of people would be complaining about the rain."

It was ridiculous, but the simple compliment made Ben's heart sing. He knew it didn't mean anything, but he locked it up in a box in his heart anyway for safekeeping.

"I'm sure it'll look different in the sunshine," he admitted, "but there's something dramatic about the rain. Like it knew we were coming."

"Pathetic fallacy," Elias said, half a wry smile on his lips. "What they call it in literature. When it seems like the weather is sympathetic to the mood."

Ben didn't know anybody else who talked like that. His heart pounded as he smiled back at Elias. God, he just wanted to drink in every word. The fact that he said such smart things like that to Ben in private made it feel even more precious. Like it was a gift. He loved that they both seemed to be as big a book-worms as each other, especially for British classics.

"Right then," Gazza said loudly from up the front. "We're going to be approaching the estate soon, just so you know."

Nerves twisted in Ben's gut. This was it. They were driving through dense forest, made gloomy by the inclement weather still raging around them. But at some point, they were going to round a bend, and there it would be.

His inheritance.

Holy *fuck*. As the estate came into view, Ben's heart dropped.

It was a goddamned *mansion*. Several stories high with grounds that stretched in every direction out of sight. How could this be all his?

He bit his lip and realized he was trembling. What if there wasn't anything he could do to make these people not hate him? What if the extended family he'd yearned for every lonely holiday wanted nothing to do with him? This was a huge responsibility, owning a whole house and a business. So many staff members were going to be depending on the decisions he made, let alone the family. What if…

For the second time in twenty-four hours, Ben was surprised as Elias slipped his hand over Ben's. But this time, he remained holding it. Ben looked over in surprise.

"Breathe," said Elias kindly. "Everything's going to be fine."

Ben wasn't entirely sure he believed that. But feeling Elias's warm skin against his, he could maybe pretend for a while.

"Okay," he agreed. "Everything's going to be fine."

Of course it wasn't, but at least Ben got to hold Elias's hand before it all went spectacularly to hell.

6

ELIAS

ELIAS KNEW HE SHOULDN'T BE HOLDING BEN'S HAND LIKE THIS. It was complicating matters. But he looked so damn terrified as they approached Whittingar Abbey that it broke Elias's heart. He told himself he was purely offering some comfort. It was an innocent gesture. Except Elias knew damn well that he wouldn't hold a regular client's hand.

The thing was, Ben wasn't a client. He was a friend, albeit a relatively new one. If Darcy or one of his other friends were distressed, Elias would probably comfort them with a friendly touch as well. It was just his own less-than-innocent feelings toward Ben that were clouding his judgment. Still, he couldn't seem to make himself let go, not when Ben was gripping back so tightly.

"It'll be okay," Elias murmured, rubbing his thumb against the back of Ben's hand. "You're not here to screw anyone over. We're just going to get to the bottom of this."

They were traveling down a cream stone driveway, the gravel crunching under the wheels as they slowly trundled through the rain toward the manor house. Even through the car's tinted windows and the gray gloom of the morning,

Elias could see it was enormous. Several stories high and who even knew how wide across. White-framed rectangular windows sat in red brick walls, with a slanted gray slate roof that had turned almost black in the rain. Green lawns flanked the driveway, and at the front, slightly scruffy-looking leafy trees swayed in the wind. There was a pile of bricks by a wheelbarrow to the edge of the circular end of the drive, and one of the first-floor windows was boarded up.

Elias pursed his lips. It didn't look like the most loved property, he had to admit.

"Is this really all mine?" Ben said.

Rather than sound excited, he seemed almost horrified by the prospect. His eyes were wide and his voice tense and squeaky. He looked from the house out over the grounds at the trees in the distance. Presumably, they were part of the working orchard business that the family ran. Although, Elias had looked up the Tipsy Blossom hard cider they allegedly produced, and it seemed their sales had been dwindling for years. Their website alone looked like a relic from the nineties and they had no social media presence at all. Perhaps they were determined to cling on to the last century for whatever reason.

"That's right, Mr. Turner," said Gazza from up front, answering Ben's question. "Miss Nancy wanted you to look after the place. Have some fresh blood around to take care of it. But Mr. Grimaldi de Loutherbergh has assumed for years and years it would all be his." Gazza tutted as they swung around the driveway, giving Elias the impression he wasn't too fond of Ben's great-uncle Kenneth. His tone was cool and his jaw clenched, but he didn't say anymore on the matter.

Elias saw Ben swallow as he craned his neck to look up at the house they were nearing. He bit his lip and Elias squeezed his hand. Ben's iron grip meant he couldn't really let go, even if he'd wanted to. It meant Elias could pretend he didn't have a choice but to continue clinging on. "D-does Kenneth know we're coming, then?" Ben asked.

Gazza hummed as he brought the car to a stop outside the large front doors. "Yes, I left word that I was headed to the airport. I'm not sure how pleased he'll be about that, but technically, I'm still under Miss Nancy's orders, so he'll just have to lump it."

Elias managed to turn his snort into a cough. Even better, he saw Ben twitch a smile. Elias desperately didn't want him to be nervous. He was almost overcome with a wild urge to suggest to Ben that he stay in the car while Elias dealt with the ominous-sounding Kenneth, but that wasn't his place. This was Ben's inheritance and estranged family. He needed to be the one to face the music.

But Elias was going to be there every step of the way.

"Right," said Gazza, looking pointedly down at Luna the cat, still lounging in the passenger seat. "What are you doing then, little missy?" Luna yawned again, then clumsily unfurled, wobbling unsteadily as her legs attempted to support her great weight. "All right, hold on, hold on," Gazza grumbled as he opened his car door.

To Elias's surprise, he pulled a small umbrella from the glove compartment, extended it as he shut the door, jogged around the front of the car, then held the umbrella out as he opened the other door for Luna. Luna looked up at him as she meowed once, then deigned to jump out of the vehicle before trotting toward the front door. Gazza followed her, dutifully holding up the umbrella to keep her dry at the expense of himself.

Cold air had whipped in from the open doors before Gazza had shut them. Ben glanced at Elias. "Do we just wait?" he asked, unsure. He shivered, making Elias want to wrap his arms around him. He had to stop himself before he did anything so ridiculous.

"I guess," he said, equally unsure. He wasn't used to being waited on. It made him quite uncomfortable if he was honest. He would rather get his own bag and brave the rain with the umbrella that he'd brought with him, but he got the sense that Gazza would take offense to that.

Before he could consider getting out of the car any further, Gazza opened one of the two double doors of the house for the fat cat, where they were greeted by several loud, excitable barks. A Corgi dog with big tawny ears and a fluffy white chest yapped at the cat, as if simultaneously telling her off and welcoming her back. Elias watched as the Corgi attempted to nudge her with their nose as they furiously wagged their tail, but the cat simply raised her paw in warning. The noisy dog scuttled backward before darting around her and running toward the car. Gazza sighed. After watching Luna saunter into the house, he trudged back to the car with the umbrella, opening Ben's door for him.

The Corgi immediately launched itself into Ben's lap, shaking its wet fur with vigor.

Elias was used to dogs, but even he recoiled in horror as they were suddenly splattered. Ben cried out and tried to protect his face. Elias realized he had let go of Ben's hand, and even though there were more pressing matters to worry about, he wondered if he'd ever get the chance to hold it again.

"Oh, *Treacle!*" Gazza yelled, pulling the dog back by its collar. "You bad boy! Get down! I'm so sorry Mr. Turner. He was Miss Nancy's and he's been playing up ever since her… well. Since she left us. Let me get you some tissues."

"It's fine, honestly," Ben said, brushing down his jacket with a grimace. The wind howled through the opened door, making him tremble even more.

"Perhaps we should get inside," Elias suggested as Treacle hopped around on the gravel, apparently unconcerned about the pouring rain.

"Of course, of course," said Gazza, ushering Ben out of the car. Rather than wait for Gazza to run around to his side, Elias slid along the backseat and followed Ben out. Of course, that meant there were now three of them trying to huddle under one small umbrella, with a barking Corgi under their feet. Even when Gazza stepped back, holding the umbrella out over Ben and Elias, it was still a tight squeeze.

"It's okay, I can hold that," Elias offered, moving to take the umbrella. But as he did, Treacle dashed toward Ben's feet, tripping him up.

Ben careened against Elias, making Elias stumble backward in shock, sending them both stumbling into the rain. Except now Ben was clinging to Elias's back, pressed chest to chest, blinking up at him in the downpour. For a second, they just stared at each other, and Elias's pounding heart felt like it was lodged in his throat. He couldn't feel the hammering rain or the icy wind in that second. All he could focus on was Ben's sweet breath ghosting against his lips, and the little flecks of gold in his hazel eyes.

"Treacle!" Gazza bellowed, lurching forward with the umbrella again. Elias and Ben sprung apart, and the unpleasant weather suddenly cut through Elias like a knife. Gazza thrust the umbrella at him before retrieving another one from the passenger side of the car. He brandished it at Treacle, who dropped his tail between his legs and whimpered. "Get back in the house! Sirs, I'm so sorry. Get yourselves into the warmth and I'll be there in a sec. *Bad dog.* Get inside!"

He forced the umbrella open then stormed behind the car. Treacle harrumphed and trotted back toward the open front door. Elias looked awkwardly at Ben, trying to hold their umbrella over both of them, but keeping a respectable distance. It was pretty much impossible. Elias decided the best option was to traverse the driveway as quickly as possible.

"After you."

"Thanks," Ben mumbled. *Shit.* Elias had probably made him really uncomfortable grabbing onto him like that. What had he been thinking? Feeling ashamed, he trudged after Ben, escorting him through the front doors, noticing the slightly peeling paint as they went inside.

The door creaked as Elias pushed it open. He allowed Ben to step ahead of him as he closed the umbrella under the narrow awning above him, shaking off the excess rainwater as best he could. Then he followed Ben into the entrance hall.

Elias had been expecting something grand due to the sheer size of the house. And indeed, the ceiling was high and the lobby area vast. But he had to admit...it was a little underwhelming. Although a crystal chandelier hung overhead, it wasn't currently switched on, making the space gloomy. Elias could just about make out a few cobwebs wafting gently between the light's arms.

He and Ben wiped their feet on the worn, coarse mat before stepping onto a faded tapestry rug. The pale pinks and blues of the rug's floral pattern were a stark contrast to the dull, dark wood of the floor. The wall panels were a slightly more faded wood, with beams made of the same material stretching over a white-washed ceiling. Elias noticed another couple of cobwebs clinging to the high corners. A foreboding oil painting of a man in historical clothing with a moustache hung on the wall. He felt like it was glaring at them.

Ben shivered and rubbed his arms as he stared, open-mouthed at the hall. His honey-blond curls were damp on his head, but they still had a little bounce to them despite the rain. "It's creepy," he whispered. Elias had to agree. He half-expected some Dickensian ghost to appear, rattling his chains and moaning.

Treacle shook himself again, sending water droplets flying over the old rug, then he trotted off down the hallway past an honest-to-god suit of armor and out of sight. Despite what Gazza had said to them about getting into the warmth, it was almost colder in the drafty hallway than it had been outside.

Elias ruffled his fingers through his hair, hoping he didn't look too bedraggled. He told himself it was because he didn't want to face Ben's imposing estranged family looking like a drowned rat, not because he'd rather Ben didn't see him in such a condition. Water was dripping off both of them and the now closed umbrella, pattering onto the threadbare rug.

"Okay, there we go!" Gazza whistled as he struggled inside with the suitcases and his still open umbrella, slamming the door closed with his foot. The entrance hall was suddenly very quiet without the noise of the rain. "Phew!"

Elias had been so preoccupied with Ben and their accidental embrace that he hadn't appreciated what Gazza was doing. "Oh, damn," Elias said as Gazza shook and closed his own umbrella. "We're staying at a bed-and-breakfast. We could have left the bags in the car."

Gazza looked at him like he'd grown a second head. "Oh, no, Mr. Solomon. I don't think Miss Nancy would have approved of that at all."

Elias and Ben shared a wary look, but before they could protest, the sound of someone bustling down the hallway grabbed their attention. "Oh, Mr. Decker," a woman's voice admonished, presumably talking to Gazza. "You're dripping all over the floor!"

Gazza looked thoroughly sheepish. "Sorry, Mrs. Hollis. I've brought our new guests, though." He perked up, looking pleased as a plump woman in her fifties or sixties rounded the corner. She was dressed in slacks and a blouse with a long sleeveless cardigan swishing around her knees. She had graying brown hair that curled down to her shoulders, and she peered at Gazza through bifocals as she placed her hands on her hips.

She sighed and gave Elias and Ben a warm but tired smile. "Oh you poor dears," she said, stepping closer and taking the umbrella from Elias's hand to drop into a copper stand by the door. "Let me take your coats. Which of you is Mr. Turner?"

Ben raised his eyebrows at Elias as Mrs. Hollis raised her hands expectantly for his coat. "That would be me." He then cleared his throat and rolled his shoulders back. "Pleased to meet you." He sounded more confident as he handed her his wet coat.

"Oh, the pleasure's all mine," Mrs. Hollis said, waving her hands dismissively. "And you are?" she asked Elias briskly, but not in a hostile manner.

"This is Mr. Solomon," Gazza piped up, sounding eager to have the answer for Mrs. Hollis.

"He's here for moral support," added Ben, giving Elias a grateful look that made his insides warm in the chilly house.

"Oh, marvelous," said Mrs. Hollis with a nod. "I'm Mrs. Hollis, the housekeeper. We're so happy to have you here. It's not been the same since Miss Nancy's passing. No, not at all. I trust Mr. Decker was on time to collect you? This weather is just appalling."

"I was on time," Gazza said eagerly as Elias also handed over his coat. He'd rather have kept it on. There was a definite draft cutting through the house. But he got the feeling it would be rude to refuse Mrs. Hollis. "And the roads weren't too bad, all things considered."

Mrs. Hollis patted his arm then hung Elias and Ben's

coats on a stand by the front door. "Good man. Okay, you get those bags put away, and I'll take the gentlemen to Mr. Grimaldi de Loutherbergh."

Where were they taking their luggage? Elias wasn't sure he wanted to stay in this unwelcoming house. They hadn't even met any of the family yet, but it was clear they weren't thrilled to have Ben there.

Sure enough, Ben piped up. "Oh, no," he said, looking between Mrs. Hollis and Gazza. "Honestly, we've booked a bed-and-breakfast and we'll be happy to get a cab there once we're done here. We don't want to be an imposition."

Mrs. Hollis scoffed. "An imposition? Miss Nancy wanted this to be *your* home. Don't be ridiculous. We're more than happy to accommodate you. Now, off you go, Mr. Decker. Everything is all sorted. Mr. Grimaldi de Loutherbergh is expecting you, Mr. Turner." She eyed up Elias. "Although I'm not sure about your...friend?"

Elias tried not to squirm as he worried about what kind of assumptions these people might be making about him and Ben. The way she'd said 'friend' like it was a question made Elias feel like she was probing as to whether they were closer than that. He thought of the UK as being a pretty progressive place when it came to LGBT rights, but he had no idea on an individual basis what to expect.

"I'm here as Ben's informal legal counsel as well as a friend," Elias assured her.

Ben nodded emphatically. "I want Elias to come with me to meet Mr. Grimaldi de Loutherbergh – Kenneth. If – if that's okay? It's kind of why he came all this way with me."

Elias didn't want to upset Mrs. Hollis, especially as she appeared to actually be welcoming Ben into the house he'd been so afraid to enter. But Elias would put his foot down if he had to. Ben shouldn't have to face anyone alone, especially not the man leading the challenge against Ben's inheritance claim.

Thankfully, Mrs. Hollis nodded. "Well, in that case, let's get a move on. Thank you, Mr. Decker," she called over her shoulder as she began ushering Elias and Ben down the hall. "Mind you stay out of the rain, now. We don't want you catching a cold."

"Yes, Mrs. Hollis," said Gazza obediently.

Elias and Ben didn't seem to have much of a choice as Mrs. Hollis marched them through various corridors and up a couple of flights of stairs. Everywhere Elias looked there were dusty oil paintings of portraits and landscapes, mirrors with chipped gilded frames, and china vases on small tables but with no flowers inside. He peeked beyond a couple of open doors and saw books on shelves with crumbling spines, and sets of china crockery locked in glass cabinets. He imagined that once upon a time it had probably been a very grand family home indeed. But now it just looked a little sad and neglected.

"I'm sorry not to give you a better welcome," Mrs. Hollis said as they bustled past a room with a huge and rather creepy-looking rocking horse standing just beyond the door. "We're a little thin on the ground these days. It's mostly been me and the kitchen staff making do, with Mr. Decker acting as our handyman. Oh, and young Antoni. He's new, but he mostly deals with the grounds and the stables. We hardly see him inside." She sighed. "I wish you could have seen Whittingar in its prime. Miss Nancy would have loved that. But, well, you know."

Elias didn't know and he was pretty sure Ben didn't either. He had no idea why his grandfather Thomas had left England, changed his surname back to his mother's maiden name of Turner, abandoned his wealth, and never spoken of his estranged family again.

Before they could discuss the matter further, however, they rounded yet another corner (how high were they going in this house?) and almost ran into a man in his seventies or eighties. He was dressed head to toe in yellow and brown tweed with an impressive curly moustache. An honest-to-god monocle was pinched over his right eye, attached to a gold chain that extended from his breast pocket. Slung over his shoulder was an antique-looking musket, complete with bayonet. He stopped, taking up the whole width of the corridor, his feet spread wider than his hips and his free hand on his hip. He glowered at Elias and Ben.

Elias very nearly groped for Ben's hand, but instinct told him that wouldn't be a good idea in front of this guy. Instead, Elias stepped marginally closer to Ben's side, as if that might protect Ben from this man's scorn.

He huffed and looked the two of them up and down before turning his unimpressed gaze toward Mrs. Hollis, adjusting his monocle with his free hand. "I see you found the Americans," he grunted in an accent that made Elias think of British Officers in World War Two films he had watched as a boy. "Pointless, if you ask me. Kenny's having none of it."

Mrs. Hollis clasped her hands in front of her and rolled her shoulders back. "We've been through this, Mr. Barnaby," she said, her tone very carefully balancing between patience, respect, and the way you might scold a naughty schoolboy. "This was Miss Nancy's final wish."

Barnaby huffed. "We'll see about that." He strode forward, cutting a path between Ben and Elias, who had to duck fast to avoid the very sharp-looking bayonet. Barnaby didn't even bother to look back as he called over his shoulder. "Don't leave them alone anywhere near Aunt Annie's silver, there's a good woman."

Just for a second, Mrs. Hollis looked utterly mutinous

before she schooled her features. "Barnaby is one of Mr. Grimaldi de Loutherbergh's cousins. We tend to call everyone by their first names other than the eldest Grimaldi de Loutherberghs. It keeps things a little simpler." She inhaled deeply, shook her hands out, then smiled politely at Elias and Ben. "Shall we?"

Elias had appeared in court more times than he could count. He'd faced some quite frankly terrifying prosecutors and had to negotiate with many seriously grumpy judges. Yet as they approached wherever Kenneth Grimaldi de Loutherbergh was hiding, he felt real nerves flutter in his belly.

Not for himself, but for what Ben might be about to face.

Fuck it. They were walking behind Mrs. Hollis down the corridor, and Ben once again looked like he might be sick. So Elias reached out and took his hand.

Ben's head snapped to look at him, and for a second Elias worried he'd made a terrible error. But then Ben's face broke into a smile filled with relief and his shoulders sagged, like they weren't carrying quite so much weight anymore.

"Thank *god* you're here," he croaked in little more than a whisper. "Don't leave me, please."

Pride filled Elias's chest. "Not a chance."

It scared him how much he truly meant that.

7

BEN

Ben wasn't sure what to think of the fact that Elias had just reached to take his hand *again*. Quite honestly, he didn't have room in his head to overanalyze it much. He was too busy telling himself positive affirmations, such as – he was small but he was fierce. He hadn't done anything wrong. He could handle whatever Kenneth Grimaldi de Loutherbergh had to say to him.

So long as he was still holding Elias's hand.

He knew logically he would have to let him go as soon as they neared wherever Mrs. Hollis was taking them, but until that moment, Ben was determined to draw every ounce of strength that Elias's touch was giving him.

It was pretty obvious that Elias saw Ben as young and vulnerable. Holding hands was how you'd treat a scared child. But for a second, Ben could pretend that Elias was treating him like a friend, an intimate one at that. Someone he felt comfortable enough to take by the hand and guide through a particularly daunting situation. It felt like they were a team, facing down a foe side-by-side.

"Right, then," Mrs. Hollis announced as they approached

another set of double doors at the end of a corridor on the fourth floor. Tall green potted plants were sitting either side of the doors and there were coats of arms hanging on the walls to the left and right, as well as more portraits that looked as if their eyes were following Ben wherever he walked. Presumably they were of former family members through the ages.

Now they'd stopped walking, Ben could hear a murmur of voices. Although he couldn't place which direction they were coming from, he felt like there were many conversations happening on top of one another. They were also muffled, as if the noise was traveling through a closed door. The rumble wasn't coming from the doors in front of them, but perhaps down the hall and around a different corner?

Who did the voices belong to? Members of his family? A ripple of nerves traveled through his body. As much as he wanted to meet his relatives, he was anxious they didn't want to meet him.

Mrs. Hollis turned in front of the dark wooden double doors at the end of the corridor. She reached up and tousled Ben's curly hair. He was so startled he didn't know how to react, so he just allowed her to proceed. "There we go. That will do."

Ben had been on a plane for several hours, not to mention that he hadn't had a shower since yesterday morning. Whatever time zone he was in, he wasn't exactly feeling his most presentable. He nervously let go of Elias and tried to brush any creases out of his clothes.

He was wearing a T-shirt with a graphic design on that he'd probably wear out to dinner, along with a cardigan, his best jeans and newish sneakers, but somehow he didn't think that was going to be good enough. At least Elias was sporting a button-down, dress pants, and loafers. Between the two of them, he was certainly the one who looked like a real adult. Stupid crush aside, Ben had meant what he'd said. He was really glad Elias had decided to take a crazy chance and come all the way to England with him. Ben felt less outgunned as he looked toward the double doors where his great-uncle was presumably waiting on the other side.

If Mrs. Hollis had noticed him and Elias holding hands, she didn't even bat an eyelid, let alone mention anything. She just smiled at Ben once she'd finished fussing with his hair, then she glanced between him and the closed doors. "He's expecting you," she said tersely. She opened and closed her mouth, then hummed for a second. "This was Miss Nancy's home, Mr. Turner," she added firmly. "Her family meant everything to her. She never got the chance to mend the ties with her beloved Thomas beyond the letters they wrote, but I think she hoped one day she might be able to get a second chance with you."

She blinked as her eyes became glassy, and Ben felt a lump rise in his throat. He wasn't sure who Nancy Grimaldi de Loutherbergh really was, but he was feeling more and more that he would have liked to have met her.

Mrs. Hollis cleared her throat. "Anyway, you just remember that. It was her last wish to have you here, and we're pleased to welcome you. Okay?"

Ben licked his lips and glanced at Elias, who nodded. "I will," Ben promised.

"All right, then." Mrs. Hollis spun on her heels, then knocked firmly on the door before opening it. She stepped a few feet inside the room and held her hands by her sides. "Mr. Turner and Mr. Solomon to see you, sir," she said loudly and clearly, looking ahead.

Ben looked back at Elias, who raised his eyebrows. "Do you want me to go first?" Elias whispered.

It would be so easy to say 'yes.' Ben wanted to hide behind

Elias and let the older, more experienced, more confident man take care of everything. But this was Ben's problem, his *life*. He couldn't hide. So he shook his head, just as a stern voice drifted from inside the room.

"Well?" it said impatiently. "Send them in, then."

Mrs. Hollis nodded once, then stepped back with her arm out toward Ben and Elias, inviting them inside. Ben only glanced back briefly to make sure that Elias was following him, then stepped over the threshold.

He walked through into what looked like an office. He was struck first by the large, extremely heavy-looking desk, made from the same dark wood that seemed to be ominously present throughout the whole house, giving it a claustrophobic feel. The dark wooden panels only reached halfway up these walls, though. The top half was wallpapered with a gray, white and raspberry-pink pattern that looked like flowers and thistles. Multiple old qualification certificates were framed and hung, and a bronze chandelier with strong yellow bulbs hovered over the desk. In the corner was a free-standing gong, its mallet perched on top of the square stand it was hanging from.

Ben wondered if Kenneth ever summoned people with it.

Mrs. Hollis shot Ben a look of what he thought was support. He hoped it was. Then she walked swiftly from the room and closed the door behind her.

The man he presumed to be Kenneth Grimaldi de Loutherbergh – his great-uncle – was sitting behind the monstrous desk studying some loose sheets of paper in a leather portfolio. He was slim with a head of thick white hair, peering down over rectangular glasses that were perched on his bulbous nose. Tiny little red veins marked the end of his nose like tree branches. He wore a beige suit with a burgundy-and-cream polka-dot silk cravat. Unlike what they'd seen of the house so far, Kenneth's appearance wasn't shabby at all. It was pristine.

Kenneth still didn't look up as Ben and Elias approached the desk. There were no chairs on this side. Ben couldn't help but feel like Kenneth didn't want people getting too comfortable in his presence.

The desk had no framed photographs of loved ones present. There was a closed maroon ledger, a fountain pen, and a two-tier wooden letter tray. The presence of a closed, slimline laptop seemed incongruous with the rest of the historic-feeling room. The only other slightly modern touches were a few of the book spines visible on the couple of bookcases that weren't faded leather.

Ben and Elias stopped a few feet from the desk so Ben didn't feel like they were looming over Kenneth. The rug beneath their feet on the wooden floor was cream with a black border. Ben thought he detected a stain or two, but figured it was rude to stare too obviously. *Damn.* This whole place felt like it was in need of more TLC than Mrs. Hollis could give all on her own. Ben almost felt sorry for the house, like it was a living thing that deserved to be loved.

Kenneth had yet to look up at them. He was still calmly reading whatever the paper was in his hand. Ben could feel his cheeks starting to heat up in embarrassment. Surely Kenneth must know that they were standing right in front of him? Mrs. Hollis had announced them.

Ben glanced at Elias who looked far steadier than Ben felt. His presence filled Ben's heart with strength. So Ben turned back toward Kenneth and opened his mouth-

"*What* are you doing here?"

A chill ran down Ben's spine. He closed his mouth again, fear prickling over his skin. Kenneth hadn't even looked up as he'd spoken. His eyes were still flicking over the paper, and Ben wondered if he was actually reading and absorbing the words, or just putting on an act.

Ben rolled his shoulders back, though, remembering Mrs. Hollis's words, and drawing from Elias standing by his side. "Excuse me?"

Slowly, Kenneth raised his gaze, fixing Ben with stormy gray eyes that made Ben want to shiver, and not in a good way. They were icy cold and had blackened depths, like Pine Cove's lake in the grip of winter.

"Mr. Turner, I presume?" Kenneth flicked his chilly gaze up and down Ben, then over Elias. He didn't bother asking for Elias's name. "You were explicitly told not to come here, and yet here you are all the same. Like a parasite, clinging to the hide of a mangey animal." He sneered, his lip curling over teeth that were yellowed from what looked like decades of smoking. "Americans are such gold-diggers. It's revolting."

"I-I'm not gold-digging," Ben said as defiantly as he could. "I wanted to understand what happened with the will. I can assure you that it was a surprise to me to receive such an inheritance, but I was excited to discover I had an estranged family, too. I wanted to-"

"You aren't any family of *ours*," Kenneth scoffed with a laugh. He looked Ben up and down again, and Ben desperately wished he'd worn something better than a T-shirt to this meeting. Shame crept over him. He'd never felt so inadequate in his life. There was no way he belonged here with these people.

But he'd forgotten for a moment that he wasn't alone.

"We were informed that Anne Grimaldi de Loutherbergh was Mr. Turner's great-grandmother," Elias said, appearing unfazed by Kenneth's hostility. "Is that untrue?"

Kenneth looked up again, fixing Elias with an icy glare. "My brother Thomas ceased to be a member of this family the second he left the country fifty years ago."

"That's a yes, then," replied Elias cheerfully. "Ben is your great-nephew, and Mrs. Grimaldi de Loutherbergh named him as her heir in her last will and testament."

Kenneth slammed the portfolio in front of him closed, his eyes burning like fire as he snatched his glasses from his face and flung them across the desk. "*This* is exactly why Whittingar Abbey should have been granted a title to accompany the estate," he snarled. "Then everything would have passed to the most closely related and oldest male member of the family, avoiding all this utter nonsense."

It was tempting to cower. Ben never felt his small stature more than when he was in a confrontation. Despite his senior years, Kenneth emanated a dangerous aura of power. Ben thought of Mr. Cabot who'd flown all the way out to Pine Cove to intimidate him, and could very well believe that Kenneth had sent him personally.

But Ben was in the right. He hadn't tricked anyone and he certainly wasn't fortune hunting. He just wanted the truth. And with Elias by his side, he felt confident to latch onto that indignation and run with it.

"Well, my great-grandmother apparently wanted to change things," he said firmly, his head held high. "I know the will makes the situation kind of difficult, but honestly, I'm so thrilled to discover I have more family, even though I never knew Nancy. I really hope we can get to know each other better and straighten out everything with the estate."

He'd been practicing that little speech since before he'd even boarded the plane. However, Kenneth didn't appear all that impressed.

"Nancy?" he repeated incredulously, rising to his feet from his high-backed chair with his hands resting on the desk. "How *completely* disrespectful. You didn't even know my mother, whose name was *Anne* by the way, and yet you barge into our family home during this time of grief?"

Ben stepped back, just a fraction. Kenneth didn't look like a grief-stricken son, but he did look like a furious predator about to strike a prey that had personally offended him. Ben hadn't meant to offend anyone, but he hadn't come here to be insulted, either.

"I'm very sorry for your loss," he ground out. And he *was* sorry. "Anne sounds like a magnificent woman."

"She was an eccentric crackpot who delighted in practical jokes." Kenneth glowered as he walked around the table, his hands clasped behind his back. Ben almost stepped back again, but he caught Elias's eye. He wasn't moving, so Ben didn't either. "Evidently, she decided to go out with a bang and give us one last headache, and here you are." He tilted his head and regarded Ben with disappointment as he stopped at the end of the desk. "Everything was perfectly in order. The will had been fixed for years. Then it appears she altered it on her deathbed, without a care for how it would affect her family. I am quite certain she was not in her right mind, and all it will take is a matter of time to prove it and reset the inheritance to how it stood before."

His words were laced with bitterness and he was practically sneering down at Ben. He may have been an elderly man, but his back was not stooped and he towered almost a foot over tiny little Ben.

Not Elias, though.

"I am right to understand, then," Elias said, looking Kenneth directly in the eye, "that you mean to challenge the late Mrs. Grimaldi de Loutherbergh's mental capacity?"

Kenneth appeared mildly irritated. "I fail to see what business that is of yours. The matter will be dealt with, then we will notify Mr. Turner of any changes in his circumstances. It would probably be for the best if you both got back on the plane you arrived on and left this matter to the family, where it belongs."

Ben saw red. He honestly had no idea why his grandfather had left England and cut himself off almost entirely from this side of the family, but again, that wasn't Ben's fault. He hadn't done anything to bring about this situation other than simply being born. But Nancy had dragged him back into it.

"Anne was *my* great-grandmother, too," he said hotly. "For whatever reason, joke or not, she saw fit to leave me this estate. I want to work through this fairly, but I'm family too. You can't shut me out."

The smile that spread across Kenneth's face was positively terrifying. "Is that so?" he asked smoothly.

Then he turned, walked toward the door, pulled it open, and marched out into the hallway.

For a split second, Ben simply stood there, dumbstruck. "Shall we follow him?"

"Probably." Elias nodded, indicating for Ben to lead the way. However, when they reached the door's threshold, Elias leaned in close enough to whisper into Ben's ear. "My god, you're doing fantastically."

Ben was amazed his knees didn't buckle. His entire body certainly shivered, sending electric jolts through his belly that made his cock twitch. *Jesus.* If there was any chance in hell he could have his way, he would make sure Elias said things like that to him in that voice all the damn time. Feeling his breath ghost over Ben's ear made even more blood thicken out his eager dick.

It was worse than when they'd fallen into each other's arms outside. That had been clumsiness.

Elias had whispered to him just now *on purpose.*

Maybe it wasn't worse? Maybe it was better?

Dear lord. Ben needed to get a grip. Kenneth was already striding down the hall like a man much younger than his years, so Ben darted out of the study to follow him with Elias by his side. Apparently, he was unaware that he'd had such an effect on Ben's trousers.

Ben was making something out of nothing. Elias had just been giving him support, not seducing him. He needed to focus on whatever was happening with Kenneth, because any idiot could have seen that his smile hadn't been even the tiniest bit genuine. He was clearly up to something, and even though Ben had only just met him, he would bet his newly acquired enormous fortune on it being no good.

Ben and Elias turned the corner of the hall, following after Kenneth, just in time to see him open a door to a room on the right. As he did, a wall of voices talking over one another escaped, hitting Ben several feet away. How many people were in there?

The thought was pushed from his mind, however, as the noise wasn't the only thing to escape from the other side of the door. Ben immediately recognized Treacle's fluffy, stubby body come bouncing out, dancing around Kenneth's feet.

Kenneth didn't hesitate as he took a swing at the dog with his polished shoe.

"Hey!" Ben yelled in horror, breaking into a run. It didn't matter that Kenneth had missed. Treacle whimpered and scampered away all the same with his tail firmly between his legs.

Kenneth didn't seem to care either way about the scared Corgi or Ben's enraged cry. He stuck his chin up as he walked into the room, all the animated voices dying down as he did.

That should have given Ben a clue as he raced to the door, but he was so upset about Treacle he didn't pause to consider what he might be running in on. Not until he reached the threshold and grabbed the doorframe with both hands to steady himself.

Then he froze.

As a result, Elias's chest bumped into his back, and Ben felt his large hand steady himself on Ben's hip. But he couldn't even enjoy the surprise contact, as his heart was too busy stuttering in his chest.

Kenneth was standing to the side of the room's entrance, his hands clasped behind his back once more, a smug expression on his face.

He was just one of several dozen faces now looking at Ben. And not one of them was friendly.

Their ages varied over several decades, the youngest in their late twenties at most, the oldest frail and stooped, possibly in their nineties. Every single one of them was dressed in black. Holy *shit.* Had they managed to crash Nancy's funeral? Ben couldn't say he liked Kenneth in the slightest from his treatment of Ben so far, but he would feel absolutely awful if he'd come storming in, wrecking a solemn event like that. Right now, he had no way to tell.

Ben recognized Barnaby with his musket, which he'd propped up against a sofa, but everyone else was a stranger. The group was divided into those sitting on an array of dark green velvet couches and those standing around them. A stone fireplace with crackling flames took up the entire end of the room, lit candelabras standing on the mantel. Ben didn't register what the large sort of diamond pattern was on the walls for a second, until he realized there were dozens and dozens of skulls mounted on the cream walls, each with magnificent antlers protruding from the top.

How many stags had died to create this monstrous decor?

Ben knew he was latching onto random details to try and distract himself from the scrutiny he was currently under from close to fifty pairs of narrowed eyes directed his way. Panic bubbled up in him. If this was his extended family, he'd never meant to burst in on them wearing jeans and a T-shirt with day-old stubble and unbrushed teeth.

He'd never felt more out of place in his life. Every bone in his body told him to run. That he wasn't worthy of standing among this crowd. But Elias was still behind him, his hand reassuringly on Ben's hip. It didn't exactly give him confidence, but it meant that he chose to stand his ground instead of fleeing. He took a deep breath, and looked back at everyone who was staring at him.

Every face that was currently scrutinizing him was porcelain white, all except two of the youngest people in the room. Instinct told Ben they were brother and sister from their familiar resemblance and body language. The young woman in a black pantsuit had an elbow resting on the edge of the mantelpiece, a phone gripped tightly in her hand, and the young man was perched on a sofa arm, his body turned toward her. They looked to be of Indian heritage or another region in South Asia. Ben wasn't sure. But he did notice that there was just a little more space between them and anyone else in the room.

The only other person about Ben's age was a gorgeous guy with a mop of dark hair and a sweater tied around his shoulders. He actually regarded Ben with something akin to curiosity. Everyone else seemed absolutely furious.

Ben's mouth was suddenly so dry he thought he might begin to cough and choke. He was vaguely aware of Elias removing his hand from Ben's hip and clearing his throat. Ben felt like he should say something, but he had no idea what.

Unfortunately, it seemed the extended Grimaldi de Loutherbergh family (as Ben assumed them to be) didn't need to wait for him to speak.

A woman who looked to be in her fifties with a bright red perm grabbed the knee of a sleepy-looking man beside her. "Harold!" she exclaimed in horror. "Is that *him?* The American?"

Harold blinked and patted her bony hand on his leg. "Yes, Mildred. Whatever you want."

"You've got some nerve, coming here," snarled Barnaby, picking up his musket. Several people around him ducked as he swung it back over his shoulder. A woman with a silver streak in her black hair deftly saved a brandy glass from going flying, then took a big gulp of its contents. "This is our family. You have no right!"

"You didn't even know Aunt Annie," added a portly man smoking a cigar. "Why would she leave it all to you? It's ours, I tell you."

"Some more than others," someone grumbled under their breath, just loud enough for Ben to hear. Presumably, he wasn't the only one from some of the scathing looks that flashed across several people's faces.

"Please don't take the house away from us," begged another older woman. She was painfully skinny and wearing bright coral lipstick, her black dress hanging off her shoulders like a sack. Next to her on the sofa was a silver-haired woman who said nothing. She had a large ruby stone necklace around her throat that she was touching with her fingertips, her lined face staring mournfully at Ben.

Panic was making Ben's heart race. "N-no, I wouldn't dream of it," he stuttered, raising his hands. He didn't realize he'd backed up until he bumped into Elias again. This time Elias rested a comforting hand on his shoulder. Ben didn't shrug him off, even though it could be sending all kinds of inappropriate signals to all these people who were already judging the shit out of him.

He needed Elias's strength.

"We only want to discuss the terms of the will and to make sure it's implemented fairly and accurately," Elias told them in a clear, steady voice.

"It's not going to be implemented at all," snapped

Barnaby. He turned around to look to his relatives for support, making several people duck again to escape the bayonet as it swung in an arc. He turned back to Ben with a nasty grin. "Aunt Annie was clearly off her rocker in the final days. We'll prove it and keep your greasy American hands *off* our fortune!"

The woman with the ruby necklace clutched it with a pained expression, closing her eyes. The skinny woman beside her nodded triumphantly, though, as did several other relatives. Interestingly, the young Indian woman huffed and shook her head, concentrating on her phone screen. The guy Ben thought might be her brother looked close to tears.

"This is all a big mistake," said Mildred with the red perm. "You should both just leave, shouldn't they Harold?"

Harold blinked and checked his pocket watch. "Well, it's close to one o'clock, Mildred," he said with a nod.

Tears stung at the back of Ben's eyes as bile rose in his throat. "I didn't mean to impose during your time of grieving," he uttered, feeling wretched. "I'm so sorry."

Several people tutted and harrumphed, making Ben feel even worse. However, the young Indian woman frowned and tilted her head as she regarded Ben. Her expression didn't seem as furious as most of the other people in the room, but it was hardly friendly. Ben still didn't feel he had any allies in the room with him. Even the young guy with the sweater tied around his shoulders appeared more curious than sympathetic.

Aside from Elias, of course. Ben was so grateful to him for his warm hand firmly on Ben's shoulder.

But really, why should any of these people give Ben the benefit of the doubt? He was a lowly outsider who was poor, with no college education, and had left his home country for the very first time only yesterday afternoon. What possible claim could he make on this estate?

Kenneth raised his neatly trimmed white eyebrows at Ben. "Well? It's clear you're not welcome. *Blood* doesn't make you family."

Sweater guy's expression was smug at that. The young Indian woman and her brother shared a dark look that Ben didn't miss, but he didn't dwell on it. He was feeling too sick.

This was exactly what he'd feared. He still had no idea why Nancy might have left him her entire legacy over all these people, and they were rejecting him as a fraud, an outsider, a fortune hunter.

He'd never felt so deeply ashamed in his life. He wasn't a greedy person. He'd come here to solve a mystery.

But perhaps it was all best left alone.

"S-sorry," he stammered again, trying not to let any tears fall and he went to step backward. But Elias was in his way, his hand still holding on to Ben's shoulder.

Elias squeezed him, making Ben want to melt into his arms and sob. "We'll discuss this further at a better time," said Elias. He shot Kenneth a stern look. "In *private*. In the meantime, we'll let you be."

With that, he gently pulled Ben out into the corridor, saving him from any further scornful looks.

Only then did Ben allow himself to cry.

8

ELIAS

Elias gave up. There was no way in hell he could stop himself from hugging Ben tightly when Ben began to sob against his chest.

He felt like his heart was breaking as he rubbed the younger man's back and shushed him with soothing noises. His skin was cold where Elias pressed his cheek against Ben's forehead. "It's okay," he promised. "Come on. Let's go. I don't want any of those assholes coming out after us."

Ben nodded and took a shaky breath in. "Yes," he croaked. "I d-don't want them to see me like this."

Elias hugged him to his side as they marched back down the drafty hall. He wasn't sure which way to head as he had no clue where their bags had ended up. It was still pouring with rain by the look of it through the windows, and Elias didn't want to leave any of their possessions in the hands of these dreadful people.

He understood that grief and inheritance matters sometimes brought the worst out in people, but Ben was a sweetheart. Just because he wasn't a pushover, they were treating him like a villain. More than that. Kenneth was actively being vindictive toward him, challenging Ben's inheritance when he had no real grounds to do so. Not to mention acting like an absolute douchebag.

Rage simmered in Elias's veins. He kept it under control for the sake of Ben. He needed Elias to keep his head for the moment. They could lose their shit about everything later.

Unfortunately, just as they began their descent to the third floor, Elias heard a door open from down the corridor and the cacophony of voices rose to greet them. He tried to hurry Ben along a little faster, but the sound of feet thumping on the wooden floor told him someone was running after them.

Shit.

"Hold on, hold on," a young man's voice called after them. However, it didn't sound hostile, so Elias turned to face whoever it was.

A guy in his late twenties with a mop of thick black curly hair jogged up beside them, stopping on the top step just above them. He had a charcoal sweater tied around his shoulders over a black shirt. His pants were black and clinging relatively tightly to his muscular thighs. Anyone could see he was extremely good-looking, but unlike everyone else Elias had seen in that room, his expression seemed to be one of kindness.

He held his palm up toward where they'd all just come from and shook his head. "I am *so* sorry about them," he said emphatically. "They're stuck in their ways and a lot of them are pretty prejudiced against foreigners, to be blunt. Anyone who can't trace their lineage back to Churchill isn't worth speaking to." He puffed his cheeks out and offered out his hand. "I'm Noah, by the way."

Elias was beyond worrying what he should or shouldn't do with regards to touching Ben. The fact was, Ben was still clinging to him, so Elias kept hold of him too. It was damned chilly in this house, so they could use being cold for an excuse if they needed to.

"Elias Solomon," he said, returning the handshake with one hand, but keeping the other on Ben's back. "And I guess you know this is Ben Turner. Are you one of Kenneth's grandsons?"

Noah blew a raspberry. "Am I one of that lot? Christ, no. I'm almost as much of a pariah as you chaps. Kenneth *is* my godfather and has a soft spot for me. But they all look down their noses when I'm around, I can tell." He gave them a crooked smile and winked at Ben. "Chin up. If they hate you, you're doing something right."

Ben wiped his face and let go of Elias, smiling warmly at Noah. Elias was deeply ashamed to admit that his heart lurched with jealousy. But that was totally unfair and completely ridiculous. Ben was allowed to smile at whoever he wanted, especially gorgeous men closer to his own age. Elias needed to remember his role here as a friend and an advisor.

"Thanks," said Ben with a sniff. "I didn't expect to be confronted by all of them like that. Did we crash the funeral?"

Noah shook his head and jogged down the couple of steps so that he was beside them, then indicated with his hand that they should continue walking. "Not at all, that was last week. She passed a week or so before that. But once they all get together, it can be a little difficult to get them to leave, especially when there's a whiff of gossip to brighten up their dreary lives. And they're so damned dramatic, so no one wants to be the first to stop mourning. Including me, it seems."

He indicated his black clothes and rolled his eyes as they walked down yet another corridor with more portraits, coats of arms, and china vases. Ben sniffed, looking at Noah with captivated eyes. Elias did his best to wrestle his jealousy back down to a manageable level. There was no denying Noah was enigmatic. Elias couldn't really blame Ben for being interested. Besides, it was good to know at least one person from that room wasn't hell bent on running Ben out of town.

"I'm sorry for your loss," Ben said sincerely.

But Noah scoffed. "It's fine. Don't get me wrong, Annie was an interesting woman whom people loved, but I'm kind of over the moping around and pretending like she was some saint."

He laughed, but Elias wasn't sure he saw the joke. "I take it you weren't close with Mrs. Grimaldi de Loutherbergh?" he asked.

"Old Annie?" Noah grimaced. "Not particularly. She never warmed to me. My grandfather worked for the family as an accountant, you see. I think she never looked at him as anything more than staff. But when I lost my parents at a young age, Kenneth took me in as one of his own." He fixed Ben with a genuine stare. "I know he's a little brash, but deep down he's a good man. I hope you get to see that."

Elias digested this new information as they once again passed the creepy nursery with the enormous rocking horse with the dead-eyed stare that seemed to follow them as they walked past. After the way both Gazza and Mrs. Hollis had spoken with such deep fondness about 'Miss Nancy,' it seemed strange that Ben's great-grandmother would hold prejudice against her staff for being beneath her. Perhaps she'd changed her ways in recent years and Noah's grandfather hadn't lived to see it?

Ben hummed and didn't appear convinced about Kenneth, either. "I'm pretty sure he hates my guts," he said to Noah. "In fact, I wouldn't put it past him to be sticking pins in a little voodoo doll version of me right now."

He slipped his hands into his pockets, giving a faint smile

as Noah laughed heartily. Elias already missed his arm being around Ben's waist. He kept telling himself that each time they held hands or embraced it would be the last. But however much he might know it was wrong, it pained him more and more each time they let go. He was already longing for another opportunity for them to be close again.

He was taking advantage of Ben's vulnerability, though. He needed to stamp it out, no matter how much it hurt his heart.

"Give it time," Noah promised, reaching over to touch Ben's elbow. Ben smiled shyly and Elias couldn't seem to quell that heartache as easily as he'd hoped. "In the meantime," Noah continued, "I'm on your side, anytime you need. I take it you'll be staying around?"

Ben looked anxiously at Elias and shook his head with a sigh. "We're not sure," Elias replied for them both. "We had plans to stay nearby, but our suitcases appear to have been confiscated. However, I can't imagine anyone would want us in the house if they're all going to be here."

Noah nodded. "They were supposed to leave again after the funeral – myself included. No one officially lives here full time aside from Kenneth. But they all treat it as a sort of way station, coming and going as they please. Mrs. Hollis hates that," he added with a laugh. "But I think they're all sticking around for the show now – by which I mean leeching off Kenneth to see how the drama with the will is going to unfold."

Elias bit his lip. "In fairness, I imagine they're quite anxious regarding the family's estate. What with the cider business and all, there's a lot at stake." *Although they didn't need to be so rude to Ben,* he added silently.

"I want to do right by them all, I promise," Ben added.

Noah tutted. "I'm starting to think more and more that Old Annie changed that will to force everyone to sort themselves out. Even though Kenneth is the logical heir, by giving you everything, it's making them question what's really theirs." He flicked a suit of armor as they passed it, making a 'ding' float through the air. "Most of them have never worked a day in their lives."

Elias detected a hint of bitterness there, but he couldn't say he blamed Noah. Personally, he couldn't abide idle people.

"So you agree I never should have gotten this inheritance," Ben said. Elias could hear his guilt.

Noah scoffed. "Oh, no, I think it's great that you've come to set the cat amongst the pigeons. It was Annie's will, she could do what she wanted. I don't envy you, facing all their wrath. But" -he sucked on his teeth- "I think you should brace yourself for the solicitors overturning it all. As fun as this chaos is, Old Annie always was a bit batty, and they'll probably be able to prove she wasn't quite in her right mind."

They arrived in the entrance hall and came to a natural halt. Elias wasn't sure where they should go in the house to find their bags, and he wasn't eager to go wandering around outside in the pouring rain. To make matters worse, it seemed their coats were now missing from the stand by the front door.

"Are you suggesting they mean to prove she was suffering from a form of dementia?" he asked, wanting to get some kind of insight into this bizarre situation. That was his job there, after all. "Are they officially questioning her mental capacity?"

Noah shrugged and ran his finger along one of the display cabinets, rubbing the dust away. "I honestly couldn't say. But Aunt Annie always was a strange one, acting on crazy whims and having all these wild ideas that would never fly. Why do you think this place is practically falling down? She was terrible with money."

He winked at Ben again. Elias had to say that issue had been bothering him. How could the estate – and therefore Ben – be worth sixty-five million dollars when the house was a shambles and the Tipsy Blossom cider business had been dwindling year after year for the past decade. It didn't make sense. Where was the money going?

"I bet you'll sort everything out, though, if the will stays as it is," Noah continued. "What is it you do for a living, again?"

Elias watched in dismay as Ben blushed unhappily. "Um, I'm a baker," he admitted.

"He's an *amazing* baker," Elias chipped in before he could stop himself, but he couldn't bear the idea of him feeling bad about himself. "His pastries are the stuff of legends."

Thankfully, Noah's face split into a joyful smile. "Oh, wow. I bet you could do *amazing* things with all the apples lying around here!"

Ben's expression shifted from distress to delight in less than a second. "One of my favorite recipes is for spiced apple muffins," he told Noah.

For a second, the two young men smiled at each other, all starry-eyed. Awkwardness washed over Elias, and he took a small step back, trying to give them some space. He was almost certain from the hints of body language that Noah was also gay. Elias shouldn't do anything to get in Ben's way if a handsome guy looked his way.

Except the moment was broken for him as an excitable Treacle came running toward them, his nails scrabbling along the floorboards. Noah jumped back, and for just a second, Elias thought he saw him sneer at the dog. But then Noah laughed and clutched his chest.

"Sorry," Noah cried. "I'm allergic to dogs and not used to having them around. This little fellow always startles me." Treacle was barking at Noah. His tail was wagging, but he was definitely directing his yaps toward the young Englishman with his ears flattened. "Off you go," Noah tried telling him firmly.

Treacle just barked more.

"Oh, *Treacle.*" Gazza's exasperated voice preceded him as he came huffing and puffing into the entrance hall to join them. "Why are you always causing trouble?"

Elias flashed back to Kenneth taking aim at the rotund Corgi, and his heart twisted. Had Kenneth ever succeeded in kicking the poor creature? Was Treacle missing his mom, Nancy, and just trying to find love from someone else?

"Oh, no," Elias said, crouching down to fuss Treacle, who was more than happy to stop barking and let him, his tongue lolling from his mouth. "He's a good boy, aren't you?" He nuzzled against Elias's hands as he rubbed and tickled him. It had only been a day and a half, but Elias was missing his own dog, Rosie.

Gazza grumbled something about muddy paw prints and shedding hair on antique rugs, but when Elias glanced up, the older guy was shaking his head and smiling.

"I'm glad we ran into you," Elias said as he stood again, brushing his hands together. "You don't know where our things went, do you?"

"Oh absolutely, Mr. Solomon," said Gazza, nodding. "We've set you up in the groundskeeper cottage. It's a guest house a little away from the main estate. We thought you'd appreciate some space."

Noah clapped him on the shoulder. "Excellent idea, Decker."

Gazza hummed and looked down at his hand. After a beat, Noah removed it. Gazza didn't look him in the eye, instead focusing back on Ben. "It was all Mrs. Hollis's idea, actually," said Gazza. "I just do as I'm told. Shall I take you gents over there now?"

Ben visibly sagged as he smiled. "That would be *wonderful,*" he said, suddenly sounding exhausted. "It's been a crazy twenty-four hours."

"Will you join us?" Elias asked Noah out of politeness. He suspected he might have been trying to prove to himself that he was perfectly fine if Ben wanted to spend more time with the gorgeous guy, but he couldn't deny his relief when Noah shook his head.

"I'll let you both get settled in, but I'm sure I'll see you soon." He waved to them as he sauntered off into the belly of the house once more.

His personal pettiness aside, Elias was happy to have someone on Ben's side who was willing to give them some information. The truth was, if Nancy's mind had deteriorated, Kenneth and the rest of the family would have solid grounds to dispute the will and have it reverted to its previous state.

Elias knew Ben wasn't in this for the money – even though there were very few people on the planet who would turn down millions, be it in dollars or pounds. But Elias was pretty sure he and Ben were both determined that this affair be conducted *fairly.* With Kenneth in the picture he wasn't convinced that was going to happen, no matter what Noah had tried to assure them.

More than that, though, Elias could see the hope that shone on Ben's face when he talked about family. As he was an only child whose parents had also been only children, Elias could understand why he would be excited to learn he had so many relatives, and why he'd be devastated by their rejection.

Elias knew all about family rejection.

He swallowed around the lump that always appeared in his throat the second he thought about his own parents, siblings, cousins and all the rest. How long had it been now since he'd spoken to any of them?

This wasn't about him. He shook himself mentally and took the smallest step back toward Ben. Firstly, they needed to settle this business with the will. Then they could maybe see about Ben forming any kind of relationship with his family.

Gazza fished a couple of large golf umbrellas out from the stand by the front door, handing them to Ben and Elias, before saying something about going to fetch their jackets. Elias was relieved they hadn't gone far. When he returned with them, they were toasty warm, as if they'd had a turn in a dryer. Elias couldn't help but feel touched by the gesture. Treacle had laid himself down at their feet, but when Gazza returned, he jumped back up, his tail wagging.

"I think this one wants to escort you," Gazza said with a chuckle.

Elias grinned, catching Ben's gaze. His expression was also amused. "We'd love a chaperone," Elias assured him.

The weather outside was just as awful as it had been before, but at least with an umbrella each that was twice the size as the ones from the car, they were a little better protected. As much as Elias had been glad that they weren't going to be staying in the main house, he now realized that he and Ben would be all alone in their own space. He hoped it wouldn't get awkward. This wasn't like staying at a bed-and-breakfast with other guests around.

Shit – he needed to cancel their reservation if they really weren't going to be staying there. Just for the moment, however, he thought he'd leave it until he saw what this cottage was going to be like. He felt better having a backup plan. Having seen the state of the main house, there was every chance they were being taken to a pokey little hut with a leaking roof and no heating.

They walked to the right of the house, toward the orchards, passing a large stable. Elias peered inside through the rain, making out the stalls and the nodding, bobbing heads of several horses, their breath cloudy in the cold afternoon air as they snorted. He also made out a muscular-looking young man dressed in jeans and a hoodie, hauling bales of hay around.

"Oh, there's Antoni," said Gazza cheerfully as they walked past. "He's only been with us since the summer. Works like a packhorse. Good lad, that one. Hi, Antoni!" He waved and the young man paused to return the gesture. Then Antoni looked down, holding his hand near the ground. To Elias's surprise, Luna the fat cat materialized from the gloomy shadows to be petted by the farmhand.

"I thought she didn't like the rain?" Elias commented.

Gazza chuckled as they trudged along the wet gravel. "She does what she wants, that little miss. But I wouldn't be surprised if she'd tricked one of the cleaners or kitchen staff to carry her out there. It's heated in the barn, you see, so she likes to sleep in the fresh hay."

As they went beyond the stable, Treacle looked torn between staying with them or going to investigate (or harass) Luna and Antoni. Eventually, the rain got the better of him, and he raced to catch up with Elias and the others under their umbrellas.

Ben was chewing his lip. "You know what's what around here, don't you, Gazza?" he asked, although Elias felt like it was more of a statement. "If I was in charge, I wouldn't know where to start with all this history."

Gazza shrugged. "We'll be here to help you, Mr. Turner. Unless you go and sack us all, that is?"

Elias got the impression Gazza was attempting to make a joke, but as Gazza glanced at Ben there was definitely a flash of worry that crossed his face. Ben, however, looked back at him in wide-eyed horror.

"I'd *never* fire anyone," he said emphatically. "Not unless they were, I don't know, doing something really bad. That would be awful if somebody new came in and changed everything – *everyone*. Oh, no, I'd never do that."

He sounded so sincere, Elias's heart ached. He wasn't sure what had happened in this family's past or why Nancy had decided to leave everything to her estranged great-grandson, but that right there was why Elias believed that maybe she had made the right decision. The house clearly needed some love and care. Perhaps fresh blood was what it needed to breathe life back into it?

Gazza looked pleased with Ben's answer as they came off the gravel driveway and continued down a dirt track through trees that were getting denser, forming a small woodland. They were thrashing in the wind and rain, so Elias didn't see the cottage until they were right on top of it. As it came into view several minutes later, Elias couldn't help but gasp.

He had always been a bit of an Anglophile, obsessed with the charm of all things British. He blamed it on his love of Dickens, Austen, Tolkien, and even children's authors like C.S. Lewis, Roald Dahl, and the more modern J.K. Rowling. Like Ben, Elias had suffered from loneliness at many points in his life, often finding friendship and escape between the pages of a book.

Seeing the cottage made his heart pang even more than approaching the grand estate. It was utterly adorable, with its thatched roof, rough cream stonework, ivy growing up one wall, and little chimney puffing out purply gray smoke. Elias blinked back tears and tried to repress the quite frankly ridiculous notion that after thirty-nine years, he had finally come home.

He hadn't realized he had stopped walking until he felt

Ben's cold hand squeeze his own. He looked down to see Ben grinning at him. After the stress of the last couple of hours, it was a huge relief to see Ben smiling at him again. But Elias wondered how much of his emotion he had betrayed on his face. He cleared his throat and tried not to feel embarrassed.

"Isn't that the most ridiculously adorable thing you've ever seen?" Ben enthused, however. He beamed as he looked between the house, Elias, Gazza, and even Treacle sitting at their feet under the umbrellas. "Is this really where we're going to stay?"

Gazza nodded, juggling his umbrella as he fumbled with the set of keys he pulled from his jacket pocket. "Technically, this is where I should be living. But me and my Jenny lived in our house in the village for over thirty years – god rest her soul – and I have no interest in upping sticks to come here. But we've made it nice and snug for you. Miss Nancy was clear on that. Apparently, her dear Thomas always loved sneaking out here, just like she used to in her later years. She thought you might like it, too."

He evidently found the right key and brandished it at Ben as he smiled. His eyes were a little watery, whether from talking about his late wife, Nancy, or both, Elias couldn't tell. He unlocked the door, then led the way inside.

Treacle shoved his way in front of both Elias and Ben, his bushy tail wagging furiously as he shook himself off, then strutted through the door as if he owned the place. Elias let Ben go first, then he followed, closing and shaking his umbrella as he wiped his feet on the mat. Gazza had been quick to grab a towel that had been hanging from a peg by the door, giving Treacle a rough dry so he didn't get muddy paws or rainwater everywhere.

The front door took them directly into a sitting room packed with mismatched sofas, armchairs, footstools, and coffee tables. There must have been half a dozen crocheted blankets draped and folded over various surfaces in the small room that would have fit comfortably in Whittingar's entrance hall. Logs were crackling merrily in the fireplace, and someone had placed several small jam jars around the surface tops filled with white flowers that Elias was pretty sure were called snow drops.

The ceiling was low and to their left was the tightest winding staircase that presumably led up to the second floor. There was a slightly crooked open wooden door on the other side of the living room that would take them through to the kitchen, where Elias could smell something meaty and tomatoey cooking. His stomach flipped over. It felt like forever since he'd eaten on the plane.

"Has someone made lunch for us?" he asked in disbelief, resting his hand on his suitcase handle. Both his and Ben's bags had been delivered just inside the front door, with not a drop of rain on them.

Gazza chuckled. "Oh, that'll be Mrs. Hollis. She can't give people two minutes here without feeding them her cottage pie. Sorry about that."

"Sorry?" Ben croaked, already kicking off his shoes in his haste to get into the kitchen. Treacle barked at him, then dashed back and forth between the two rooms.

Gazza pointed at him. "He's already herding you. Watch that. He can count – all Corgis generally can. He'll get upset when I leave – oh, unless you want me to take him back to the house?"

Ben and Elias looked at each other. "He can stay with us?" Elias asked.

Gazza nodded as he also toed off his shoes and walked into the kitchen. "There's some tinned food for him in the cupboard, I'm sure, and usually a bowl you can put out for water. Ah! There we go." The sound of water running was followed by the clatter of china on tiles.

Elias finally got his wits together and removed both his damp jacket and shoes, hanging the jacket on the coat stand by the door. He stashed both the umbrellas into the bucket he assumed was meant for that purpose. Only then did he get to join the others in the warm kitchen, where Gazza was pulling out a dish from the oven that was topped with golden, cheesy mashed potato.

Elias's mouth watered, but not as much as his heart ached as he watched Ben spin around, looking at everything.

The kitchen was just as cramped as the living room and also slightly crooked, but unlike the enormous stately home, it didn't feel claustrophobic with all that dark wood. The floor tiles were white, as were the painted walls, with light, roughly hewn wooden beams crossing up the walls and over the low ceiling. Elias almost had to stoop, especially with the various pots and pans hanging down, all a bright royal blue and so heavy looking he reckoned they'd make pretty effective weapons if you really needed to smack somebody. A small herb garden tray was sitting on the window sill, thriving despite the time of year, and a clock was mounted on the wall, telling the time in Roman numerals. There were more jam jars with snowdrops, as well as an impressive collection of teapots in all shapes and sizes that ranged from ancient-looking to Ikea.

As Ben spun around and Gazza fetched some plates, Elias noticed there were also dozens and dozens of photo frames that were hung on the walls and standing on every surface, both in the living room and in the kitchen. Gazza wafted floral oven gloves over the cottage pie as it rested on the counter, then apparently noticed Elias's interest in all the pictures.

"Oh, yeah," he said warmly, nodding to himself. "Since I never did move in, Miss Nancy put a lot of her old photos out here. Those are all of her when she was a girl, before she married Charles. He passed away all the way back in eighty-four, god rest his soul. But she always was an independent sort."

Elias picked one photograph off a shelf. "Was Nancy in the war?" he asked, unable to stop the admiration from creeping into his tone. But the young Nancy – probably only just in her twenties – looked damned happy in her bottle-green uniform and round tin helmet.

"Absolutely," said Gazza, slicing up the cottage pie to dish two portions onto plates. Treacle danced hopefully around his feet, obviously angling for a taste. "She was a searchlight operator. She talked about it a lot. Nancy always believed people should do their part, war or no war. All right!" He held out the two plates. "That's lunch. The cupboards are pretty full, but if you need anything, just give us a bell on the number by the phone. I imagine after all that traveling, you'll need some rest."

Before Elias knew it, Gazza was putting his shoes back on, petting Treacle goodbye, then heading back out of the door with his umbrella into the pouring rain.

Leaving Ben and Elias all alone in this beautiful cottage, with a piping hot lunch, and an already faithful dog at their feet.

He'd never even imagined such a picture of domestic bliss.

Elias hovered in the kitchen, his cottage pie clutched in his hands, watching as Ben curled up on one of the sofas, flinging a blanket over his legs, first checking that Treacle was dry enough, then inviting him to hop up beside him. Ben scooped up a morsel of gravy-covered potato from his plate with a single finger before offering it out for Treacle to lick off. He then looked up at Elias, making him startle.

"Is everything okay?" Ben asked.

No, it wasn't.

Because there was only so much Elias could do to fight this. In that moment, it was suddenly and rather painfully clear to him.

He was falling for Ben, hard.

Maybe the perfect, rustic English setting wasn't helping Elias think realistically. Or maybe it was just the fact that he had finally gotten the chance to spend a couple of days with the young man he'd been admiring for a year and a half, and now his crush had gotten wildly out of control.

But he couldn't say any of that to Ben. Beautiful, sweet, fiery Ben. So instead he settled himself on the sofa adjacent to Ben and Treacle, doing his best to smile.

"Everything's wonderful," he assured him, despite his inner turmoil saying otherwise.

How the hell was he going to get through two weeks of this?

9

BEN

Ben blamed the jetlag. It *had* to be the jetlag.

Because why else would he wake up at five in the afternoon from a deep sleep to a cold fireplace, wrapped up on a sofa, with a dog huddled at his feet.

And, oh yeah, Elias pressed up against his back with his arms wrapped around Ben like an octopus.

Ben froze, frantically searching his memory. *Oh god.* At some point a few hours ago (he had to assume) he had a vague memory of waking up shivering his ass off. His lizard brain must have kicked in from his camping days with his parents. Because when you were cold out in the wilderness, you snuggled with whoever was closest for body heat.

Mortified, Ben remembered how his mostly asleep brain had reasoned it had been a perfectly acceptable idea to drag himself off his own couch and drop down onto Elias's, spooning the two of them close together to warm up under several blankets. A robust Corgi acting like a pair of slippers had obviously encouraged him back into a solid REM cycle, and only now was he waking up and realizing exactly what he'd done.

It was *fine*. No damage had been done, yet. He just had to gently extract himself from Elias's arms and move back to his own couch, pretending like nothing had happened. So long as Elias hadn't surfaced in the past couple of hours since Ben's humiliating, semi-conscious relocation, he'd be none-the-wiser.

Except Ben didn't have that kind of luck, and he should have known it.

Doubtless sensing Ben's movement, Treacle suddenly burst to life, barking like they were under attack and jumping down off the sofa, kicking up half the blankets with him. Ben gasped and made a split-second assessment whether or not he had time to remove himself from Elias's personal space. However, Elias's response to imminent danger was apparently to cling onto Ben like the world was ending.

"Huh?" Elias cried, wrapping his arms tighter around Ben's chest like a vise and even throwing his damned leg over both of Ben's. "What's...where...?"

Shame like Ben had never known flushed through him. How the *fuck* was he going to explain that his sleepy, possibly nightmare-riddled brain had decided that the only place he'd felt safe and warm going back to sleep was in Elias Solomon's arms? He'd never in his life wanted the ground to swallow him up more.

Except...Elias grunted, probably regaining full consciousness if he'd been sleeping as deeply as Ben had been. "You're cold," he mumbled, rubbing Ben's arm and chest. "*Really* cold. Did the fire go out?"

Ben was almost too afraid to breathe. Why wasn't Elias mad or freaking out that he'd crawled onto his sofa with him? They were tangled under several blankets and Ben was certain his hair – made wilder and curlier by the rain – was smooshed all in Elias's face. Instead, he glanced over his shoulder to see Elias give the dead fireplace a disgruntled look.

"Damn it," Elias growled right by Ben's neck, sending naughty feelings straight to his cock. If Elias was going to keep murmuring in his ear, Ben could only be so responsible for the way his dick got happy. Not that Ben would ever do anything about it.

Although…he wanted to cringe as a sudden, appalling image flashed through his mind. It would be *so* easy to turn around and press himself against Elias, showing him just how fucking turned on he made Ben.

Instead he bit his lip so hard he was worried it might bleed. "I-I'm sorry," he stammered. "I think I was so out of it, I sleepwalked over to you."

But Elias confounded him further. He rubbed Ben's arm again and huffed. "I'm glad you did. You're icy. It'll take a while for me to get the fire going and heat up the cottage. *Don't* move. Keep as much heat under these blankets as you can while I fix it."

Ben might have been shivering he was so cold, but inside, he melted like ice cream on a warm summer's day. *Jesus fucking Christ.* How could Elias not know what he sounded like when he talked like that? Ben wanted to lap it up, bottle it, and save it for exactly this kind of rainy day.

Ben's parents were loving and supportive, but they were very timid. They never liked to take charge. So Ben wasn't used to someone simply *telling* him what was going to happen. It made him feel secure in a way he'd never really known.

If he ever had a boyfriend, that was what Ben would want him to be like.

But why couldn't Elias be his boyfriend? a traitorous voice demanded in his head. Was Ben reading all these signals totally wrong? If there was nothing going on between them, would Elias really hug him like that? Would he climb over Ben, making sure he was still securely snuggled up under the many blankets while he ran over to relight the fire and heat up the cottage they were now suddenly staying in together?

He was being stupid. Elias was just being protective and responsible.

Right?

Elias flung another of the crocheted blankets around his shoulders before adding another couple of logs from the basket by the mantel into the grate. He crouched down, using a wand lighter to get the flames going with the aid of a starter brick, then proceeded to poke at the fire as it flourished into life.

Ben pillowed his hands under the cushion his head was resting on, cocooned in his blanket nest to keep him warm. He watched Elias work, his heart aching at Elias's sweet little frown of concentration as he fussed with the positioning of the logs. Then he stalked off into the kitchen, muttering about searching for a thermostat to adjust.

Ben would have just kept piling blankets on. He might have braved restarting the fire, but he had just assumed the cottage was warmed by the heat from the fireplace. However, there were radiators on the walls – old clunky ones, but they were there. Of course Elias would see that and go do something about it.

Maybe Ben could learn a thing or two about being a responsible adult while he was here. Speaking of which, he reached out for his phone only to discover it was on three percent battery. Sighing, he reluctantly dragged himself out of the blanket fort, keeping the fluffiest one around his shoulders, and went over to open his suitcase. It took him a minute to remember the padlock combination, and then of course the charger was all the way at the bottom of the bag.

By the time he yanked it out, he was feeling unreasonably

irritated. At himself for always being so damned disorganized, but also unfairly at Elias for just being so near yet so unattainable. Ben's heart needed to shut up with this stupid pining. Elias was simply being nice. Best-case scenario, he might be up for a quick fuck with a cute twink. But he wouldn't look at Ben as boyfriend material. What the hell would a twenty-three-year-old have to offer a mature, sensible lawyer?

The final straw of his little tantrum came when he eventually found a plug socket in the wall, only to discover that it was a completely different shape to a regular one. There was no way his charger was fitting into that.

"What the fuck is this fucking fuckery?" he snapped, blinking back angry tears as he slumped cross-legged to the floor. Treacle trotted over and rested his head on Ben's thigh, looking up at him with big dark eyes. Ben sniffed, and gently stroked his fur, feeling sheepish already. He was fully aware that you needed a power adapter in other countries, but somehow he'd failed to pack or even buy one.

So naturally Elias came and crouched down beside him, holding out exactly the adaptor Ben needed.

"Oh," Ben said, feeling even more embarrassed. "Thank you. But what will you do?"

Elias pressed the adaptor into Ben's hand. "I have several. Why don't you go claim one of the bedrooms upstairs and plug your phone in there? I checked on my way to the bathroom earlier, and there are two. The heating's on now, so you should feel the place warming up soon enough."

Ben was torn. The logical side of him was still mad at his own inefficiency at not packing something so essential as a plug adaptor. But the other side of him was winning out, the one that basked in Elias's care and attention like it was sunshine.

He tried not to let his heart throb too much as he smiled gratefully back at Elias. "Thank you," he said again, but with more enthusiasm. "Honestly, I'd be completely lost without you, wouldn't I?"

Elias winked at him. "I think you'd be just fine, but I'm happy to help."

With that he wandered off, tidying their plates into the kitchen, and setting down some food for Treacle. Once the dog left Ben's side, he didn't really have an excuse to sit on the floor any longer. So he made himself get up, shove everything that had tumbled out of his suitcase back into it, then haul the bag upstairs.

There was a master bedroom and a slightly smaller one that Ben suspected was meant for a child from the single bed. He didn't feel right taking the larger one. He couldn't picture Elias cramming himself into the single bed. It seemed undignified. So Ben was happy to take that, dropping his suitcase to the floor and plugging his phone in by the wooden bed frame. There were more photos in frames here, but mostly of dogs. Ben wondered if they were all pets Nancy had owned over the years.

Feeling travelworn and generally icky after napping on the sofa, Ben decided to brush his teeth and have a hot shower. That also gave his phone a chance to power up, so by the time he headed downstairs, he was feeling a lot less cranky.

The kitchen was clean, the blankets were all folded neatly back on the various furnishings, and Treacle was asleep on his back by the crackling fireplace, his stubby legs pointing up in the air. Elias had changed into a chunky sweater and was curled up with some reading glasses on, absorbed in the same textbook he'd been looking at on the plane.

Ben was overcome by a wild urge to go over to him and

snuggle by his side. *Damn.* This was going to be a challenging few days if his thoughts kept drifting in that direction without his say-so. He was going to be exhausted, not to mention more than a little heartbroken.

He hadn't realized he'd been staring until Elias looked up. Ben felt his cheeks heat up. "Uh, I like the glasses," he said stupidly, waving his hand at his own face. "They suit you."

Elias smiled and nudged them up his nose. "I usually wear contacts, but my eyes were feeling like sandpaper. Did you work out how to use the shower okay?"

Ben tousled his damp hair, guessing that's how Elias had known he'd freshened up. He was so observant. "Yeah," said Ben shyly, leaning against the stair banister. "I've left it on a good setting. You just need to pull the lever. Although, I noticed that they have this weird two-faucet system. One for hot, one for cold?"

Elias rolled his eyes. "Tell me about it," he grumbled with a grin. They spent the next few minutes talking about the oddities they'd discovered in the house, and the general differences they'd already noticed being in the UK. Then the conversation stalled. Ben became aware that he didn't have much to say that wasn't inane chitchat. Just because *he* had never been to another country before didn't mean Elias would also find novelty in simple things like strange brands of food and unfamiliar-looking trees.

"Um," he said, rubbing his arm. "I think I might go for a walk."

Treacle was awake and springing to his feet before Ben had a chance to draw another breath. The Corgi barked excitedly and scampered over to Ben while Elias laughed. "You said the magic word," he told Ben, rising to his feet. *"Walk.'* Are you all right to bring him along? I found a leash when I was organizing things in the kitchen."

"Oh, sure," Ben said. He'd never taken a dog for a walk before by himself, but how difficult could it be?

"He's probably okay off the leash," Elias said. He came back into the living room holding a length of worn leather with a metal clip at one end and a loop for your hand at the other. "But I'd take it just in case. You're lucky. It looks like it's stopped raining, but it might be a good idea to take one of the umbrellas? We have several."

Ben would have probably wandered out in his slippers if he wasn't careful. He was beginning to appreciate that sharing a living space with someone highlighted both of your domestic habits pretty damn fast.

"Uh, sure," he said as he fished one of the small umbrellas out of the wicker basket by the door and shoved it into his pocket. "Good thinking. Oh – did you, um, want to come with me?"

If he was honest, the whole point of going for a walk was to clear his head and shake off some of this stupid crush that had been building. He could feel he was getting locked in and obsessed thinking about Elias. That often happened when he was immersed in a project. But this wasn't like when he got all-consumed with a TV show for days on end, or when he couldn't stop making macaroons until the recipe was perfected. This was a person.

He'd done the same thing at school when he'd first realized he was gay. For months he'd been unable to stop himself daydreaming about his young math teacher, Mr. Marquez, simply because he was seeing him at least once a day. As soon as Ben went up a grade and got a different teacher, the crush quickly faded away.

However, it felt rude not to ask Elias to join him, especially when he was helping him get out of the door. But thankfully, Elias shook his head. "I've finally gotten warm. I think I'm going to see if I can find something to watch on my tablet. There doesn't appear to be a television in the house."

Ben realized he was right. He hadn't seen a TV around at all, certainly not in the living room. There were, however, a lot of books. "Or something to read," he said enthusiastically gesturing at the bookcases. "I bet there's something good over there on the shelves."

"Or something trashy," Elias added with a laugh. He walked over to inspect the shelves. "I wouldn't mind a raunchy sort of romance."

Ben was sure his face flamed bright red just thinking of leaving Elias alone to read about ripped bodices and heaving bosoms. Would that get him off? Ben admired the hell out of a lot of women, but he couldn't say he'd ever felt anything sexy about any of them. Who was to say Elias wouldn't enjoy something like that, though?

Oh, *god*. Would he go jerk off in his room or the shower while Ben wasn't there? Ben couldn't decide if he was horrified by the idea, or so turned on he could get hard himself.

He needed to get out into the cold, *now*. "Okay," he said, jamming his shoes back on his feet and his arms through his jacket. "I'll leave you to your, um, reading. Stuff. I'll be back in a little while. Bye."

Before he could blabber anymore, he opened the door so he could march out of the cottage and into the dark evening air. It was still pretty cold, but at least it had stopped raining for the time being.

For a second, Treacle looked unsure if he wanted to follow, his head swinging to look between Ben and Elias, just like he had between them and Antoni in the barn earlier. Oh, this was what Gazza must have meant about herding. Treacle was trying to keep them all together.

Well, that wasn't going to happen.

"Come on," Ben said brightly to the dog. "We're going to go for a walk. Don't you want to come?"

Eventually, Treacle seemed to work out what his options were, and dashed out after Ben. He almost closed the door without looking back, but he realized Elias was watching him with a fond expression. At least, that's what Ben hoped it was. He waved lamely at him.

"See you in a bit."

Elias raised his hand, waving back once. "See you."

Ben shut the front door and took a deep breath in the dark. *Elias was just being nice,* he told himself for the millionth time. It didn't mean anything.

It had been about half past six when he'd last checked a clock, but he realized as he hurried down the dirt path that he'd left his phone behind. Well, it was probably a good thing to take a break from everything for a while. He wasn't going to be gone long and hadn't found a wi-fi network yet to connect to anyway. He could check his Facebook any time. But this was his first chance to explore real English woodland.

There was a very small voice in his head that reminded him that this entire estate was *his.* He could come and go whenever he wanted. But that concept still seemed so farfetched that he pushed it away. Noah had cautioned him that it was likely Kenneth's solicitors would reverse Nancy's last changes to her will if she'd been suffering from dementia like a lot of people had been suggesting.

Ben chewed his lip as he and Treacle made their way through the trees, heading back toward the house and the orchard. It had been kind of Noah to come after them and offer some insight into the whole situation. Ben wondered if they might become friends, even if the rest of the trip was a bust. He was sure that Noah's body language had suggested he was interested in men. It was an intuition Ben had developed over the years that was usually pretty accurate.

At least Noah was someone Ben could have a reasonable crush on. They were a similar age, after all. But Ben's heart wasn't logical. It was still back in the little cottage, pining over Elias in his dorky sweater and adorable glasses.

It wasn't just Ben's heart that was trying to override his head, though. His dick was still ready to perk up at a moment's notice, apparently still quite aware of the effect snuggling up with Elias earlier had caused him.

Urgh, maybe he needed a mindless fuck. Once he got wi-fi, perhaps he should try opening Grindr. Would there be other guys on it in such a rural area? There was only one way to find out.

The thing was, once Ben got locked on to something (or specifically in this case, someone) he couldn't move on that quickly. The idea of a random hookup right then seemed like *cheating* on Elias, which was utterly ridiculous. Ben was a free man. He could do whatever he wanted.

Yet he knew he wouldn't be using Grindr anytime soon.

He picked up a stick and threw it for Treacle, who barked and excitedly chased after it before bringing it back. It was a game they could both enjoy as it soothed Ben's mind, its repetitive nature dragging him away from the thoughts that were spiraling out of control.

He was so engrossed, however, he wasn't fully aware of the direction he was walking. There weren't any lights out this far, but his eyes had adjusted to the gloom and the moon was almost full. So he could see the muddy path quite well, he just wasn't entirely sure where he was.

So when he heard a noise, he practically jumped out of his skin. "Hello?" he called out, his breath a cloud of smoke in the cold.

The noise had been a sort of creak. Now he definitely heard somebody sniff. "Who's there?"

Damn. He wasn't sure who would want to see him from the family, but there was a chance it could be a member of staff and they had all been kind so far. So Ben forged ahead, keeping his wits about him.

The first thing he saw was somebody leaning against a fence with their back toward him. It looked like they were on the edge of a paddock, and Ben was pretty sure he could make out a few horses in the distance with coats draped over their backs.

The person by the fence was wearing a thick, three-quarter-length coat as well as a scarf and a hat that looked like it could be a beret. Only as Ben got closer did he see a braid of long dark hair down their back, cluing him in to the person's identity just before they turned around.

It was the young woman from the antler room, the Indian-looking one who had stood with the guy Ben had assumed to be her brother. As her gaze landed on Ben, her eyes widened and her jaw set. "Oh, it's you," she said. Her accent was as close to the Queen's English as anyone else who Ben had heard speak so far from the family. But Noah had said that the Grimaldi de Loutherberghs were hostile to outsiders, and he wondered what they thought of these two. Were they family members? How had that come about?

Ben took another couple of steps so they could see each other, although the young woman turned to lean back on the fence again. "I'm sorry. Do you want to be alone?"

She shrugged, slowly rotating her phone between gloved fingers. "It's your house. You can do what you like."

Ben hated that. Guilt welled up inside him, but he paused before he spoke as Treacle ran up to the young woman, his bushy tail wagging like crazy.

"Oh, hello, darling," said the woman warmly, reaching down to rub his head. "I wondered where you went."

"He came out with us," Ben explained, approaching the fence. "So Gazza said we could keep him with us for the time being."

The woman looked up at Ben, then out through the trees. "You're staying at Aunt Nancy's cottage?" she asked thoughtfully.

Ben's guilt crept up a notch. Having felt like the cozy cottage was his and Elias's little sanctuary away from judgmental gazes, he now worried that they had in fact blundered into something much more personal.

"Goddamn it," Ben moaned, leaning against the crooked wooden fence and dropping his face into his hands. "This is awful. I've come in and intruded on everything. I didn't ask for any of this. I'm so sorry."

The woman grunted. "Yeah, it's fucked up," she said, making Ben look up from his hands at her. "But...I know it's not your fault. A lot of people are angry, but it kind of makes sense to me."

Ben blinked and straightened up. "It does?"

The woman smirked, but there was both sadness and fondness in the expression. "Nancy always liked an outsider. I'm Anika, by the way." She shoved her hand toward Ben.

"Nice to meet you," said Ben quickly, seizing on her hospitality and shaking her gloved hand eagerly before letting her go. "So, Nancy is your aunt?"

Anika shook her head, looking back out over the paddock at the horses. "She's my grandmother's aunt, but we always called her that too. Elizabeth – my nana – is Kenneth's cousin, although she barely says a word to him or anyone else these days. You might notice her around. She always wears a great big ruby necklace my grandad bought her."

"Oh, yeah," Ben confirmed. "I saw her during that car

crash earlier, in the antler room. I felt like I was facing a firing squad."

She chuckled fondly, then shook her head. "My dad's her oldest son. A lot of people didn't like his choice of wife, but Nancy…"

Anika swallowed and spun her phone in her fingers again. "I'm sorry," Ben said. He wasn't sure what it would feel like to be the only brown members of a stuck-up family, but after his experience today, he could get an idea.

Anika laughed, though, and looked back at him. "You'd think my mum being an actress would help. Google 'Kavya Bhat' sometime. You've got a pretty famous second aunt or whatever it would be."

Ben felt like his chest eased a little. The little things Anika was sharing with him felt like secrets. "I didn't think I had *any* family," he told her. "No cousins, nothing. It's a bit of a shock discovering all of this."

Anika's brow furrowed. "Be careful who you trust," she said darkly. "Sorry to sound all melodramatic, but things aren't always what they seem around here." She looked Ben up and down. "Which is why I'm glad you don't come across as a total nutter, but the truth is you've got us all by the purse strings now, literally. Some people rely on their stipend and had plans for what they thought their inheritance would be."

Ben considered her for a moment. "Some people?"

Anika licked her lips. "Yes," she said. "Not me. But for *some* people, it is – or was going to be – the difference between freedom or a thoroughly miserable life. Kenneth has ideas about the kinds of jobs people in this family should do. The way they should live their lives. He wouldn't be afraid to leave anyone destitute if he didn't like their decisions."

A chill ran down Ben's spine. Was she implying that Kenneth had already done that to someone?

Anika scoffed and shook her head. "Kenneth has held all

our inheritances over our heads for decades. He always said he was the one in charge, it was just a formality that Nancy had the last say, and that would no longer be the case once she passed. And then *you* came along." She licked her lips and pushed herself away from the fence, making Treacle's enormous ears perk up from where he'd lain down on the damp grass. "I wonder what *you'll* do to keep everyone in line."

"What if I don't want to keep everyone in line?" Ben asked, raising his eyebrows. "What if I just want my family to be happy?"

Anika tilted her head. "Then I don't think you'll last long, but I wish you well." She slid her hands into her pockets and walked away from the fence. "Oh, and tell your boyfriend to be less handsy. People around here see what they want to see. So they'll either turn a blind eye for as long as they can or read into every tiny detail and blow it out of proportion. Not everyone in this family is okay with gay people."

"Oh, n-no!" Ben spluttered, waving his hands at her. "I mean, I *am* gay. We're both gay, actually. But he's not my boyfriend! He's just a friend, a lawyer."

Anika scrutinized him for a second, then nodded. "Good. Remind him of that, then." She wandered back down the trail into the trees. "Bye, Treacle," she called over her shoulder. "Be a good boy. And, Ben?"

"Yeah?"

She gave him one last playful smirk. "Don't be a twat, and I'm sure we'll get along just fine."

Ben was left standing alone in the near dark. Well, almost alone. Treacle was snuffling around by his feet, then he picked up the stick again, as if hoping Ben would start throwing it for him once more.

But Ben leaned on the fence again, lost in his thoughts for a while longer. He wasn't sure if Anika liked him or not, or if he could trust her. However, what she'd said about Kenneth lording the entire family's wealth over their heads like the Sword of Damocles fitted in with what Ben had seen of his personality earlier.

Was that why everyone was so upset? Did they think Ben would take their fortune from them? He would *never* leave anyone destitute.

It sounded like Kenneth might, though.

Ben drummed his cold fingers against the wooden fence, watching his smoky breath and wishing he'd put a pair of gloves on. Had he even packed any? He hoped so.

Anika had assumed Elias was Ben's boyfriend.

Why?

He sort of remembered that Elias had rested his hand on Ben's shoulder or something when they'd met the entire clan at the threshold of the antler room. Was that enough for her to make an assumption? Or had she noticed something else?

Ben was ashamed to admit that his heart skipped at the idea she might have seen something more. A look, perhaps?

Elias *hadn't* been mad to find Ben asleep in his arms just now.

Ben's stomach swooped. What was he thinking? That he might have a shot with Elias, no matter how slim?

If so, what could he do about it?

He exhaled, puffing his cheeks out as the cloud of condensed air floated around him. He could take a chance, that was what he could do. He had the ideal opportunity. It was just the two of them, all snuggled up in that cute little cottage.

But what if it backfired? What if he'd been right all along, and Elias just thought of him as a dumb kid? They'd then be stuck together in that same tiny house.

He finally picked up the stick Treacle had been dutifully dropping over and over at his feet, throwing it back down the path, hoping he'd be okay to find his way back to the cottage. It felt like he'd suddenly come to a crossroads, and a decision had to be made. Did he pursue his feelings for Elias, or preserve the friendship that was blossoming between them and not risk changing anything?

Whatever direction he went, he felt like he couldn't ignore this any longer. Time to pick one or the other.

ELIAS

BEN HAD BEEN GONE A WHILE NOW.

Elias had spent some time hunting for a book he might like, then decided to unpack his suitcase instead. To his surprise, Ben had taken the smaller bedroom, leaving Elias the main one with the big double bed. Seeing as this was Ben's trip, Elias had assumed he'd take the lead, leaving Elias in the spare room.

For a minute, Elias had debated waiting to unpack until Ben returned so he could offer to swap, but he was itching to find some order in the chaos of the last few days. He reasoned that he could easily still switch rooms if Ben wanted, it would just take a little longer to repack if necessary. Besides, Ben's version of getting unpacked was apparently to shove his suitcase in the corner of the room and allow the contents to explode quite spectacularly. Elias wondered if he still meant to come back to it, or if that's how he intended to proceed for the next couple of weeks.

Two weeks. That was a long time to face spending with someone who was taking up more and more room in Elias's brain. He'd almost had an aneurysm earlier when he'd woken up to find a beautiful, perfectly snug, slightly chilly Ben cuddled up against him. He'd smelled so *good* and Elias had been able to feel his fluttering heartbeat through his clothes.

It had taken everything Elias had to let him go. He told himself over and over that he was doing the right thing, even though it felt completely wrong to pull away. It was as if he and Ben were magnetized toward each other.

He physically shook himself where he'd come to a halt in the middle of the landing. "Focus," he said out loud, then checked his watch again.

He should have asked how long Ben was intending to stay out. It had been over an hour now and Elias's insides were beginning to gnaw at him. What if Ben had gotten lost in the dark?

Ultimately, it was Elias's job here on this trip to protect Ben, so he retrieved his phone to give Ben a call. But it rang out, and after taking a quick look in his room, Elias found the cell on the nightstand, plugged in and on silent.

So Ben was out there all alone and without a phone?

That was it. Before he could reason himself out of it, Elias gave in to his primal instinct and shoved on his boots, coat, hat, and scarf to go looking for his friend in the woods. Using the flashlight on his phone and the illumination from the almost full moon, he began to hunt through the trees. It was fucking freezing and the ground was slippery with mud from the downpour earlier.

"Ben?" Elias called out. "Are you out here?"

For a while, he stuck to the path, swinging his light back and forth. But by the time he reached the other side of this particular copse and could see the stable and main house again, his imagination was starting to get the better of him.

What if Ben had tripped over a tree branch and twisted his ankle? Or worse, hit his head? What if he'd met some sort of madman out here? Elias should have gone looking ages ago. Ben had probably been lying on the cold ground, hurt and afraid, waiting for rescue.

"Ben!" Elias shouted, breaking into a run as he headed back into the woods. The cold air was painful on his exposed face and hands. He should have worn gloves. Had Ben worn gloves or even a hat? "Can you hear me? BEN!"

The faint sound of a dog barking was music to his ears, making relief flood through him. Of *course* he was with Treacle. He wasn't alone at all. But Elias still kept running, following the sound of the Corgi's happy barks. "Elias?" Ben called out. Elias tried to swallow the lump in his throat. Ben was *fine.*

"I'm coming!" Elias cried back, still running through the mud, his feet squelching. "Are you okay?"

He finally broke through the tree line to see Ben sitting on a damp wooden log. He was shivering as he hugged himself and his breath was condensed in the freezing air, but he seemed otherwise fine. He looked up, his face splitting into a big smile as Elias stopped to catch his breath. "Hi?"

Elias rested his hands on his knees and took a deep breath before standing up straight again. "Sorry, I thought you'd gotten into trouble or something. Did you? Are you all right? You'll freeze to death on that log."

Ben stood suddenly, his hands dropping to his sides. His eyes went wide, then he clasped his hands to his chest. "Let's go to dinner," he blurted out.

Elias blinked. "Huh?" he said stupidly.

Ben swallowed and bit his lip. "Uhh. I got a bit lost, so I sat here and was looking up at the stars, getting hungry, thinking about restaurants I'd researched before we got here, and you've been so nice helping me with everything, then you appeared, looking for me, being nice again, and I suddenly thought that I could take you out to dinner, to say thank you." He finally paused long enough to take a deep breath. "Unless you don't want to. That's totally fine too. I mean, it's a pretty stupid idea, uh…"

He was all flustered and Treacle was looking at him like he'd lost his mind. But Elias's heart was in his throat. Ben wanted to go to dinner?

Like…on a date?

No, that was *ridiculous*, Elias told himself sternly. Ben was just being considerate. But Elias couldn't deny he loved the idea. Even if it was just as friends, spending time together one-on-one was deeply appealing.

"No, no," he spluttered as Ben's face fell, presumably at Elias's hesitation. "It's not stupid at all! I'd love to! Where did you have in mind?"

Ben opened and closed his mouth, then a laugh bubbled up his throat before he slapped a hand over his jaw. "Uh. Well, there's this cute little pub in town. I feel like you're supposed to try a pub when you're in the UK, yeah? The food had really great reviews, and, um, I liked the photos. It looks cozy. Like a hobbit hole."

Elias's heart ached from cuteness. Why did Ben have such an effect on him? Out of all the guys Elias could have met over the years, why was it this young man who was sending him head over heels? It didn't matter that in theory there were better matches out there for Elias. Older guys in similar fields to him. Ben was the one who made his heart sing.

"That sounds wonderful," he said sincerely before he could second-guess himself. He tried not to get too excited when Ben's face blossomed into a bright, relieved smile.

But why shouldn't he? Ben had invited him to dinner. Just the two of them. Why couldn't Elias get his hopes up that Ben felt the same way as Elias did?

Because then Elias might have to finally admit how he really did feel.

This wasn't some dumb crush. Elias didn't just think Ben

was cute or pretty or young, even though he was all those things. He was also kind and talented and fierce. He made Elias feel both calmer and more excited every time their skin brushed. He made a room better just by being in it and Elias realized he wanted to be in any room Ben was in.

It suddenly occurred to Elias that he'd never felt like this about someone this much younger than him before. He'd been so preoccupied worrying whether his feelings were right or wrong, deep or superficial, but he hadn't until that very moment appreciated that they weren't a trend. It wasn't like he always went for guys of a certain age. In his twenties he'd had friends who weren't interested in guys unless they were at least ten years older, and honestly Elias had never seen anything wrong with that.

So what was he trying to work out here? That it was better or worse that he didn't usually go for guys much younger? Because if that was a problem, Elias would be a hypocrite considering he never once judged any of those friends when *they* were back in their twenties. And if he had any single friends now, would he judge them if they showed up with a partner a decade or two younger than them?

No. So, what? Why was this realization helping him feel less guilty in that moment?

Was it because he was finally admitting to himself that he really liked Ben as more than a friend, and although he was aware their age gap could cause an issue, when push came to shove, Elias didn't see Ben as a twenty-three-year-old? He just saw him as amazing. Wonderful. The man who was slowly but surely stealing Elias's heart.

Only if Ben felt the same way though. Elias was still hung up on their imbalance of power. He would *never* want to put Ben in a position of feeling he was unable to refuse Elias's advances.

So Elias would ask him. Listen for any hint of a rejection, and take it with grace.

If he was waiting for a better opportunity, he doubted he'd get one. Ben had literally just asked him out to dinner. This was the perfect chance for Elias to test the waters and see where they both stood.

He stepped closer. If possible, Ben's eyes got wider. As their breath was coming out in visible clouds, Elias realized he could tell that they were both holding it in. What should he do? Reach for Ben's hand?

Lean in for a kiss?

Unfortunately, that was the moment Treacle decided he wasn't getting enough attention, so he let out a string of fervent barks, hopping around through the tacky mud on the ground. Elias jumped back and laughed, relieved when Ben did the same. So long as they were both on the same page, it was easier to not feel as embarrassed about what almost happened, and if he'd been about to make a huge mistake.

"Shall we go back to the cottage to freshen up and leave this troublemaker somewhere safe?" Elias asked, pointing his phone flashlight toward Treacle, whose tongue lolled out as he panted and grumbled some more. "Then we could try out the restaurant?"

"Great," said Ben, starting to walk forward. "Although, it's just a pub. It's not very fancy, I don't think, but it's quaint. If you'd like-"

"Uh, Ben," Elias interrupted, pointing with his phone again. "It's back that way to the cottage."

Even though it was dark and the flashlight was turning everything either eerily blue or casting it in deep shadows, Elias was sure Ben blushed.

"Right, yeah," Ben stuttered with a sheepish laugh. "I told you I was lost."

Elias was pretty sure he was lost too, in a completely

different context. The hopelessly romantic kind. He sighed and followed Ben and Treacle back along the path, trying not to worry that he was making a mistake taking his vulnerable heart out to dinner with this delightful young man.

"So, yeah, we don't have to go to the pub..." Ben began saying, sounding nervous.

Elias touched his elbow and they stopped to look at each other in the bluish glow of Elias's phone. "Cozy and quaint sounds perfect," he assured him. Ben smiled bashfully and nodded, so they continued walking.

They made their way back to their vacation home in a few minutes with Elias leading the way. Ben didn't seem all that bothered that he'd gotten himself stuck out in the woods, like it was a fairly usual occurrence. Elias would have lost his mind, he was sure. But Ben was simply delighted that some of the lights were on in the cottage and he sighed deeply once they stepped back inside to the warmth.

"Meet you back here in fifteen minutes?" Elias asked. Ben nodded and once they headed up the stairs, they went their separate ways to their rooms. Elias attempted to suggest they should swap, but he barely got the words out before Ben scoffed.

"Don't be crazy. You need the grown-up room." He then shut the door and Elias heard rummaging sounds almost immediately.

The grown-up comment made him hesitate. If that was how Ben saw him and their relationship, was Elias about to cross a line and make a horrible mistake? What if Ben saw him as some kind of *dad* figure. Again, Elias passed no judgments on what other consenting couples did. But that really wasn't his kink. He didn't want to be anybody's daddy.

He balled his fists. This overanalyzing was going to be the death of him. If this age difference was such a big deal, he needed to walk away, now. If it wasn't, if – as he suspected –

he just liked Ben for Ben and his age was simply something that was a part of him – then Elias had to stop stressing so much over it.

Did he want to go to dinner? Yes. Was he interested in being more than friends with Ben? Hell fucking yeah. So that was it. Time to do what he promised himself he'd do this year and stop living life in the shadows. Time to grab it with both hands.

He was worried he wouldn't have time to shower. But he got himself through the bathroom, changed into a nicer button-down than the one he'd travelled in, styled his hair, and put on cologne, then *still* beat Ben back down to the living room. Unfortunately, that gave Elias time to panic that he was overdressed, but when Ben finally did emerge, he was wearing a pretty stylish cardigan over a fun T-shirt with a graphic design of a record player and musical notes. His jeans were tight and showed off his ass and thighs when he gave Elias a spin, making Elias's cock throb. He smelled kind of like his baking, too. A sort of cinnamon spice that got Elias's mouth watering.

They'd both dressed up and were looking slightly nervously at one another.

Was this a date?

If it felt like a date and looked like a date, then surely it was a date, right? Elias knew he should ask, but he was too afraid of the answer. By *not* asking, it was Schrodinger's cat, and he could remain both on and not on the date.

He knew he was being a wuss, but he didn't care. He would rather live in the happy limbo a little while longer.

That *didn't* mean he couldn't compliment Ben, however. "You look great," he said as casually as he could.

"Thanks, you too," said Ben. He licked his lips, and for a moment, they just kind of stared at each other. Then Elias remembered he was supposed to be in charge here.

"I looked for an Uber," he said, holding up his phone, "but it's pretty nonexistent out here in the middle of nowhere. So I ordered a cab. They should be here soon, if you'd like to head out to the driveway?"

"So organized," said Ben with a smile, shrugging on his coat. Was it Elias's imagination, or had his breathy words been kind of sexy? Like he was turned on by Elias's efficiency.

Or maybe he liked Elias taking charge.

That was an interesting concept that Elias hadn't been prepared for. But Ben had been happy for him to handle everything on this trip, which soothed Elias's anxiety. In the past, he'd been told off for being bossy and controlling, when he'd never meant to be either. But perhaps he and Ben balanced each other out in that way?

One thing at a time. He was getting carried away. They needed to get to the pub, then see how they fared having dinner together, just the two of them.

Shit. What if Elias ran out of things to say? What if Ben thought he was boring because he could remember VHS tapes and had no idea what the appeal of Snatchat was.

What if-

"Are the stars different in England?" Ben asked, spinning on the spot as he looked skyward by the driveway. Their taxi wasn't there yet, or had gotten lost. Either way, they had a second to spare.

"Uh, yes, I think so," said Elias as he also craned his neck. "The only one I really recognize is Orion's Belt. Oh – and the Big Dipper. That's it there, isn't it?"

When Elias glanced back down, Ben was grinning at him as Elias pointed skyward. "Maybe it's not such a different sky, after all?" Ben murmured.

They were interrupted from speculating further as headlights swung across the dark evening. Gravel crunched and their cab pulled up along the drive. Elias had been able to instruct the driver to stay far enough away from the main house that they shouldn't cause any upset. The last thing he wanted to do was anger any of Ben's relatives any further.

Unlike Kamran, this taxi driver wasn't chatty at all, just letting Elias and Ben listen to the radio playing pop hits. Ben chattered on about a couple of his favorite artists of the moment, some of whom Elias had even heard of. He sent a silent prayer of thanks to Darcy's teenage children as Ben gave him a particularly delighted look for knowing who Lizzo was.

That took them through their drive down several country lanes, and then both Elias and Ben were captivated by the charming scenery, even in the near dark. The tiny town of Horncaster was gorgeous. All the houses were mismatched in size and height, but they all seemed to be made from the same cream stone with triangular thatched roofs. The cab crossed over a fairly wide river, its dark waters rushing through the town at a considerable rate. The bridge was also made of stone and had three arches that Elias's childish imagination pictured trolls living under. The street lamps looked like the old-fashioned wrought-iron ones that made Elias think of Narnia.

This whole trip was like a library brought to life. When Elias had hung his clothes up in the free-standing wooden closet earlier, he had legitimately reached through to press his hand against the back to make sure it had been solid, and wasn't a secret portal to a magical land. He'd felt like a dork, but at the same time, it gave him a thrill of joyful nostalgia too.

Horncaster looked like the kind of town that should always be covered in snow. Or like it should have a sassy little old lady solving crimes. Or be home to a witch that was secretly looking out for everyone.

It made Elias's heart swell, and apparently he wasn't the only one. "Oh my god," Ben said softly, his breath misting up the car's window where his nose was pressed too close to the glass. "How is this even real? Do people actually live here?"

It was on the tip of Elias's tongue to say that Ben could very well be living in this town, or right next door to it, if Nancy's will held up. But he sensed it might be a good idea to take an evening off talking about Ben's family and the estate. Besides, Elias had something else completely different on his mind, namely matters of the heart, and he'd rather not bring Ben's mood down.

"It makes me think of Charles Dickens," he said instead.

Ben turned excitedly to face him on the back seat. "Or Thomas Hardy," he agreed. Elias found it far more attractive than he probably should have that Ben was into the same books as him. But his heart fluttered nonetheless.

The cab came to an abrupt halt on what might pass for a high street around these parts. The buildings were all still quaint and made of stone with thatched roofs, but there was some sort of small grocery store, a post office, and a pharmacy across the street, their modern signage at odds with their historical facades. Elias looked through the car's window to see a wooden painted sign hanging above the door that read 'The Owl and the Pussycat Inn.' There appeared to be a lot of people inside, even though it was a Monday night.

"Is this where we're going?" he asked Ben as he handed over a banknote to the driver and told him to keep the change. Ben nodded and opened his door to exit the car.

"It's not exactly Aquarium, is it?" he said, sounding slightly nervous.

Elias supposed Ben was used to the raucous bar back home. Had he ever been to a pub or – for that matter – ever been taken out by a man for dinner? Elias had been to a lot of similar establishments in other American cities, not to mention European pubs when he'd traveled in his youth.

"Pubs are usually very casual," Elias assured him once he'd also gotten out of the cab and the driver had pulled away. Elias held out his arm, inviting Ben to go first. He only realized he'd placed a hand on Ben's lower back to guide him after he'd done it. But he was just offering Ben some comfort when he was nervous. Besides, if Elias was going to confess that he had feelings for Ben, he might as well give the poor man a heads-up now.

To Elias's relief, Ben didn't shrug him off. If anything, he leaned into the touch.

As they pushed through the heavy wooden door they were hit by a wall of warmth, light and the sound of a lot of people talking happily. Under all the chatter an old Queen song was playing. The white ceilings were low and propped up by wonky wooden beams, similar to some of the rooms they had seen at Whittingar Abbey. Archways to the left and right led to two different rooms, each with a step up from the barroom they'd walked into. There were people sitting at small tables here just drinking, but the tables beyond the archways appeared to lead to dining areas where people were eating.

A throng of people was propped up at the bar itself, some placing orders with the focused-looking staff, some patiently waiting to, and the rest appeared to have settled there with a gaggle of friends, talking and laughing. The carpet felt slightly uneven and sticky underfoot, and even though the place looked clean, there was a whiff of stale beer and cigarettes, even though Elias had read that Britain had been nonsmoking indoors for over a decade.

Elias loved it immediately. It was messy and crowded and slightly grubby, and yet he got that same feeling he had at the cottage. This was home.

"Wow," said Ben, drawing his attention. Elias watched him looking around like Harry Potter in Diagon Alley for the first time. On the walls were framed satirical political drawings from what looked like old newspaper and magazine articles, as well as black-and-white photos of what might have been famous people or beloved locals. There was even an old portrait of the queen from her coronation back in the fifties.

"Where do you want to sit?" Ben asked breathlessly. "Oh, no, wait. We have to order at the bar first the travel blog said. What shall we get to drink? Is it true English beer is warm? Can I get bangers and mash?"

Elias chuckled affectionately at his enthusiasm as Ben practically skipped his way up to the bar. "We can get whatever you like," Elias promised him as he followed.

Elias was slightly concerned how they might be received in a small town, but the barmaid with several face piercings and purple streaks in her hair was delighted to hear they were American tourists. She let Ben try a couple of local ales before pouring him a full pint of the one he liked, then confirmed that they would need to order food at the bar and pay there and then. She allowed them to sip their drinks while they checked out a menu and she got to serve another patron. When they didn't have bangers and mash on the menu, she promised Ben they could whip up some mashed potatoes, sausages, gravy, and peas, just for him.

"We'll even throw on a Yorkshire pudding for you, love," she said with a wink.

Elias followed Ben's lead on the traditional English food and ordered fish and chips. They then took a mini tin bucket with a number painted on the side that was filled with cutlery, napkins, and packets of various sauces. After wandering around the packed pub for a minute, they got lucky and spied a couple leaving a cozy corner table near the crackling fireplace, and Ben dashed to claim it before a member of bar staff could even get over to clear the dirty plates off.

"This was a great idea," said Elias, sipping his beer once the table had been cleaned. He figured he could have one and see how he felt. Technically, he could probably drink more than he did, but he was out of the habit and preferred not to mess around when it came to his health.

But for Ben, he would make an exception.

Ben was still looking around in wonder, but he pulled his attention back down to Elias and grinned, holding out his pint glass. "To our continuing adventure," he proposed.

Elias was happy to toast to that.

For a while they people watched and talked more about the differences between Europe and America. Ben looked up what a Yorkshire pudding was on his phone, explaining it was a small bowl-shape made of baked batter. Before Elias knew it, Ben was rattling off recipes, clearly excited to try and make them himself. "I think I could use muffin tins," he said eagerly.

Elias rubbed his chest discreetly where his damn heart was aching that much. Just seeing Ben so happy and engrossed in what he loved filled Elias with such joy.

When their food came, Ben immediately offered Elias a bit of gravy-covered Yorkshire pudding to try, then Elias held out some battered fish on his fork for Ben. He'd often heard that English food was bland but had long suspected that was an outdated stereotype. Sure enough, everything was delicious. They even agreed to split a slice of treacle tart and custard in honor of a certain naughty dog, probably currently asleep on one of their beds knowing him.

They talked about their upcoming plans for Thanksgiving, Christmas, and for Elias, Hanukkah. He brushed off talk of his family, saying he had plenty of friends who he shared various celebrations with. Ben explained his family usually kept things pretty low-key, too.

Elias found himself staring at Ben as he took a sip of his second pint. He wasn't drunk by any means, but it had been a while since he'd indulged and he was definitely feeling light and floaty.

Ben caught him looking and blushed, glancing away as he grinned.

Was this a date? It had to be a date.

"So," Ben said, toying with an unused fork. "How come you've never been to England before? You seem to really love it all here – which I totally get, by the way. But how come it's taken you this long to visit?"

Ice rushed through Elias's veins.

He could skirt around the issue, of course. There were several ways he could answer that question without delving into something he hadn't prepared himself at all for to talk about tonight. He'd been so hung up over finding an opportunity to let Ben know that he liked him quite a lot. But now this question had been asked, and Elias didn't want to hide. The whole point of all his resolutions before he turned forty was to live a better, bolder, more open life.

He'd spent so much time avoiding talking about this subject. But it wasn't just his new determination that made him want to be honest. It was because Ben had asked, and Elias wanted to be completely straight with Ben. He deserved to know everything.

Elias cleared his throat, and reminded himself that he had *nothing* to be ashamed about. Ben was looking at him curiously, and had probably realized by now that he'd asked a pretty loaded question.

"I was restricted from flying internationally for a few years," Elias explained. "Until around 2010, to be exact. Internally was fine, but not outside America. After that, I was just sort of in the habit. I needed this push to leave the country, to take my dream trip."

Elias could hear his voice was tight. It had been so long since he'd discussed this with anyone. It had become old news in some ways, but suddenly in that moment he could feel the raw pain creeping up on him again, as fresh as that first day.

"I visited Berlin and Amsterdam during college, but then…"

Ben was watching him carefully, making Elias's skin burn. Was it too late to back out of this?

"Then you got busy with work?" Ben prompted.

"No," Elias said. "Then, in 2003, I was diagnosed as HIV positive."

The words hung in the air between them. A lump rose in Elias's throat and he focused his gaze on where his thumb was rubbing the condensation on the side of his pint glass. People carried on their conversations around them to a chorus of laughter and cutlery clinking and scraping on plates.

Ben reached over and removed Elias's hand from the glass, clasping it between both his own, rubbing the knuckles with his thumb. Elias gasped softly, looking at their hands. Most people moved further away when they heard Elias's diagnosis. Not reach over to touch him.

"I'm sorry," Ben said quietly.

Elias let out a shaky breath. It was like all the air whooshed back into the room. He hadn't realized how muffled everything had been sounding until it went back to normal. He managed a sort of chuckle, feeling light-headed. "No, it's okay. Thank you. By 2003 the treatment was already so much better. It's just been a long while since I came out to anyone new, and it's like I'm suddenly back in that room, hearing I was going to…to…"

To die.

Because Elias grew up in the eighties and nineties, when gay men were on a ticking clock. They all knew it was just a matter of time before they were diagnosed and then their days would be numbered. So in that moment with that doctor telling him his test results, all the logic and reasoning in the world that good treatment was now available couldn't stop Elias's initial, devastated reaction.

It was difficult not to fall right back into that panic, even though he was sitting in a pub a million miles away and sixteen years later.

But Ben was still there, rubbing Elias's hand, bringing him back to the here and now. "I can't imagine," he said sympathetically. "I've read a lot about it...seen it in films. It always felt like an awful nightmare that was in the past. But...it really wasn't that long ago, was it? Are you...okay?"

Elias sniffed and managed a more robust laugh of relief. His diagnosis had forced him to come out to his parents, who had disowned him on the spot. Luckily he had already moved out by then, but he hadn't seen them – or any of his family – since that day. It wasn't a unique story, but it had framed his coming out experience ever since. He once had a work colleague recoil in horror. They had apologized several times, but the damage was done. He'd had people act okay, then stop calling him. He'd been refused membership to a gym back in Seattle.

But Ben was still firmly holding his hand, stroking it, watching Elias wide-eyed to hear if he was doing all right.

"Yes," Elias said, both answering Ben's question and reminding himself. "I'm good. It's kind of simple these days. I just take one pill each morning, as well as keeping healthy, and now I pretty much have the same life expectancy as anyone. But there's a lot of emotional baggage still, I guess. For myself and other people."

Ben nodded, looking visibly relieved. "I bet. So that means you're undetectable?" He sounded like he was trying out the word for the first time, but Elias was impressed at his knowledge. A lot of people still had no idea what that meant.

"Yes," said Elias again, even more emphatically. He even went so far as to rub Ben's hand back. "So long as I stay on my meds, my viral load is so low it's undetectable and I can't pass the virus on, even if the other person isn't on PrEP. In a lot of ways, life is pretty normal again. But it took a while to get back there."

Ben took a long, shaky breath in. "I feel like anything I'd say right now would be dumb and insensitive."

Elias blinked at him. "Why? Don't think that. What's on your mind?"

Ben chewed his lip, staring at their hands. It was like the physical touch was giving him strength. "I'm glad you told me because it's an important part of you, and I'm enjoying getting to know you. But at the same time, it doesn't change anything, and I want you to know that. Not that I think it's unimportant, just that I don't see you as any different. I'm not...I'm not afraid of you or it. Does that make sense? I hope that's okay to say."

Elias squeezed his hand to get him to look up. When he did, he was sure Ben could probably see the tears pooled in his eyes, but Elias also gave him a big smile. "It's *really* okay to say. I...okay, so I met a guy a few months after I was diagnosed. I told myself I could make it work. I fell in love with him, I really did. But I was just so terrified of infecting him, or dying and leaving him behind, that I wrecked it. I pulled away until we had nothing left and I lost him anyway. So if we're going to...be friends...I want to be honest and talk through anything. I'm not ashamed."

"So you shouldn't be," Ben snapped hotly. He was only small in stature, but he puffed himself up impressively in his seat. "You've got nothing to be ashamed of! It's a terrible illness that practically wiped out a whole generation of gay men, not to mention the crisis in Africa and anyone else who's got it, and people are still prejudiced, and I'm so fucking happy you're being treated and are okay-" He broke off as he became visibly more and more upset.

"Hey, hey," Elias said soothingly. Before he could second-guess himself, he reached over to brush away an escaped tear on Ben's cheek with his thumb. "It's okay, sweetheart."

He brought his arm back as Ben sniffed. Their other hands were still entwined, and for a moment, they simply stared at each other. It was like the air was heating up around them.

Elias swallowed around the lump in his throat. He was feeling light-headed again, but he was pretty sure it wasn't from the booze or the emotion of reliving some of his trauma. Ben's skin felt so warm against his and their gazes were still locked. It was like Elias couldn't quite get enough air into his lungs.

"Shall we maybe head back to the cottage?" Elias suggested. He'd almost said 'home,' which would have been ludicrous. "Or we could get another drink-?"

"Let's go back," said Ben, nodding, then he laughed and wiped his eyes again. "This was really lovely, but it might be nice to go somewhere quiet now." Elias agreed.

Ben pushed his chair back, then let go of Elias's hand. He felt the loss immediately, but once they'd bundled up again and made their way out into the night, Ben surprised Elias by grabbing his hand again, once more cradling it with both of his either side. He leaned his arm against Elias's, and his head on Elias's shoulder as he took in a shaky little breath.

Elias was almost too afraid to move. He didn't want to do anything that might scare Ben off. But he was also keen to get off the street and back to the safety of their cozy little cottage. Talking about his diagnosis made him feel vulnerable. So he carefully extracted his phone from his pocket and dialed the same taxi company he had before. They were based in the village and knew the pub well, so promised to have a car to him within a few minutes.

Elias didn't know what to do once he put his phone away again. Ben seemed to be thinking about what he'd said, hard. He had a crease in his brow and was staring intently at the sidewalk while they waited.

Which made Elias ask the question: was Ben snuggling up to him out of affection, or just sympathy? Sympathy would be okay, he supposed. It had been a tough conversation, after all. But Elias didn't want Ben's pity on its own. He was more than just his diagnosis. He couldn't help but hope that Ben was clinging to him because he cared for Elias as a whole.

Only one way to find out.

"Are you okay?" Elias asked.

Ben looked at him like he was in a bit of a trance. "Huh?"

"It looks like you're freaking out. I understand if this *does* change some things. I can't pass the virus on, but we're still sharing a house and-"

"What?" Ben interrupted indignantly. "No! I don't – what? You think I care about that? I-" He seemed to trip up on the word and cleared his throat. "I was thinking of everything you've been through. You've had so much hardship that I've never really had to think about with the advancement in medical treatments. Yet here I am, getting upset because of a silly family feud when I could potentially be a millionaire, and you've had to face your own *mortality*. You must think I'm so stupid and selfish, and I'm really sorry-"

"Whoa," said Elias sternly. He kept his hand between Ben's gloved ones, but he stepped in front of him to hold his other shoulder and scowled down at him. "I don't think *any* of those things. I think you're smart and kind and tough and

I'm so happy we're getting this chance to become friends. Ben, you're amazing. Just because you didn't have to go through the AIDS crisis doesn't make me think any less of you. I'm glad for you. I'm *glad* you hopefully won't have to say goodbye to friends like I had to. I'm *glad* that if you ever get the same diagnosis, you'll know there's so much hope for the future. But most of all, I'm just so glad to be with you here right now."

Their breath was coming out in steam clouds between them. There was a light above the pub and streetlamps, but it was still pretty dark. Elias tried to search Ben's wide hazel eyes to get a clue as to what he was thinking.

But nothing prepared him for Ben shooting up onto his tiptoes and crashing their mouths together in a cold, desperate kiss.

Instinct took Elias over as he pulled Ben closer to him, their lips moving against one another. However, just as Elias's heart was catching up and beginning to feel elation, Ben snatched himself away, horror clear on his face.

It was also the moment their cab pulled up.

"Taxi for Solomon?" the cabbie asked, leaning out of the window.

"Oh my god, I'm so sorry!" Ben gasped, tears in his eyes. "I never meant – I didn't – I can't-"

Elias felt his heart break. It was a pity kiss. Of course it was. "It's fine," he said gently.

"No, it's not!" Ben cried wretchedly.

Elias hated himself for causing him so much pain. All his hopes that Ben might feel the same way as he did were dashed like a ship on the rocks. *He* was the one who had been selfish, confusing Ben like that.

"Look, let's go back to the cottage-" Elias began.

But Ben shook his head. "I-I think I need to be alone for a bit."

That was the final knife in Elias's chest. "Of course. You take this cab, and I'll get another one, okay? Do you have your door key?"

Ben frowned and fumbled in his pocket while their cab driver huffed loudly. "Uh, yes. But you-?"

"I'll be fine," Elias assured him, faking his best bullshit lawyer smile as he steered Ben to the car and opened the back door for him. "You just get yourself back to the cottage and stay warm, all right? I'll follow on and we can talk some more, or forget it all happened, okay?"

Ben sniffed and looked miserably at him. "Okay," he repeated in a whisper.

As soon as Elias closed the door, the impatient cab driver sped off down the lane, leaving Elias standing alone in the shadows.

He put his hand over his eyes and did his best not to cry. So that was that. The kiss had been a mistake, and Ben wasn't interested in him as a lover. He'd suspected as much all along and should never have reciprocated the kiss. He was supposedly the more mature one here, with more life experience. He needed to pull himself together and comfort Ben as a *friend*. And he had a taxi ride home with which to compose himself, and pretend like his heart wasn't cracked in two.

It was just a stupid crush on someone who had never really been available to him. But when Ben had initiated that kiss, Elias had dared to hope, just for a second. Now it was back to reality, and any hopes Elias might have been nurturing needed to be squashed back down and forgotten about.

Just like he always did.

BEN

"*Stupid, stupid, stupid!*" Ben snarled through his tears, punctuating each word with a savage pummel to the dough he was kneading.

When he'd returned to the grounds, he couldn't face going back to the cottage. He had to *do* something, and the best way to take his mind off anything was to bake.

Usually.

Luckily, Mrs. Hollis had answered when he'd rung the bell at the front door of the main house. Ben wasn't sure he should really go back in there – it felt like he was trespassing. But Mrs. Hollis had not only been awake when she greeted him but still dressed – it was only about half past nine, after all. Her face had also fallen in concern at the sight of him.

"Oh, petal, what's the matter?" she'd asked

It had taken Ben a great deal of determination not to burst into tears and throw himself into her arms, but he'd managed to retain his composure. "This might sound crazy, but is there any chance I could borrow the house's kitchen? I don't have any baking supplies. I can pay you back-"

She'd scoffed at the notion and ushered him right in. "It's

your kitchen right now. We won't miss a bit of flour. The staff have gone home for the night. You use whatever you like."

Which was how Ben had ended up thumping dough in the middle of the night. He didn't want to overwork the pastry or let it get too warm, so he forced himself to put it in the fridge while he worked on the pie filling, then began aggressively slicing apples, filling the air with their fresh, crisp tang.

The kitchen was enormous, at least three times the size of the space they had at Rise and Shine. Ben had felt a little overwhelmed when Mrs. Hollis had first led him in there, but at the end of the day it was just like any other kitchen, just with more surface area. Unsurprisingly, the faded wooden cabinet doors and drawers squeaked and got stuck when you tried to open them. The utensils were clean but their style was about thirty years out of date. When Mrs. Hollis had left Ben to his own devices, he'd spent a little while looking over a shelf filled with cookbooks from the seventies and eighties, wondering how many people had thumbed through their spotted, dog-eared pages over the years.

But Ben hadn't needed a recipe once he'd discovered a basket of fresh apples from the estate's orchard. Instinct took over and allowed him to feel his way through as he began combining flour, butter, sugar, and other ingredients. He was already halfway along before he realized what he was creating were apple pies. Unfortunately, as soon as he broke out of his baking trance, that meant his other thoughts came tumbling back in.

Thoughts of Elias.

How selfish was he? *Childish, sex obsessed, inconsiderate.* All these words were flying through his mind as he attacked the apples, wiping his face with the back of his hand as he went, the tears mingling with the sticky apple juice on his fingers. He didn't care he had nice clothes on. He was now covered in flour despite finding an apron to borrow. He had sugar and lemon juice in his hair, probably making the unruly curls stick up at all angles.

It didn't matter. It wasn't like anyone was here to see him. Well, except Luna, who had slunk into the kitchen despite almost certainly not being allowed in there. Ben had tried to gently shoo her off, but she'd yawned at him and dropped her fat butt in the very corner by the door and begun licking her paws like she owned the place. Ben supposed it didn't matter, so long as she stayed away from the work surfaces.

He sniffed as he heated the sugar with several spices in a saucepan, bringing the mixture to a boil. The comforting aroma and the sound of the sauce simmering filled the quiet room, keeping Ben and Luna company. Ben took a deep, shaky breath, and tried to bring some order to his thoughts.

Honestly, Elias had shared an intimate, painful truth about his life and what had to have been an extremely difficult period in his past, and Ben had fucking *kissed him.* What exactly had it been about a potentially deathly illness that had turned Ben on? Had he listened to Elias pouring his heart out and thought 'this seems like a good time to make out'?

Urgh. And he'd been so *sweet* afterward, immediately forgiving Ben's impulsive, completely inappropriate behavior. Ben quashed another sob as he savagely stirred the boiling mixture. He respected Elias so much. He didn't want to infantilize him, his experience, or his illness, but how could Ben *not* admire someone who had been so strong to overcome adversity and still become such a competent adult?

The worst part was the holding hands had felt too good and right, even more so than when they'd been in the car or facing Ben's family. It was like Ben's hand was meant to slip into Elias's that easily, all the time. Ben had just been trying to comfort Elias and convey how awesome Ben thought he was. Then he was saying all those lovely things, his face so close to Ben's, and Ben hadn't been able to fight the urge to taste his lips any longer.

He'd practically assaulted the man, during a moment of vulnerability, no less. Ben was a total dick.

The noise of his timer brought him back to his senses. He took a second to wipe his face on a sheet of kitchen towel, then he tipped the chopped-up apples into the boiling liquid, stirring vigorously, then bringing it down to a simmer. He wasn't particularly following any recipe, just going on instinct from the hundreds of pies he'd made before. The kitchen was well stocked for what he needed, so he'd made a mental note of all the supplies he'd borrowed. He was tallying up their cost, intending to leave a twenty-pound note for the kitchen staff's compensation.

Normally, he could completely lose himself in baking, like it was meditating. But nothing was dulling the horrible shame in his guts that evening. His chest ached and his eyes were sore from crying.

If Luna hadn't bolted across the kitchen to make her silent escape out another door, Ben probably wouldn't have noticed anything. He was so busy stirring his simmering filling, he didn't even hear the kitchen door opening.

But Luna could move surprisingly fast considering how fat she was. Ben startled, thinking it was Kenneth or another angry family member ready to shout at him and kick him out.

It was not.

"Hi," said Elias softly, resting his hand on the edge of the door, only half his body visible.

Ben froze and tried not to hiccup. "I thought – how did you find me?"

Elias came all the way inside and shut the door. The lighting in the kitchen was a bit dim, probably because they usually relied on light from the big windows to the left. But unlike when Ben had gone out walking, there was no light from the moon now on this cloudy night, and the dim yellow bulbs hanging from the few pendants above the central island counter just made the place kind of gloomy more than anything.

Ben hoped that would at least cover some of his blotchy face, but it also made Elias's expression kind of hard to read with so much of it being thrown into shadow.

"You weren't at the cottage," Elias said as he took his jacket off and draped it over a section of counter space that wasn't being used. "I got worried, so I took a look around the woodland again. But then I saw lights on in the house." He gestured to Ben's pot, reminding him to stir the hot filling again. "My mom was a stress baker, and I just wondered…"

He smiled sadly. Ben sniffed and figured the mix had probably had long enough, so poured it into a large ceramic bowl that was probably older than he was to allow it to cool.

"I'm so sorry."

Ben looked up, concerned he'd spoken out loud and not even realized it. But no…it was Elias who'd said that.

"*You're* sorry?" Ben said incredulously. "Why would *you* be sorry? I'm the one who kissed you at a deeply insensitive moment. I'm the one who disappeared like a child and made you worried, hunting through the woods in the dark *again*. *I'm* sorry!"

Elias shook his head. "I'm sorry because I led you on."

"You…what?" Ben was suddenly acutely aware of just how much flour and sugar he probably had smeared all over him and really wished it wasn't.

Why would Elias be leading him on?

"I understand why you'd regret it," Elias said kindly,

stepping closer. God, his soft brown hair was practically glowing like a halo in this gentle yellow lighting. "A lot of people pity me when they first hear about my condition, but it's okay, I promise. I'm fine and we can just forget it ever happened."

But Ben was angrily waving his hands, sending little flecks of pastry dough flying. "Pity you? Elias, I absolutely do *not* pity you. You're one of the most impressive people I've ever met. Sure, we were talking about something really fucking tragic and I got all in my feelings, but that's not why I kissed you."

Elias had become very still, resting one of his hands on the central island. He was a few feet away, staring at Ben. Ben's heartbeat was leaping in his throat as he tried to control his adrenaline while he worked out what the hell was going on.

"Why *did* you kiss me?" Elias asked slowly.

Oh fuck. Should Ben come clean? What if Elias thought Ben had lured him here to Wiltshire under false pretenses to seduce him? What if he was repulsed that someone so immature could think they'd have a chance with someone so successful and accomplished?

Well, at the moment Elias thought Ben had kissed him out of pity for revealing his HIV diagnosis, and Ben couldn't live with that. So long as Elias wasn't suffering from his condition, Ben didn't give a fuck what his status was.

"I kissed you..." Ben said slowly, unable to keep eye contact, so he stared at his cooling apple pie filling instead. "Because...I think I might...sort of...like you. But you were in a vulnerable place, and I should never have done something so selfish! If I upset you, I'm so deeply sorry."

Elias was quiet for so long Ben had to look up. When he did, he saw Elias licking his lips. "I was only upset when you pulled away."

Ben felt himself blink, but honestly, he wasn't even sure this was his body anymore. *What* had Elias just said? "Huh?" Ben grunted inelegantly.

They were now staring at each other, not looking away. In his peripheral vision Ben could tell Elias's chest was rising and falling, and his Adam's apple bobbed as he swallowed. "I know you're a lot younger than me," Elias said, "so I don't want to make you uncomfortable-"

"I'm not uncomfortable," Ben interrupted impatiently, stepping forward. "I'm confused and possibly about to pass out from stress. What do you mean 'when I pulled away'? Did you *not* want me to pull away?"

Elias raised his eyebrows. "There's sixteen years between us-"

"And I'm twenty-three!" Ben cried, slapping his hand down on the counter. He took another step forward. He could smell Elias's cologne, fresh like the ocean, and his spicy man musk. The scent Ben had woken up to on the sofa earlier. "I can make up my own mind about these things. We had a date, my heart was hurting for you, I wanted to comfort you and it came out in a stupid kiss that I thought was totally ill-timed. But are you saying you didn't want that kiss to end?"

Elias blinked several times, looking as confused as Ben felt. "It *was* a date?"

Ben licked his lips, wishing his heart rate would slow down and stop making him feel so dizzy. "I thought so," he admitted. "I kind of hoped so. I was trying to decide how I felt. No, not how I felt. I know how I *feel*. I was trying to decide what to do about it."

He could have been mistaken, but Ben was sure he saw Elias's hand edge closer to his. "How do you feel, then?"

"I already said," Ben grumbled. "I think I like you. Like... not just as a friend. As in I'd quite like to kiss you again right now. But I'm so *boring* compared to you and you're here helping me, so you might feel obliged-"

"You're the reason I come to Rise and Shine every day," Elias blurted, looking utterly terrified. Their gazes locked again and Ben stopped breathing. "How can you *possibly* say you're boring? We're literally in the middle of some twentieth-century political family drama. You make Hobbit jokes and midnight pastries, and even though it both baffles and horrifies me that you never seem to know where your passport is, I kind of love that too. You stood up to your great-uncle and were nice to Treacle and..." He cleared his throat and swallowed, his breathing heavy. "I guess I'm trying to say I like you, too. But-"

"No!" Ben yelped, holding a finger up as his feet nudged him even closer. "No buts! Why does there have to be a but?"

Elias sighed and shook his head. "I'm broken," he said, his voice catching. "And I *don't* just mean my HIV status," he added as Ben opened his mouth to protest exactly that. "It's what my diagnosis did to me and my ability to be in a relationship. It's the years it made me hide away. You deserve someone like you, young, and-"

"Stupid?" Ben snapped. "Obsessed with YouTube and memes? Still fretting about what the hell to do with their lives?"

Ben knew not everyone his age was like that. In fact, he didn't blame people of his generation for being like that at all. But it wasn't what he found attractive. He found confidence and stability a fucking aphrodisiac. That didn't necessarily mean an older man, but Elias had it in spades so why was he going to complain about a few years between them when that had given him the maturity Ben craved in a partner?

He stepped closer. They were practically chest to chest.

His blood was roaring through his ears and his mouth was dry as he panted.

"Besides," Ben said breathlessly, just a hint of hope and excitement bubbling in his stomach. "Who said anything about a relationship? Don't you think that's jumping the gun?"

Elias studied him. "You're not looking for anything serious?" Ben didn't miss the anxious hint of disappointment to his words. Ben could have teased him, but he didn't feel like playing, not after days – fuck, weeks, *months* – of a potential misunderstanding.

They liked each other. More than liked.

"I'm not looking to date anyone I haven't given a test run in the sack," Ben hissed, not caring if he sounded crude. His cock was throbbing in his jeans, begging for release. Elias's skin looked so tasty, especially his neck. Ben wanted to lick and suck and bite it. *Jesus*, how many times had he jerked off to Elias before he even knew his name? Imagining him deep inside Ben, fucking him slowly, fucking him *hard*.

And now he was here, right in front of Ben.

But Elias's breathing was shallow and his eyes were wide, like he suddenly wasn't sure of what they were doing. As difficult as it was, Ben forced himself to take a breath and calm down. Then he took that final step, and rested his hand gently against Elias's chest. He heard Elias's breath hitch.

"Or we don't have to do anything," Ben offered. "I'm still not sure what's going on. I'll be honest and say I've never had a boyfriend so I don't know what I'm looking for. All I know is that I *want* you."

Elias licked his lips and closed his eyes with a pained expression. "I'm so out of practice these past years," he all but whimpered. "I've dated. But sex?"

"We don't have to do *anything* you don't want to," Ben

growled meaning it. His dick would get over it. Elias's feelings were ten times more important.

A wave of anger threatened to engulf him for what this virus had taken from Elias. Not just for the health scare but also for what other people's opinions had done to him. As much as Ben was about to explode from desire and lust, his heart won out easily. He wanted what *Elias* wanted.

Elias's eyes were still closed, but he suddenly lifted his hand and fumbled to squeeze Ben's fingers which were resting over his heart. "I want you *so badly*, sweetheart," he rasped. "Just show me how."

Oh…dear god. *That,* Ben could do.

With pleasure.

1 2

ELIAS

BEN LAUNCHED HIMSELF INTO ELIAS'S ARMS. LITERALLY. HE stepped back and fucking jumped, making Elias stagger a couple of feet. But then Ben's legs were around his waist, and his arms were around his neck, and his hard cock was pressing into his stomach, and his lips...

Oh, *god*...his lips.

They crashed into Elias's mouth frantically, his tongue already slipping through and begging to be allowed entrance.

Elias granted it.

Ben's kisses were hot and needy. His fingers were digging into Elias's back and tugging at his hair. His crotch was rutting against Elias's stomach, stabbing him with his raging erection.

Elias had his hands under Ben's ass to hold him up and around his back to make sure he was pressed as tightly as he could be to Elias's chest. Their mouths devoured one another, teeth clashing and clicking in their desperation to kiss harder, deeper.

This had been *exactly* what he'd wanted.

Elias turned, depositing Ben onto the island counter so

his hands could roam free. A cloud of flour puffed around him from where he'd been making pastry. His mouth tasted sweet, possibly from sampling the applesauce filling.

How long had Elias dreamed about touching those honey-blond curls? They were silky and slightly sticky under one hand, while the other became familiar with Ben's slim waist, his surprisingly firm thigh, and his delicate neck. His skin was hot and his breath warm despite the chilliness of the drafty old house.

Elias couldn't remember the last time he'd made out frantically with someone. He'd kissed several guys on dates over the past few years, but there had always been a part of him that had been reserved. He'd been open with all of them about his HIV status, but Elias suspected he'd still held himself back, always afraid to commit or get too close.

It wasn't like that with Ben.

Ben was demanding *everything*, and Elias wanted to give it to him.

His heart was racing and his cock was throbbing, rutting against the friction of his pants and the inside of Ben's thigh. It felt like Elias had been living in his fantasies for too long. He jerked off pretty regularly and made good use of a lot of toys, conjuring up all manner of wild scenarios for him to get off to. But it was as if he'd forgotten how fucking *hot* it was just to kiss a gorgeous guy with the desperation of a drowning man bursting through the water's surface and sucking in air.

If Elias wasn't careful, he might come in his briefs. But that made him pause and think. What *did* he want here? What did Ben want? To fuck?

God, Elias gave a full-body shudder at the idea of getting down to it right here on the countertop. He hadn't fucked like that since college, when he was up for all the dick he could get. That felt like a lifetime ago, almost like it had happened to someone in a novel rather than him.

Was this Elias rediscovering who he was? Or was he just playing pretend at the man he used to be?

"Hey?" Ben said breathlessly, pulling away from their kisses and cupping his hands either side of Elias's face. His hazel eyes darted back and forth as he searched Elias's expression. His breath escaped in sweet little puffs of air that ghosted over Elias's tingling lips. Ben's mouth was red and shiny from making out, and Elias just wanted to dive in and claim it again. But Ben was giving him a serious look.

"What?" Elias ran his hands up Ben's thighs and held him around his slim waist. God, he fit perfectly under Elias's touch.

Ben rubbed his thumbs gently against Elias's checks. "It felt like you were pulling back?"

Elias rested their foreheads together, then lightly kissed the tip of Ben's nose, tasting a hint of flour. "I was thinking," he admitted.

"About what?" Ben asked.

"About feeling like my old self, like I was in college. Your age. It's kind of scary," Elias admitted.

Ben nuzzled their noses, then pulled back a little so they could see into each other's eyes. "Why?"

"I'm not sure I know how to be that guy anymore," Elias tried to explain. "Do I even want to be him? He got me into trouble."

But Ben shook his head. "He did no such thing. These things happen. You don't deserve to be punished for the rest of your life for one reckless moment. That guy is just a part of who you are now. You can tap into him without becoming him again. Not that you could, I don't think. Not after going through so much else since."

Elias arched an eyebrow and studied Ben until he squirmed, making little clouds of flour lift off the counter.

"What?"

"You keep saying you're young and inexperienced and immature."

Ben frowned at him. "Yeah?"

Elias chuckled. "I call bullshit. You're plenty wise, Ben Turner."

Ben scoffed but his smile suggested he was pleased. He moved his hands to the back of Elias's neck, caressing the short hairs there. "Come here," he murmured.

Elias gladly brought his mouth back down to meet Ben's. These kisses were lest fervent. They were sweeter, more leisurely. Ben hummed as Elias drifted his fingers up and down his back, feeling the material of his clothes moving over his skin.

Elias couldn't remember the last time he was so eager to get somebody else naked. He was so focused on Ben, he wasn't worrying about his own body. Despite logically knowing how much his rigorous workouts with Swift had done him good, he was still kind of nervous about taking his clothes off. It was difficult for him to entirely trust his body. It had been his enemy for so long.

But Elias had seen a therapist for a while last year for that very reason, and he was determined to stop punishing himself, like Ben had said. His body wasn't the enemy. It was his ally, a warrior that had survived a great battle and was now his faithful companion on their journey forward in heart, body, and soul.

It was nice to try and *not* think about it. To be neutral. His focus was mainly on how Ben felt against him and under his hands, as well as Ben's feelings – if he was happy and getting what he wanted. Elias would rather just not think about himself at all, unless it was in relation to Ben.

Damn. He couldn't quite believe this was actually happening after all this time. He still wasn't entirely convinced their age gap wasn't a problem like Ben was saying. But the fact of the matter was they were two consenting adults, and they both appeared very clear about what they wanted.

Elias hummed and kissed Ben's neck, loving how Ben moaned at his touch. "I'm not sure what to do with you," Elias whispered, enjoying their openness. He'd been with a lot of guys who thought it was sexy to be mysterious. Elias had often felt that was a poor excuse to bottle everything up and not deal with issues until they exploded.

He liked that Ben seemed eager to talk about how they were feeling.

More than eager.

He squirmed and groaned, fisting the back of Elias's shirt "I'm pretty sure," Ben said in a deliciously breathy voice. "I've got lots of ideas. There's a list. It's alphabetized."

Elias laughed and kissed Ben through his grin. "I'm so glad you made a move. Otherwise, we could have kept dancing around each other forever."

Ben gave him a considered look. "Have you really been coming to the bakery just for me?"

Elias waggled his eyebrows. "I don't know. The pastries are okay, too."

Ben surprised him by tickling Elias's sides, making him jump and yelp. How long had it been since someone had felt comfortable enough to be so free in touching Elias's body?

Years.

"Okay, okay," Elias said through his chuckling. "The pastries are amazing and so are you." They stopped laughing and looked at one another, their hands resting gently on each other's chests. Elias sighed and brushed back one of Ben's slightly sticky curls. "I got butterflies in my stomach every time I saw you. But I never knew what to do and felt a bit creepy, to be honest."

Ben snorted. "Why? Was my unashamed flirting not clear enough for you?"

"Apparently not," Elias admitted, shaking his head with a lopsided smile. "I thought you talked to everyone like that."

At that, Ben dropped his head back and really laughed. "You think I ever talked to Sunny Perkins like that? He'd have cuffed me around the head. Old Mrs. Morse from the dog grooming parlor would have fainted."

"Really?" Elias teased, then decided to go the whole nine yards and put on a terrible attempt at a British accent. "You never once told Mrs. Morse you wanted to butter her crumpet?"

Ben hooted and covered his face. Elias basked in the moment, watching Ben being so happy and carefree in his arms when he'd been upset before. But he *had* been crying because of Elias.

"I'm sorry there was a miscommunication," Elias said, nuzzling their cheeks together. Ben's laughter became more of a hum. "I don't like the idea I made you cry."

"I made myself cry," Ben replied, his hands back in Elias's hair.

But Elias took a few seconds to consider Ben. "I can't promise I won't make you cry again. I...I meant what I said earlier. I feel broken. Like I've forgotten how to be with a man. Physically and emotionally. I've been in a sad little bubble for a pretty long time."

Ben's expression was serious as he rested his hands on Elias's shoulders. "I'm sorry," he said softly. "But...I can try and show you how happy this makes me, if that might help? No one has a crystal ball. This might not work. We might want different things. But right now, I just want to touch you and not stop. I want to explore every inch of you."

Elias's mouth went dry and his cock perked up again. He might have forgotten how this went, but it seemed to remember exactly where everything fitted together and how damned incredible it could be.

"Fuck," Elias breathed, ghosting his lips over Ben's. "Can I take you back home?" He didn't care he'd said 'home.' It was their space for now and the word felt right.

Ben pulled back and looked guiltily at Elias. "Uh...my apple pies?"

Elias chuckled. "Oh, I see how it is. Pies before guys?"

Ben snorted with laughter and lightly bashed Elias's arm. "Never, *ever* say that again."

"Sure," Elias promised with a kiss to the lips. "How about I help you finish the pies, then we can go back to the cottage?"

"You want to bake with me?" Ben asked. Elias was about to protest that Ben had done most of the work already, but the spark of delight in his eyes told him that not many people had offered to spend time with him and his passion. Maybe he'd never baked with a guy he liked before?

Elias felt honored.

"I'd love to," he said, looking down at the bowl with the thick, sticky apple filling. "But you'll have to tell me what to do. My mom tried to get me to help her make babka once or twice, but I was more interested in licking the filling off the spoon."

In an instant, Ben's eyes became dark and sexy. "Oh, I'm sure we can find something for you to lick later."

Elias slapped his thigh playfully, even though his cock was done playing and would much rather have gotten serious there and then. But this was special. *Ben* was special. Elias wanted them to take their time and do it right, whatever 'it' might turn out to be.

So he followed Ben's instructions and helped him fill a

dozen small pies with applesauce and then lay little tops on them all. As they waited for the pastries to cook, they kissed a while longer, but then Luna came strolling back in with a loud meow and flopped dramatically onto the kitchen floor, causing both Elias and Ben to laugh. They sat down beside her, taking turns to scratch between her ears and over her enormous belly until she batted them away when she'd had enough.

They stayed on the tiled floor, getting gradually colder, but Elias didn't care. Ben's hand was entwined with his and his head was on his shoulder as he talked sleepily about some of his old favorite recipes and other things he wanted to try with the Whittingar Abbey apples.

But as their previous passion cooled, doubt started to creep into Elias's guts. What was he doing here? Was he being responsible? Ben sounded like he hooked up with a lot of guys, which was *absolutely* fine, but was this just sex for him? If he wasn't really interested in dating, should Elias get involved? Elias was pretty certain he was becoming attached to the gorgeous young baker. Was it fair to have sex when there was a risk Ben could get infected? Was a one-night stand worth that?

There was no risk. Undetectable meant undetectable. Fact. There just wasn't enough of the virus in his system anymore for it to be able to transfer over. But over the years, sex had become something sinister to Elias. How long had it been since he'd done anything more than frot or trade hand jobs? Even blow jobs made his instinctual brain hesitate and pull away.

Could he give Ben what he wanted? Or had that ship sailed for Elias? If Ben wanted casual sex and Elias wanted something more long term, maybe they just weren't compatible.

So the question was, did Elias pull back now and keep

them safe? Or fumble through with whatever might come next at the risk of his heart? It was so much easier not to rock the boat and keep things as they were. Perhaps they were just two friends who shared a kiss one night?

But he wanted *more.* It was like his brain had already made up its mind and absolutely couldn't wait to get Ben into bed. But his body was freezing up at the prospect. What was wrong with him? He'd been daydreaming this moment might come ever since Ben started working at the bakery a year and a half ago. Why the hell was he second-guessing himself now?

As he sat there on the cold kitchen floor, waiting for the timer to go off for the delicious-smelling pies, he really wasn't sure what he should do. All he knew was that he wanted to protect Ben, and himself as well if he could help it. He just wasn't sure what the best way to do that was.

Or if he was strong enough to distance himself from Ben now, even if that was the right thing to do.

But he guessed he was going to find out, sooner rather than later.

BEN

Ben gripped tightly on to the covered plate of small pies as he and Elias walked back toward their cottage, nerves dancing in his belly. He probably could have managed the plate with one hand and held Elias's with the other. But in that moment, it seemed like a convenient safety blanket to hold it with both, just while he gathered his wits.

He wanted this, desperately. But he couldn't remember the last time he'd taken a man he already cared about to bed. Sure there had been guys that he'd dated for a while who he'd become fond of, but he wondered now if that had just been a case of familiarity. It wasn't like he'd cared about any of those guys like he did Elias, as evidenced by the fact that they'd always drifted apart before becoming anything official, like boyfriends.

He'd certainly never felt as strongly about anyone before bedding them for the first time. *God,* at least he hoped Elias wouldn't just want to fuck once then be done with it.

Ben had felt it important to be honest earlier. He'd never had a boyfriend, and wouldn't consider dating a guy until he knew they were compatible in bed. That absolutely didn't mean he wasn't open to the idea of becoming a couple. In fact, the thought of Elias being his boyfriend made him want to pass out with joy. He couldn't believe he'd ever be that lucky.

But first things first. Ben needed to see what happened when they closed the door on their cottage and shut out the rest of the world. He might have been nervous but he was still practically vibrating with desire. He wanted to see the night through to the very end. In the morning they could consider where that left them, or which direction they wanted to head in next.

They were being guided down the dark path by a swishing silvery tail. As they'd left the main house, Luna had decided she wanted to head back outside, whether Ben and Elias tried to stop her or not. She was obviously very familiar with the grounds as they'd seen her outside plenty of times, so Ben didn't see any harm in letting her out.

When they neared the cottage, however, a *very* excited Corgi face appeared at the window, clearly visible where they hadn't pulled the curtains. And then the barking began. Treacle's tail wagged like crazy as he *bork bork borked* through the window at Ben, Elias, and their tour guide cat.

Luna stopped at the racket, her tail flicking in apparent suspicion. Then she turned (Ben could have sworn she stuck her nose in the air) and shot off in the direction of the stable. Treacle stopped barking. Ben would also have sworn the poor little fella looked extremely disappointed.

"Aww, sorry, Treacle," he said as he let himself and Elias in through the front door. "I'm afraid it's just us. Is that okay?"

Treacle quickly recovered, jumping down from where he'd been standing up against the back of an armchair to look out of the window. He launched himself at the two men, barking happily again.

"Okay, yes, hello, hello," Elias said cheerfully after he'd

shut and locked the door. He knelt down to fuss Treacle and Ben recalled how he'd mentioned he had an Irish Red Setter back in Pine Cove.

Ben hadn't thought of home much since they'd arrived in England. He bit his lip as he placed the pies down on their own small kitchen counter. If they made a go of being together here in England, would it survive everyday life back in Washington?

Ben was getting *way* ahead of himself. He'd said first things first, and that was what they should do. Tonight might be a disaster.

However, he had the strong feeling it wasn't going to be.

Elias came to join him in the kitchen. Treacle had obviously been asleep before their arrival, as now he'd said his hellos he dropped back into his dog bed and rested his head on the edge with a grumble. As if he was pleased things were back to normal, but he wanted to let them know he was still unimpressed at being left on his own for the evening.

Thanks to Elias's skills with the thermostat, the cottage was now lovely and warm, unlike when they'd first arrived.

Perfect for taking all your clothes off.

"The pies made it in one piece?" Elias asked, standing just close enough to Ben that he could detect his scent. It was like the air was crackling with electricity between them.

"Seems like it," said Ben, indulging in making polite conversation for a second.

They had only taken a few of the apple pies with them, leaving the rest for the kitchen staff to discover in the morning along with a thank-you note and a twenty-pound bill. Ben and Elias had shared one of the pastries before they'd left. Naturally, Ben had to do a taste test for quality control purposes. It didn't hurt that he'd also gotten to kiss some sugary crumbs from the corner of Elias's mouth.

But as Ben regarded Elias standing in the kitchen, he was

pretty sure that something wasn't quite right. Elias had taken off his jacket but now he was fiddling with one of his cuffs and flicking his gaze between Ben, the plate of pies, and out of the dark window.

Ben also removed his coat to hang from the back of a chair, then stepped up to Elias and rubbed his arm. "Are you okay?" he asked. "We don't have to do anything if you're worried or having regrets."

"No regrets," Elias said immediately in alarm. His eyebrows shot up, then he cleared his throat and rubbed his face. "Christ, I don't know what's wrong with me. A gorgeous guy who I have a massive crush on is begging me to go to bed, and I'm freaking out for no reason."

"If you're freaking out, then there is a reason," Ben insisted. "But that's okay."

Elias frowned at him. "It is?"

Ben nodded and rubbed his arms again. "You just said 'gorgeous guy' and 'massive crush' in one sentence. If that's true, I'm pretty sure we can work anything else out."

Elias laughed softly and nuzzled their noses together. "Maybe I should stop doing so much thinking and talking, and start doing more of other things."

As much as Ben was down for 'other things,' he wasn't an asshole. Elias was clearly processing some stuff and had said it had been a long time since he'd been with a guy. Ben wasn't sure if he meant any sex or anal or even making out with anyone, but whatever the case, Ben wanted to take things slowly.

"How about..." he said, then chewed his lip. "We try lying down and cuddling, then some kisses. See how that feels?"

Elias's eyebrows crept up dubiously. "You're changing your mind?"

"Nope," Ben told him with what he hoped was a cheeky smile. "But I don't see any reason to rush into anything. And

I *never* just cuddle. I had a sort of best friend slash boyfriend in high school and we used to do that kind of thing before he moved away. But these Grindr guys always want to jump into fucking. They never take a moment to chill. It'll be nice."

The relief on Elias's face was clear, making Ben glad he suggested it. He was so desperate not to screw this up, he'd take any little victory he could. That expression made him feel like he'd made the right decision with his idea.

So they kicked their shoes off and left Treacle downstairs, gently snoring. Ben threaded his fingers through Elias's, leading him upstairs to the master bedroom. "Is this why you let me have it?" Elias asked. Ben was thrilled to hear a hint of teasing back in his words. "Because you planned to sleep in here anyway?"

Ben winked over his shoulder at him as they went through the door. *"May-be,"* said Ben, matching the playful tone. Elias closed the door and let Ben pull him toward the bed. A quick glance at the nightstands told Ben which side was Elias's, so he chose the other side.

Wow. He realized before he lay down that Elias had apparently unpacked everything from his suitcase. His phone charger was plugged by the bed and he had a metal water bottle on a coaster as well as his box of medication and his passport, all lined up perfectly neatly. There were no clothes in sight, suggesting they were hung up or folded away.

Ben never really saw the point in doing all of that, as he'd just have to put it all back in the suitcase in a few days. But he had to admit that Elias's room felt cozier for it.

"Is everything okay?" Elias asked. He was already laid out on his side, his head propped up against his palm with his elbow jammed into his pillow.

He looked *delectable.* How could Ben resist a tableau like that?

He dropped onto the mattress, bouncing before he also

lay on his side, wriggling his way next to Elias so they were facing each other. "Everything's great," he said, meaning it. There was no point voicing his concerns that Elias's tidiness was just further proof that he was so much more mature than Ben. Who knew? Maybe Ben would still be a messy disaster at forty, too.

Elias dropped the arm that had been holding up his head so Ben could rest his neck on it and they could both lay their heads on the plump pillows. Ben tried sliding his hand over Elias's hip and waist, then rubbing his back. It felt sumptuous.

"God," he breathed. Their faces were only inches apart. "I so wanted to kiss you on the couch earlier."

Elias chuckled. "You mean when you burrowed your way under my blankets like some kind of vole?"

Ben wasn't even sure what a vole was, but he still laughed. "I genuinely did sleep walk," he said. "But I could have ended up in worse places."

Elias licked his lips and rubbed Ben's back. "I didn't want to let you go," he murmured.

"You don't have to now," Ben promised.

They kissed leisurely, mouths and tongues meeting over and over again. Elias tasted like sweet beer and apple pie, and his couple of days' worth of stubble scratched at Ben's chin, making his toes curl in delight.

It wasn't long before hands began to wander.

"Is this okay?" Elias asked as he skimmed his fingers across Ben's lower back, causing him to shiver. He nodded.

"Very okay. Good," he grunted. Elias grinned and kissed him some more, allowing his hand to drift slowly up and down Ben's spine and along his hip.

Ben followed his lead, gently pulling Elias's shirt out of his pants. Ben knew they both had their concerns about this age gap between them, but *fuck*. Elias had *abs*.

"Oh my god, your body," he mumbled against Elias's lips as he began undoing buttons with more urgency. "Is this okay? I have to feel them."

"It's fine," Elias said fondly, watching as Ben's fingers flew up his shirt. "I've been working hard on them. It's nice to show them off."

"Oh," Ben groaned as he reached the last button and flung the shirt open. "Please, show them off. But mostly to me." Elias laughed.

With the shirt open, Ben discovered a silver necklace hanging against Elias's firm chest. The slim chain looked shiny and new, but the pendant was perhaps older judging from a few tiny dents and scratches Ben could make out.

It was an unfamiliar symbol to Ben. It could have been a lower case 'n' with a tail added on the left. It also kind of reminded Ben of the mathematical pi symbol, which he only knew because he'd spelled it 'pie' all throughout high school, clearly showing where his interests lay.

He wondered if Elias wore this necklace every day, but something told him now was not the time to ask. Instead he ran his hands up those delicious abs and sighed deeply. "I just want to smother you in chocolate sauce and let you rise for twenty minutes."

Elias laughed harder, stroking Ben's messy hair. The action encouraged Ben to dip his head and capture one of Elias's nipples in between his lips and suck.

"Oh, fuck," Elias cried out, bucking in the most beautiful way, then dropping his head back down on the pillow. His fingers were still carding through Ben's hair as Ben continued to suck and lick and even graze the now hard nub with his teeth.

He guessed they were doing more than just cuddling.

Elias's hands were gripping harder in his hair and on his hip. Ben took the initiative and swung his leg over to straddle Elias, grinding his groin down against Elias's as he reclaimed his mouth. His cock was protesting again in his jeans, but this time, there was actually some promise of relief in sight.

Elias pushed Ben's cardigan off then held the hem of his T-shirt, raising his eyebrows. Before he could ask if it was okay to remove, Ben yanked it over his head and flung it to the floor, rolling his hips over Elias's, making him moan.

But then Elias placed his palms on Ben's soft, slightly rounded belly, and Ben got the impulse to flinch away. Usually he felt super confident in bed. Was this what happened when you actually cared about a guy before you got naked with him?

"Sorry," he mumbled. "I'm all squishy."

A look almost like anger flashed over Elias's face. In less than a second he'd sat up, grabbing the back of Ben's head to crash their mouths together in a quite frankly filthy kiss. "You are fucking *gorgeous*," he growled against Ben's lips.

Ben trembled, his horniness tripling in the blink of an eye. "Oh my god," he breathed. "Where did *this* Elias come from? I-I like him. He can stay, please."

Elias licked his lips, looking at Ben through his eyelashes. It was as if something had been unleashed from within him.

It was erotic as all fuck.

"I was wondering if you liked me taking charge of things," Elias murmured against Ben's lips. It felt weird keeping his eyes open when they were this close. But Elias hadn't shut his, so neither would Ben. It was like Elias was already inside Ben, it was that intimate.

Ben managed to nod. "Y-yes." It wasn't like he was meek during sex. Quite the opposite. But maybe this was part of his obsession with Elias being mature and having his shit together. Ben was turned on by confidence and competence, in everyday life but especially in the bedroom.

Elias didn't say anything, he just cradled Ben as he rolled them around so Ben was now on his back with Elias towering over him.

Oh, yes. This was good.

It also meant Ben could push Elias's shirt off and discard it by his T-shirt and cardigan on the floor. The silver pendant swung from Elias's neck. Now they were both bare-chested, and the skin-to-skin contact as Elias leaned down to kiss him felt incredible. Ben let his hands roam over Elias's firm chest and well-defined arms while Elias sucked at his throat and collarbone.

But then Ben reached for Elias's belt buckle…and felt him freeze.

"Sorry," Ben said, immediately withdrawing his hands as they looked at one another. "You're supposed to be in charge.

Elias frowned, however. "No, it's not that." He sounded confused. "I don't know why I panicked. I want you to undress me."

Ben tried running his hands gently down Elias's arms. He seemed fine with that. Elias exhaled and bit his lip. "Sorry."

"No." Ben shook his head. "You said it's been a long time. You might be having some kind of instinctual reaction that your brain isn't controlling."

Elias arched an eyebrow down at him, but he didn't look annoyed. "You make it sound like PTSD or something."

Ben shrugged. "Maybe it is something like that?"

Elias appeared to chew that over for a minute. He laid himself next to Ben, who turned to face him on his side, pleased when Elias placed a hand on his bare hip. "Maybe. But I want to have sex?"

"If your body is disagreeing," Ben said slowly, working out what he was trying to say as the words came out, "perhaps it needs a while to warm up to the idea. Like I said, we can just lie here and cuddle."

Elias blinked. It felt like that had finally pulled him from his deep thoughts since the moment of panic. He smiled warmly and pulled Ben into an affectionate hug, nuzzling his face into the side of Ben's neck and causing Ben to shiver.

"There you go again," Elias said. "Being all wise."

"My generation is just therapy obsessed," Ben scoffed, but he couldn't deny that hearing Elias say that made him flush with pride. It just seemed logical to him that if Elias hadn't had sex in a long time because his diagnosis had made him wary of intimacy, he might have some lingering hang-ups the first time he tried to fuck again.

Elias kissed his neck and sighed. "That's a good thing," he said softly. "I've known too many guys who just bottle everything up." Ben agreed that was no good for anyone.

For a while, they kissed and caressed and cuddled in a tangle of limbs. Their skin was slightly damp, their hair kept falling into their eyes, and Elias's lips looked as red and tender as Ben's felt. Despite the road bumps during the evening so far, Ben felt a deep sense of contentment.

He wanted to ask Elias what he wanted, but gut instinct told him to just carry on rolling with their make-out session and see what happened. Sure enough, it wasn't long before Elias began massaging Ben's ass, grinding their crotches together once again. Ben had an idea. Maybe Elias might feel less vulnerable if Ben was vulnerable first?

"Undress me?" he murmured.

Still lying side by side, Elias rested their foreheads together, their lips a fraction of an inch apart as Elias appeared to consider Ben's words for a second. Then to Ben's delight he dropped his hands down to Ben's jeans and started hungrily undoing them, slipping his top hand over the curve of Ben's ass.

At which point Elias froze, but this time not in a bad way. His hand was resting on the bare skin of Ben's backside. "Are you wearing a jock-strap?" he whispered. Ben nodded, his pulse elevating in anticipation. Elias looked down as if to double-check that the pouch securing Ben's straining cock was indeed being held in place by the two bands around his thighs, leaving his ass exposed and ready. "You wore that to dinner?" Elias rasped.

Oh, yeah. He liked Ben's little surprise. "Uh-huh," Ben purred.

"For me?"

Ben chuckled. "I wear them for me, whenever I go out or want to feel sexy. But I half hoped you might get to enjoy it, too."

Elias's eyes practically rolled into the back of his head. He maneuvered Ben so he was straddling Elias again, then stroked and squeezed Ben's cheeks with both hands. "Oh, *sweetheart,*" he groaned.

Ben held himself up with both his hands on Elias's chest, watching as he explored Ben's ass. Ben shivered as he ran a finger between his cheeks and rubbed his hole. He hadn't prepared to bottom tonight, but if they were just going to stick to foreplay it felt amazing.

Suddenly, Elias leaned up to kiss Ben again enthusiastically, pulling him down and onto his back. Then Elias undid his own belt and pants, kicking them and his socks off, but keeping his briefs on. This felt like excellent progress to Ben as Elias crawled on top of him, laying his full weight over him and rubbing their hard cocks together through their underwear. Precum was already leaking through the fabric as they rocked together, kissing frantically.

"Elias," Ben murmured, digging his fingers into his back muscles and hooking his leg around the back of Elias's knee. This felt good, *really* good. Maybe not quite as amazing as slippery dicks rubbing flesh to flesh, but they didn't have any lube with them anyway. So the material actually felt pretty nice as Ben let Elias's cock grind against him more and more vigorously.

"Ben-?" Elias cried out. Ben could hear the question without him needing to ask it. He was building to a climax, too. Ben was *perfectly* happy to come like this.

"Yes, yes," he whispered against Elias's neck, clinging to him as they sped up, chasing release...

Elias bucked as he came in his briefs, grunting and shuddering as he rode out his orgasm. Ben breathed deeply as he did, holding him tightly to his chest until he felt Elias stir back to his senses.

"Holy fuck," he breathed, pulling back to kiss Ben on the mouth. "That was..." He trailed off, looking down between them. "Did you...?"

Ben rubbed his arm and smiled, trembling a little. "Not yet."

Elias's eyes went wide. "Do you want me to...should I...?"

So Mr. Take Charge Elias wasn't a permanent fixture and might need some further coaxing out. That was fine. Ben knew how he wanted to finish, but if Elias wasn't comfortable, he could just dash to the bathroom quickly.

"Can I jerk off for you?" Ben asked, nuzzling his nose against Elias's cheek and looking him in the eye. Elias appeared to take a moment to process what Ben had said, then nodded. He scooted up alongside Ben, slipping his arm underneath Ben's neck and placing his other hand on Ben's soft tummy which he'd felt self-conscious about a little while ago, but now couldn't care less about. Elias apparently liked it, so that was good enough for him.

Lying on his back, Ben pulled his cock free of its pouch and spat on his hand as most of his precum had been absorbed by his underwear. Then he wasted no time beginning to stroke himself while Elias held him. His gaze kept drifting between Ben's lips and his hand moving on his cock, like he couldn't quite believe this was happening. Ben felt like a superstar, basking in all the attention Elias was giving him.

They kissed and rubbed noses as Ben began to climax again. He didn't want to string it out, so he moved his hand faster, relaxing as his body built and built before finally releasing. His orgasm crashed over him like a wave as he jerked and shot his load over their chests and the bedspread. Luckily it managed not to go above their shoulders. Sometimes Ben loved nothing more than a face full of hot cum. But what he and Elias had just shared felt gentler than that.

"Was that okay?" Elias rubbed Ben's arm as they hugged. It took Ben a second to muster up enough energy to talk again.

"Okay?"

Elias glanced down between them. Ben got the impression his lover was questioning whether what they'd done was good enough.

The thing was, Ben loved sex. All sex. It almost didn't matter what he did with a guy. What was important was how he felt while they were fucking. And he wasn't sure he'd ever felt a deeper emotional connection with *anyone* before.

"Oh my god, Elias? That was *amazing*." He tucked himself back into his jock strap for dignity's sake, then managed to nuzzle himself in even closer against Elias, slinging his leg over Elias's and cupping the side of his face with his hand. "I can't believe we're here. I can't believe you feel the same way as I do. It was perfect and simple and sweet and gives us a great starting-off point."

To his surprise, Elias laughed, mirth shining through his eyes. He caught Ben's lips for a kiss, then caressed his fingers through his damp hair. "Starting-off point?"

Ben wasn't ashamed. He didn't particularly want to leave this bedroom now they'd found their way into it. He'd happily spend the next two weeks getting to know every delicious inch of Elias's beautiful body.

"I told you," he said, nipping at Elias's earlobe. "There's a list. It's alphabetized. I can definitely think of at *least* twenty-six things I'd like to do with you."

Elias regarded him affectionately, rubbing the back of his neck. "You're not disappointed it wasn't real sex?"

Ben gave him a stern look. "All fun times with orgasms count as 'real sex' in my book. But if you want to get all top verses bottom, do you have a preference?"

"For 'next time'?" Elias asked with a raised eyebrow. He didn't seem opposed to the idea at all, much to Ben's relief. "I used to bottom a lot. But I honestly don't know these days."

Ben nodded, tracing his fingers along Elias's warm skin. "I tend to bottom most of the time, too. But we can experiment and see how we fit together."

Elias considered him for a few moments. "So this isn't just a one-time thing for you?"

"Not unless that's what you want," said Ben, praying it wasn't. But Elias sighed in relief.

"No. I – I'd like it very much if we tried again."

"And again. And *again.*" Ben waggled his eyebrows, making Elias laugh. But then Elias wrapped his arms around Ben and hugged him close, rocking them slightly. All of a sudden, tiredness hit Ben like a brick wall. Heavy food on top of sex and jetlag was making him crash hard and fast. "Sleepy," he murmured.

"Do you want to stay here with me?" Elias asked.

Ben nodded. He should have asked if that was what Elias wanted, but he wouldn't have asked if that wasn't his intention, right?

Ben was vaguely aware that Elias turned and reached

behind him. Then he grunted an apology and slipped off the bed. Ben was about to protest, but Elias returned a few moments later with some tissues to clean them off. Why was being so organized such a damn turn-on? Ben had to wonder in his sleepy haze. He'd have just passed out then woken hours later covered in cold cum. *Ew.* But of course Elias had thought ahead.

"Thank you," he mumbled as Elias got him to wriggle so they could pull the comforter back. Ben squirmed so he had his own pillows under his head, then Elias came to spoon beside him.

"Turn around," Elias whispered. Ben did as he'd been asked, so his back was to Elias's chest. He realized Elias must have quickly changed into clean underwear as he nestled his soft cock between Ben's exposed ass cheeks. He didn't usually sleep in his jock-straps, preferring to be naked, but he'd keep his modesty for Elias's sake. Besides, he was about three seconds from blacking out, and had no energy to pull it off even if he'd wanted to.

"Goodnight," he uttered, feeling immensely safe as Elias got his octopus arms and legs wrapped around Ben's body again. God, if he could have assured the Ben who'd woken on the couch that afternoon that this was how their night would end, he wasn't sure he would have believed it. But it had, and he was incredibly glad.

Who knew what this meant for tomorrow or when they got back to Pine Cove? But for now, Ben was more than happy to drift off, Elias's lips brushing the back of his neck and his necklace pendant pressed against Ben's shoulder blade.

ELIAS

It had been a while since Elias had suffered from true jetlag. Traveling between states made you tired, but there was nothing like an eight-hour time difference to really wipe you out.

So even after dinner, late-night baking, heart-to-hearts, and some surprising but wonderful sex, Elias still found himself wide awake at four o'clock in the morning and there didn't seem to be anything he could do about it. By the time it reached five o'clock, Elias's thoughts were starting to drive him nuts, so he resorted to checking his work emails even though he'd promised himself he wouldn't while he was on vacation. When the clock hands hit six and Ben was still fast asleep, Elias decided to take Treacle for a walk.

He took his medication with water, having decided on the plane the day before to stick to his usual routine rather than try and worry about compensating for the time difference. Then he bundled up and tried to keep Treacle from barking when he went downstairs, getting the dog outside as quickly as possible. It was still dark, so Elias didn't venture far, choosing to potter around and around the same little loop a few times rather than get lost.

The rain had held off, but the woods smelled rich and earthy from the weather day before, the mud fresh and squelchy under Elias's boots. Birds were chirping in the barren tree branches, waking up the day. Treacle wagged his bushy tail non-stop as he ran around smelling everything, regularly trotting back to check that Elias was still following him. As they ventured back toward the cottage at just past seven o'clock, dawn was starting to break, sending pink and orange streaks across the horizon.

When Elias peeked silently back into the bedroom, Ben was still fast asleep. The covers were half kicked away from him, his arm over his head and his foot hanging off the side of the bed, his curls looking like a bird's nest. He looked so angelic in a disheveled sort of way. Elias decided not to disturb him yet, instead going to take a shower.

The trouble with lying in bed and going for a walk was that neither of those things had done much good in taking Elias's mind off the night before. Not even his work emails had been able to distract him. He'd opened three separate ones before accepting that the words were going to just swim around in front of his eyes because they weren't anything to do with Ben.

Elias took a deep breath, scrubbing every inch of himself under the streaming hot water. Not because he felt dirty or anything like that, but because he felt the need to apply some real pressure on his body, to feel it alive under his hands.

He was so confused. There were so many questions he was wrestling with and not nearly enough answers.

Was he happy with what had taken place last night?

Fucking hell, yes. He'd been dreaming of Ben for months and now it seemed they were going to take a shot at being together. Not to mention that the sex had been amazing.

Although it seemed strange for Elias to call what they'd done sex. In his day, that would have just been 'making out.' But Ben had seemed pretty adamant that what they'd done counted fair and square. Elias was glad. He wanted their night to matter.

Was Elias having second thoughts?

Maybe. It was impossible to deny that he and Ben had heaps of chemistry going on between them. In the end he wasn't sure they'd had any choice but to give into their raging lust for one another, even if the result had been a little tame. But Elias remembered plenty of times where anal had been awkward or outright painful. What he and Ben had shared was sensual, intimate. But did they have anything more than that between them? What did they really have in common?

What did Ben want out of life or a relationship? If he had ideas about taking Elias out clubbing on the weekends or bungy jumping off cliffs, then they were going to have an issue. Similarly, if Ben had no interest in long dog walks or Netflix binges, Elias wasn't sure what he really had to offer him in the long run.

What had happened when Elias had frozen?

That he thought he might have had an answer to. In fact, Ben had kind of gotten there on his own, too. It hadn't mattered that Elias had been turned on and eager for a wild night of fucking with his hot new lover. Something in him had slammed the brakes on, like it was a matter of life or death. Maybe somewhere inside him, Elias wasn't done seeing his body as the enemy that had betrayed him. The mere thought of getting totally naked had sent him into a complete tailspin.

But then Ben had discovered a work-around. In that moment of panic, Elias would have sworn he'd lost his erection and wasn't going to come anytime that night. But

Ben had been patient and sweet, changing up their plans and waiting until Elias felt comfortable again.

And that brought him to his final question as he stepped from the shower and towel dried off.

Didn't Ben deserve someone better than Elias?

Ben was always putting himself down. Even if it was in jokes, he didn't seem to realize that he was amazing. Elias was pretty confident he could tell *and* show him how wrong he was, but shouldn't he have the opportunity to do that with someone his own age? They were at different stages in life. Shouldn't Elias be giving Ben the opportunity to go crazy in his twenties with someone he had more in common with?

Cradle snatcher. That's what people used to call guys who dated someone much younger than themselves. There was older and then there was 'old enough to be your dad.' Darcy and Elias's other friends back in Pine Cove might have said they'd support anything between him and Ben, but what would Ben's friends say? Would they be horrified?

Elias rubbed the condensation from the mirror to look at his reflection, and tried to put his rational brain into play. The lawyer one that looked at facts, not emotions. Was there really anything wrong with a bit of an age gap when both men were well above the age of consent? As Ben had rather hotly reminded Elias the night before, he was twenty-three, and more than capable of making up his own mind.

Elias rubbed his face, feeling the stubble so deciding to shave. As many doubts as he was having, he also couldn't resist the urge of looking as good as he could for Ben when he woke up. He was apprehensive Ben was going to regret it all or change his mind and say once was good enough to scratch his itch. It was superficial, but Elias hoped maybe if he looked his best, Ben wouldn't toss him away so easily.

No, Ben wasn't that shallow. Was he?

How well did Elias really know him?

Shit. He'd been in such knots he'd forgotten to bring any clean clothes into the bathroom with him. Well, it was getting close to eight o'clock now, so Ben might be awake and then Elias wouldn't have to worry about disturbing him by going back into the room and rummaging through his drawers and closet.

But if he was awake, that meant Elias was out of time. He'd have to face the music and see how Ben felt about the night before.

Resigning himself, Elias collected up his dog-walking gear, folding it all into a pile. Then he crossed the chilly hall with just a towel wrapped around his hips. He might need to take another look at that thermostat.

He knew he was thinking about the central heating just to distract himself as he gently knocked then cautiously opened the bedroom door.

Ben was awake.

He looked up from where he was on his phone, snuggled under the covers, looking breath-taking. His curls were a mess and he had lines from the pillowcase indented into his cheek and forehead, but to Elias, he was beautiful.

Especially when he broke into a dazzling smile. "I thought I heard you in the shower. Have you been up for a while?"

God, Elias felt like he'd already done a day's work he'd been awake so long, but to Ben, he just smiled. "I took Treacle for a walk. I – oh!"

As if he'd heard his name, Treacle came barging through the door, almost knocking Elias over in his eagerness to reach Ben, presumably now that he'd heard Ben's voice. But his legs were too short to enable him to jump onto the bed by himself, which was probably a good thing when he was left alone in the house. For now, Ben was laughing and patting the mattress, encouraging Treacle to keep trying to reach him, so Elias placed his clothes pile on top of the dresser, then gave Treacle a boost up.

The small dog was a lot heavier than he looked, though, and in the process of Elias lifting him, his towel slipped.

Almost falling entirely off his hips.

Elias managed to catch it just in time to keep his dick covered, gasping as he did. His heart skipped, and he glanced up at Ben, his immediate response to be embarrassed. But Ben was dragging his bottom lip between his teeth, before looking up at Elias with eyes of pure sin.

Then there was a flash where he seemed to pause. He was possibly remembering Elias's hang-ups from the night before and his moment of inexplicable panic. But…none of that came to Elias then. Under Ben's sultry gaze, Elias forgot his fleeting embarrassment.

He just felt sexy.

His heart skipped again for an entirely different reason. He stood up straight, deliberately holding the towel with his hand next to his belly button so it fell and barely concealed his cock. With Ben looking at him all wide-eyed and breathless, he felt something strange.

It was almost powerful.

"See something you like?" he rasped.

Ben's hazel eyes flicked up and down Elias's body and he let out a little puff of air, his mouth curling in a wicked grin. "Not quite, but I got a good preview."

Elias laughed. He wanted to talk before anything more physical happened between them, but he was suddenly quite sure that something *was* going to happen, and that made him oddly calm.

"Would you like some breakfast?" he asked as he wrapped the towel back around his hips.

Treacle was headbutting Ben, so he chuckled and started petting him, but then he blinked up at Elias. "In bed?" Elias nodded and Ben smiled bashfully, dropping his gaze back down to Treacle. "How romantic," he mumbled.

Yes, it was, Elias realized. He kind of loved that.

Ben was determinedly looking at Treacle. Elias wondered if he was doing it to give him a chance to dress with a modicum of privacy, so he turned and grabbed some briefs from one of the drawers. As soon as he wasn't swinging around anymore, he took a little time to pick out a pair of jeans and a Henley that he knew brought out his green eyes well.

"I'm not sure what there is in the kitchen," Elias said as he pulled some socks on and found his slippers. It was probably terribly fuddy-duddy, but he couldn't bear to travel without his slippers.

Ben dropped his gaze deliberately to Elias's crotch, then slowly dragged it back up again. "I'll eat anything," he said, his voice hoarse.

A mix of pride and embarrassment flushed through Elias's body. He almost walked into the side of the door in his haste to escape the room, stammering something about being sure of finding toast and eggs.

He was glad he had a bit of cooking to occupy him for a while. While his hands were busy and he was watching several things at once, his thoughts were less likely to stray.

Although he was pretty sure he'd answered the question as to whether or not Ben was interested in having sex again. But Ben had also appeared to find the idea of Elias cooking him breakfast romantic. It had been a purely practical suggestion when Elias had made it. They had to eat, after all. But then Elias took a moment and wondered if he had *ever* cooked breakfast for a lover.

He couldn't recall that he had.

There was a distinct possibility that Mrs. Hollis had snuck back over to the cottage while they'd been at dinner last night, as the fridge was definitely fuller than it had been when Elias had glanced at it the previous day. As a result, he was able to whip up some eggs, toast, bacon that looked more like Canadian bacon than American, and hash browns that came from the freezer in funny triangle shapes. However as much as he hunted, he couldn't find a coffee machine, or any coffee other than a dusty old jar of instant granules. There *was* a large box of tea bags, though, so he made them a mug each of that using the kettle, figuring 'when in Rome.'

It was tricky, timing everything to be ready all at about the same time, but Elias just about managed it. While he'd been hunting for the coffee pot he'd come across some lap trays, so he loaded up the first one and brought it upstairs to Ben.

"I wasn't sure if you took sugar in your tea, so I brought the pot up," he said as he shouldered his way in through the door.

Ben chuckled. At a glance he looked to have put a T-shirt and some sweatpants on. It wasn't that Elias didn't want to see him naked again as soon as possible, but he appreciated Ben respecting his wishes to take things slowly. Being dressed would make it easier to have a conversation first, if one needed to be had.

"I haven't drunk much tea," Ben admitted, "but knowing me, I'll probably load it up with more sugar than liquid."

"I drink a lot of green tea," Elias told him as he placed the tray on Ben's lap. Treacle immediately tried to get his nose in the eggs, but Elias swooped in and dropped the cheeky devil back down at the floor. "Don't look all betrayed at me like that," Elias grumbled at him, raising an eyebrow. "You still have food in your bowl downstairs."

Treacle harrumphed and trotted off, most likely going to check if Elias was telling him the truth.

Ben sipped his mug of tea then grimaced and reached straight for the sugar bowl. "Oh, look! It comes in cubes!" He added three lumps, stirred the tea, then sighed deeply after another sip. "Much better. Have you got breakfast, too?"

Elias nodded, reminding himself he couldn't spend all his time making moon eyes at Ben, musing about how sweet he was. He hurried back down to load up his own plate and then returned to Ben in bed. Treacle was happily chewing on some kind of rawhide treat by the empty fire grate. Elias thought it might be nice to get that going again later, even though the central heating was doing a good job of keeping the cottage warm after he'd fiddled with it again while cooking breakfast.

"This is nice," Ben commented, nibbling on some toast. "Thank you."

"You're welcome."

They stared at each other for a second, before Elias turned his attention back to his breakfast on his lap. But Ben wasn't going to let him off the hook that easily. "So. Last night."

"Yes," said Elias, glancing at him with a shy smile.

Ben bit his lip but he was still smiling. "Everything okay?"

Elias took a moment to chew and swallow some eggs and buttery toast, then sipped his tea. "Yes," he said firmly. "I'm sorry I'm cautious. It's been so long since I spent the night with anyone, let alone..." Oh *god*, he'd almost said 'dated'! He and Ben weren't dating! How could he be so hesitant on the one hand, yet almost suggesting they become boyfriends in such a hurry? He was all muddled.

"Let alone?" Ben probed. He'd inhaled most of his breakfast already and now seemed more interested in Elias while he cradled his mug of tea.

Elias took a breath. Ben was *interested*. That was a good thing. Maybe Elias shouldn't be writing himself off so quickly. But he wasn't going to blabber on about being boyfriends or whatever and go scaring Ben off.

"Let alone sex," he said instead, trying not to blush. He was almost forty. He could say 'sex' without giggling like a schoolboy. "Thank you for being kind and patient. I mean – it was all pretty great."

Ben grinned and placed his tray on the nightstand, turning to give Elias his full attention. "It was, wasn't it?"

In a flash, Elias's appetite vanished. It was replaced with a squirming sensation in his belly, and a dry mouth despite the tea he'd gulped down. He followed Ben's lead and removed his tray and the remainder of his breakfast from his lap.

"Ben," he said, not even sure what he was going to say. "I can't promise-"

"Stop," Ben said, raising his eyebrows as well as his hand. "I like you. I have for ages. Do you like me?"

Ages? It took a second for Elias to remember how his voice worked. "Uh, yes. Very much."

He tried to hold Ben's gaze, but he felt his cheeks heating up and he wasn't confident enough to keep his eyes level. He looked at his fingers pulling at each other in his lap, until Ben's hand also came into view, claiming Elias's right one between both of his, rubbing the knuckles.

"Then it's that simple," Ben said, as if it was. "You're hot and kind and clever. I like sharing your bed. Does it have to be anything more than that for now?"

Elias wasn't sure. Did it? On the one hand, he'd be lying if he didn't admit he had several doubts they were compatible as boyfriends. So maybe a more physical thing was preferable. But he was no *good* at the sexy stuff anymore. What if he kept freezing up again like he had the night before? He would hate to let Ben down or disappoint him.

"Or…" said Ben, the playfulness gone from his voice. He

sounded nervous. "If you'd rather just leave it at what happened last night, we don't have to-"

Elias only thought for a split second before he darted forward and stopped Ben from talking the best way he could think of. The kiss was just lips pressed against each other, but he felt Ben melt against him before he cupped the side of Elias's jaw and hummed. Elias hummed back.

"Last night was wonderful," he murmured against Ben's mouth. "I – I'd like to explore that some more. Please."

Ben's reply was more kissing, their lips parting to allow their tongues to dance. "More," he agreed as they slid down under the covers, their limbs becoming entwined as their stomachs rubbed together.

They weren't the only things rubbing. Elias couldn't remember the last time he was this readily horny. Not since his carefree college days, he was pretty sure, where he'd had so many men to play with and his secret was still safe from his family.

There was a risk he might have gotten melancholy at that thought, but Ben tugged at the T-shirt he'd only just put on. "I have an idea," Ben said devilishly, rolling and slipping out of bed. Elias almost had time to feel disappointed, but it was clear Ben wasn't done with him from the filthy kiss he leaned down to give him. "How do you feel about getting naked for me?"

Elias took a steadying breath, rubbing his nose against Ben's. The panic didn't come. "Good," he said hoarsely. "Very good."

Ben kissed him firmly before grinning. "Then you better have your clothes off by the time I get back!" he called over his shoulder, dashing out of the bedroom door.

After a moment of trepidation Elias hurried to comply. His heart was pounding and his dick was throbbing. What was Ben up to? Was Elias being irresponsible with this whole 'go with the flow' idea? He huffed and flung his naked body back under the covers. He'd been sensible enough for one damn lifetime. He could afford to be a little reckless and have some fun, right? This was a reasonably safe kind of reckless, after all.

Ben's footsteps alerted Elias that he was heading back up the stairs – *running* up them from the sounds of it. Elias's heartbeat increased in anticipation. Ben appeared back through the door, closing it behind him, and resting his back against the wood.

He held up a squeezy bottle of something, wiggling both it and his eyebrows.

It was honey.

Elias couldn't help it, he laughed. "What are you up to?" he asked incredulously. Ben skipped back over to the bed, dropping down to sit next to where Elias was lying.

"I told you that you looked edible," he said, his voice sultry. "I thought maybe I could help you relax, if you'd like?"

Elias was pretty sure he gulped. If Ben was suggesting what he *thought* he was suggesting, Elias could add that to his rapidly growing list of things he'd never done before.

That traitorous panic threatened to rise again. Whatever Ben had in mind, Elias was pretty sure he was going to be left feeling exposed and vulnerable. Things he hadn't allowed himself in years with another man. Yet here this young guy was, making sex fun, practically begging Elias to break down his walls so they could share something unforgettable together.

"O-okay," he managed to stammer, smiling. Ben's eyes were dancing with excitement, and that was difficult to ignore. His enthusiasm helped Elias relax, just like Ben had promised.

Ben clicked the cap of the honey open, squeezing a droplet onto his index finger. Then he reached over, touching the sweet tip to Elias's bottom lip, making Elias's heart skip a beat altogether. Logic and reason faded away as his tongue automatically darted out to taste the sticky nectar.

"Lie down," Ben whispered with a wink, "and think of England."

Trying not to tremble, Elias shifted in the bed, lying on his back with his head on the pillows. For a second, he worried that Ben was going to rip all the covers off. Instead, he tugged them just a little, exposing Elias's chest, the comforter resting on his hips and covering his modesty.

For now.

Then Ben straddled Elias's hips, turning the honey bottle upside down, drizzling a good squeeze over Elias's abs.

He couldn't help the moan that escaped his lips at the sensation, already confident of what was about to happen. Sure enough, Ben clicked the cap shut again, dropping the bottle beside him, then dipped his head to take a slow, long lick up Elias's stomach, lapping up the sticky spread and making all Elias's muscles contract.

"Holy fuck," Elias rasped.

He ran his fingers through Ben's curls, watching him kiss and lick at the honey, tracing patterns along Elias's abs, obliques, and even darting his tongue into his belly button. *Damn,* Elias was glad he'd taken that thorough shower. His skin was clean and fresh for Ben to enjoy himself with.

And unless Elias was very much mistaken, Ben was enjoying himself a *lot.* He looked up at Elias through golden lashes, humming as he touched and kissed Elias's ticklish skin. The funny thing was, Elias *did* feel just as exposed as he feared he would, but it was far from demeaning.

It was invigorating. Empowering.

Ben crawled up his body with a look in his eyes that made Elias think of a wild cat. He grinned wickedly as he captured Elias's mouth for a deep, sensual kiss. His lips and tongue were sweet and tangy from the honey, his hands hot against Elias's chest and arms.

"Do you trust me?" Ben murmured.

The question caught Elias off guard. He almost flinched. Trust was something he'd become very bad at in the bedroom. After he'd been diagnosed, he'd never wanted to pass on the virus the way he'd had to experience. But the answer escaped his throat before he could overthink it.

"Yes," he uttered. Because it was true. Even though they were only just getting to know one another, he *did* trust Ben already.

Ben's hazel eyes were dark with lust, and they flashed with something exhilarating at Elias's answer. "Lie on your front. Relax. You've taken care of me in so many ways. Let me take care of you now."

Elias swallowed in trepidation, but he nodded. Ben gave him a sweet kiss, then jutted out his chin, indicating Elias should roll over.

The sensible part of his brain fretted for a moment that he was getting honey on the sheets. But sensible wasn't really the name of the game in that moment. The bed already had sweat and cum on it, so what was a little honey as well? There were bound to be clean sheets somewhere for later.

Elias hugged his pillow, looking over his shoulder as he got comfy. Ben grinned and pecked a sweet kiss to his lips before drizzling a line of honey down Elias's spine, kissing and licking his way down Elias's back.

Getting closer to his ass cheeks.

Elias couldn't stop his eyes from fluttering closed as Ben massaged his non-sticky shoulders and neck, rolling his groin against the back of Elias's thighs. Then he stroked down his ticklish ribs as he kissed Elias's lower back and hips, gently nudging the covers down, gradually exposing Elias's ass cheeks.

Elias took a deep breath, his eyes still firmly closed as he determinedly tried to relax like Ben had asked him to. To begin with, Ben kissed his cheeks and kneaded where they met the top of Elias's thighs. Then he nuzzled along the crack with his nose, his breath tingling on Elias's sensitive skin, making him shiver.

The click of the honey cap meant Elias guessed what might be coming, but he still nearly jumped as Ben held his right cheek aside and drizzled some honey over his hole with his other hand. But then he was pushing both cheeks aside and lapping with his tongue against the tight ring of sensitive muscle, making Elias moan into his pillow. He tried not to squirm too much, but it was almost impossible.

He'd quite forgotten how much he fucking loved being eaten out.

Back in his college days, this had been his preferred way to stretch out before anal, but lately it had felt far too intimate with men he didn't really know, not to mention he'd stayed clear of penetrative sex for the most part. But now, feeling Ben kiss and lick and probe with his lips and tongue, Elias was in heaven. He could take this for hours.

It seemed Ben felt the same. Elias lost track of time as he relaxed into a puddle of goo, everything but his pleasure fading away as Ben tenderly looked after him. But at some point, he must have started grinding his hard cock against the mattress looking for release. Ben came away from his ass with a kiss, then he was breathing against Elias's neck as he nipped at his earlobe.

"Do you want to turn over and I'll finish you off with my mouth?"

For a second, that damned panic threatened to creep in and shatter Elias's bliss. But instead, he took a deep breath and allowed his eyes to flutter open and regard Ben's flushed face.

"I haven't got any condoms," he said.

To his surprise, Ben smiled. "I know," he said, gently caressing the side of Elias's face.

"Are you on PrEP?" Elias asked directly. Logically, he knew Ben didn't need to be, but he thought it might help calm his nerves if he was.

However, Ben shook his head. "No. But I trust you when you say you're undetectable. If it helps you feel better, though, you can warn me, and we can finish with my hand. But I need you in my mouth. Now."

Holly fuck. Elias had assumed after their discussion yesterday that Ben would be more submissive in bed than this. But it seemed more like it depended on his mood. Elias had to admit that he equally liked to be taken charge of from time to time. As Ben had said, to just lie back and think of England, but in a good way.

He nodded. "Okay." His voice was hoarse but steady. However, it took a moment to steel himself before rolling onto his back in all his naked glory, exposing his stiff, weeping cock to Ben.

Ben groaned and licked his shiny lips, already reaching for the honey. He took his time enjoying spreading the sticky substance along Elias's length, chuckling as Elias bucked and cried out in pure desire. Ben licked and kissed along the shaft and tip before finally swallowing Elias fully.

For someone so young, he deep-throated with ease, reminding Elias that his age was no indication of experience. Rather than feeling threatened or jealous however, Elias privately thanked the men who had come before him for their part in helping Ben to become such a confident lover.

As Ben sucked and swallowed, Elias carded his fingers through those glorious curls, drinking in every second of such an erotic sight. His mouth was hot and tight around Elias's dick, so perfect. Ben looked back at him, holding his gaze as he urged Elias to completion. It took an embarrassingly short time for Elias to feel his climax rising, but Ben *had* been teasing him from behind for a fair while.

"Ben!" Elias managed to grunt, giving his hair a slight tug as his hips bucked.

True to his word, Ben popped off his cock immediately. But his hand was there in a flash, jerking Elias's rock-hard cock, and he moved so he could kiss Elias's lips. "Come for me, gorgeous," he murmured.

Elias gripped Ben's shoulders, tasting his own intimate flavor as they kissed and finding it invigorating rather than off-putting. In less than twelve hours, he'd gone from having a borderline panic attack at the thought of getting naked, to reveling in his boldness.

Ben made him feel free.

He cried out again as his orgasm peaked, spilling over his belly and Ben's hand. He buried his face against Ben's neck, his breathing ragged and his eyes squeezed shut as waves of ecstasy rolled over him. It was perfect.

Almost.

After a moment or two, his senses started coming back to him, then he kissed Ben messily and happily. "You," he uttered, pulling at Ben's sweatpants. "Your turn, sweetheart."

Ben's smile shone on his damp face as his eyes danced, and he hummed. "Sweetheart," he repeated, grinning. "I like that."

"Do you?" Elias may have been blissed out and groggy from his high, but he was also aware he was bestowing a pet name on Ben not even a day into…whatever this was between them.

"I like it a lot." Ben kissed him again and nuzzled their noses together. "I'm okay, if you're too tired."

Elias scoffed. "You're like a fucking tent pole," he said

with a laugh. "I'm underconfident, not selfish. I could suck you off?"

Ben shivered and ghosted his breath against Elias's lips. "Could I fuck your face?" he whispered in a counteroffer. "You look so cute and relaxed laid on the bed. I don't want to move you."

If Elias hadn't just come quite explosively, he would be hard again. As it was, he still trembled, his mouth going dry in anticipation. This was why he liked bottoming with the right kind of guy. Sometimes it was the best feeling in the world to just be held down and fucked.

"God, yes," he rasped. "Can you be more naked, please?" he asked, fumbling with Ben's T-shirt. He knew he'd been a bit shy taking his clothes off, but Ben didn't seem to have any such issues, to Elias's delight. Sure enough, he had all his clothes back off again in a flash, grinning as he crawled up Elias's body, angling the shiny red tip of his rigid cock to rub against Elias's parted lips.

Elias relaxed against his pillow as Ben pushed his cock into his mouth, holding Elias's hair as he thrust his dick toward the back of his throat. He didn't push Elias too far, though, and expect him to deep throat. He seemed perfectly content with shallow thrusts, watching hungrily as Elias sucked him.

Elias ran his hands up and down Ben's legs and over his ass cheeks, feeling the beautiful peach fuzz on his skin. Everything about Ben was soft and light and lovely. Elias remembered how much he'd used to adore giving head, knowing he was offering his partner something so sensual and intimate. He was willing to lie back and let Ben use his mouth for as long as he wanted.

Sadly, but unsurprisingly after all their foreplay, it didn't take Ben long to climax. "I'm going to come," he cried screwing up his face.

Elias gripped his ass firmly, telling him that he wanted to take the load. Ben responded right away, speeding up then suddenly halting to erupt down Elias's throat with a shout. Elias swallowed obediently, drinking every drop and letting Ben soften in his mouth before he pulled out.

"Holy shitballs," Ben said with a shaky laugh, dropping down to spoon Elias's side. Elias automatically turned to hug his lover tight. The room was thick with the scent of sex and musk. Wintery sunshine was spilling through the net curtains, making the bedroom feel like it was glowing.

"Yeah," Elias agreed roughly, not able to muster the energy for anything much more elaborate. All his strength was going into cradling Ben as close as possible to him, their legs entwined, Ben's head on Elias's chest.

It was funny in a way. As their heart rates slowed and the sweat and cum cooled, it wasn't the blow jobs that Elias was marveling at, although they'd been excellent. It was the fact that he was lying there, totally naked and exposed, with the man who'd stolen his heart so many months ago, feeling completely at ease.

Maybe it was simply because Elias had gone so long without intimacy in his life, and Ben was the first one in a long time to break down his walls. But Elias felt that any old hook up wouldn't be making him feel this way. No. It was Ben, specifically, that was making him radiate confidence for the first time in years.

With Ben, he felt as if he'd finally come home.

15

BEN

"Wʜᴀᴛ's ᴛʜɪs?"

They'd been lying quietly together on the bed in the post-orgasmic glow for several minutes. But as usual, Ben hadn't been able to keep his thoughts still for long, and he was curious about Elias's silver necklace. He was deliciously naked aside from the chain around his throat, the pendant that had been resting on his chest now between Ben's fingers.

He glanced up to see Elias looking thoughtfully at him. Oh, damn. Had Ben made a *faux pas?*

"Sorry, if it's private," he mumbled, letting the sort of 'n' shaped pendant go. But Elias picked it up himself, looking at it fondly.

"No," he said gently. "I mean, I guess it is quite personal. But I don't mind talking about it. It's my *chai.*" He made a guttural sound at the start of the word. "C-h-a-i."

"Like the tea?"

Elias chuckled, the sound a soft rumble in his chest, then repeated the word. "It means life, and also represents the number eighteen."

Ben reached out to touch it again. "Is that Jewish?"

Elias nodded. "I got it for my eighteenth birthday from my parents. It's a traditional present."

He paused and bit his lip, looking troubled. Ben wanted to ask why, but experience had taught him that sometimes it was better to keep his mouth shut and wait. So instead, he rubbed Elias's collarbone, showing him he was there for him if he wanted to continue talking. After a moment, Elias spoke again.

"When I was diagnosed with HIV, I was your age. Twenty-three. I hadn't come out to my family as gay. I knew they wouldn't like it. But I didn't feel I could hide my HIV status. I didn't *want* to. I so desperately needed their support. I was scared, and deep down, I believed they would still love me, no matter what." He blinked, his eyes shiny. "They did not. They cut me off that day and I haven't seen any of them since."

Ben couldn't help but gasp. "What? Not ever?"

Elias shook his head, still looking down at the necklace. "I was living in Seattle at the time. By the time I returned to Pine Cove, my parents had moved back to be nearer my aunt, and my brother settled with his wife in her home town, or so I heard through the grapevine. I don't even have addresses for them. When the chain broke on this a few years ago, I considered finally taking it off. But...it's the last thing I have of them."

A single tear slid down his cheek. Ben's heart ached and he reached up to wipe it away with his thumb, cradling the side of Elias's face. "What *assholes*," he said thickly, unable to stop his own eyes from burning.

Luckily, Elias laughed. He sniffed and hugged Ben tighter. "Damn right," he mumbled. "But there's a part of me that could never really blame them. It's what most people did."

"What do you mean?" Ben asked.

Elias scrubbed his face and breathed out, then he flung the comforter over their lower halves, presumably to feel more comfortable and less exposed. Ben was fine with that. During sex he was pretty confident naked, but his body didn't half compare with Elias's toned form. It was easier to talk in a more modest state.

"I couldn't hide my diagnosis," Elias said sadly. "I got what I thought was the flu several months after I think I was exposed. By then I was with my ex-boyfriend, so I told him right away. Luckily we'd been practicing safe sex, so he was never infected. But the drugs I started on were quite brutal, so I needed to inform my law school and eventually had to make up a semester for all the time I missed."

He sighed and stroked Ben's hair. Ben smiled sympathetically at him when their gazes met. He couldn't imagine what it was like to receive such life-altering news, but he was starting to get an idea.

"It was like coming out all over again," Elias continued. "Except in 2003 people were pretty okay with me being gay. But the stigma around HIV and AIDS was still rampant. By the time I graduated, every single friend of mine had drifted away. Especially those that had started having kids. They didn't want me within a thousand feet of them."

The bitterness in his voice was clear. Anger bubbled in Ben's chest. "But that's fucking awful," Ben said through gritted teeth. "Did *everyone* abandon you?"

Elias gave him a pained smile. "Not my ex, but I was already sabotaging that relationship, utterly terrified to get too close to him. In the end we split as amicably as we could, and I moved to be nearer the only friends who had never dropped me. My high school buddies. My family might no longer have been in Pine Cove, but Darcy and the others were as good as family to me by then."

Ben wasn't too sure what to say. He felt so childish and ill-qualified to try and comfort Elias when faced with such a horrifying string of events. "I'm so sorry," was all he could muster.

Elias stroked his hair and kissed his forehead. "It's okay. Over the years, I've realized I was so lucky I contracted the virus when I did. Ten or even five years previously, I might not have been able to access the drugs out there now to beat this thing." He laughed ruefully. "Don't get me wrong. I've been on some shockers. Some I had to take every four hours, even through the night. Some that made me suicidal. It hasn't been a picnic, but I'm still fucking here. I'll be forty next year, and I decided that was it. I was going to start living again, because so many others never got that chance."

His voice was thick toward the end of his little speech, and they lay there in silence for a few minutes while Ben processed everything he'd said. *Fuck* Elias's family and so-called friends. How could they only see him for his diagnosis, not as a human being? Ben got that people were scared, but Elias was still a person who needed to be loved.

"I'm so glad you're still here, too," Ben murmured, his temple resting on Elias's chest again.

To his surprise, Elias chuckled. "Well, this is cheery pillow talk. You only asked what my necklace was. I should have just said a birthday present and left it at that."

Ben shook his head and looked back up at him. "No, no," he insisted. "I want to know about you, even the sad stuff. Thank you for sharing that with me. I'm sorry I can't be better support."

Elias leaned down and pressed a sweet kiss to his lips. "You're great. Just listening is better than so many other people have done in my life."

Pride warmed Ben's chest. He wanted to be better than all

of those assholes. He wanted to be special to Elias, even if he didn't have much to offer him in return.

The sudden sound of Treacle barking from downstairs made them both startle. Ben strained his ear and just caught the sound of someone knocking at the door.

"Shit," he hissed. Elias was still covered in drying cum where they hadn't cleaned up yet, so Ben threw himself out of bed and shoved his way back into his T-shirt and sweatpants, dashing down the creaky, uneven stairs.

Even if Elias had been presentable, Ben figured he should probably answer the door anyway. This was technically his estate, his family, and his problem. He should be dealing with any visitors. He wasn't sure who he might meet on the other side, however: friend or foe. Luckily, when he yanked open the door, he was pretty sure it was a friend.

"Morning!" Noah cried cheerfully, his breath coming out as a puff of condensation in the crisp autumn air. It was an entirely different day than when they'd arrived yesterday. Gone was the gray and gloomy sky, replaced with brilliant blue and fluffy white clouds drifting gently by. The air smelled fresh and earthy after all the rain, and the wind was only a light breeze that teased at the bare tree branches.

Noah was as objectively handsome as he'd been the day before, with a square jaw, thick, light brown hair, and blue eyes. He appeared to have a good body under the sweater and puffy vest jacket he was wearing. His jeans were tight over bulging thighs and his rain boots clung to his large calves. But Ben's heart didn't even flutter. It was still firmly upstairs with Elias in their messy bed.

That didn't mean he wasn't still happy to see Noah, however. He was one of the only people from the house Ben felt was on his side. Apart from the staff, who all seemed fiercely loyal to Nancy still and therefore apparently Ben as well.

"Noah, hi!" Ben said cheerfully. "What brings you here?"

Noah looked Ben up and down, presumably taking in his disheveled state. "I was hoping to issue you and Mr. Solomon an invitation, but I'm terribly sorry if I woke you. Is the jetlag being a beast?"

Ben almost blushed. *No, but Elias is a bit of a beast in the sack,* he thought devilishly. He cleared his throat and attempted to mask his lust with a cough. "Yeah. I've never left the States before, so it's a bit of a shock. What kind of thing did you have in mind?"

Noah's gaze flicked back up. Had he been ogling Ben's crotch? Ben was more and more certain they batted for the same team. Unfortunately, he wasn't looking for any new recruits now. He was happy with the partner he had.

"Oh, right, yes." Noah beamed, flashing perfect white teeth. "Kenneth asked me to extend an invitation to come shooting with some of the family."

Ben felt his mouth drop open as several questions flashed across his mind. "Kenneth…what?"

Noah shrugged, shifting on his feet and making the mud squelch. It was only then that Ben noticed that Treacle hadn't come to the door to greet him. Maybe he knew that Noah was allergic?

"I told you Kenneth's bark is worse than his bite," Noah said with a wink. "I'm not saying he's ready to welcome you into the fold or that he's reconsidering his challenge on the will. But I think he'd like a chance to get to know you better, even if only to see what your aim is like."

He chuckled, clearly seeing this all as a positive. But Ben was still unsure.

"And…shooting?" he questioned. However, Noah waved his hands and shook his head.

"Clay pigeon shooting," he explained. "Flying disks. Perfectly humane. Although in the good old days, the game *was* used in the kitchens after. But people frown on that sort of thing for sport these days."

Ben couldn't honestly work out if Noah thought that was a good or a bad thing. In either case, Ben was relieved. He wasn't a vegetarian or anything, but he hated the idea of blood sport just for fun – even if it did end up in a pie in the end.

Aiming at flying disks, though? That actually sounded pretty fun. And Ben was open to anything that might improve his relationship with his extended family. Which was how he and Elias found themselves showered and dressed in their warmest clothes and sturdiest boots, traipsing through the grounds of Whittingar Abbey an hour later.

"Are you sure they're not just trying to lure us out to the middle of nowhere to 'take care' of us?" Elias asked over the wind as they followed Noah down the dirt path. Ben snickered. Treacle was happily trotting by their feet, his tongue lolling out of his mouth.

"It had crossed my mind," Ben replied, glad he'd brought his hat and gloves this time. "That or they have a big bonfire they're going to throw us on."

Elias shuddered and grinned. "Don't," he said playfully.

It was subtle, but Ben felt the electric charge between them as Elias bumped their shoulders together. Ben would have thought that given his background, Elias would have been shy of even any hint of PDA, but Ben couldn't say he minded. In fact, he wanted more.

The party came to a halt in a clump not long after that, at a destination everyone else seemed to recognize but Ben couldn't see any real markers on the path. They were very much out in the open, looking out over wide, rambling fields of grass, well away from the estate, stables, and the orchards next to them. Ben inhaled deeply, filling his lungs with fresh air.

There were around a dozen family members ahead of Ben and Elias, several of which Ben recognized from that awful encounter yesterday in the antler room. Ben might have felt embarrassed if any of them had been paying him the slightest bit of attention, but they all seemed to glance his way, then pretend he didn't exist. However, none of them had seemed surprised at Ben and Elias joining them in their morning excursion, so Ben assumed someone had informed them of their attendance. Maybe Noah?

"Isn't this weather delightful, Harold!" Mildred with the red perm exclaimed, tapping her husband on the shoulder as she squinted up at the bright blue sky.

"I shouldn't think so, Mildred," Harold replied, cleaning a pair of spectacles on a monogrammed handkerchief. "Maybe after supper?"

"Rochelle," the very skinny woman admonished, looking at the younger woman with the silver streak in her wild dark hair. "Is that really a good idea?"

Rochelle smirked and took a long drag from a silver hipflask. "It's the only way to get through this balderdash, Mummy. I assure you." She licked her lips and regarded Ben and Elias with interest before sauntering off from the group and lighting a cigarette.

Ben tried not to read too much into it, but she hadn't outright snarled at him like the portly man smoking another cigar had done. It struck Ben that they weren't all in black like they had been yesterday. Maybe that was progress if they were moving on from their excessive mourning?

Aside from Noah in his blue denim jeans, the rest of the party was a sea of tweed, brown, beige, and bottle green. They all appeared to own the exact same pair of rain boots, down to the make and color, including Noah. Ben tried not to feel like he'd somehow gotten it wrong for not having a pair, too. Neither did Elias, after all.

Noah had been on the phone most of the walk up from the house, leaving Ben and Elias by themselves. Just as Ben caught eyes with Anika, hoping they might have another chat, Noah closed his call and came bounding over. Anika very clearly turned her back then, moving slightly further away with her brother. That was a shame. Ben wondered what that was all about.

"Apologies for my rudeness," Noah announced loudly to Ben as he stopped beside him. "Just some silly business with my landlord. It's all sorted now." Ben liked Noah, he did. But he was starting to notice that he only addressed Ben, never Elias. Ben wasn't comfortable with that.

Ben bumped Elias's shoulder and looked fondly up at him. "Anything Elias can help with? He's a lawyer, after all."

Was it Ben's imagination, or did Noah's smile seem somewhat fixed now?

He was saved from answering as two Jeeps revved into sight in the distance. "Ah, here comes Kenneth," said Noah rather than responding to Ben's question. He began walking toward the four-by-fours, extending one hand out in more of a salute than a wave.

"Shit," Ben grumbled. He was only human. It didn't matter how well his personal life was going with Elias, he'd still been humiliated by his great-uncle yesterday, and still didn't entirely understand what was going on with the will.

Elias rubbed his back. "It's okay. Noah said Kenneth wanted you here."

"Yeah," said Ben dryly as the Jeeps tore over the grass toward the gaggle of people. "I'm still not entirely convinced there isn't going to be a firing squad directed at us." Elias hummed and didn't look convinced either.

The first car squelched to a halt. Before the driver had

even killed the engine, Barnaby swung the door open, almost taking out the cigar man as he jumped out and swung his musket over his shoulder. A miserable-looking old bloodhound dropped heavily out of the passenger seat, too, immediately seeking Treacle out to snap and growl at before trotting after Barnaby as he walked away without speaking to anyone. Treacle whimpered behind Ben's legs.

The next car held Kenneth, who exited the Jeep like he was a member of the royal family, looking snootily down at all his lesser relatives as they rushed to fawn over him. Not all of them, of course. Anika and her brother stayed well back, and Rochelle took another swig of whatever was in her flask, regarding Kenneth shrewdly.

"Beautiful day for a shoot!" Mildred cried, clasping her hands in front of her bosom. "Excellent idea, Kenneth. Wasn't it an excellent idea, Harold?"

"Yes, Mildred," Harold agreed. "Especially if we go on Tuesday."

He held his hand out toward Kenneth to shake, but Kenneth ignored them both. Instead, he strode out to where the guns and ammunition were being set up on two folding tables by the Jeep's drivers, selected a weapon, then marched off without a word. After getting over the shock of Kenneth's rudeness, Ben realized with a happy surprise that the drivers had been none other than Gazza and Antoni, the strapping guy who had been moving the bales of hay around the stable yesterday.

Treacle raced to greet the two members of staff, whereas most of the family didn't seem to speak or acknowledge them in any way as they picked out guns for themselves. But Treacle's enthusiasm gave Ben and Elias an excuse to wander over to the table without feeling awkward, otherwise Ben wasn't sure he'd have had the courage. Especially when Noah's phone started ringing again. He cursed and removed himself from the group for a second time and started shouting, his words swallowed up by the chilly wind.

Most of the other family members had dispersed by the time Ben and Elias reached the table, clearly knowing what guns they wanted already. Ben didn't have a clue, but Gazza's beaming smile meant he didn't feel nervous or out of place about it.

"I didn't know you chaps were coming?" Gazza said, leaning over to shake their hands. "Antoni, this is Mr. Turner and Mr. Solomon, our guests from America."

"Please," Ben said, shaking both their hands. "Ben and Elias."

"It's nice to meet you," said Antoni with a slight hint of some kind of European accent Ben couldn't place. But then his eyes lit up over Ben's shoulder. "Oh, hello, Mr. Bhat. And Ms. Bhat."

Anika and her brother smiled as they joined Ben and Elias. "Good morning, everyone," said Anika cheerfully. "How are we all?" Ben didn't miss the way she glanced at Noah, still ranting on his phone several feet away, then smiled back at the rest of them. "What a lovely day for a spot of violence."

Gazza chuckled and handed her a shotgun. "We're very well, thank you, Ms. Bhat. Oh, how'd that big presentation go with your bosses? They finally listening to you?"

Anika expertly cracked the shotgun, checked the barrels, then snapped it shut again, looking through the sight. "Oh, the same as usual," she said heavily, holding the gun with both hands across her front. "None of them listen to me because I haven't got a penis. Thank you, Mr. Decker. This particular model will do nicely."

"Here you are, Mr. Bhat," Antoni said a little breathlessly, offering another of the weapons out to Anika's brother.

His brown eyes widened and a smile twitched at his lips.

"Oh, um, thank you, Mr. Kolton." Unlike his sister, he accepted the gun gingerly, like he wasn't sure what to do with it.

Speaking of Anika, her eyes flashed over to where Noah had just closed his call. "Right, we'll go find ourselves a dugout then, shall we Raj?" She touched her brother's elbow and steered him away. "Have fun everyone! Try not to shoot anyone you're not supposed to," she added in a mutter as she and Raj marched off.

"Sorry about that," Noah said breezily, trotting back over to Ben and Elias by the table. "More silly business stuff. Oh, did you just meet the Bhat Brats?" He chuckled and shook his head. Antoni gave him a murderous look and Gazza huffed, his breath escaping as a particularly large cloud of condensation.

"Now, now, Mr. Beaumont," he said tiredly. "You know Miss Nancy hated all of that."

Noah waved his hand dismissively. "I'm only teasing. Sorry, they just annoy me. Reg is such a wet blanket, and Kiki just *won't* take no for an answer, if you know what I mean." He rolled his eyes at Ben, who wasn't sure he did. Was Noah implying Anika was interested in him, and that Noah didn't appreciate that? "Come on, let's get you chaps kitted out. After all that hot air yesterday, it'll be good to let it all loose today. Has either of you ever shot before? Oh – you're American. I guess you would have."

Again, Ben wasn't sure what Noah was implying by that, but at least he was still smiling as he looked over the few shotguns he had remaining. In no time, they all had guns in hand, and spare ammunition.

"Kenneth will want us to pair off," Noah continued saying to Ben and Elias. "It's safest not to have two newbies together. So, Decker, why don't you look after Mr. Solomon, and I'll take our Ben here."

Ben opened his mouth to protest, glancing at Elias. But Noah was already steering Ben away.

It was kind of ridiculous, but being separated from Elias gave Ben mild anxiety. He was completely out of his depth here and Elias was like his anchor. It appeared he wasn't the only one, as Treacle danced on his toes, swinging his head back and forth between them as they got further away. In the end, he chose to stay with Elias and Gazza. Ben knew it wasn't fair, but he couldn't help but feel a slight pang of disappointment.

"Right," Kenneth's voice boomed out over the dispersing crowd. He flung a filthy rag that looked like he'd been using to clean his gun at Antoni. It splatted against Antoni's chest, making him flinch as he caught it in his hands before it fell to the ground. Kenneth didn't seem to notice. "You all know where to go, so get going. We start in ten minutes."

Ben clearly didn't have a clue where he was supposed to go, but it was equally as clear that Kenneth didn't give a crap about that. Luckily, Ben had Noah to escort him. "Are you really sure it's okay we're here?" Ben asked. "I feel like a leper."

Noah laughed and clapped him on the back. "Don't worry, that's normal. You just have to wear them down. If you're going to run the family now, they'll need to get used to you. You seem pretty decent, after all. Unlike other people we've had to put up with." That was hardly reassuring. Ben was starting to suspect that Noah had invited him and Elias of his own accord, not Kenneth. But why?

Noah's situation was curious. He spoke as if this was his family, but he wasn't biologically related, just Kenneth's godson. There was the connection with Noah's grandfather, Ben supposed, and presumably his father before he'd passed. And then there was the fact that Noah didn't seem to actually *like* anyone here.

Before Ben had a chance to inquire further, Noah spoke again. "You want to watch that lawyer of yours," he said as they approached what looked like a man-made mound. It was built up in a small hill on one side, then hollowed out on the other in a kind of U-shaped bunker. Ben assumed this was where they shot from, but he was distracted by Noah's comment.

"What do you mean?"

Noah smiled at him and nudged him with his elbow. "I think he's interested in you."

No shit, Sherlock, Ben thought, hiding his grin. "Well," he said slowly instead. "Would it be a bad thing if he was?"

Noah shrugged as they took their positions behind the dugout. "Just be careful. It's different now you have money."

Something icy cold slid down Ben's spine. *Money? What?* He looked back down the way they'd come from, but Elias, Gazza, and Treacle had moved out of sight behind the Land Rovers. "Elias isn't interested in money," Ben said softly. "He has his own."

"Oh, good," said Noah happily as he rested on the lip of the dugout. "So he was interested before you got the inheritance?"

Ben opened and closed his mouth. He'd been about to say that he had been, but then two things stopped him. The first was Anika's warning to play their relationship close to their vests as a lot of the family would use them being gay as yet another reason to hate Ben. But the second reason made him feel sick.

Elias had *said* he'd been having feelings for Ben before the inheritance had come through.

But had he? Really?

What did he actually see in Ben? Elias was a successful lawyer, and he'd been through so much in his life, a lot of it quite traumatic. His diagnosis, not to mention losing his relationships with family and so many friends due to stigma and prejudice. Ben had lived a simple, pretty carefree life. He probably seemed dull and shallow to the likes of Elias.

Until he had potentially become a millionaire.

No, that was *horseshit.* Elias wasn't like that. He couldn't be faking the kindness and tenderness he'd shown Ben, could he? Sure, they had an age gap, but the chemistry was undeniable.

"Hey," Noah said gently, pulling Ben from his reverie. He touched Ben's elbow and smiled kindly at him. "I didn't mean to upset you. I just wanted to offer some advice. I've had just as many gold-digging fellows try it on with me as the ladies, but the men can be aggressive where the women are devious. I don't know if it's better or worse when they find out I'm essentially penniless," he added with a rueful laugh. "But you'll need to protect your heart now. That's just the way it is around this family."

"Right," Ben said in a bit of a daze. He was sure Noah meant well, but he couldn't really believe that of Elias, could he? He was a lawyer. He was plenty well-off already. Rich, even.

However, there was rich, and then there was *rich.* Ben had read that the motives for most crimes were sex and money. Could Elias really be after his fortune? Ben was loathed to think so, but Noah was right. His circumstances would change dramatically if the will stayed as it was. He needed to think with his head, not his cock.

Or his heart.

"I'm here for you, Ben," said Noah with the utmost sincerity. His eyes were wide and he rubbed Ben's arm, giving him a sympathetic half-smile. "You know you can trust me, right?"

Ben nodded automatically, not sure who to believe. Him or Anika. "Thank you," he said, shaking himself and searching for the first distraction he could grab on to that would change the conversation. "But what do you mean penniless? Sorry, only if you don't mind me asking."

Noah gave him a curious look. Ben wondered if he'd put his foot in it again, like he had with the *Chai* necklace earlier. Noah didn't look upset, more like he was working out how best to articulate his response.

"Oh," said Noah eventually, running his fingers over the shotgun handle like a caress. "Does that mean you don't know why your grandfather, Thomas, fled to America?"

Ben physically reeled at the turn in conversation. What the hell did his grandfather have to do with anything? "Uh, no," he admitted, his confusion clear in his voice.

"Bugger," said Noah, sounding genuinely sorry. He rubbed his brow and shook his head, huffing out little clouds of steamy breath. "Okay, well, I guess someone has to break the news. That explains a lot. Okay. Well, I'm sorry to say he fled the country in shame. He and my grandfather were business partners. They invested a considerable amount into a railway venture in the sixties that your grandfather gambled away. It ruined my family. My grandfather was completely bankrupted. Thomas used the last of his money to escape to America and never returned. Perhaps now you understand why Kenneth took me in and the rest of the family distrusts you. My family never recovered. Kenneth did what he could for me, but old Nancy never wanted to give me a penny. I don't know why."

For a moment, all Ben heard was white noise, feeling like he was going to throw up. He thought he'd been stunned at the idea of Elias only being interested in him for his money, but to discover this about his beloved grandpa was nothing short of devastating.

"Oh, god," he said faintly, resting against the side of the

dugout. The wind whipped around his head as blood rushed through his ears.

He covered his mouth with a gloved hand, staring out over the horizon at the bright blue sky and rolling muddy fields. If that really was true, he felt even *more* wretched about swooping in and snatching this inheritance away from the rest of the family. He had no right to claim it at all!

"I'm so sorry," he told Noah, meeting his gaze. "I honestly had no idea. I never knew why my grandfather emigrated. My family is very private. Fuck, I feel terrible."

But Noah gave him a warm look and squeezed his arm. "No, darling. It's not your fault in the slightest. I hate having to tell you that and let you down about someone you clearly loved. I like to think he was extremely remorseful and grew to become a better person. No doubt the man you used to know. But you should have all the facts."

At that moment a whistle rang out and Noah immediately switched his attention back to his shotgun, crouching down and aiming into the sky. He fired at the same time as several other shots rang out, cracking apart a number of clay disks as they tore through the air, but Ben was hardly paying attention at all.

This was too much. His grandfather – Grandpa Tom who'd taught him how to make Victoria sponge and custard tarts – was a despicable traitor. Had he really ruined Noah's family for generations, then fled like a coward? Ben checked the time on his phone. He wanted to call his dad right away, but his parents weren't likely to be awake yet. His dad had never even hinted at any such thing – would he even know?

And then Ben was ashamed to admit his more pressing concern was what Noah had said about Elias. Ben wanted to think there was no way in hell Elias was only interested because he thought Ben was going to become a millionaire, but Noah was *right*. Until that letter had arrived, Elias hadn't spent more than two minutes strung together talking with Ben.

Now he was in his bed.

Was *that* why Elias was so hesitant to have sex? Because he wasn't attracted to Ben at all?

No, *no.* Ben believed everything Elias had told him about feeling vulnerable with his HIV status. Unless Elias was a major con artist, Ben couldn't believe he was faking it.

But that brought him back around to his core worry since this whole thing had started.

What the hell did Elias see in Ben?

Not only was Ben nothing all that special, but he'd now discovered he was descended from someone with a history of devious behavior. Elias was a *lawyer.* Even if he wasn't just sniffing after Ben's inheritance, why would he want to associate with someone with such a criminal history?

Ben tried his best, but he couldn't really join in with the shooting after that. Noah tried valiantly to cajole his spirits, but Ben's mind was a complete mess. He needed some time alone.

"I need to go for a walk," he informed Noah in between the next rounds, leaning his gun against the dugout. "I'll stay away from the shooting range. Give my apologies to Kenneth."

Noah tried to dissuade him, but Ben was already walking away, trying not to cry. He didn't really care if Kenneth thought less of him for leaving early – it didn't seem like his opinion of Ben could get much lower anyway, and rightly so from the sounds of it.

Ben didn't deserve this inheritance if what Noah had said was true. It would probably be for the best if Kenneth and the rest of the family overturned the will.

However, that shame was nothing compared to the dread when Ben thought about Elias. He'd tried not to get his hopes up, but after all those months to finally know what it was like to kiss Elias, to be with him so intimately, had felt more like winning the lottery than Nancy's inheritance ever had. Ben wasn't sure what he'd do if it turned out to be all lies.

He needed time to think.

Alone.

16

ELIAS

IT WAS PETTY AND CHILDISH, BUT ELIAS DIDN'T LIKE THE IDEA of Noah whisking Ben off.

He couldn't shake it. No matter how much he tried to tell himself he was being an asshole, that he trusted Ben and he could spend time out of Elias's sight, for god's sake, worry was chewing at his guts. Because there was *something* about Noah that bothered Elias.

Unfortunately, it was probably that he was young, handsome, and more than likely came with far less emotional baggage than Elias did.

Jealousy and insecurities were ugly, *ugly* emotions. Elias had no time for either of them. But logic didn't seem to want to come into play no matter how hard Elias tried to shift to that brain.

The thing was, he hadn't been that vulnerable with any man in years, let alone the one he'd been pining after for over a year. He tried cataloging all the reassuring things Ben had said, but all they'd really agreed was to take things slowly, one step at a time. No labels. Ben had no obligation to be faithful to Elias.

Why wouldn't he go with someone fit and healthy who was closer to his own age?

Urgh. Elias was fed up with his own mind already. This wasn't attractive, and more to the point, it wasn't who Elias was. He wasn't clingy or possessive. At least, he hadn't been before. But he just felt so fragile around Ben. Like Ben was going to come to his senses any moment and run a mile when he thought about how the two of them couldn't possibly have a future together.

That was the opposite of taking things slowly. Jesus. Elias was going to come across as desperate. Just because he was letting his imagination run away with him, picturing a relationship unfolding between him and Ben, didn't mean that was what Ben was thinking at all. He was young and vulnerable. Coming back out of their little cottage bubble to face his family again had proven that.

Speaking of which, Elias surveyed the scene as Gazza took him to get settled in a dugout with Treacle, safely out of the firing line. The various Grimaldi de Loutherberghs were strewn out along the shooting range, which was completely different from the gun ranges Elias had been to back home. Those were all in a straight line with targets, indoors or outdoors. These dugouts seemed to be in a wavy sort of line along hilly terrain, with the clay disks apparently going to be fired by sling-shot contraptions into the air from an assortment of angles, to simulate pheasants taking flight in a traditional shoot.

The only people who appeared to have paid Ben any attention, let alone shown him kindness, were Anika and Raj, and – to be fair – Noah. As well as Gazza and Antoni, of course, but Elias found himself having a *lot* more time for the people who worked at Whittingar Abbey than those that lived there. Antoni had left as soon as Gazza had walked

Elias to his dugout, saying he needed to go check on something.

Gazza must have caught Elias staring at the siblings, because he nudged his side and jutted his chin toward them. "They get that a lot," he said, his tone somewhat cautionary. "But I can assure you that they're part of this family, more so than other people I could mention."

"Oh, no!" Elias spluttered, mortified. "I was interested as Ben mentioned he'd spoken to the woman, Anika. They seem less hostile than most everyone else. I wasn't – I didn't mean to imply-"

"Whoa, whoa," Gazza interrupted him with a laugh. "Okay, that's good. Sorry to jump to conclusions. It's just what a lot of people think when they see Anika and Raj. Just coz their skin don't match, don't mean they ain't welcome here at the home. Miss Nancy was *very* clear about that."

Elias watched from a distance as the brother, Raj, slumped against the dugout, dropping his head in his hands. His sister, Anika, placed her own gun down and hugged him, rubbing his back. "Is everything okay?" Elias asked Gazza, concerned.

Gazza snorted. "It's not my place to comment on family business," he said gravely. "But their mum isn't exactly the nurturing type. She headed back to Bollywood the second she could, and their dad was always more interested in fancy parties than either of them kids. They were barely here a day for the funeral before jetting off again. I don't blame Anika or Raj for moving to London the first chance they got when they turned eighteen. It's never easy for them to come home, I think."

Elias frowned at him. "So why are they still here?"

Gazza raised his eyebrows. "Again, it's not my place, sir. But I think they have a vested interest in the outcome of this will and their inheritance. More than others." A whistle rang out, catching Gazza's attention. "Oh, here we go! Apologies, sir. You'll have to wait for the next round now, but let's get you set up and ready."

Elias craned his head as several clay disks catapulted into the cloudy sky, shotgun cracks ringing out through the cold air as almost all of the disks were obliterated into shards and dust. Treacle barked his head off, wagging his tail at the excitement.

"Aren't you shooting?" Elias asked.

"With the family?" Gazza replied, sounding scandalized, then he laughed. "Oh no, Mr. Solomon. I'll just be giving you a hand. There we go." He handed the loaded shotgun back to Elias, encouraging him where to perch. The adrenaline was already starting to tingle through Elias's system.

From their dugout, Elias couldn't see Ben behind the Land Rovers, but he hoped he was having fun.

There. That was more like it. He didn't need to be anxious or threatened. Ben was his own man, and he would come back to Elias if he was confident and independent, not needy and anxious. If Ben was interested in Noah, so be it. Elias only wanted to be with Ben if that's what he wanted, too.

And really, after two pretty spectacular sessions in bed, how could Elias doubt himself that badly? He knew it had been a while, but that had been *hot,* and they still had so much more they could try.

There was a reason the saying was 'opposites attract.' It was entirely possible that all the reasons Elias were telling himself a relationship wouldn't work between them could actually be why it *would* work. He just needed to give it a chance.

"You missed," a snooty voice drawled, making Elias turn around. Unfortunately, he was greeted by the sight of Ben's great-uncle Barnaby, still swinging around his ancient-looking musket like he was in the Boer War. His miserable-looking bloodhound growled at Treacle, who in turn wagged his tail and barked indignantly back. Elias smiled as the stumpy little fellow put himself between Elias and Gazza, and Barnaby and his bloodhound.

"I wasn't ready," Elias said jovially, not wanting to appear rattled in front of this rude old man.

Barnaby huffed and muttered something that sounded like 'Typical Americans, late for everything.' Elias ignored it.

"Is there something wrong with your dugout?" Elias asked him pleasantly but pointedly.

Barnaby rubbed his walrus moustache under his nose and sniffed. "No, no. Just keeping an eye on everything. Don't want anyone getting shot now, do we?" He cackled, and Elias couldn't help but wonder if he was joking or not. "Decker, make sure you clean the equipment after the gentleman is done. I know they have different standards across the pond. Give everything a good disinfectant."

A chill ran down Elias's spine. "What's that supposed to mean?"

Barnaby chuckled, a hollow, nasty sound. "Oh, nothing old boy. Just a little joke. I'm sure you're perfectly *clean.* Come, Augustus!"

The bloodhound bayed at the snapped command, obediently trotting after his master who was already striding over the grounds, apparently unconcerned that the next round of disks might fly out at any given moment.

Elias looked at Gazza, who was frowning after Barnaby. "What was that about?" Elias asked, feeling distinctly queasy.

"I'm sure I don't know, sir," Gazza grumbled, still scowling after Barnaby. "Come on, they're going to blow the whistle again any second."

Elias did his best to pay attention. He didn't want to make any mistakes with a gun in his hands, after all. But Barnaby's words had thrown him. He was sure it was just a coincidence. However, the reference to him being 'clean' was too close to a slur against his HIV status. But Barnaby couldn't possibly know about that, could he?

It appeared Elias wasn't the only one Barnaby wanted to needle in his tour around the dugouts. He stopped by Anika and Raj, too. Elias was too far away to tell what was said, but poor Raj hugged himself and hung his head while Anika placed herself between her brother and Barnaby, her arms folded and looking a lot like Treacle had when he'd been protecting Elias and Gazza.

The next round fired, and Elias didn't want to miss out again, so he whipped his gun around and took aim. It was exhilarating, although he wished he'd been able to share the experience with more friendly people. Not that he didn't like Gazza, but everyone else felt like they could switch targets and fire at him or Ben at any given moment.

Not Anika or Raj, he hoped, but when he next looked after this round of disks were done, they had vanished. He hoped Barnaby hadn't said anything too upsetting to them.

For a while, Elias allowed himself to become absorbed in the sport. It wasn't like going to the gym or playing tennis, but it was a different kind of physical activity that still required concentration. Even though the cracks of the gunfire were loud, there was still something oddly soothing about it.

"You did right good there, Mr. Solomon," Gazza said after the final round of shots were done. He took Elias's gun from him, nodding with apparent sincere appreciation. "Nice aim. The family will like that."

Elias wanted to make a biting comment about preferring to be liked regardless of how he handled a firearm, but he was distracted. Everyone was beginning to mill around now that they were finished shooting. Noah emerged from behind the Land Rovers with a swagger. The dugout was still hidden, but it was a bit strange that Ben hadn't followed Noah back down the path. Noah seemed more interested in pulling his leather gloves from his fingers than he did Ben's whereabouts.

"Thank you, Gazza," Elias said genuinely. "I'm just going to check on Ben, if that's okay?"

Gazza shooed him away. "Of course it is, sir. I'll take care of all this."

Elias thanked him and made his way around the dugout with Treacle loyally trotting by his side to intercept Noah. But before they reached one another, Ben's dugout came into view from behind the Land Rover.

Ben wasn't there.

"Noah," Elias called out with a wave, trying to sound friendly. "Is everything okay?"

Noah stopped walking, tilted his head, and considered Elias as he approached along the narrow dirt track on the open, hilly field. "Yes, perfectly fine," he said, sounding mildly confused.

Elias and Treacle came to a halt. Elias decided it was probably best to just be direct. "Where did Ben go? Is he all right?"

Noah laughed, not so subtly looking Elias up and down, then shifting slightly away from Treacle who was no longer wagging his bushy tail. "I'm sure he's fine. We talked about some important things. He needs a real friend around here. I think he needed time to digest everything. Why don't you give him some space?"

Elias chuckled, but there was no mirth in it and he certainly didn't smile. "Ben and I are just fine, but thanks for your concern."

A dark look flashed across Noah's eyes. "Are you, really?" he asked, his voice silky smooth. "Why don't you give Ben a choice instead of manipulating him?"

Elias was so stunned, he couldn't think of a response before Noah smirked and nodded at Elias.

"Good day, Mr. Solomon."

What the hell had just happened? Elias had never once controlled or manipulated Ben. He'd only ever wanted to help. Surely Ben couldn't think that of him, could he? Was that just Noah's opinion or maybe even *him* trying to manipulate circumstances to his advantage? Whatever way he looked at it, Elias wasn't happy.

He needed to speak to Ben.

Treacle grumbled as Noah sauntered off, waving to Rochelle with the silver streak in her hair who was still nursing her hipflask. She flipped Noah the bird then marched off. Noah rubbed the back of his neck, then carried on walking.

Elias was left standing there like a chump. Treacle bumped his ass against Elias's mud-flecked jeans, before trotting down the other way down the path. The party was generally dispersing, clumping off together, paying no mind to Elias as usual. He might as well have been invisible.

He was used to being ignored. By just existing, Elias offended a lot of people. He wasn't going to waste energy worrying about these snooty bastards when he was concerned about Ben. *Fuck* Noah. Besides, Treacle seemed to be on a mission. Elias wondered if he'd gotten a whiff of an interesting scent or something, because he was determinedly making his way back toward the house. He was practically running.

"What's the matter, boy?" Elias asked, striding fast to keep up, his breath coming out especially steamy as he put a little exertion in. "Can you smell Ben?" he asked hopefully.

Treacle barked and sped up.

But he wasn't heading toward the house, after all. He took Elias in the direction of the horse stables. They hadn't been in them so far, just walked past. However, right then Treacle dashed through the main doors, bold as brass.

It was around midday, so several of the horses were out in the fields, but Elias could hear a strange noise as he followed Treacle down to the last stall. Treacle was whining and panting, like he was distressed. "What is it, little fellow?" Elias asked.

"*Shh,*" a human voice gently chided back.

Frowning, Elias made his way to the end of the stable where Treacle had come to a stop – or at least as much as he could when he was anxiously dancing on the spot. Elias softly chuckled at him, then looked up to see what was going on in the stall.

Antoni was sitting with his back against the stable wall. He was covered in sweat-streaked grime that hadn't been present back at the shoot. His black hair stuck up at odd angles, and his sweater was straining against his bulging biceps and pecs. His arms rested on his dirty cargo pants, calloused hands that looked like they could punch through a wall dangling between his knees. If Elias was honest, he was the sort of guy Elias wouldn't want to meet alone in a dark alley.

Which was why it was so surprising to discover him with a serene smile on his face, looking at Luna the cat who was in the corner of the stall.

And she wasn't alone.

"Holy shit," Elias whispered in delight, forgetting all his earlier worries. "Are those kittens?"

Antoni nodded as Elias crept over to him. Elias had to laugh. He'd assumed she was just a very fat cat, but it turned out she'd been pregnant this whole time. Treacle was still dancing fretfully, looking like he wanted to dash over to his feline frenemy, but Elias put his hand out.

"No. Good dog. Give her some space. Is she all right?"

He sat down next to Antoni, who nodded again. "I've done this many times." His English only had a hint of what Elias guessed to be a Polish accent from his name. "Back home. Cats like to get on with it themselves." He pointed to the bales of hay in the stall. "I had a feeling today would be the day, so I rushed back to clean out this stall, all for her." He grinned. "Welcome to the cat hotel."

Elias laughed softly. "That's so good of you," he marveled.

Antoni shook his head. "I like to do it. We must take care of our four-legged friends. Look - she already has two, and now she's working on her third."

Sure enough, there were two wobbly-looking newborns snuggled up on some towels that had been placed on top of the hay. Antoni had a stack of clean-looking ones folded next to him as well as a bowl of warm water by one of the infrared lamps. Luna was under another one, pushing and wriggling away, working on kitten number three. She already had a ginger one and a brownish-black one.

"So you knew she was pregnant?" Elias asked, jutting his chin at the towels. "I just thought she was fat."

Antoni snorted. "Yes. The little madam has been yowling for some days now, showing off for all the attention. I guessed the diva would be taking mainstage soon. I must say, she is doing magnificently. She's a lovely cat." He tilted his head and looked at the snooty cat with such warmth and attention that Elias took back his earlier thought. If he was alone in a dark alley, perhaps Antoni was *exactly* the kind of man he'd want by his side, for protection.

Elias shook his head and covered his mouth, feeling quite emotional. To see a life come into the world was something he'd never thought about much before, let alone experienced. But here these little kittens were, their eyes shut and their fur sticking up in wet clumps, taking their first breaths and fumbling around the fluffy towels that had replaced their mom's warm belly.

It was precious and quite remarkable.

With a sudden loud meow and a firm wiggle, another baby came free in its amniotic sac. Elias was alarmed at first to see the fine membrane still around the kitten, but Antoni held a hand up when Elias went to move, then shook his head. "Mummy should fix it," he said with a smile, joy shining in his eyes.

Elias had definitely judged him unfairly. This guy wasn't a thug at all. Just because he was big and had some tattoos peeking out from under his cuffs and collar didn't mean he wasn't kind or caring.

Sure enough, he knew what he was talking about. Luna licked and fussed at the sac until it broke and the kitten tumbled free. Then she kept cleaning her new baby, making it look more like a cute kitten rather than a drowned rat, until the little guy yawned and took his first deep breath.

"Wow." Elias was suddenly overcome with gratitude that Treacle had brought him here to experience this moment, and Antoni had graciously allowed him to share it with him. Sometimes, the universe just brought you to where you were supposed to be. "Do you think she'll have any more?"

Antoni nodded. "At least one more, from the size of her. Would you like to stay? I have tea." He pulled a thermos from out of the hay, giving it a wiggle. Elias laughed and accepted the little plastic cup that came on top, while Antoni drank from the flask itself.

They passed the time talking a bit about their home towns (Elias had been right with his guess at a Polish accent), comparing mountain ranges. But mostly they sat in amicable silence, making sure that Luna didn't need their help. Treacle eventually lay down next to Elias, never taking his eyes off

Luna as she began the whole process again for kitten number four.

Raised voices caught Elias's attention. He couldn't quite make out the words, but he was pretty sure two people were coming closer to the stable, and they were having a disagreement.

No, they were distressed.

Elias knew he shouldn't butt into other people's business, especially in this family, but the whole reason he'd become a lawyer was to help people. The urge to go investigate was too strong. "Are you all right here for a minute?" he asked before he stood up.

Antoni nodded and stroked Treacle, who looked to be going absolutely nowhere while Luna was still in labor. "We're fine."

So Elias stood, brushing the hay and dirt from his jeans, then made his way down the stable. He wasn't trying to eavesdrop, but he was pretty intuitive at sensing when a disagreement could turn more hostile, and he wanted to try and prepare himself for what he was about to walk out into.

"Stop meddling!" a male voice, sounding tearful.

"I'm not meddling," a woman replied. "I'm worried *sick*. This has got to stop!"

"Don't you see?" the guy begged. "That's exactly what I'm trying to do!"

Nope. Elias wasn't going to snoop anymore. As he neared the large opening to the stable, he cleared his throat, loudly. Then he stepped out into the sunshine and much cooler air, away from the lamp heaters.

It was Anika and Raj, walking side-by-side on the path that skirted around the stable toward the little cottage Elias and Ben were sharing. Well, stomping might be more accurate than walking. Anika had her hands stuffed in her coat pockets, her long hair braided down one side under a bobble hat.

Raj was strikingly handsome in a slim, delicate sort of way, wearing a three-quarter length navy coat. He also sniffed like he'd been crying. "Oh, it's you," he said as the siblings came to an abrupt halt in front of Elias.

"Hi," said Elias, unperturbed. "Is everything okay?"

Raj opened and closed his mouth, then hung his head.

Anika huffed and rubbed her brother's back. "We're just trying to work on a little problem."

"Anything I can help with?" Elias asked, genuinely meaning it.

The siblings shrugged. "I doubt it," said Raj heavily. "It's all family nonsense. I suspect you're getting used to that by now?"

"Yes," said Anika eagerly. "Where is Ben? How's he doing?"

That was an odd segue.

"Anika, leave it," Raj muttered, but Elias still caught the vibe between them. The siblings shared a look for a second. Elias remembered playing that kind of tug-of-war with his own brother when they had some silly secret. Not like when Elias had grown up and his secret hadn't been so silly anymore. These two were clearly having a spat, but Anika looked like she definitely wanted to help her younger brother, just like when she'd put herself between him and Barnaby earlier.

"I'm not sure where Ben went," Elias admitted to break the tension. "I lost him after the shooting."

He'd texted Ben while he'd been sitting in the stable, but so far, he didn't look as if he'd even read the message, let alone replied to it. Noah's words made him feel sick every time he replayed them in his head, but there was no sense doing that. He needed to ask Ben what had happened. But there was something that still needed his attention right at that moment. He couldn't just abandon Luna.

He jerked his thumb over his shoulder and grinned at the siblings. "I don't suppose you guys like cats, do you? That big one Luna is in here having kittens."

In a second, all crankiness was forgotten between the pair of them. They both gasped, going wide-eyed and rising onto their tiptoes in a way that illustrated just how closely they were related. "Kittens?" squeaked Raj.

"Can we see?" Anika asked.

Elias was glad. Whatever their squabble was, hopefully it wasn't too serious as they both put it aside so quickly. He gladly led them back through the mostly empty stable, the warm hay smell greeting them as they reached Luna and the three babies she had so far. Almost four, from the looks of it. She'd been busy while Elias had been off talking.

"How's she doing?" Elias asked as the siblings cooed. They sat next to Antoni and Treacle, not caring that their expensive clothes were getting dirty.

Antoni hummed. "She's tired," he said, his gaze still on the cat. But then he glanced at the siblings, resting his gaze on Raj. "Oh. I'm sorry. Ms. Bhat, Mr. Bhat. I know I'm still on duty-"

Anika waved a hand and blew a raspberry. "This *is* work. And don't call us that. It makes us sound like Kenneth and all our aunts and uncles. "I'm Anika and this is Raj."

"I know," Antoni murmured. Elias realized he was still looking at Raj, who also seemed to have noticed and looked away. If his skin was paler, the blush would probably have been pretty obvious.

Elias would have been more interested in that little interaction, but the fourth kitten had come free, and Luna was attempting to break the amniotic sac again. But Antoni was right. She was tired and it wasn't working. Elias glanced at Antoni, who had immediately become serious again. "That's not right, is it?" Elias asked.

"Hmm. We might need to help." Antoni reached for one of the clean towels, but then he offered it to Elias. "Would you like to help Mummy Kitty out?"

"Me?" Elias said, feeling a sense of urgency. The kitten was still in the sac, and Luna had lay down next to it, looking defeated. "What do I do?"

"Just rub with the towel until the lining breaks, and clean the tiny one until he breathes. You can do it." He smiled, pushing the towel into Elias's hands. Elias wanted to insist Antoni did it if he'd done this sort of thing before. But as much as he didn't want to jeopardize the newborn, he also had a flush of confidence he hadn't felt in a while.

He could do this.

"Okay, little dude," he said as he crossed the few feet over to the cats, crouching down by the litter. "You've got this. Come on, time to wake up." He rubbed the membrane just like Antoni had said, and it soon gave way. Luna had almost gotten there. But she didn't look to have the strength to try and clean the new baby, so Elias gently rubbed at the fur with the clean towel.

The kitten still wasn't moving.

"Should I rub his chest or something?" he asked anxiously. Antoni came to crouch beside him, as did Anika and Raj. Treacle shoved his snout under Elias's arm, wanting to see as well.

Antoni hummed. "Keep doing what you're doing," he said gravely. "But that's a small one. Might be the runt. It's okay if he doesn't make it."

No it goddamned wasn't.

Elias bit his lip and scowled. "Come on," he muttered, continuing to rub over the tiny little guy's body. He was a silver tabby, just like his mom. Elias wasn't going to be defeated by this. The poor little mite deserved as much of a chance as his siblings. "You can do it. Look, your brothers and sister are waiting to meet you. You've got this, champ."

He rubbed the tiny creature all over, drying his fur so it stuck up all over the place. But he still wasn't moving or breathing.

Antoni laid a hand on Elias's shoulder. "It's okay," he said. "I'm sorry. These things just happen sometimes. You can stop."

Elias shook his head and blinked back tears. "Just another few seconds," he rasped.

Antoni patted his back. "Of course."

It was probably hopeless. Antoni was right, this little fellow was quite a bit smaller than the others. But he still deserved a chance.

However, after another minute, Elias stopped. His efforts weren't doing anything. He heard Anika sniffle next to him. Maybe it just wasn't meant to be. Elias swallowed and stroked the damp fur between the kitten's flat, teeny ears. "I'm sorry, little man," he whispered.

The kitten twitched.

"Oh!" Raj cried. Anika shook Elias, and Antoni leaned in closer to the litter. Even poor, exhausted Luna lifted her head.

"Keep going!" Antoni said, beaming at Elias. Holding his breath, Elias began rubbing the tiny creature's body, feeling him twitch again before he gave a big yawn.

"You did it!" Anika shrieked, clapping her hands. Elias laughed and gently wrapped the smallest kitten up in a bundled bit of towel, leaving enough room that Luna could shuffle over and begin licking him herself. Elias gently stroked both their heads, then carefully petted the other three newborns, before sitting back on his heels.

"Damn," he said, shaking his head. "That was kind of

intense." But the pride he felt was the best kind of adrenaline. He'd been so undermined by Barnaby and Noah earlier. To trust his gut and get something right was incredible. He touched a fingertip to the top of the tiny guy's head. "Well done, champ," he said.

That kitten was a survivor. Just like Elias.

And so was Ben. The longer he'd been gone without contact, the more worried Elias was getting, especially after Noah's nasty jibes. Elias needed to find him. So he shook himself and looked at Antoni. "That's possibly enough heroics for one day. I should probably keep looking for my friend. He's been gone a while. Are you okay from here?"

Antoni clapped him on the shoulder. "Of course. Thank you for sharing this with me – all of you." He glanced at Raj who hummed and became very interested in a piece of hay he was rolling between his fingers.

"Are you going to see Ben?" Anika asked as Elias stood. He nodded at her, then she jumped to her feet too. "Great! We'll come with you!"

"We will?" Raj asked. Then he took a look at Antoni and scrambled up as well. "Uh, yeah, we will." Was it Elias's imagination, or did Antoni look disappointed?

Treacle didn't even look at Elias as they left. He just forlornly rolled onto his side and kept looking at Luna. Luna appeared to have fallen asleep. Elias laughed ruefully on the Corgi's behalf. It was an unlikely friendship. Treacle harrumphed and wriggled a little closer to the litter.

Elias walked with Anika and Raj out into the sunshine, taking in a breath of cold, fresh air. He was sure Antoni would have saved the kitten, too. But…maybe Elias was meant to be there that afternoon to keep trying for a little longer. Elias touched his *Chai* under his sweater, feeling something he hadn't in quite a long time. Was it purpose? Like he was on the right path, after all? He thought of the *mitzvot, Tikkun Olam.* There was a lot to be said for repairing the world, one shard at a time.

"I'm going to see if Ben is back at the cottage," Elias said, spurred on by his success. He didn't want to be worried about Ben. He was a grown man who could take care of himself. All the same, Elias felt like he wanted to check in, if only to soothe his own nerves after what Noah had said. "Do you want to come?"

"Oh, no, that's fine," Raj said, glaring at Anika. "We don't want to trouble him-"

"Yes, we do," argued Anika.

Elias held his hands up placatingly. "Is this about your inheritance? Because Ben wants to honor Nancy's wishes and make sure everyone gets what's fairly theirs."

"See," Raj cried, holding his hand up. "You're being greedy."

Anika jabbed a finger back at him. "Not everyone has the same idea of fairness around here! And I'm not money-grubbing. This is about freedom!"

Raj scoffed. "Stop being dramatic. I'll fix this, all right?" But he swallowed and his eyes looked glassy, like he was close to tears again.

"Oh, *Rajiv-bhai,*" Anika said, rubbing Raj's arm. "Please. Let me *help.*"

Elias looked between them. "Can Ben help, then? Because I'm sure he would."

"Raj is being blackmailed," Anika said bluntly. Elias raised his eyebrows in shock as Raj cried out and shook her hand free.

"You have no business telling that to a complete stranger!" he snapped. He scrubbed his face, making his cheeks shine in the wintery sunlight. "Either I'll get the inheritance to pay it or I'll find another way."

Elias shook his hands. "Whoa, whoa, whoa. Why would you pay this person?"

Raj chewed his lip and looked sadly at his sister. "Because they know something that could ruin the family."

"Oh bull *shit!*" Anika balled her fists and stamped her foot. "No, it won't. But it *will* make Kenneth so furious that he would disown Raj. Raj needs that money for his career and he shouldn't give a *fuck* what this blackmailer says. It's the twenty-first century!"

Elias continued looking back and forth between the two of them, still missing several puzzle pieces. "You know I'm a lawyer. Not here, but I could still probably help, if that's what you want. But only if you want to tell me what's going on."

Anika took Raj by the shoulders and looked purposefully into his wet eyes. "Elias will *understand,*" she said, raising her eyebrows and nodding at him. "He *and Ben* will understand." He tilted her head, like she was talking in code, then gently brushed his tears away with the backs of her fingers.

Raj blinked and looked as if something dawned on him. "Ohh. Um." He grimaced and shook his head. Then he closed his eyes and breathed deeply, before peeking back at Anika. "Are you sure?"

"One hundred percent," his sister replied.

Raj took another couple of breaths. "I'm *gay,*" he blurted out suddenly, and in a flash Elias was pretty sure he cracked the secret code, too. "My ex is threatening to go to the tabloids with photos unless I give him fifty thousand pounds. The family would be disgraced. Kenneth would most certainly cut me off without a penny."

Elias felt relieved and horrified at the same time. He'd been beginning to worry that Raj had done something *wrong.* He wasn't happy he'd been put in this situation, but this was *fine.*

"Fuck that asshole!" he cried, throwing his hands up. The

siblings both stepped back slightly, their eyebrows raised. Elias laughed to stop himself from cursing more. "Anika's right. That's not a scandal, that's pathetic. I'll tell you what you do right now. You release your own blog or an article for Buzzy News or whoever if you think they'll really care about such a story. Hell, just write a public Facebook statement if you want. But you come out as gay first and take all your ex's power away. He doesn't get fifty grand for not outing you! No, fuck that. Then to hell with Kenneth. Ben *will* take care of you. You say you need your inheritance money for work?"

"Raj is an amazing photographer," Anika said, beaming and rocking on her tiptoes again. "But Kenneth is determined to make him an accountant. He's just being cruel, honestly. See, Raj! That fixes both your problems. Just remove Kenneth and your evil ex from the equation! Elias, you're a genius."

Elias thought of something. "Wait, so it's not Barnaby causing you trouble? I saw him giving you grief during the shoot."

Anika blew a raspberry. "Him? No. He's just a sad old man who likes kicking people while they're down."

"And not Noah?" Elias asked, recalling the looks Anika had given him and the way she'd steered her and Raj away from him.

"Narcissist," said Anika with an eyeroll. "Annoying egomaniac, but not a blackmailer."

Elias released a breath. "Well, that removes both of *them* from the equation, too, in that case."

Raj didn't seem as convinced. "It can't be that simple…can it?" He asked uncertainly.

Elias's new confidence from saving the tiny kitten was still thrumming in his veins. He clapped Raj on the shoulder. "Of course it can. Let's go find Ben, then you'll see."

Anika hugged Raj and jiggled them both. "I told you it would all be okay. I *told* you!"

Elias smiled at them both as they began walking toward the cottage. Yes, it *would* all be okay. They just had to find Ben. There was probably a perfectly reasonable explanation as to where he'd gone to, like when he'd gotten lost in the woodlands around their cottage. He was just a little haphazard like that. And Noah was a douchebag. Elias had sensed it when they'd first met. Elias wouldn't believe a word he said until he got Ben's side of the story, which he was sure would be totally different.

And if a knot of worry tried to lodge itself in Elias's gut, he refused to pay it any mind.

Because everything was *fine.*

17

BEN

As most of the family were preoccupied out on the shoot, Ben felt safer entering the house after his ordeal yesterday. Not that it gave him much comfort. He was still alone with his thoughts, which were all pretty vicious right about then. But at least it was quiet and there wasn't anyone around to confuse him further.

He ran his hand over his face and unzipped his coat. Everything that Noah had said about his grandfather and Elias was now rolling around with all the other insecurities that had been piling up. How he was feeling dumb and childish compared to Elias, how he was basically poor white trash to these people who would never accept him as family.

How could he have felt so happy that morning in bed with Elias, only to have crashed so far down now? Did that just prove it was irrelevant how hot their chemistry was between the sheets if everything they had fell apart like a house of cards the second they stepped outside the front door? Was Elias right when he'd said their age gap and life journeys were too wide apart and incompatible?

No. No, that wasn't what Ben wanted. If he liked Elias this much, then they could figure out all that stuff.

At least he hoped.

He most likely wouldn't get any answers on that front until he drummed up the courage to talk to Elias. Ben's plan was to head back to the cottage in a little while, when the shoot was over. But he'd purposefully come inside the main house first, feeling like this was where he needed to be to search for knowledge. Why had Nancy brought him here when he clearly didn't belong? Did she know what Gramps had done all those years ago when he'd fled to America?

It wasn't like there was anyone here to give Ben the answers he was yearning for. He was probably being silly, but he felt like maybe he'd find what he was looking for in the very walls of the house. If this legacy was supposed to be his, maybe it would send him a sign?

Jesus, this was such a mess. How could his dad have never told him about his grandpa's shameful history? Was it really possible his dad didn't know either? Had Grandpa Thomas left his shame and disgrace here in England when he'd fled?

Ben chewed his thumbnail, wandering aimlessly through the chilly corridors of the Abbey. The house had a sort of damp smell to at and it was creaking against the wind outside. What he really wanted was to run right back down to the kitchen and whip up some spiced apple muffins or banana cake or almond bear claws. But the staff would be there now, more than likely preparing lunch for when the shooting party returned.

How could Nancy have thought that Ben deserved this house? He looked around at the slightly faded and peeling wallpaper that must have once been so luxurious and grand. How many generations had lived in this place? Elias had told Ben that most British estates had been handed over to the National Trust over the last hundred years to be preserved as historical sights, or turned into fancy schools. Whittingar Abbey had survived all of that. So many centuries. Was that all going to fall apart with Ben?

He wondered idly if there had been any other shocking surprise heirs in the past? Probably not. As far as he understood, there was always a strict way these things were done, handing the property down to the eldest surviving male, like Kenneth had said, just without the benefit of an actual title like a lordship. Ben was so far from being that, he might as well have been sweeping the floors of this once grand place.

Not that there was anything wrong with being employed here. In fact, all the staff he'd met so far had been a thousand times nicer and warmer than almost all of his so-called relatives. But no one was asking any of them to run the whole house and the business, not to mention sort out people's inheritance. Which was a shame really, because Ben would bet good money that the likes of Mrs. Hollis could do a far better job of it than he could.

He groaned and trudged up another flight of stairs, running his finger along a banister that was in dire need of a good varnish. How long was the contention of the will going to take? Would it be better or not if the court ruled in his favor? Surely Ben didn't deserve any of it after the way his grandfather had behaved. The hostile manner in which he was greeted right from the moment he set foot on the estate all made so much sense now. Honestly, what had Nancy been thinking? Was it really some kind of final joke from beyond the grave?

Ben had to say he didn't find it particularly funny.

When Ben thought about how much of a mess his life was right now, it was tragically all too clear that Elias could very well want him just for his money. And if he didn't end up getting any, did that mean Elias would be straight back to his fancy lawyer friends, forgetting all about the immature baker he'd had a five-minute fling with?

That was what was really troubling Ben at his core. He knew he should be most worried about the house, the failing Tipsy Blossom cider business, the millions of pounds of inheritance, and the expectations of so many people. But deep down, he was a selfish child, and he just wanted the guy he liked to like him back.

More than liked. Ben's heart *ached* for Elias. He wasn't sure if he could bear it if it had all been a lie.

He scuffed his foot against the worn carpet. It had taken all his strength not to just go straight back to the cottage and crawl into Elias's bed again where he had felt safe. But like it or not, he *was* an adult, and he couldn't hide from his problems forever. But he didn't know how to fix them.

All he knew was what his heart wanted, and that was Elias.

But what if Elias didn't feel the same way? What if he just wasn't interested in Ben for his heart, only his wallet?

Ben huffed, trying to be brutally logical. Out of everything he was worrying about, that had to be the most ridiculous. Elias wasn't like that, at all. But try as he might, he just couldn't shake the thought from his mind, or make everything he was feeling any less painful.

Damn Noah. Like Ben didn't have enough conflicting him already, Noah had to go and drop two more bombshells on him. The crazy thing was, all Ben wanted to do was go talk to Elias about it, but he didn't want to bring more insecurities to what they already had. That wasn't going to make Elias like him. Confidence was attractive, not whining.

So Ben needed to get his head together before he went back to find Elias. He wasn't able to go down to the kitchen, but his aimless twisting and turning happened to lead him to perhaps the other best room in the house.

The library.

Ben almost missed it. The door was only partially ajar, and if he hadn't happened to glance in at that precise moment and spot a row of book spines, he probably would have walked straight past. As it was, he stopped in his tracks, then gently pushed the door open further to reveal a slightly crooked mahogany bookshelf crammed full of leather-bound books. There were no tatty paperbacks here, although some of the books looked like they might be a bit cracked and had suffered some sun damage.

Ben didn't care. It was as if his troubles melted away as he walked further into the room and inhaled the comforting smell of warm leather and old paper. It was beautiful in here, with more dark wood bookcases, a light gray stone mantelpiece, brass chandeliers, chocolate-colored leather sofas and armchairs, terracotta rugs, and watercolors of countryside landscapes hanging from the wooden panel walls. Large bay windows let in a good amount of wintery sunshine, but even then there were pockets of gloom, and it took Ben a moment to realize he wasn't alone.

"Oh, I'm so sorry," he spluttered, jumping back. The figure had been mostly obscured by the back of the armchair that was facing the unlit fireplace. "I didn't mean to disturb you," Ben added genuinely. "I thought everyone was out shooting. Or at least watching the shooting. I didn't...I'll leave..." He trailed off, feeling like a babbling fool.

The figure rose from the seat and turned around. She was one of Ben's older relatives, wearing a cream, chunky-knitted cardigan, tweed skirt, maroon slippers, and beige tights. She was clutching a lace-trimmed handkerchief to her chest, which made Ben glance at her neckline. There, poking out from underneath her white blouse, was a very distinctive ruby necklace.

"Oh," said Ben happily as he took another step inside the

library, allowing the door to swing shut slightly. "You must be Elizabeth, Anika's grandmother. It's a pleasure to meet you. Properly, I mean. I know we sort of met yesterday. Was it yesterday? Jetlag is so brutal. I, um…"

He was jabbering again, so he stopped, embarrassed. No wonder all these people thought he was a dumb Yank. Elizabeth looked at him with wide eyes surrounded by wrinkles. Laughter lines, he noticed, but she certainly wasn't laughing now. In fact, from her watery-looking eyes it appeared that she'd been crying by herself in this chilly library.

"Is everything all right?" Ben asked gently when Elizabeth didn't respond to his prattling.

Elizabeth opened and closed her mouth, her eyes darting around the room. Dust motes floated through the beams of sunshine coming through the windows. "Yes, yes," she croaked, like she wasn't accustomed to using her voice. "Fine, dear." Before Ben could ask anything more, she bustled forward, clutching her hanky even closer, and not looking at Ben. "I'm sorry," she mumbled as she headed for the door.

Ben frowned, watching her go. "For what?"

"Everything," Elizabeth told him, not pausing in her shuffle or looking back as she pulled the door open and disappeared through it.

Ben blinked, once more alone. Although he had a lot on his mind, he couldn't see how any of it could be the fault of Anika and Raj's grandma. It was kind of nice to get some sympathy rather than hostility from some of his extended family, but he was worried that she'd been weeping. Perhaps she'd been close with Nancy and had come here for a moment to mourn. Once he'd flicked the lights of the chandelier on, he quickly noticed upon closer inspection that all the watercolors on the walls had a signature that could very well have been her name. Had this been a special room of hers?

Ben turned on the spot as the lightbulbs warmed up and glowed brighter. He found himself smiling, and thinking this was possibly the most at ease he'd been inside this house yet. Even more so than the kitchen, as he'd been upset then, thinking he'd messed everything up with Elias. All he could think now was that he wanted to share this library with Elias so badly, as he loved his books as much as Ben did. It was so peaceful, yet full of life between so many pages of literature.

As Ben wandered around the room a few times, inspecting numerous titles on the leather spines, he felt calmer. He had been getting himself so wound up but he needed to remember that none of these worries were a matter of life or death. So what if these people didn't like him? He hadn't done anything malicious to them. And it was unfortunate if his beloved grandfather had made a bad decision decades ago, that had nothing to do with Ben. The chips would fall where they may. If the will stood up to being contested, then Ben would do the best he could to be fair and responsible. If the estate and everything reverted back to Kenneth, he honestly wished the family luck. He didn't like their chances under the thumb of that old bastard.

He wasn't sure if he should touch the books or not, so rather than find something to read like he would have wanted to, he curled up on one of the couches and pulled a woolen blanket over him. He looked out the windows at the blue sky, fluffy white clouds, and brownish-green land. He was on the third floor, so the view of the orchards and surrounding fields stretched on for miles, giving him a deep sense of peace and contentment.

He must have dozed off, because the next thing he knew the grandfather clock that had gently been ticking in the corner chimed on the hour. Ben snuffled and stretched.

Jetlag was weird. It wasn't just wanting to sleep at odd times. It was an exhaustion that seeped right down into your bones.

Carefully folding the blanket back up and draping it over the sofa once more, Ben moved to take a closer look out the windows. It appeared as if the shooting party had only just broken up, as he could see little figures moving around in the distance. His heart panged, thinking of Elias. Ben hadn't meant to run off and leave him like that. He'd just wanted to get some space from Noah and the family.

His heart twisted, not knowing what to think. In the heat of the moment, what Noah had said made a lot of sense, playing into Ben's darkest fears about Elias. Simply put, that Ben wasn't good enough, and the only explanation that made sense was that Elias was only interested in his fortune.

But after some time alone and a nap, Ben was feeling less vulnerable and more logical. How much water did that theory really hold? He stood by the library window and replayed all his and Elias's highlights from the last few days, especially the last twenty-four-hours. The way Elias had held him tenderly after they'd made love didn't exactly scream of a gold-digger.

Yes, Ben had his doubts. But didn't everyone going into a new relationship? Ben might not have had a long-term boyfriend before, but he'd dated a bit and had a lot of hookups. A couple of times he'd felt that spark of wondering whether or not it was going to turn into something special. But Ben had never felt it this strongly, ever. Didn't he owe it to himself to explore that further, to give it a chance to flourish?

He lightly touched some of the book spines as he made his way back out of the library, the leather soft under his fingertips. He felt rejuvenated. Sometimes, good things happened because you *made* them happen. There was no point sitting around waiting for opportunities to fall into your lap. Like his inheritance. He hadn't earned that, he was quite sure. But he wanted to earn Elias's admiration.

Maybe even his love.

Smiling and feeling a little giddy, Ben jogged down the stairs, planning on heading back to the cottage. It was so tempting to think he was heading back 'home.' That's what it felt like. Of course he'd never admit that to anyone, it was ridiculous. But no one would ever know if he didn't say it out loud, and it made him grin a bit broader as he strode toward the front door.

Unfortunately, it opened before he could reach it.

His great-uncle Kenneth was plunged into dramatic silhouette by the bright winter sunlight shining from outside into the gloomy entrance hallway. Ben stopped short. Kenneth was the last person he wanted to see, but he was now blocking the door and there was no way for him to walk past him. Shit. If only he had left the library two minutes earlier, he could have avoided them bumping into each other.

Kenneth was alone, presumably having left other people to clear up his guns. It seemed to Ben that no matter how much the likes of Mildred and Harold tried to suck up to Kenneth, he wasn't particularly interested in any of his relative in a caring way. So it wasn't really a surprise he had returned from the shoot on his own.

He allowed the door to slam shut behind him, staring at Ben with a curled lip, his shoulders back and his hands hanging by his side, looking like they could ball into fists and swing a punch in a split second, despite his senior years. His woolen suit was dark brown and he wore the same uniform bottle-green rain boots as everyone else had been sporting.

"Just *what*," he snarled slowly, "do you think you're doing in *my* house?"

A spark of fear flashed through Ben, but he needed to defend himself. He wasn't afraid of this man's fists or his bad opinion. "I thought it was open to all the family," he said with his chin up.

Kenneth huffed like a bull in a matador ring, and advanced a step closer. "Those who have been *invited*. You were given the blasted cottage for a reason. Did you come to pilfer the family jewels?"

Indignantly, Ben put his hands on his hips. "Of course not," he shot back. He wished he could muster up something wittier, but under the circumstances he was just glad his voice didn't shake. "You invited me on the shoot. I thought you were interested in talking this through?"

Kenneth dropped his head back and laughed, a chilling sound that rang through the shabby entrance hall. "I did no such thing. Noah has some scheme in mind. I couldn't care less. You are a minor inconvenience that will be crushed under the heel of my boot soon enough. The idea that you have any real claim over this estate is as preposterous as it is vulgar, you common little thief."

A lump rose in Ben's throat. "I'm not a thief," he stammered. "I didn't ask for any of this."

Kenneth loomed over him, jabbing a crooked finger in his face. "Oh, but you'll accept it anyway, won't you? Greedy little Americans, always taking what isn't yours."

Ben had to splutter indignantly at that. "Hello! The British Empire? That's all you guys did!"

The puce color that rose on Kenneth's cheeks and his bulbous, spider-veined nose as he clenched his jaw was unnerving, but Ben refused to take a move back. He'd known this fight was coming, and it was important that he stood his ground.

Kenneth's eyes were dark as he lowered his hand. "Let's be perfectly clear, *mongrel*. I would rather die than see this family's legacy tarnished. Your grandfather shamed us all and fled over the Atlantic with his tail between his legs. You are *just* like him, it's easy to see. Utterly without any kind of honor or decency. I will burn every inch of Whittingar Abbey to the ground and allow it eternal glory rather than suffer the contemptable indignation of allowing your sort to destroy its reputation."

Ben's heart was beating in his throat and his eyes burned with tears. So much for trying to tell himself that Kenneth couldn't frighten him. He was trembling so badly he wanted to pass out.

"You – you would take everything from everyone?" he managed to stammer.

Kenneth smiled nastily and raised both his hands, palms up. "We would rise from the ashes like the mighty phoenix." He slid his eyes up and down Ben. "Those of us who were worthy, that is. I think it's time you abandoned this folly and scuttled back off to the colonies, don't you?"

Ben balled his fists. "Elias and I aren't going anywhere," he snapped. "You may not like what Nancy's will said, but it's legally binding."

Kenneth dropped his hands and chuckled softly. "Ahh, yes. Your plague-ridden friend. I'm particularly disgusted you let him onto our grounds. Our investigator found out *all* about him, and your little bakery. Tell me, how *is* the sale going with The Happy Baker Inc?"

Icy coldness flushed through Ben's entire body. "W-what?" he uttered.

Kenneth smirked and clasped his hands in front of him. "You thought we wouldn't dig up every little fleck of dirt on you both? Your families? Your friends and coworkers? Oh, we're only just getting started, but really, you've made it too easy. The skeletons practically walked out of the closets themselves." He looked at Ben with utter revulsion. "And speaking of *closets,* if I was opposed to your little insurgence before, imagine my horror when I found out the both of you were nothing but dirty queers, daring to set foot in my glorious ancestral home. I will *not* stand for it!"

Ben really didn't want to cry, but the dual tears slid down his cheeks anyway. His hands were shaking and his knees felt like they might give way on him at any moment. Try as he might to utter a single syllable, his mouth just opened and closed like a guppy. He didn't think he had ever felt so small in his entire life.

"In case you were under any mistaken impression that I was bluffing, let me spell it out for you," Kenneth continued, smiling maliciously. "I may think twice about engulfing several centuries worth of history in flames," he said, holding his hands up to indicate the house, "but I wouldn't even blink an eye to purchase that pathetic little establishment you are currently employed at and razing it to the ground. And as for your friend..." Kenneth hummed in glee. "Wouldn't it be a shame if something happened to invalidate his insurance policy?"

A wave of nausea washed over Ben so forcefully he thought he might puke right then on the hundred-year-old rug he was standing on. "You'd seriously try and fuck with Elias's HIV medication?" he cried, not believing his own ears. "You couldn't – there's no way-"

"You have *no* idea what I'm capable of, young man," Kenneth whispered silkily. "It's not my fault your medical system is so corrupt. One little glitch and who knows if dear old Elias could get what he needs at an affordable rate ever again."

The tears were streaming down Ben's face now. He didn't even need to blink or sob. They were just dripping from his chin as he stared in utter horror. How could anyone threaten the life of another human being like that? It was the most abhorrent thing Ben had ever witnessed.

"I-I'll go," he managed to croak. "Please. Don't hurt Elias.

And don't ruin the bakery. It's not mine. You'll destroy people's lives."

Kenneth chuckled. "That's no concern of mine."

"Still," Ben stammered. "If I have your word, I'll renounce any claim I have. You'll never hear a single thing from me again. Just promise me…as a *gentleman*…your word that you'll leave them both alone."

His hunch paid off. Appealing to Kenneth's status and class looked like it made him feel even more puffed up and superior than he already was.

Kenneth shook his head, finally taking a step back. At least Ben felt like he could take a breath again, but he was no less crushed. His whole world felt like it had come plummeting down around him. "Pathetic," Kenneth huffed. "Very well. I will have the driver ready for you in fifteen minutes. With or without the lawyer, I don't care what he does. But you will leave the country tonight. Do you understand."

"Y-yes," said Ben.

Kenneth cupped his hand behind his ear and leaned forward, looking to the side. "Yes…*what?*"

Ben hated himself. He detested what lows he'd been dragged to. But he balled his fists and did what he had to do. *"Yes, sir,"* he whispered.

Kenneth stood up straight once more, looking remarkably smug. "Good dog. Now *fuck off* before I change my mind."

With that, he strode out of sight, leaving Ben shivering in the entrance hall of Whittingar Abbey.

But not for long.

He had a plane to catch.

He ran all the way back to his and Elias's beloved cottage, sobbing the entire time.

1 8

ELIAS

Something was very wrong.

The cottage was lifeless, the lights all off. When Elias jogged up the stairs to check if Ben was napping (after all, his disappearing could be explained simply by jetlag) the bed in his room was empty. Elias could have assumed Ben was elsewhere, in Elias's own bed even, but with a jolt he realized Ben's suitcase was gone. However, there were still mismatched socks under the bed, a Chapstick on the dresser, a sweater draped over the banister, and Ben's electric toothbrush plugged into the wall in the living room, because that was naturally where he'd keep it.

Anika and Raj were waiting politely by the front door, but they raised their eyebrows in concern at Elias's return. "He's not here?" Anika asked.

Elias shook his head slowly, still confused, and rubbed his mouth. "No. And some of his stuff is gone. But not all of it. Let me try calling him." Except when Elias got out his phone, he realized Ben had finally replied to his text.

Elias's stomach dropped when he read it, though.

"What?" said Anika, immediately on alert. She stepped closer to Elias and Raj followed. "Is something wrong?"

Elias managed to nod.

"Did you get a text?" Raj asked, clearly concerned. Elias didn't blame him. Elias had promised Raj that his future was safe in Ben's hands, but now…

"He said," began Elias, clearing his throat, "'I've made a terrible mistake. Thank you for all you've done, but I'm heading back to America now. Please stay and enjoy the rest of your vacation. I'd keep away from the house now, though. Maybe you could go to that nice B'n'B in the town? Maybe we can catch up when you're back home, but I understand if you never want to see me again. Ben.'"

"What the *fuck?*" Anika exploded.

"What happened?" Raj asked, his hand on his chest. "Did you guys have a fight?"

Elias shook his head, feeling dizzy. "No, no. Everything was fine. Why would he think I'd never want to see him again? Oh, except Noah said-"

"That *shit* weasel!" Anika cried, interrupting. "I should have known he was up to something. He keeps telling everyone I'm obsessed with him, no matter how much I tell him to fuck off. It's no surprise he'd try his tricks on Ben. He likes toying with people," she added darkly, looking Elias dead in the eyes. "What did he say to him?"

"I'm not sure exactly," Elias replied, racking his brains. "He told me to stop controlling Ben, but I truly don't think I was."

"No, you probably weren't," said Anika, shaking her head and sharing a look with her brother, who sighed. "He's a gaslighting prick. I'm sorry. But he must have said something really fucked up to make Ben flee the country."

Elias began pacing the room and rubbing his temple. The

cottage was chilly again. *Fuck.* What he wouldn't give to light the fire and cuddle up with Ben and some hot tea. He stopped rubbing his head and rubbed his chest instead. It was almost as if he could feel his heart actually breaking.

"Ben never felt like he belonged here," he said, more thinking out loud than replying directly to Anika. "No matter how much I tried to tell him, he was convinced he was too young, too stupid, too poor to have anything to offer this family. He was so desperate for their approval, though. Their love." Elias blinked back tears, unable to stop himself from feeling like he had somehow failed Ben by not making him see just how precious he was.

Raj scoffed and Anika tutted. "Yep," she said ruefully. "These sharks will sniff any blood in the water and devour you whole."

"They sense weakness like a sixth sense," Raj added bitterly, although he held his head high and folded his arms defiantly.

"But..." Elias said, still scrambling around trying to comprehend what had happened. "Ben was just here. How could he have left so fast? He doesn't have money for a last-minute plane ticket. Why wouldn't he at least say goodbye to me?"

"What destination airport?" Anika demanded, getting her phone out of her pocket.

"Uh, Sea-Tac," Elias said, distracted. Ben was *gone?* Were all Elias's fears valid after all? He'd tried so hard to quash his insecurities and look at the evidence that he and Ben were forming a real connection together, but perhaps it had all been wishful thinking.

Raj placed his hand on Elias's arm. "I'm really sorry, mate," he said sincerely. Elias wouldn't have blamed Raj for being furious that Ben had abandoned him to his blackmailer, but he seemed more concerned with Elias in that moment.

"Okay," said Anika, looking at her phone and scrolling rapidly through. "It looks like he could get an indirect flight tonight to Frankfurt where he could get the Seattle flight at crazy-o'clock tomorrow morning for just over three hundred quid. Does that sound like something he'd try and do?"

Elias shrugged helplessly, feeling off-kilter, like he was on a boat at sea. "I mean, maybe? But he'd still have to get a train ticket to the airport…or call a cab…he didn't even know the route between here and Heathrow when we landed. How…?"

The frantic knock at the door made them all jump. Elias shook himself, then moved to open it, revealing a distraught-looking Mrs. Hollis. "Oh thank *goodness* you're here!" she shrieked.

Elias had only known her a couple of days, but he didn't take her as a woman who usually shrieked. Sure enough, Anika and Raj looked more than a little disturbed. She flapped her hands and marched into the cottage, furiously wiping her rain boots on the doormat before slamming the door after her. She'd tied a headscarf on and was now attacking the knot under her chin to get it back off again.

"I was too late! I couldn't stop them! Not that I could have, really, but I would have *bloody* tried!" She gave up with the knot, ripping the scarf off still tied and leaving her hair in a cloud of wispy static.

"Mrs. *Hollis*," said Anika, sounding scandalized. Presumably, she was a woman who didn't usually swear, either.

However, Mrs. Hollis had been driven over the edge, so it seemed. She was vibrating with rage as she rocked on her heels and jabbed a shaking finger toward the main house. "That – that *wretched man* told Mr. Decker to drive Mr.

Turner to the airport, and he was crying his eyes out, the poor soul! I don't know what on Earth happened, but that boy was rattled to his core and *Mr. Grimaldi de Loutherbergh* wouldn't even let me make him some tea to take with him!" Elias knew enough to appreciate that was the gravest sin here, as far as she was concerned. "What's happened? Did you boys spat?"

Elias was very glad they had not in fact quarreled with the look she nailed him with. "No, no," he assured her, waving his hands. "Everything seemed fine-"

"Noah got involved," Anika said, folding her arms and glowering.

"Oh, *well* then," Mrs. Hollis griped. She smoothed down her hair and folded her headscarf into one of the pockets in her waxy green coat. "That explains a great deal."

"Maybe it's not too late?" Raj said, optimistically. "How long ago did he leave?"

Mrs. Hollis shook her head. "Not more than ten minutes ago, love," she said. "But why would he rush off like that? Why did Mr. Grimaldi de Loutherbergh insist he take the car?"

"Because he wanted to make sure Ben left," suggested Elias grimly. He reread the text Ben had sent. "It might not be Noah after all. I think Kenneth threatened Ben and is trying to get him out of the way of the will."

"No!" cried Anika. She shoved her hands in her hair under her bobble hat and looked at Raj with a gasp. "No, no! Kenneth can't get everything back."

Raj licked his lips and shook his head. "This isn't about me, *Anika-didi*. We need to make sure Ben's safe. He's all alone and it sounds like he was distraught."

"Crying his *eyes* out," Mrs. Hollis confirmed, wringing her hands.

Elias thought his heart might genuinely crack in two. He

wanted to click his heels like Dorothy and be by Ben's side that instant to hold him and kiss the top of his head through his beautiful curls and tell him everything was going to be okay.

Raj fixed Elias with a look, pulling him from his wretched thoughts. "You should go after him," Raj said.

Elias swallowed, rereading the text yet again. Doubt was slithering through his mind. "But what if he doesn't want me to?"

He was accosted by three very loud indignant voices all yelling incoherently. "Do you love him or not?" Anika demanded when the cacophony died down.

Elias blinked, then looked between the three of them. "I don't know?"

Anika smacked his arm. "Yes, you do!"

Did he?

As a lawyer, Elias was used to thinking about every tiny detail. But now wasn't the time for analysis and logic. He switched off that brain and let his heart take charge. How did he feel when he closed his eyes and pictured Ben's gorgeous smile, excitable nature, kind heart, and sexy, *sexy* body?

He opened his eyes again. The three of them were waiting with their eyebrows raised for his response.

"I think...maybe I do love him?"

Raj whimpered and clutched his chest. Mrs. Hollis beamed and smiled.

Anika flung her arms toward the door. "Then what are we waiting for? Let's go!" She danced on the spot and offered Elias her fist to bump. He did so, feeling silly, but also laughing.

"Don't you need a car?" Mrs. Hollis asked.

Anika blew a raspberry. "I've got that covered. But we need to hurry, or he'll get through check-in. Once he's in departures, we won't be able to follow."

"Unless Elias buys a ticket just to follow him." Raj grinned as he winked at him.

Anika rolled her eyes. "You watch too many rom coms."

"No, that's a brilliant idea," said Elias, clapping Raj on the shoulder. "But let's try and get to him before that. I need to check something here first, though."

"Oh," said Mrs. Hollis. She wagged her finger as she pulled a clunky old push-button phone from out of her anorak. "Let me text Mr. Decker. I'll tell him to use the backroads and buy you some time."

"Don't tell Ben," said Elias, worry eating through his chest. "Whatever Kenneth used to frighten him might convince him to run faster if he knows we're coming."

Mrs. Hollis shook her head. "When he's driving, Mr. Decker gets his texts read to him in the little earpiece he wears. So Ben won't hear or see." She began walking toward the kitchen, pecking out the message on her phone with her index finger. "Hurry now. Anika's right. You should go as soon as possible."

"It looks like the M25's clear," said Anika in surprise as she looked through her phone again. "I guess miracles really do happen."

"What do you need to get?" Raj asked.

Elias shook his head. "It's more that I want to check something. Give me a minute?"

"Okay, but then we're *going*," said Anika, still concentrating on her phone. "I'm fast, but I can't fly."

Elias knew time was of the essence, but he had to stop and marvel for a second. *Thank you,* he said with as much gratitude as he could muster. "You guys don't even know us, and you're going to such lengths."

Raj smiled. "Of course. You're family."

Anika blew another raspberry. "Fuck *family*. Fuck those arseholes in particular. We're doing this because you're *nice*.

Nobody seems to be nice anymore! It's like it's a weakness. I don't care about riches or power." She poked Elias's chest and sniffed. "I care about the kind of person who doesn't give up when someone is relying on them. Even if it's a sodding kitten." She sniffed again and blinked rapidly. "Now go and do whatever it is you need to do. Go! Run!"

Elias chuckled and dashed back upstairs, pretty sure he knew where he needed to look. Thankfully his hunch paid off, and he grabbed what he was searching for right away. He actually hoped it wouldn't be necessary, but just in case…

As he jogged back down, Mrs. Hollis was also walking back in from the kitchen. She waved both her hands at him. "Just a little something for the journey," she announced.

Elias wanted to know how she had whipped up three Ziploc-bagged sandwiches and what was probably a thermos of tea so fast, but he wasn't really surprised. "Thank you," he said, throwing his arms around her and hugging her tightly. She squeaked and laughed.

"Are you coming?" Anika asked Raj, but he shook his head.

"Thanks," he said as he took his sandwich from Mrs. Hollis, "but I'll leave the daring car chase to you two. I, um, have something I have to do here."

Anika looked intrigued, but she smiled and nodded before kissing his cheek. "It'll all be all right," she promised.

Raj nodded at her, then Elias. "It will be," he agreed firmly. "Now, go! Gazza can only take so many country rounds before Ben'll get suspicious."

Elias laughed fondly as he followed Anika out of the door. "I don't know. Ben isn't particularly observant like that. But I don't want to waste another second."

Logically, he knew he could just see Ben when they both got back to Pine Cove. But something in his heart was telling him it would be way too late by then. If he didn't want to lose

Ben forever, he had to stop whatever madness was happening right now.

He just had to pray Ben would be happy to see him. That he was fleeing from something awful Kenneth or Noah or both had said, not anything Elias had done. As they marched up the dirt path, Elias mulled over what he'd said back in the cottage.

Did he actually love Ben? Could you fall in love that fast? Or had he, in fact, been falling slowly in love for a year and a half and not even realized it? Did he even remember what love felt like after all these years? All he knew was that when he thought of Ben being ripped away from him like this, it was as if he'd lost a limb. His heart was aching so much it felt physically painful. He would do *anything* right now to make Ben feel safe and loved.

He needed him back in his arms, and that was all that really mattered.

A sharp bark pulled him from his reverie, and he turned to see Treacle scrabbling on his stumpy legs as he tore from the stables to catch up with them. "I thought you were looking after your girlfriend?" Elias asked, bemused.

Treacle barked several more times, falling into step with Elias.

"He said that Luna can look after herself," Anika told him with a grin. She could move damned fast for a petite woman. She was swinging a set of car keys around her finger, taking them to the back of the estate. "Come on, keep up! Google Maps says we should make it in good time, but there could be an accident at any time on the motorway, and then everything will be buggered."

Elias jogged so they were striding side-by-side. "I'll make it right," he promised. "I'll help your brother. We won't let him be ruined."

Anika bit her lip and nodded. "Thank you. That would be great. But right now, let's just focus on *you*, okay?"

"I'm not used to that," Elias admitted.

Anika hummed. "You know, Ben said you weren't together when I asked."

"We probably weren't," Elias admitted, shaking his head. "We still aren't really now."

Anika scoffed and turned her head to raise an eyebrow at him. "I beg to differ. But maybe that's something you should clear up when we get to him."

"If we make it in time," Elias said gloomily.

"*When*," Anika repeated.

Elias knew he shouldn't have been surprised, but as they rounded the house and came to a long, covered carport, the vehicle that flashed when Anika pressed the fob on her car keys was a bright yellow Aston Martin, all sleek curves and shiny wheels.

"*That's* your car?" Elias asked incredulously.

Anika waggled her eyebrows and skipped sideways over to the driver's seat. "I got a *great* secondhand deal. Get in, lover boy."

Elias shook his head and opened the passenger seat…only for Treacle to hop straight in. "Oh, no. Come on, boy. You can't come to Heathrow. That's not a place for dogs."

"You can waste your time trying to stop him, or you can just accept defeat graciously and *get in*," Anika cried, dropping into the driver's seat and starting the engine with a roar. "We are *out* of time!"

Elias at least managed to brush some of the dirt off the leather before he clambered inside. He and Treacle shuffled awkwardly until Treacle was sitting on his lap. Elias barely got his seat belt on before Anika was tearing out of the estate, gravel flying on the driveway behind them as they sped away.

Elias just hoped luck was on his side. Had he used all of his up earlier when he'd saved the tiny kitten? Or did he have just enough left to stop Ben from disappearing off into the sunset and taking Elias's heart with him?

He guessed he would just have to wait and see.

19

BEN

"I'm sorry about the slow journey, sir."

Ben blinked from his stupor in the backseat. "Slow?"

Gazza nodded solemnly. "There's been an accident, you see. That's why we're having to take all these, uh, back roads. I'd normally want to make sure we get there as fast as possible, I promise. But this accident, it's clogged everything up. So, uh, sorry."

Ben knew he was groggy, but he didn't understand why Gazza sounded so flustered. "I hope nobody got hurt," said Ben, slumping down a fraction more against the BMW's upholstery.

"Oh, no, I don't think so," said Gazza quickly. "The traffic report said…an oil spill. So just a lot of oil to clean up."

"Do you think we'll still make the flight?" Ben asked.

Gazza nodded. "Uh, yes, I'm sure we will. You've got a lot of time before check-in."

Ben didn't really care, other than he didn't want to sleep at the airport if he couldn't make it to Germany. At least there he would only have to wait a few hours before his flight back to the States. But he was desperate to leave England as soon as he could. He felt like Kenneth had spies checking up on him, and he couldn't risk pissing off that fucker any more than he already had. What if he sent Mr. Cabot after him again to chase him out of the country? Ben shivered, not liking his odds if Mr. Cabot decided to really threaten him like he'd implied back at Rise and Shine.

God, that felt like a lifetime ago.

Ben swallowed down a fresh wave of despair. Guilt and horror were competing for which could try and eat him alive first. Ben would never in a million years have intentionally jeopardized anyone else, but he believed Kenneth when he'd said he had the power to flatten Rise and Shine, not to mention threaten Elias's medical insurance.

Who would do that? Those pills were literally the only thing between Elias and a cruel death. Ben would let himself die first before he subjected Elias to that. Of that he was crystal clear.

He didn't have the energy to feel relief, and nothing right now could make him happy, but he did appreciate the luck of being able to get such a cheap flight home simply by suffering a layover in Frankfurt. He was pretty sure they still had seats available, but he wasn't set up on his phone with the right apps or credit cards, so he had just decided to book and pay when he got to the airport. He was pretty sure he could do that, but honestly, he was so drained right then there was no way he could try and navigate that much admin by himself.

Oh *god*, he wished Elias was there with him. He'd have everything taken care of, no problem. But he hadn't been at the cottage, and ultimately Ben had decided not to call him and try and get him to pack and leave, too. Kenneth had said fifteen minutes, and he'd damn well meant it. Besides, Ben was so ashamed he couldn't bear the idea of Elias seeing him like this.

Hopefully, they'd be able to meet up again when they both got back to Pine Cove, like he'd suggested in his text. But really, had this all been a dalliance that had never meant to last more than their time in England? How could Ben have ever really thought they could make it as a couple outside of this little bubble?

The truth was, they'd never gotten the chance to find out, and they probably never would now. But Ben would accept that if it kept Elias alive.

Jesus Christ, how had it come to this? Ben's life was making fucking cupcakes, not life and death! How far would Kenneth have gone? Would he have gotten Ben's parents fired from their jobs as well? How about Ben's friends, like Emery? What could Kenneth do to him?

Ben didn't trust Kenneth as far as he could spit when he'd said he wouldn't hurt anyone to spite Ben, even if Ben did what Kenneth wanted by leaving and promising never to return. Ben had to trust that he was so beneath the likes of Kenneth that he wouldn't bother messing with him so long as Ben let him have what he wanted.

At what cost, though? He kept thinking about Anika's words in the forest. She'd been pretty convinced that Kenneth was trying to ruin other people's lives in the family, too.

Ben didn't know any of the specifics of that, though. He had to work with the facts he had, and the primary concern was Elias's health. That was it. He could continue to beat himself up, or accept he was doing the best he could.

Logically, he knew that. But his heart continued to torment him all the way to the airport.

The drive was a couple of hours long, like Gazza had warned him. In all that time, Elias didn't message him back, even though the little ticks told Ben that he'd read the message. He probably hated Ben now, and he couldn't say he blamed him. He'd just abandoned Elias to those hyenas. At least it wasn't him they were mad at. Kenneth had said he didn't mind if Elias got on a plane or not. He was probably so confident in his own power that he didn't see Elias as a threat. It was Ben he wanted out of the country.

So Ben would go, even though he felt extremely shitty about it.

Goddamn it. He wished he'd never set foot in Whittingar Abbey. He'd fucked everything up, most of all with Elias. He could maybe have coped if he had never known what it was like to be held in his arms, to see his confidence coming back to life before Ben's very eyes, to have shared such special, intimate moments together. But it was as if Ben had opened Pandora's Box, and there would be no shoving those emotions back inside. He would be forever grateful they had gotten to spend at least some time together, and in the future that might help it hurt a little less. But right now, all Ben could think of was everything he had lost, and all the opportunities he would now never get.

Dread filled him as they approached the ramp that led up to the massive structure that was Heathrow Terminal Five. As much as he was anxious to do what Kenneth wanted and stop him hurting anyone, Ben so desperately didn't want to leave this dream behind. For all there had been unpleasantness on this trip, he'd also experienced some of the best moments of his entire life.

Would he ever be as happy again as he had been when Elias had kissed him? When he'd told Ben he was beautiful and perfect, and they had lost themselves in bliss together? He felt complete when he was with Elias. He made Ben feel like he could actually *do* things for once.

So that was what Ben was going to do now. He was going to do what was right. Whether Kenneth would have ever really committed arson on Whittingar Abbey, or bought out

Rise and Shine, or worst of all tampered with Elias's medical insurance, Ben would probably never know. But he'd rather forsake his own happiness on the off chance that the old man was just that fucking crazy.

"Uh," he grunted as Gazza pulled up to the drop-off point.

Ben's legs were like jelly, feeling quite separate from his brain, apparently determined to sabotage any attempt to exit the car. Saying 'thank you' didn't seem nearly appropriate for everything they had been through, but what else *could* he say? 'It was nice to meet you, but I feel like my whole world is ending right now'? Gazza had made Ben and Elias feel welcomed when a lot of people had been outright hostile. Ben would never forget his kindness.

They got out of the car, and Ben watched as Gazza effortlessly yanked Ben's suitcase and carry-on from the trunk of his BMW. Ben gripped the handles and took a deep breath, willing himself not to start crying again.

He'd run out of tissues to blow his nose on.

"Please look after Elias," was what he managed to say in the end. "I'm not sure if he'll still be in the cottage or if he'll go to the town…but if you see him…"

"We'll take good care of him, sir," Gazza promised him solemnly. He stuck out his meaty hand and cleared his throat. "Well, best of British to you," he said, nodding as they shook. "Sorry, that means good luck. It was a pleasure to have met you. I'm sad things didn't work out the way you wanted, but Miss Nancy would have been glad to know you saw the house. That we got to meet you. I – we all – do really wish you well."

Ben swallowed before he replied. "Thank you," he said thickly. "It was an honor."

Before he could start bawling again, he turned on his heels and dragged his cases with him through the double glass doors as they automatically swooshed open for him.

It was time to say goodbye to England, and everything it had held dear for Ben.

London Heathrow was apparently the busiest airport in Europe, in fact, one of the busiest in the whole world. He could well believe it as he looked up and down the departures area of just this one terminal, feeling completely lost in the sea of bustling people. It was mid-afternoon now, and the sky beyond the floor-to-ceiling windows was growing dark as the evening drew in.

If only he had Elias's hand to hold, maybe he wouldn't feel so completely overwhelmed. But there was no one to help him now. He had to help himself. So he took a long, deep breath, and began searching for the airline check-in desks that would apparently start him on his journey back home, trying not to feel like he was walking to the gallows.

He thought of how, only a couple of hours ago, he'd pictured that little thatch-roofed cottage when he'd said the word 'home.' How wrong he'd been.

When he eventually found the desks matching the low-budget airline he wanted, the line wasn't too bad. He had a few hours still until the flight he hoped to catch, so no rush, really. Not unless Kenneth had sent Mr. Cabot after Ben to frog-march him onto the first plane available. But that was just being ridiculous. No one was following him.

No one cared that much, though. He was beyond contempt as far as most of his so-called family were concerned. Nothing to worry about now he was out of sight. They were probably right. Ben had been a fool to think he could ever fit in with high British society.

Without him really noticing, he'd reached the front of the line. A plump, middle-aged Black woman with enormous natural hair beckoned him to her station. "Good afternoon," she said in a Scottish accent with a big, bright smile. "May I take your passport, please?"

"Actually," Ben said, "I haven't bought a ticket yet. Booked a flight, I mean. Can I do that now?"

The woman – Kwen her name badge read – raised her perfectly painted eyebrows at him. "Oh, that's highly unusual."

"I'm sorry," said Ben genuinely. "It's all extremely last minute. I've had a terrible day," he couldn't help but add. He managed to blink back his tears, at least.

"Oh, love," Kwen said sympathetically. "Okay, let's see what we can do for you. Where are you heading to?"

"Seattle – Sea-Tac," he said, holding out his phone to show her the screen. "I've found the flights I want, if that helps?"

Kwen nodded, typing away rapidly with long, sparkly purple nails. "Sure. Okey dokey, let's have a look at your passport and see what's possible."

"Yes, I…"

Ben felt the blood draining from his face as first denial, then dread filled him.

His passport.

He didn't remember picking it up.

He checked his coat pockets, then his jeans, then the outer pockets of his luggage, just in case by some miracle he'd packed it somewhere in there yesterday. But it was nowhere. He wasn't even sure where he'd put it back at the cottage. But it was pretty evident it wasn't here with him now.

He could feel Kwen watching him with increasing concern as he tried to keep his panic at bay. "I-I think I left it behind," he said, choking back a sob. He stood up straight again and covered his mouth with his hand. "Oh, god, what do I do?"

"Hey, hey, it's okay," Kwen said urgently, reaching out her hand. Ben gave her his, letting her give it a tight squeeze. She nodded at him, her glittery eyes wide. "Don't worry now, love. How far away is it? Could you get it couriered?"

"W-Wiltshire." Ben hiccupped, checking his phone.

Oh, *fuck.* His battery was only at eleven percent. How could he have let it get so low? Had he even packed the charger from the living room? He'd basically just closed up his suitcase and ran. He barely had the money for the flight. How much would a courier cost? Would they even be able to get into the cottage? They probably wouldn't have time to get the passport to Ben before he had to board the Frankfurt flight anyway.

Why was he so *useless.* His passport was the most important thing – the *only* thing he really needed – and he'd left it behind. Ben could feel people in the line behind him getting fidgety. There was another clerk serving, but Ben was monopolizing fifty percent of the check-in desks.

"I have to catch this flight," he said, trembling as he looked at Kwen through blurry eyes. "I have to get out of the country."

"Son," Kwen said, suddenly serious. "Are you in trouble? Do we need to involve the police? Has someone threatened you?"

Yes. "No, I just...I just really need to get home. I'm so sorry. I'm wasting your time-"

"Not at *all* darling. This is my job. Now, take a wee second and blow your nose." Kwen let go of his hand and offered him a tissue that she produced from somewhere in the hidden depths of her desk. Ben took it gratefully. "Now, we'll find a solution, don't you – sir? I'm sorry, sir, there's a queue."

"It's okay," gasped a breathless voice, like they'd been sprinting. "I'm not flying anywhere. I just thought my friend might need this."

Ben had been too busy loudly blowing his nose to really

hear the voice as the man came up behind him. He hadn't even registered the American accent.

But when a hand slapped down an American passport onto the desk, Ben jumped and snapped his head around in shock.

It was Elias.

Of course it was Elias.

2 0

———————

E L I A S

THANK GOODNESS THAT ANIKA HAD CHECKED THE AIRLINE BEN was likely to be traveling with so they'd driven to the right terminal. There was a *big* difference between them, apparently. She'd skidded to a halt at the drop-off point up the huge ramp that led to the right part of the airport, where Elias had jumped from the Aston Martin and sprinted through the doors of Terminal Five into departures and along the check-in desks.

Ben was so small, Elias had almost missed him. But there he'd been, standing at the front of the line. Elias didn't care who stared, or when the clerk tried to stop him skipping ahead. He just knew he had to get to Ben.

And now there he was, his blotchy face stained with tears as he looked between Elias and the passport Elias had just produced. Elias had been almost certain that Ben would have forgotten it, and when he had, he secretly banked on it holding him up. He thanked the heavens to be given this chance to set things right.

Ben's mouth was hanging open. "How – what?"

"Oh!" the clerk cried happily. She was Kwen according to her name badge. "Is this his passport? That's amazing!"

She reached for it, but Elias looked at her and held his hand up. "Actually, I'm really hoping that Ben doesn't need it after all, ma'am. But that's up to him."

"How are you even here?" Ben squeaked, tearful, his puffy eyes red and wide. Even though he was disheveled he was still so beautiful. Elias's heart skipped a beat as he brushed one of the stray tears from his cheek away with his thumb.

"I followed you," Elias said with a sad laugh. "I don't know what scared you so badly, but I'm *here* for you. I want to help. Please don't leave."

Ben sobbed and flung himself at Elias, clutching at the back of Elias's jacket with both hands as he buried his face against his chest.

Someone tutted in the line. "There are *other* people here, you know," a man called out.

"And you'll kindly wait your turn, sir," Kwen replied loudly in a Scottish accent. Her colleague was still serving, so Elias didn't feel too bad. She made a shooing motion with her hands toward Elias and Ben. "Go on, lad. What is it you have to say?"

"I thought," Ben said between sniffles and hiccups, wiping his eyes as he leaned back from Elias to look at him. "I – Kenneth said-"

"What did that asshole do?" Elias growled. His blood began boiling in a flash, but he did his best to remain calm for Ben's sake.

Ben took a couple of shaky breaths. "He threatened to burn the house down. He said he'd buy the bakery back home and flatten it. He...he..."

Ben dissolved into a fresh wave of sobs. Elias hugged him tightly, stroking his hair and kissing the top of his head, just like he'd been so desperate to do. "What?"

"He said he'd mess with your insurance. Your…*medication.*"

Elias's blood went from boiling to icy in a second. He was going to *eviscerate* that heinous man. Poor Ben. Poor, darling, Ben. "No," Elias said as gently as he could. "He can't do that, sweetheart."

"He said I had no idea what he was capable of," Ben whispered.

Elias laughed darkly, kissing Ben's forehead. "And *he* has no idea what *I* am capable of. I was a big city lawyer for years, remember? He was just trying to scare you. He has no power. He knows the will rules in your favor and he's making a last Hail Mary pass to try and save his ass."

Ben chuckled wetly. It was the most relieving sound Elias had heard in years. "If that was a football reference, you don't know your audience very well." Elias laughed, too.

"You know what I mean, though," he said warmly.

Ben sniffed, holding Elias tighter. "I do."

A tissue appeared between them, being waved by Kwen. "You silly wee man," she chided Ben gently as he took it. "Did you seriously run away from this fine fellow?" She hissed and shook her head. "It sounds like he's a keeper to me." She waggled her beautifully painted eyebrows at them.

Elias smiled at Ben, hoping that was true, but Ben bit his lip and looked anxious.

"What, sweetheart?" Elias asked.

Ben gulped and grimaced. "Noah…Noah pointed out…he said you only became interested in me after the money."

Much like Mrs. Hollis, Elias was not one to shriek. But he did then. It was kind of a strangled bellow as he seized either side of Ben's face and planted a firm kiss right on his lips. "That…*shit weasel,*" he cried, borrowing Anika's rather apt insult. "Ben, I hate to break it to you, but I'm already kind of rich. I don't want a penny from you! I loved you when you were serving me croissants!"

Kwen gasped, but Elias didn't dare take his eyes off Ben's hazel ones. For a good few seconds, Ben didn't move. Someone in the line huffed *'Americans.'* Then Ben licked his lips and blinked. "Y-you love me?"

Elias nodded. The more he said it, the more he realized it was true. "Yes. And it has nothing to do with this inheritance or anything. Of course it doesn't! The only relevance it could possibly have is that it finally brought us together. When I thought I'd lost you today, it was like my heart cracked clean in two. I *need* you, Ben. Not for anything you have, but for who *you* are."

Kwen sniffed and dabbed her own eyes with one of the tissues. "I tell you now," she said to Ben. "If you dunnae take him, I will."

Elias twitched a smile, but he still wasn't sure how Ben was feeling. "I've been falling for you for months," Elias said gently. "This past week has just shown me what I already knew. That you're the man for me."

Ben opened and closed his mouth. Elias could already imagine the protests he was working on. But then he finally spoke. "I really find it hard to believe someone like you would feel that way about me, *but*" -he added firmly when Elias made to interject- "all I know is that I don't want to be without you. You're amazing. I think this might be what love feels like. If that's the case…then maybe I can try working on the rest by other things. Slowly. But…if we want to be together, we should. Right? Nothing else matters."

Elias barked out a happy laugh, cupping Ben's face again to kiss him properly, then hug him close. "No, it really doesn't. So," he said, hardly daring to believe this was really happening. "Does that mean you won't be leaving? Can we let this very nice lady get back to her job?"

"Och, don't mind me," Kwen said with a laugh. "This is better than any telly I've seen lately. There're no urgent flights to check in yet." Some people in the line sounded like they disagreed, but if Kwen didn't care, then Elias didn't care.

Ben chuckled and wiped his eyes again. However, his face dropped once more. "I don't want to go," he said bitterly. "But Kenneth told me I had to leave the country tonight."

Elias shook his head. "He's got no power, remember? His contesting of the will has no legs. The house, the estate, the business, it's all yours to do with as you see fit. We could call the cops on him just for making those threats. He thinks we won't, but I'll have absolutely no hesitation."

"He said they wouldn't believe me over them," Ben mumbled miserably. His expression looked like he wanted to believe Elias, but was too afraid to.

Elias smiled and brushed a wayward curl back. "It'll be *us* against him. I'm sure Anika and Raj would help, too."

Ben frowned. "Really?"

Elias nodded. "Anika drove me here. There might be someone else waiting in her car as well. What do you say?" He waggled his eyes at Kwen, who looked to be holding her breath. "No fleeing the country tonight?"

Ben looked down, chewing his lip, apparently thinking. "Okay," he said eventually, looking back up. There was something shining in his eyes that Elias couldn't help but think was hope. "I trust you."

Those three words were almost as amazing as the other three words Ben had more or less said moments ago. But trust was just as important as love to Elias in a relationship. He knew they would fail before they even started without it.

Kwen whooped and clapped her hands, her glittery eyes shining. "Och, yous two have made my day. Now, off you trot. Go get this all sorted. And *you*, young man." She slid

Ben's passport over her desk and arched a single eyebrow threateningly. "Put that somewhere safe. Understood?"

"Yes, ma'am," Ben mumbled sheepishly, taking it from her and putting it in his pocket. Elias logged that was where it had gone, making a mental note to check before the next time they came back to this airport.

He held his hand out for Kwen to shake. "Thank you so much, ma'am," he said sincerely. "I hope you have a pleasant evening."

"I will now!" Kwen said with a chuckle, waving them off. "All right, next please! Can I take your passport?"

As they left the line, Elias took Ben's suitcase by the handle to wheel, letting him steer his carry-on, and hugged him tightly to his side. A couple of young women with multicolored hair gave them thumbs-up and wild grins from where they were waiting. Elias smiled back with a nod.

"I'm *so* glad I caught you," he murmured, feeling Ben sigh deeply against him as they walked. "Gazza must have driven you around the block once or twice so we could make it in time."

He chuckled but Ben frowned up at him. "He *did* say something about it being a slow journey."

"Mrs. Hollis got him to delay so we could catch up to you," Elias confessed. Ben's mouth dropped open in surprise, but Elias shook him gently where his arm was wrapped around his shoulders. "I told you, it was a team effort. Fuck Kenneth, honestly. There are people at Whittingar Abbey ready to *fight* for you, sweetheart."

Ben frowned, his eyes glassy, but he also smiled, looking at the shiny floor as they walked toward the short stay car park where Anika had promised she and Treacle would be waiting. "I want to fight for *them*," Ben said with a nod. "Anika said Kenneth had ruined people. I don't want that to happen to anyone again. I want it to be fair. I...I think that's maybe why Nancy left me everything. She hoped I'd be a neutral party?"

"I'll catch you up in the car, but yes, that's exactly what he's trying to do." Elias kissed the top of Ben's head, flushed with pride to hear him talk with such conviction. "I think you may be right about Nancy," he said warmly. Then he sighed. "It's entirely possible that there's a big fight coming. Whatever happens, I'll be by your side, okay?"

Ben turned his face to look anxiously up at Elias. "Are you mad I left without you? I wouldn't blame you if you were," he added hastily before Elias could answer. "But Kenneth only gave me fifteen minutes to get out. He said you could do what you liked. But if I didn't leave right then, I thought he'd do something awful-"

"Shh, shh," said Elias, interrupting to stop them in the middle of Departures and hug him tightly, chest-to-chest, and rub his back soothingly. "I understand. I really appreciate you looking out for me and the others. You have such a big heart, darling. It makes me furious that Kenneth took advantage of your kindness. But he won't get away with it."

Ben blinked up at him. "He won't?"

It wasn't like Elias to smirk, but much like shrieking, that seemed to be par for the course that afternoon. "Oh, baby," he purred. "No, he fucking won't. Now, can I *please* take you home? My bed has been cold without you."

Ben chuckled nervously, but he also ran his hands up Elias's chest. "You haven't been in it since we left it this morning, have you?"

Elias waggled his eyebrows. "No, but I have a hunch it's still been cold."

Ben rolled his eyes and laughed properly. "Oh my god," he said with a giggle. "Where did shy Elias go?"

"He remembered life's too damn short," Elias told him

sincerely, caressing the side of his face tenderly. "And he got a glimpse of what losing you might feel like today. He fucking hated it."

Ben laughed, but it was a timid sound. "You, uh, really love me, huh?"

Elias didn't want to be flippant, so he considered for a moment before he spoke. "I know it's fast. We're just at the start of this. But thinking I'd never get to hold you in my arms again was like I couldn't fully breathe. I *ache* for you, Ben Turner. I'm done second-guessing the age gap and my HIV status and everything else. There is no good reason we shouldn't be together, if that's what we want."

Ben closed his eyes and clenched his fists around the material of Elias's jacket. "I want that *so* badly."

For the first time in hours, Elias finally felt the last of his tension melting away. The panic was over. Everything was going to be okay. "Then let's go home. There's a roaring fire and snuggle times with our names on it."

Ben grinned, opened his eyes, and bit his lip. "Yes, there is," he agreed.

BEN

BEN WAS REALLY OVER ALL THE CRYING HE'D BEEN DOING THAT afternoon. However, as they approached the bright yellow car that apparently belonged to Anika, he realized he had a few more tears left in him after all.

Treacle's enormous ears popped up first, like swiveling satellite dishes, followed by his big fluffy snout. The second he caught sight of Ben and Elias through the window of the fancy sports car, he began barking his head off, jumping his back paws on the seat and scrabbling his front ones on the glass.

That broke Ben. Dogs didn't lie. That little fellow was so beyond excited to see Ben again. He'd definitely made a mistake abandoning Whittingar Abbey so soon. Ben whimpered and hugged Elias tighter, letting the tears fall as they approached the car. Anika jumped out from the other side and raced over to Ben with her arms thrown open.

"You are a *wanker!*" she declared as she pulled him away from Elias and hugged him fiercely.

Ben laughed and allowed her to rock him back and forth. "Thanks for the big dramatic rescue," he said sheepishly.

"Did Elias have to buy a ticket and chase you through security?" she asked, looking between them both.

"Sadly not," Elias admitted. He put Ben's suitcase and carry-on in the trunk and slammed it shut with a satisfied grin. "It was still pretty dramatic, though."

Anika slapped Ben on the back. "Raj will be disappointed, but it's still good to have you back, mate. I'm sorry Noah was such a wanker."

"It was more Kenneth, actually," said Elias darkly, coming around the car to hold Ben's hand. "I think something needs to be done about that."

"Let's plot on the road," Anika suggested, marching around to the driver's seat. Ben was still not getting used to it being on the wrong side of the car. "Traffic still looks good, but I don't trust it and I rather not get back home at midnight."

It was just after four o'clock. With any luck they'd be back at the cottage at six. What would happen after that, Ben wasn't sure. But with Elias by his side, he was confident it would turn out okay.

After they'd been barked at, jumped on, nibbled, and slobbered over by Treacle on their way inside the car, Ben and Elias managed to crawl into the cramped back seat. It was probably only meant for one person, but that was all right, because Elias seemed to want to keep Ben wrapped in his arms with Ben's legs draped over his lap.

"I'm not going anywhere," Ben promised, secretly loving the attention.

Elias nodded against his neck. "I know," he said. "Just making sure."

Anika stuck her fingers down her throat and made a retching noise, but then grinned at them both in the rearview mirror. "You guys are gross, you know?" She winked as she reversed out of the parking space. Treacle panted and generally looked pleased as punch with having the whole front seat to himself.

The drive back to Whittingar Abbey went surprisingly smoothly with only a little bit of traffic to slow them down. They didn't end up plotting anything, as Ben spend the whole journey dozing in Elias's arms. After all the adrenaline and emotions combined with the jetlag, he was exhausted. Elias stroked his hair and rubbed his side, occasionally murmuring sweet nothings and calling Ben his sweetheart. Ben wasn't sure he deserved any of that, but he didn't have the strength to fight it.

When he wasn't sleeping, Ben was musing on the particular way his heart was aching. This could very well be love, he reasoned, although reason and logic didn't seem to be playing much of a role in how he was feeling. It was as if with Elias he finally felt whole, even though he hadn't noticed anything had been missing before this trip. It was strange and terrifying but definitely quite wonderful, all at once.

Ben also knew he'd do anything to protect this feeling. Just like he'd do anything to protect Whittingar Abbey, whether his family wanted him to or not.

"Did Elias tell you about the kittens?" Anika asked suddenly as they got closer to the estate. She excitedly looked at Ben in the rearview mirror as he shook his head. "What? Tell him!"

Elias chuckled. "It turns out Luna wasn't fat. She was pregnant. We saw her giving birth."

"She had kittens!" Ben cooed. "That's amazing."

"No," Anika said impatiently. "You're telling it all wrong! Honestly – Ben. The runt of the litter wasn't going to make it but Elias wouldn't give up rubbing his little chest, and he woke up! Your boyfriend is a hero!"

"Oh, we haven't discussed labels-" Elias began, but Ben waved him quiet.

"It doesn't surprise me in the slightest that my *boyfriend* was kind and determined," he said, locking gazes with Elias.

Elias raised his eyebrows. "Are you sure?" he asked quietly. "I don't want you to feel pressured."

Ben huffed and blinked back the tears that were still there waiting to spill in an instant. "You rescued a god damned kitten. As if I couldn't love you anymore," he said, with only a fractional hesitation before using the 'L' word. It felt amazing to say that out loud like that. "So yes, I'm sure I want to be boyfriends."

"Grooooooss," Anika teased with a cackle from the front seat. But Ben was too busy kissing Elias to really mind.

Someone had left a few lights on in the cottage, so it looked warm and cozy when they pulled up a little while later. Anika helped them to clamber out from the back seat and haul Ben's suitcases out of the trunk then drag them down the woodland path. Elias couldn't seem to keep himself from constantly giving Ben little touches on his arms, his back, even his hair. Anticipation bubbled in Ben, like Champagne waiting to escape from the pressure of its bottle. He couldn't wait to get Elias alone again.

"Come on," Anika said to Treacle after she'd hugged Ben and Elias. "Let's leave these two lovebirds alone. We'll catch you later, yeah?"

"Thank you for everything," Elias said, offering her his hand. She scoffed, batted it aside, and threw her arms around him for another hug.

"I wasn't sure what to make of you guys, but I think Ben listened to my very wise words," she said as she and Treacle walked down the path back to her car.

"And what words were those?" Elias asked.

Ben and Anika shared a grin. *"Don't be a twat,"* they said in unison.

After Ben and Elias had waved them off, Elias took the suitcase handles once more and dragged them up to the front door, where he opened it for Ben. "I'm glad you didn't get on that plane," Elias said, ushering him inside, "for lots of reasons, obviously. But I think you left half of your stuff behind, and it was making me twitch."

He laughed while Ben blushed, looking around the living room and counting at least three things that he had indeed forgotten in his haste to flee the country. Ben hugged himself and looked at Elias through his eyelashes. "But I've got you to keep me in check now, haven't I?"

"Damn right."

Elias slipped his arms around Ben, kissing him softly. Ben had never been kissed so much in his whole life. He hadn't put much stock in it before, thinking it was just something you did to show you wanted to fuck. But with Elias, he would have been happy doing nothing else for hours.

"Why don't you take your things back upstairs?" Elias suggested after a while. "You can put your bags in my room, if you want?"

"Explode my mess all over your tidy space?" Ben asked incredulously.

But Elias just grinned. "Yes," he said firmly, rubbing Ben's arms and looking at him fondly. "You do that, and I'll get the fire going. Sound good?"

Ben stood on his tiptoes and pressed a light kiss to Elias's lips. "Sounds wonderful," he murmured.

After another couple of kisses, Ben broke off again, otherwise they'd never do anything else. Humming and smiling, he lugged his suitcase and carry-on up the stairs, doing as he was told and taking them to the master bedroom.

But when he opened the door, he let out a yelp then burst out laughing.

"Elias!" he called down the stairs. "You have to come see this!"

Tears of mirth were better than all the other ones Ben had experienced that day. He wiped them away so he could see Elias's reaction as he also entered the room.

"Oh dear *lord*," he cried, slapping his hands to his cheeks as he took in the state of the room, shaking his head.

There was wedding confetti all over the bed along with what looked like real red rose petals. Half a dozen flameless candles – the kind powered by batteries – were standing on the dresser and nightstands proving ambient lighting for the room. Also on the dresser was Champagne chilling in an ornate silver bucket, with two saucer glasses standing by it and a box of fancy-looking chocolates.

But the real kicker was the pump action bottle of intimate lubricant standing proudly on Elias's nightstand, as well as a box of condoms, and a pair of fluffy pink handcuffs.

"Mrs. *Hollis!*" Elias cried when he spied those, going beetroot as he covered his eyes.

"You think she did this?" Ben asked, laughing incredulously and picking up the lube bottle.

Elias snorted and lowered his hands again. "Anika and I left her here when we went to go get you. So, yes, that would be my guess."

Ben inspected the label on the lube appreciatively. It was high quality. "Good for Mrs. Hollis, the little minx," he said, grinning.

"No, stop," Elias said, waving his hands and laughing.

Ben waggled his eyebrows. "Make me."

The atmosphere changed on a dime. Elias stopped chuckling and flapping, instead focusing all his attention on Ben as he took a step forward. He was like a cat stalking its prey. Ben's heart fluttered and he swallowed as his mouth suddenly felt dry.

He never thought he'd get to experience this again. He tilted his chin up slightly, inviting Elias in as he closed the gap between them. Ben shivered as Elias cupped the side of his face and kissed him tenderly. As their mouths parted and their tongues stroked together, Elias slid his hand around Ben's back, splaying his fingers out and holding their bodies tightly together. Ben could feel his cock straining in his jeans, and he ground against Elias's thigh, showing him how much he wanted him.

Wordlessly and still kissing, they managed to walk the few steps back toward the bed, tumbling onto the mattress, sending the confetti and petals fluttering everywhere. Ben laughed as Elias pinned him down by straddling his hips. Then he plucked the lube he'd still been holding from Ben's hand that. He looked at it thoughtfully.

Ben could see some resignation behind his eyes, so he reached up and caressed Elias's cheek to bring his attention back to Ben. "Do you want to top me?" he asked simply.

Elias's mouth became a little 'o' of surprise. He looked between Ben and the lube. "We've got condoms," he said as if he was thinking out loud.

But Ben shook his head. "We don't have to use them, though."

Elias frowned and moved to lie down on the mattress so they were facing each other. Ben preferred being pinned down, but he appreciated that they were more equally situated like this. "Ben," he began tentatively, "are you sure?"

Ben linked their hands together and rested them over his heart. "I trust you when you say you're undetectable."

Elias bit his lip and nodded. "I have been for years," he said soberly. "I get regular checkups."

Ben pressed his lips against Elias's knuckles. "I want to do whatever is going to make you feel the most comfortable and confident. But I would really love for there to be nothing at all between us. If you're comfortable topping, that is? I could try it, but-"

"No, I'd love to," Elias said, resting their foreheads together.

Elias breathed deeply for a moment, perhaps considering what would make him feel best. The last thing Ben wanted was to trigger any unpleasant reactions for him. So his plan had been to lay out some options and ask directly for what he wanted. Now the decision was in Elias's hands.

"Sorry," Elias said, shaking his head.

"No," Ben countered immediately, rubbing the side of Elias's neck. "There's nothing to be sorry for. I might not have had a boyfriend before, but I'm good at talking through sex. It's so much better when everyone gets what they want out of it."

Elias closed his eyes and grimaced. "I want to go bareback so badly. It's been so long, and I want that with you, but there's a voice in my head saying I'm being irresponsible."

"Are you?" Ben asked. Elias knew far more about his HIV status than Ben did, after all. "I went to the clinic not long ago and everything came back fine. But if you want, we can hold off and go together."

Elias gritted his teeth and opened his eyes. They were blazing. "I want to make love," he said, gripping Ben's hand tightly. "I want to be a god damned man, not just my condition. I don't want to be having this clinical discussion when we could already be naked and slippery and breathless." Ben's heart skipped a beat as he let out a breath. Wow, yeah, he wanted that too. A lot. "I know I'm undetectable and that means I can't pass this on to you. Those are the facts."

"Then no condom," Ben said, holding the side of Elias's

face and looking him square in the eye. "I'm making the decision. I trust you."

Elias exhaled. Like Ben had hoped, taking the responsibility away from him seemed to have done the trick. "Okay," Elias said, nodding and managing a small smile.

Ben bit his lip, grinning and leaning in for a sweet kiss. "Don't get me wrong," he whispered, rubbing their noses together. "I still love shy Elias. But I wouldn't mind hot, commanding, sex-crazed Elias back from the airport. That guy looked like he could pin me down and give me a real good fucking."

Elias groaned and also bit Ben's lower lip, dragging it between his teeth. "I don't know what depths you pulled him out from. I've *never* felt this sexy with anyone, even when I was young, dumb, and full of cum."

It was Ben's turn to groan, rolling his hips against Elias's, finding the bulge between his legs. "Fill me with cum," he whispered.

There was a scramble as they shrugged their way out of their sweaters and T-shirts, kicking off their shoes and socks. Elias was wearing a belt, whereas Ben wasn't sure he even owned a belt, so they got him out of that together. Next it was their jeans.

Ben's fingers were fumbling with his fly when Elias batted his hands away and pushed Ben onto his back. Ben's heart skipped a beat and he felt perspiration appear in a wave over his body. Jesus Christ, Elias bossing him around was *seriously* hot. Ben watched as Elias gave him a devilish look, then began tracing kisses down his chest, pausing to suck one of his nipples.

"Oh, fuck," Ben gasped, already writhing under his touch. Elias held onto Ben's hips and Ben ran his hands through Elias's soft hair. Ben had felt anxious last time, comparing his soft tummy to Elias's hard abs, but now he didn't give a shit.

When Elias licked the slightly round bit just under his belly button and above his jeans, Ben whimpered in pleasure.

"You're so gorgeous," Elias rasped. He nuzzled his nose against Ben's erection through the denim, breathing through the material against his sensitive skin. "Tell me you're wearing another jockstrap."

Ben bit his lip and silently thanked his past self. "I wanted to be sexy for you," he admitted.

With a moan, Elias slipped his hands between the mattress and Ben's ass, squeezing hard. "You're always sexy, baby."

Ben's breathing was all fluttery, not quite getting enough air in his lungs and making him dizzy. He loved it. "So are you," he said, trying not to let his voice shake too much. "Did you like it when I ate you out before? When I stuck my tongue in your tight hole and kissed you?"

Elias growled and crawled up the bed, capturing Ben's lips for a filthy open-mouthed kiss. "I loved it, baby," he said. "I want you to do that before you fuck me for the first time, okay? Whenever you're ready. Not tonight. Tonight, I'm in charge. I want to take care of every tiny moment of your pleasure and hold you while I make us both come."

Ben could feel tears in his eyes. How many different kinds could he have in one day? He squeezed his eyes shut and gasped. "Holy shit," he uttered, digging his fingers into Elias's back. "I'll come in my jeans if you keep that up."

Elias bit his earlobe. "You'll come with my cock in your ass, gorgeous baby. Understood?"

"Elias, yes," whimpered Ben, grabbing his face to kiss him and rut their groins together. But Elias was on a mission, so he broke away and moved back down Ben's body. He made short work of the button on Ben's jeans, but then he took the zipper between his teeth, his gaze locked with Ben's as he dragged the fly downwards.

Ben didn't dare blink as he watched Elias kiss his hard dick through his cotton underwear, mouthing it and making it tingle with his hot breath. "Please," Ben begged, not sure what he was asking for other than 'more.'

Elias wrapped his fingers around the waistband of Ben's jeans and tugged them over his ass. Ben lifted his hips to help, then watched as Elias slide them the rest of the way down his legs, discarding them on the floor. He kissed his way back up the inside of Ben's thigh, gently stroking his cock through the cotton, teasing him. Then he squeezed the shaft, hard, making Ben gasp and groan.

"Turn over, gorgeous," said Elias, running his fingers along the elasticated fabric of Ben's jockstrap. "I want to fuck you into the mattress."

Ben was panting as he flipped, grabbing a pillow to shove under his head. While he did that, Elias retrieved the bottle of lube and squeezed a good amount onto his fingers. After that, Ben sort of lost track of everything that wasn't Elias rubbing his entrance and probing a single finger through the tight ring of muscle.

Ben used his breathing to help him relax, his hands grabbing fistfuls of the duvet and scrunching up whatever rose petals and little bits of confetti were still lying around. Elias laid himself against Ben's side, the denim of his jeans rough and delicious against Ben's goose-bumped skin. He kissed along Ben's shoulder and neck before seeking out his mouth. Ben looked at Elias through his eyelashes as he pushed his fingers inside, stretching Ben out.

"Like that," Ben said breathlessly, giving Elias little fluttery kisses on his lips. "Feels good, just like that."

Often, Ben didn't spend too much time prepping for anal, but that was generally with more confident and experienced tops. Not that Elias was coming across as nervous right now, but he'd said it had been a while and he used to bottom most of the time. Ben really loved the idea that they would switch roles in the bedroom. Topping didn't particularly interest him usually, but with Elias it was different. He wanted to do anything and everything to please his stunning lover, especially if he wanted to be eaten out beforehand. Ben had a feeling topping with Elias might be very fun indeed.

When Ben was feeling more relaxed, he reached back and pawed at Elias's jeans. "Get these off and fuck me, please," he said trying not to slur his words. But the cottage was so warm, and the candlelight dim. Ben felt such deep contentment after Elias had taken his time completely undoing all of the stress that had felt like it was going to destroy Ben earlier.

"Of course, darling," Elias said in his terrible attempt at a fancy British accent.

Ben snorted as Elias knelt up and began undoing his fly. "I don't think you know how funny and cute you are," Ben said. He wasn't sure why, but giving the compliment made him embarrassed. He blushed, so he turned his face into the pillow. Perhaps it was saying things like that out loud that made him realize he was admitting just how much he did love Elias. There was a vulnerability in acknowledging deep feelings like that.

Fingers gently caressed under his chin, encouraging him to turn his head and open his eyes. He was greeted by the sight of a naked Elias, leaning on all his knees and other hand, looking down at Ben, his cock hard, wet, and straining from lust that Ben had caused.

"Hello, beautiful," Elias said, smiling warmly. "You're helping me discover all kinds of things about myself. Don't hide away."

Ben sighed, gazing up at him adoringly. He would have found such behavior in himself nauseating with anyone else. But with Elias, it felt perfect.

"Okay," he promised.

Using more lube, Elias came up behind Ben and aligned the tip of his cock with his entrance, pushing inward. He lay on top of Ben, smothering him with his whole body as he pushed further inside him. Ben gasped and moaned, taking the slight burn from the intrusion and making it pleasurable, knowing it would soon fade. Elias intertwined the fingers on their right hands and kissed along Ben's neck and spine. His skin and hair were damp, dripping sweat onto Ben as they kissed and Elias bottomed out.

They breathed deeply in tandem, allowing Ben to relax. But Ben was used to this side of things. He wasn't sure how much Elias had topped in the past, if ever. "How does it feel?" he asked, grazing their noses and lips together.

"Fucking incredible," Elias replied breathlessly. Ben laughed, making Elias smile. "Oh, god, baby. You feel so good. It's like nothing else."

Ben leaned up to kiss him sensually, nipping at his mouth and rubbing their stubbled chins. "You feel amazing, too. You can move, I'm okay."

Elias nodded, kissing Ben's lips once more before pushing himself up slightly to draw back and plunge inside Ben again.

Ben wailed, taking much joy in knowing they were in the middle of nowhere and could be as loud as they liked. Living with his folks still meant he always had to go to the other guy's place or make out in a car or restroom. Feeling like this was 'their' bed and there wasn't anyone else around for almost a mile made him feel even more relaxed and content.

He jerked suddenly as Elias shifted his angle and found Ben's prostate as he was speeding up his thrusts. "There, there, there!" Ben cried, rutting his ass back to meet Elias stroke for stroke. However, it wasn't long before Elias pinned his hips down and started fucking him hard and fast.

Ben could have easily come like that, but Elias's

enthusiasm was at a new high. "On your back, baby," he gasped, slipping out and moving to the side to free Ben's legs. Ben immediately did as he was told. As soon as he flipped over Elias was yanking his jockstrap down, flinging it across the room where it got caught on a drawer handle, much to Ben's delight, then hoisting Ben's ankles over his shoulders.

Ben's cock bounced on his belly as Elias shoved his way back inside Ben. Wordlessly, they both leaned in at the same time for a kiss, then Elias grabbed Ben's thighs and started plowing into him.

Ben groaned as Elias lifted his hips off the bed to get a better angle. Ben seized the bedsheets to try and give him some purchase, staring into Elias's eyes the whole time, the both of them grunting as they thrust together again and again. It was messy and sticky and ungainly and Ben fucking loved every second of it.

"I'm going to come," Elias managed to utter as their timing went off. Ben tried to go limp, allowing Elias to use his body so he could climax. With a bellow, Elias buckled forward as his orgasm washed over him. Ben panted, watching with delight as Elias shook, regaining his senses after such a high.

Ben had done that. He wasn't sure if it was right or wrong to feel proud, but he did anyway. He wanted Elias to be happy more than anything. He deserved it.

With a final gulp of air, Elias shuddered and rolled his neck, glistening as he grinned down at Ben. "Your turn," he said mischievously.

He pulled his softening cock out of Ben's tender ass, moved back, then swallowed Ben's length all the way down his throat in one flawless move. Ben yelled and bucked, but Elias held his hips down in a way Ben was becoming quickly addicted to.

It didn't take long. Ben was tired and emotional and so

turned on he could have shattered into a thousand pieces. Elias's hot mouth, lips, and tongue were heaven on his sensitive cock, but watching his beloved Elias pleasuring him was what really tipped him over the edge.

"Elias!" He managed to shout in warning, but Elias didn't seem to care. He just kept swallowing again and again as Ben's orgasm hit, coming down his throat hard and fast. He dropped back onto the mattress, feeling boneless as Elias eased off, taking the time to kiss and lick Ben's shaft as it softened.

Finally, on shaking limbs, Elias crawled back up the bed and flopped beside Ben, wrapping him in his arms like he had when they'd awoken on the couch together the day before. Ben sighed, pretty sure he'd never felt this safe and loved in his whole life.

"That was beyond incredible," Elias mumbled against his neck.

Ben stroked his back and kissed his temple. "Completely," he agreed. "Thank you."

Elias blinked and lifted his head to look him in the eye. "For what?"

"For trusting me," said Ben simply.

Elias's lips were red and swollen, his hair sticking up in clumps, and his face blotchy as he smiled back at Ben. It was possibly the most beautiful he'd ever looked. "Thank you for trusting me, too," he said.

They held each other tightly, and Ben knew in his heart, no matter what, they were going to be okay.

22

ELIAS

"So…what happens now?"

Elias lifted his head and looked down at Ben. They had migrated from the bedroom to the living room via the bathroom. Another thing Elias had forgotten he used to love was showering with a boyfriend. Even if it was in a poky little bathtub with a flimsy curtain and water that flashed cold every now and again without warning. Showering with someone was intimate without having to have penetrative sex, which since his diagnosis had been the kind of intimacy Elias had preferred. Or it used to.

He was pretty relaxed after that spectacular fuck, he had to say.

But he reveled in being able to wash Ben after the day they'd both had. Massaging conditioner through his hair and running a soapy pouf over his boyfriend was deeply sensual without chasing the high of an orgasm. Ben had confessed that he'd had awkward fumblings in showers before, but never just taken the time to wash a lover.

Elias's body was no longer his enemy. It was a proud and loyal warrior, and he felt that most with Ben's hands caressing their way all over it, washing away all the stress and the worry and the fear they'd put themselves through in the past twenty-four hours. It had been a roller coaster for sure.

But Elias had wanted to take a moment for himself to reflect. For both of them to have the time to reflect, but especially taking time for himself, which he hadn't historically been very good at. He wanted to be proud, though, that he'd moved past the terror that had been holding him back from sex, and was in a stronger place now. Ben had been patient and understanding, and making the decision about the condom had allowed Elias to trust the facts and ask for what they both wanted.

To be as close as two human beings could possibly be together.

And he'd done it topping. If his twenty-something self knew that one day Elias Solomon would feel amazing in a reversed roll, he probably wouldn't have believed it. That was the power Ben had over him, he guessed. And he hoped he did the same for Ben.

They were stronger together.

Elias hadn't had a chance to get the fire going before Ben had discovered Mrs. Hollis's delicious little surprise. They were going to have to send her flowers or something for that, Elias was determined. But once they'd pulled some sweats on, Elias had been on a mission to light the grate. He'd become obsessed with the idea of curling up in front of a roaring fire as much as they could while they were still staying at the cottage.

While he'd been poking the logs, Ben had slipped away into the kitchen. Apparently, the rose petals and lubricant hadn't been Mrs. Hollis's only sneaky gift. Ben had squealed in delight when he'd discovered the cupboards had been replenished with a reasonable number of baking supplies. In a matter of minutes, he'd managed to whip up some kind of chocolate cakes in mugs using the microwave which were insanely delicious. The man really did have a talent. More than one, if Elias recalled from their bedroom adventures so far.

Cake with hot tea and blankets on the sofa had made for a seriously good snuggle. Elias had felt himself just dozing off when Ben had asked his question. "What do you mean?" Elias asked, gently brushing back a clean, damp curl from Ben's forehead. "What happens now with us?"

Ben blushed and looked away for a second. "Not really," he admitted. "I'm feeling pretty good about that, shockingly. I figured we'd just try dating and spending time together – that's what couples do right?"

Elias's heart felt like it glowed with warmth from within his chest. "That's what I want, for sure," he said, capturing Ben's fingers to plant a little kiss on them. "To just be a normal, regular couple."

"There's nothing normal or regular about you," Ben said with a laugh, caressing the side of Elias's cheek, but he didn't really understand.

"Ahh," said Elias, knowing he sounded bitter-sweet. "But that's all I wanted for so long after my diagnosis. To be 'normal.' And I thought there would be something wrong with an age gap relationship, but now I see that was just my stupid hang-ups."

Rather than laugh or tell him he was stupid, Ben regarded Elias with sympathy and kindness. "I still maintain that you're extraordinary," he said, laying a hand over Elias's chest. "But no, there's nothing abnormal about two people being in love."

They kissed leisurely with no aim of going anywhere with it. Just for the pleasure of kissing. It was a perfect moment that Elias would bottle up forever to keep in his heart. But he wasn't done taking care of Ben that evening yet.

"So what did you mean?" he asked after a while.

Ben fiddled with the end of one of the blankets. "What happens now with the house? Kenneth? I'd be lying if I said I wasn't scared shitless of him. I thought I was going to piss my pants before."

It would have been tempting to lose his temper, but the person Elias was mad at wasn't there. So instead he kissed Ben's forehead and rubbed his back. "He's just a bully and I eat those for breakfast, I promise."

Ben chewed his lip and considered Elias for a second. "Please don't take this the wrong way," he said, worrying Elias immediately. However, he needn't have fretted. "But," Ben continued, "I want to stand up for myself."

Elias smiled as warm pride flooded through him. "Hell yeah," he said, meaning it. "In which case, I'll help you work on some things and be there by your side, one hundred percent. But you're right. It's your fight, and you can win it. I believe in you."

Ben took a big breath in, grinning. "That feels so good to hear, thank you. I love my parents, I really do, but they're both very much about not rocking the boat, even if the other person is in the wrong. I grew up believing that for so long. But" -he kissed the tip of Elias's nose and grinned at him- "someone recently told me several times that life's too short."

"It damn well is," Elias growled, kissing Ben on the lips. Ben hummed and wriggled deliciously in Elias's arms.

"It's not just about me with this, though," Ben explained. "There are so many other people involved. It's kind of easier to fight for them than just myself, you know?"

Elias did. That was his whole career, after all.

He'd explained Raj's situation to Ben while they'd been drying off after their shower. They were now aware of his particular predicament, but if Kenneth was used to dangling people's inheritance over them like the Sword of Damocles, there could be others he was making just as miserable. Elias had been thinking about it, and he was pretty sure that could very well be another reason Nancy had wanted to give control of the estate to an outsider. Maybe she'd hoped that her long-lost great-grandson would be fairer than her son.

Elias nodded and went to assure Ben that he wasn't on his own, when he remembered something. "Oh, damn. I texted Anika asking what she was planning on doing with regards to the family while I was stoking the fire. I wonder if she replied."

He reached for his phone where it had been resting on the coffee table. Earlier, he'd gently nudged Ben until he'd remembered to plug his in. For someone who almost never left the house without a hundred percent battery, seeing how low Ben's was all the time gave Elias anxiety.

Elias frowned as he read Anika's reply text. "Oh. It says-" There was an urgent knock at the door. He raised his eyebrows at Ben. "-that she's on her way over. That was a bit freaky."

Ben shrugged as he untangled them from the numerous blankets so they could go answer the door. "We're coming! We're coming!" he called out with a chuckle as the banging came again.

Anika had her fist raised to knock once more when they opened the door. She arched an eyebrow at them. "Oh, excellent. I was worried you'd started shagging again with all that yelling about coming."

"Oh my god," said Elias, covering his eyes as Ben laughed.

"Not yet," he said, waggling his eyebrows just as Elias lowered his hand again. "Do you want to come in? It's cold."

"Thanks, but we haven't got long," Anika said as she wiped her feet on the doormat and stepped inside. Over her shoulder she had something slung – it looked to be two suit bags.

"What's going on?" Ben asked, looking at Elias. But he had to admit he was equally in the dark.

Anika huffed and laid the suit bags over the arm of the sofa with a flick of her arm. "In a word: mutiny. Kenneth has called a big family dinner. People are coming in from London and other places again."

"The ones who only just left after the funeral?" Elias questioned. He was aware that the party that had been around since his and Ben's arrival was not the entire Grimaldi de Loutherbergh clan.

Anika nodded. "Precisely. My aunt Josephine is getting the Eurostar from *Paris* for crying out loud. I think Kenneth is confident he scared you off, Ben, and is declaring victory."

"Which is legally preposterous, but whatever," Elias grumbled. He wasn't a violent man by nature, but he had to flex his hands as he longed to grab Kenneth and shake some sense into him. What a greedy, corrupt, and spiteful man.

"Exactly," agreed Anika. She placed her hands on her hips over her coat and looked between Ben and Elias. "But two can play that game. How do you feel about a little *coup d'etat?*"

"You want to overthrow Kenneth?" Ben asked uncertainly.

Elias shrugged and rubbed Ben's back. "Technically, he's the one staging the coup. Your great-grandmother couldn't have been clearer about leaving the estate and business to you. You're just defending what's rightfully yours. All of yours," he amended, nodding at Anika.

"That's just it," said Anika. "Ben, when you talk about being fair to the family, I know you mean the ones still living. Kenneth is completely obsessed with our ancestry and, somewhat ironically, I'm pretty sure it will be our undoing if he's not stopped. I mean, you've seen the state of the house, it's practically falling down. And from what I can tell from online research, the cider business isn't faring much better." She rubbed her mouth and shook her head. "It's so frustrating watching it all fall apart and not being able to do anything."

"So I go and challenge him," said Ben, looking petrified but holding his head high. Elias took his hand to hold. "This ridiculousness needs to be put to a stop. He's holding people hostage by hoarding all the money for himself, like Smaug the dragon on his pile of gold. And you're right. It's not as if he's investing it wisely. What's he even doing with all these millions?"

"I'd love to think it was something interesting like a sex dungeon or an outrageous smack habit," grumbled Anika, "but it's probably just sitting in an account in the Cayman Islands for him to stroke all the pretty numbers when he gets bored."

The savageness in her voice seemed to give Ben a burst of strength. He stood up just that bit taller. Elias felt a rush of pride. Like Ben had said, he should fight for himself. But that didn't mean Elias couldn't be right next to him, cheering from the sidelines.

"I say," Elias suggested, "that we head over and inform Kenneth that if he doesn't stop this nonsense immediately, we'll begin legal action. We probably should have done that from the start."

Anika shrugged. "You were trying to be amicable. Fuck that now. He's declaring war." She pointed at the suit bags on the sofa. "You'll need to change. This is a proper family affair, so that means posh as fuck. If you want these people to take you seriously, you have to speak their language, and that means bling."

Ben blanched. "I don't have any bling," he mumbled. *Urgh.*

Elias hated how that was his Achilles heel. It took only a split second to have him feeling like he wasn't good enough again.

But Anika grinned. "That's why your fairy godmother is here. You *shall* go to the ball!" She waved her hand at the sofa. "I've labeled the bags. You have a suit each and all the trimmings. They're Alexander McQueen and they're only rented, so for the love of *god* don't spill anything on them, or I'll cry."

Elias's jaw dropped open. "How did you find us McQueen at such short notice?"

Anika winked, then spun around to head toward the door again. "Darling, I'm just that fabulous I'm afraid. Now – can you meet Raj and me by the service entrance in half an hour?"

Ben nodded. "Luckily, we just showered," he said proudly.

"I know, sweetie," Anika said with a grin. "The place stinks of sex. You boys are terrible." She blew them a kiss and pulled the door open as Elias and Ben blushed in embarrassment. "Half an hour!" she barked. "Looking pretty! Chop chop!"

And with that, she was gone.

Elias turned to Ben as he rubbed his face and took a deep breath. "Fuck," Ben said, looking at Elias with a weak smile.

But Elias shook his head and stepped over to hug him tightly. "Nope. None of that. You're in the right. You've got this, baby. Now let's get glammed up. I *would* be scared of being late for Anika. But not of Kenneth. He's a dinosaur."

Ben chuckled with a hint of glee in his eyes that gave Elias a thrill. "Then let's go be meteors."

"That's my boy," said Elias.

It looked like they were both warriors now.

23

BEN

IT WAS AS IF THEY WERE WALKING INTO BATTLE. BEN TRIED TO remain positive, but he didn't have much experience in managing his adrenaline. Elias looked perfectly calm as they walked up to the dirt track from the cottage. Ben supposed he'd had countless appearances in court to harden his confidence. Ben had barely even been in a school play. He had nothing like that to fall back on to calm his nerves.

But he had Elias.

He could do this – he *wanted* to do this – and knowing Elias was with him might mean he'd actually succeed.

Kenneth's reign was over.

Ben wasn't sure when his great-uncle had started calling the shots, presumably when Nancy's heath had begun fading over the last decade or two. But it was clear that Whittingar Abbey and the Grimaldi de Loutherberghs were in need of saving from him, and that had been Nancy's intention in giving Ben everything. She had trusted him with her family, their lives, their *legacy.*

Ben wasn't going to let her down, nor himself. He could do this. After all, he had the man he loved standing shoulder to shoulder with him, giving him strength he never knew he could possess.

"Are you feeling okay?" Elias asked as they crunched up the driveway from the sanctuary of their cottage toward the main house. He squeezed Ben's hand and gave him a tight smile.

"I think so," Ben replied, thinking the more times he said it out loud, the truer it would be. "The armor helps."

Anika hadn't been kidding when she'd said she'd gotten them Alexander McQueen. Ben had only had one off-the-rack suit in his life for going to proms and homecoming dances. He'd just changed the corsage and tie each time. It had been obvious that Elias was impressed with the designer alone, but when Ben had actually seen the suits Anika had picked for them, he'd gasped. She'd even gotten their measurements right. It was like witchcraft.

Elias was wearing a white jacket with a black open-collar shirt and pants. The jacket had a random black pattern on it that had taken Ben a moment to realize was broad paintbrush strokes. Ben would have thought that would have looked tacky, but it was utterly cool. His own suit was a more classic black three-piece with a white shirt. The jacket and pants had a subtly embroidered asymmetric pattern that ran from his left shoulder to his right hip, depicting a flock of butterflies. Along with the suits, Anika had provided shined shoes, pocket handkerchiefs, cufflinks, and a pair of watches that were probably worth more than Ben's yearly salary, if not much more. It was all on loan, but that still didn't stop Ben from feeling like a million bucks.

Elias looked stunning, but that hadn't exactly been surprising. As far as Ben was concerned, he looked gorgeous in everything. What had genuinely been a bit of a shock was when Ben had looked in the mirror at himself.

He looked like an *adult*. Not a boy playing dress-up in his dad's clothes. But a grown man.

It helped Ben to step out of the door with determination, his shoulders rolled back. It was strange, but the fact that the suit was slightly flamboyant – in other words, a little gay-looking by some people's standards – actually gave Ben more confidence. He might have been given a boost by the expensive watch and cufflinks, not to mention the threads. But declaring that yes, he was gay, and proud to be there with his boyfriend, was actually pretty empowering.

He would have thought that blending in more would have made him feel better able to face people so above his class status. But funnily enough, being authentically himself was giving him far more of a backbone.

It seemed he wasn't the only one.

"Oh, brilliant, you're bang on time," Anika said happily as they approached the service entrance that would lead them into the house via the kitchen and old servants' quarters. It probably wasn't an appropriate route for the supposed heir to the family fortune, but as Anika had said, right now they were staging a coup.

Much like Ben and Elias, Anika and Raj looked ready for battle. Despite the cold, Anika was wearing the most beautiful black-and-blue lace sari with a matching shawl over one shoulder. Her wrists jangled with about twenty silver bangles each. She wore a detailed hoop on one side of her nose and a sort of necklace on her head with the pendant lying perfectly on her forehead. She looked like a Bollywood star, just like her mom.

Equally, Raj was wearing a long cream jacket with pink rose petal design, a black T-shirt, silk cream baggy pants, and a large statement gold necklace. Ben wasn't sure if it was the gorgeous clothes making him glow, or if something else had brightened his smile. But he was looking like Ben was feeling.

An upgraded version of himself.

All four of them were choosing to celebrate what made them different from the rest of the family, and embrace that with pride.

"Those suits," Raj gushed. "You did such a great job, *Anika-didi.* Give us a twirl!"

Ben laughed as he spun around. "So what's the plan?" he asked once they had finished admiring each other's ensembles.

Anika took a deep breath and nodded, tapping her phone against her palm before slipping it somewhere inside her sari. "Honestly? I think just going inside, showing that you – *we're* – still here, and that nothing has changed.

"I checked in with the solicitors again while we were getting changed," Elias said, sharing a knowing look with Ben, who was aware of this already. "It's impossible to get anyone on the phone there, but they finally got back to me. Apparently, they're aware of Kenneth's complaint, but as one of their partners was present when Nancy made the changes to her will, they're fully confident of her mental capacity. They assured me she knew exactly what she was doing."

"So Kenneth hasn't got a leg to stand on," said Anika hopefully.

"Unless they can prove Ben somehow influenced her decision," Elias said with a shrug. "But considering he didn't even know she existed until less than two weeks ago, after she had passed, I'd say that was also a flimsy defense at best."

"He's doing what he always does," said Raj grimly. "Trying to bully everyone into following him."

Anika nodded in agreement. "To be fair, he *is* very good at that." She looked around the small group. "None of this will matter if they all still support him. We need them on our side, or nothing's going to really change." She took her brother's hand and gave him a sympathetic look. Raj inhaled, then nodded firmly.

"It has to change," he announced. "Time to bring this family into the next century."

Ben clapped Raj's shoulder, then took Elias's hand, so they were all connected. "Then let's do this."

His insides trembled with the last of his nerves as they walked through the ordinary-looking door into the depths of the kitchen. It felt totally different filled with people running around and shouting. Dozens of pans were bubbling and simmering away as the many staff prepared food for the family.

"It's a buffet spread," Anika explained, "not a formal dinner as it was all so last minute. Everyone should just be sort of milling around." She fixed Ben with a look. "Brace yourself," she said, taking his hand and giving it a squeeze. "There's a hell of a lot of them, now. But I think – I *know* – once they understand that you're here to protect us, they'll get on board."

"They're just used to Kenneth and his overlord ways," Raj agreed. "They don't know there could be another way."

Ben took a final deep breath as they walked down a corridor he hadn't been down before, the sound of conversation rising as they approached a set of double doors. Anika squeezed his hand again, then let him go, and Elias leaned over to give him a tender kiss on the cheek.

It was the final push of courage he needed. He was ready. Time to stand his ground. They opened both the doors, all four of them entering side-by-side.

Anika hadn't been wrong about the family hanging around, in a way.

They were having a ball.

For the second time in two days, Ben found himself

standing at the threshold of a large room filled with dozens and dozens of people. This room was twice the size of the one with all the stag antlers, with a high, arching ceiling, crossed swords mounted over shields hanging from the walls, many enormous portraits of proud-looking men, and blazing chandeliers. Chairs had been pushed to the edge of the room, but most people were standing and talking, taking glasses of Champagne from silver trays floating around on waiters' hands.

"Oh, for *heaven's* sake," the portly cigar man snarled a few feet away from them. Several people around him were engulfed in his pungent cloud of smoke. Ben didn't recognize them as they tilted their heads to look in confusion at him after cigar man's scorn. As Ben's nerves fluttered, his eyes flicked over the crowd, seeing Anika had been right. Everyone was done up in tuxedos and ballgowns. The four of them didn't look overdressed at all. Although, their styles were certainly out of place in the sea of more traditional formalwear.

"Here we go," Ben muttered. He hoped he'd been quiet enough that only his three friends had heard him as more heads began to turn. It was like a ripple traveling through the room, as a hundred or so people gradually fell silent, one-by-one. Classical music continued playing over a sound system, saving them from completely awkward silence.

Near the front of the throng, Rochelle's skinny mom covered her mouth, looking horrified. Her heavily beaded dress looked like it was going to drag her fragile frame to the floor if she wasn't careful. Rochelle herself was wearing a loud pink cocktail dress, her wild hair in a messy bun. She blatantly took a photo of the foursome on her phone, snickering gleefully as she swigged from a tumbler of whiskey.

"Well, really, Harold," Mildred huffed, addressing her

husband as well as the fussy-looking middle-aged women clumped around her. "I thought we were done with this silly business. Weren't we done with this silly business?"

Harold inspected the sandwiches on the plate he was holding. "No, I think they're crab, Mildred."

Ben felt dizzy, but then Elias's hand slipped against the small of his back, and he found a puddle of courage somewhere in his expensive shoes. He dredged it up, like water from a well. He was an ally to most people in this room, whether they knew it or not.

A low buzz of chatter was starting to fill the room again over the music, and although people were still looking their way, they also starting glancing at one another and whispering behind their hands. Elias moved away again, although Ben wished he could have kept his hand on his back. He was probably trying not to cause a scene before they'd even started, though.

"Bugger me sideways," Noah said with a cackle as he all but skipped up to the quartet. "I though Kenneth had scared you off. This is hilarious."

"Not really," said Elias dryly as Ben scowled at Noah. He couldn't help but feel like he'd been hoodwinked by the handsome young Brit.

Before they could speak any further, another hush filled the room in a second.

This time, someone cut the music.

In the silence that followed, everyone's eyes snapped back toward the quartet, but now they were wide. Almost fearful. A chill ran down Ben's spine.

"I see," a menacing voice drawled from behind them.

Ben and Elias immediately sprung to one side as Anika and Raj leaped to the other. It took Ben a moment to realize that their united front had just been divided. Kenneth was standing in the middle of the open double doors in a black three-piece suit and cravat, looking like he was about to attend another funeral. His cold, dead eyes traveled over Ben and Elias, then the Bhat siblings, a nasty smile curling over his yellow teeth.

"How amusing."

Clasping his hands behind his back, he strolled leisurely into the ballroom, every single pair of eyes locked on him. You could hear a pin drop as he reached the front of the throng and slowly turned on the spot. He was now the head of the crowd, all of them facing off with the four outsiders. Noah seemed to realize this divide too, and nipped back to align himself with Kenneth and the rest of the Grimaldi de Loutherberghs.

"I thought I made it perfectly clear what would happen if you remained on my property, Mr. Turner." Kenneth fixed Ben with a glare, but his demeanor was calm, like he wasn't upset in the slightest. In fact, there was a quiet glee radiating off him, like he was excited by what might come next.

Ben wanted to be sick. Elias had seemed so sure that Kenneth couldn't do all the terrible things he'd said, but in that moment, it was difficult for Ben to imagine this despicable man couldn't do anything he wanted.

"Well, technically, this *isn't* your property, is it, Uncle Kenneth?" Anika said, placing her hands on her hips. The four of them were able to move closer together again now Kenneth had passed between them, giving Ben a little reassurance. "It never was and it never will be, and that's why you're so cross."

"What do you know about it, silly girl?" one of the relatives snapped from the crowd that had knitted closer together behind Kenneth. Kenneth smirked at the comment, but Anika didn't flinch.

Ben was doing this for her and Raj as much as anyone. He rallied himself.

"Yes, you were perfectly clear," Ben said, projecting his voice as best he could. He wanted everyone to be able to hear this. "You said that you would burn down Whittingar Abbey rather than let me inherit it."

A collective gasp rose up from the crowd and a flurry of murmured voices traveled through the room. Kenneth laughed. "Utter poppycock," he announced. "If I ever said such a thing, it was obviously in jest."

"Yes, because you're famous for your sense of humor," Anika said pleasantly in a way that undoubtedly read as sarcastic. Was it Ben's imagination, or did several people in the crowd nod in agreement with her?

"Of course he wouldn't do that – *would he?*" people were murmuring.

"You weren't joking," Ben said firmly, anger bubbling in him. God, he'd been so terrified yesterday, when he had fled the house. Kenneth didn't get to pretend that had never happened. "You were threatening me. Just like you threatened to ruin my employer back in the US. And threatened other people's inheritance and livelihoods in this very room. And then you made *explicit* threats to cut off my friend Elias's life-saving medication. Or was I wrong? Were all of those just jokes, too?"

People in the crowd were frowning and shifting uncomfortably on their feet. Ben had a feeling that reminding them that Kenneth was wielding their financial security against them might curry some favor. But maybe some of them were kind-hearted enough to hear the way his voice cracked when he mentioned Elias's medication and insurance being in jeopardy. To Ben, that and the potential destruction of Rise and Shine were the worst offenses. But he was also sure there were people among the throng that were in perilous or miserable situations thanks to Kenneth, just like Raj was.

"I find you very tiresome," Kenneth said with a sigh, turning away. "Get out now, and I *might* forget this all happened."

"*No,*" Ben snapped, trying not to let the adrenaline pumping through him make him dizzy. Kenneth stopped halfway between turning away completely, then glared at Ben from the corner of his eye. Ben wanted to hold Elias's hand, but just knowing he was there beside him was enough to help him go on. "Nancy named me as her heir in her will and you know there's nothing you can do to change it. And unlike you, I want what's *best* for this family. Not for them to be scared of me!"

The reactions around the room were varied. Some people gasped or tutted or shook their heads. But some frowned in consideration. Was Ben getting through to them?

"How preposterous," Mildred said with a haughty chuckle. "Isn't it, Harold?"

For once, Harold said nothing.

Kenneth sighed and turned back around to face Ben once more. "This is extremely tedious. A child playing a part, trying to negotiate business with the adults."

To Ben's surprise, his words did nothing to him. Even yesterday, they would have been devastating. But thanks to Elias, he now knew they weren't true. He *was* an adult, and he wasn't going to put himself down anymore.

"You had one chance to run off with your tail between your legs," Kenneth continued. "It's not my fault idiocy obviously runs in your particular vein of the family. No bother. I shall be calling immigration services to have your visa revoked with immediate effect. You'll never set foot in this country again."

"Actually," Elias said cheerfully. "Ben qualifies for an ancestry visa, as his grandfather was British. He could move here indefinitely if he wanted to."

Kenneth looked like he'd sucked on a lemon. "This is *our* estate, *our* family. We will not be cowed by outsiders!"

"Foreigners, you mean," said Raj, nodding sagely. "Yes, we know how you feel about them, Uncle Kenneth."

"Oh for heaven's sake," he snarled. "Not this again. Your mother has always been welcomed here."

"Because she's highborn, rich and famous," said Anika coolly.

"Look, I'm not here to take anything from anyone," said Ben fiercely. "Quite the opposite. I intend to honor my great grandmother's wishes and see that everyone and everything are looked after. Starting with this sad, neglected house. It doesn't look like it's had an ounce of love given to it in a generation, if not two."

That got the attention of several people. "You'd change the house?" Rochelle's mom asked, clutching her boney chest.

"No, Mum," said Rochelle by her side. "He's saying he *wouldn't* burn it down. Which, personally, gets my vote." She gave Ben a thumbs up, and even though he couldn't really tell if she was being snarky or not, he chose to take it as a sliver of support.

He shook his head. "Not change, restore. It's gorgeous, but everything is threadbare, faded, and chipped." He threw an accusatory glare at Kenneth. "You say I'd waste the family fortune. But what exactly have *you* been doing with it?"

"Keeping the estate afloat," Kenneth snarled.

"Badly," Anika added, her arms folded and her chin in the air. "And that makes it extra obscene that you've been withholding funds and promising to leave people penniless if they don't live how you want them to. You've been doing a pretty poor job of that yourself."

"Oh god, Anika, give it a rest," said Noah, rolling his eyes. "You don't know what you're talking about."

"I've got more of a clue than you, you leach," she shot

back. "Just because you're his pet favorite now, doesn't mean he wouldn't drop you in a flash."

Noah scoffed, looking at Kenneth. But Kenneth didn't look back at him, and Noah's smug look wavered.

Instead, Kenneth's eyes slid to Raj, who only flinched slightly. "It is *my* responsibility to protect the reputation of this noble family when others would see it torn to shreds. British aristocracy is a dying breed! We have to defend our heritage!"

"By making people miserable?" Ben asked, shaking his head. "Why are you the one who gets to say what's acceptable in the twenty-first century, anyway?"

"Because we live or die by our traditions!" Kenneth bellowed, his fists balled. "I wouldn't expect a filthy American to understand. This is so far beyond your comprehension, *boy.*"

"Just like his grandfather," Barnaby sneered. It was strange to see him without his musket perched over his shoulder, but Ben was sure it couldn't be too far away. "An utter disgrace. At least Thomas knew when to abandon ship and preserve a little dignity."

This was the part of the confrontation that Ben had been dreading. He looked between Noah and Kenneth, raising his hands and nodding. "I know my grandfather let you all down," he said, with sincere regret. "I know he bankrupted your family, Noah, and disgraced the Grimaldi de Loutherberghs. But I was never aware of any of that. I'm not him, I swear." He felt like he was betraying the memory of his beloved grandpa, but he had to admit to his mistakes.

Or did he?

"No!" a pitiful voice screeched out. There was a murmur of surprise through the crowd, and they began parting. *"No!* I will not hear it! Not *one* more time!"

"Granny?" Anika said in surprise as, sure enough, small,

fragile-looking Elizabeth pushed her way to the front of the throng, clutching her ruby necklace as always. Anika shared a confused look with Raj, who shrugged, apparently equally as in the dark.

"Lizzy," said Kenneth. Ben was shocked to hear the fury contained in that one word. His fists had clenched and his usually dead eyes were blazing with anger. "This is *not* appropriate."

But Elizabeth stopped pawing her rubies and brandished a trembling fist at him instead. Kenneth blinked and took a step back. "Enough! For fifty years, I've stayed quiet!" she screeched. "After all, there was nothing I could do to undo it, was there? But you *broke* your mother's heart, and I won't have you ruin this strong young man's life as well!"

Ben was a little taken aback at being called strong. He wasn't used to that. But he supposed he was, in a way.

"Lizzy, calm down," said Barnaby impatiently.

"I won't have it from you, either!" she snapped, tears running down her face.

Anika stepped forward and wrapped her arm around her grandmother's shoulders, so Raj followed to hold her hand on the other side. "What are you talking about, Granny?" Anika asked her softly.

Elizabeth produced a lace handkerchief from up the sleeve of her bejeweled dress and dabbed her eyes. "Thomas and I were always close, you know?" she told her and the rest of the room. "He was different. *Delicate,*" she added pointedly. Her face crumbled as she scowled at Kenneth. "You could *never* stand how close he was with your mother. So you discovered his secret and threatened to send him to *jail!* Your own brother!"

Ben covered his mouth, feeling sick. He was starting to suspect what Elizabeth was trying to say.

"No, no," said Noah, stepping forward and shaking his

hands. "He and my grandfather were in business, and Thomas gambled it all away. That's right, isn't it, Kenneth?"

But Kenneth didn't answer. He was glowering at Elizabeth.

"Oh, your grandfather bankrupted his own damn self on the horses," she snapped at Noah. "That was just a convenient excuse to chase Thomas away. Your grandfather was in on the whole scheme, along with Kenneth and Barnaby. The three of them, they all tricked Thomas! He was gentle and loving and born just the way God meant him to be! There was nothing *unnatural* about him. But you would have seen him behind bars! Or pumped full of chemicals! You, Kenneth, saw the perfect chance to grab the family fortune for yourself from your older brother and you took it. Thomas had to flee to America to save his life. Shame on you all. I say *shame!*"

Anika and Raj were both looking down at her with open mouths. Ben could feel the tears in his eyes as he hiccuped back a sob. Elias moved to hold him around his shoulders. "My grandpa was gay?" Ben asked in little more than a whisper.

Elizabeth sniffed and dabbed her eyes again. "I believe he loved your grandmother *very* much, darling, in his own way. I think she might have even understood and looked the other way when he found a…a special friend. Thomas could only ever say so much in his letters, you see. He was afraid." She flashed her eyes at Kenneth again. "But our Nancy cherished every one he sent. She never forgot about her darling boy, the rightful heir of Whittingar, wrongly chased away." She grinned at Ben. It was almost savage, which made it kind of breath-taking. "I have no doubt she decided to set it right as best she could with you, dear Ben."

So many emotions and thoughts were flying around Ben's head he didn't know where to begin. Noah filled in the momentary pause for him, though.

"No," he said with an uncertain laugh. "That's not right. Tell her, Kenneth. You wouldn't…you didn't…" But it looked as if a sad realization was dawning on Noah's face regarding his godfather. He blinked and stepped back, his brow creasing as he continued to look to Kenneth for an answer, but Kenneth refused to acknowledge Noah.

A vein was ticking in Kenneth's temple as he clenched his jaw, staring daggers at Elizabeth. "I don't deny it," he said eventually, jutting his chin in the air. "How could I allow our family name to be tarnished by a *pervert?* We did what we had to do to save everyone from the disgrace! And that is what I am doing right now. Mr. Turner, you will kindly take your plague-ridden friend and *leave my house at once!*" he roared.

To Ben's surprise, Elias just huffed and shook his head. Kenneth was trying to shame him for his HIV status, but Ben had a feeling that wasn't going to work anymore.

"No," said Ben calmly.

It was almost funny to watch Kenneth losing his shit. "I will not have one in this house! Do you hear me? Let alone two of you queers! *Get out!*"

"Well tough," said Raj loudly.

"*Raj-bhai,* no," Anika whispered, but Raj shook his head.

"No, I won't hide anymore," he said firmly. "I know you've suspected for a long time, Uncle Kenneth. But yes, I'm gay. And," he added, clearing his throat nervously, "I-I'm dating the farmhand, Antoni."

"The *help?*" Barnaby stuttered. One of the aunts near the back looked like she swooned in shock, and several other family members covered their mouths with the scandal of it all.

Ben wasn't sure what they were more upset by. The fact that Raj was gay or that he was dating so beneath the family's class. But he thought it was absolutely marvelous Raj and

Antoni were together, though. Ben hadn't known a thing. He flashed Raj a supportive grin, which he shakily returned.

"No," said Kenneth stubbornly, shaking his head and staring at the marble floor. "No, I won't have it. If word gets out-"

"You mean like the Medium article I published a few hours ago?" Raj asked, raising his eyebrows. "Yeah, sorry. That cat's not going back in the bag, I'm afraid. I think several other news sites might have republished it."

Damn. Raj worked fast. Ben was even more impressed.

"Get out." Kenneth spat flecks of spittle and pointed at the door. "You're dead to this family. Do you understand?"

"Now, just one minute-" Elizabeth began as Anika looked ready to lunge for him.

"Wait, hang on," Rochelle said loudly, lifting up a finger as she knocked back the rest of her whiskey. "Are we kicking out all the queers? Because I'm bisexual. Does that mean I can sleepover on the weekends or…what?"

"My goddaughter is a lesbian," said one of the women still engulfed by the cigar man's cloud of smoke. She wafted at it irritably, then stepped away, looking rather indignant. "What do you mean, this is a problem?"

Rochelle's mom looked absolutely disgusted. "You mean to tell me," she spluttered, tears in her eyes, "that for all this time, we thought Thomas had done us wrong. When it was just *you*, making up lies!"

"Tiffany," said Kenneth in a patronizing tone. "He would have ruined us all!"

"He was prepared to marry a woman and keep quiet," Elizabeth cried. "He was dutiful! It was *you* who threatened to destroy him and us!"

"And now you're trying to ruin everyone anyway," Ben said, not quite believing the indignation he was seeing from so many people on behalf of his grandpa. He was so relieved that he had never betrayed anyone or forced them into bankruptcy after all. This made so much more sense! But he was so sad and angry that Kenneth still ran him from his family. "The business is failing. No wonder the house is falling apart! You're nothing but a miserly old man, sitting on his pile of gold."

"Oh, like you'd do any better," Kenneth scoffed. "What do you know about running a business?"

Ben shrugged. "Not much," he admitted. "But Anika does."

There was another wave of hush that befell the room as heads turned to stare at a stunned-looking Anika. "I'm sorry – what?" she said, her eyebrows raised.

"You're one of the most organized people I've ever met," Ben said with a grin. "Besides, we looked you up online. Mr. Decker was right. You're criminally underappreciated where you currently are. I bet if anyone can make Tipsy Blossom thrive, it's you."

"Oh, yes," said Elizabeth slightly breathlessly, nodding. "Yes, that sounds like a splendid solution."

"What about the family stipends?" cigar man asked. "The properties in London and France? Will you protect them, too?"

"What about our charities?" asked another of the women. "They rely on us."

Ben nodded, trying to look them all in the eye as he swept his gaze around the room. "I have to go over the books with an accountant. We'll use a fine-toothed comb. But family investments will be protected. I want to see us thrive. Not be held back by a misplaced notion of ancestry."

"You can't be serious," Mildred spluttered. Her cheeks were burning red as she looked between Kenneth, Ben, and everyone else. "Harold, tell him! He's being extremely rude to cousin Kenny right now."

Harold sighed. "Actually, Mildred, it sounds like the boy is making an awful lot of sense." Harold offered Ben a sad smile as his wife's mouth dropped open. "I always quite liked Tommy, myself."

Ben's attention snapped back to Kenneth as his lip curled over his yellow teeth. *"Ungrateful,"* he snarled. "The lot of you! Greedy bottom feeders. I'd think *very* carefully about whose side you're on right now."

Unfortunately for him, Ben was pretty sure that was *exactly* what people were doing. He and Kenneth stared at each other for several seconds, but Ben could feel the atmosphere shifting in the room. He dared to let hope bubble in his chest.

"I *do* believe it was what Aunt Anne wanted," said one brave soul from somewhere in the midst of the crowd.

"I want to know I'm going to be taken care of," added an old dear.

"The house *is* a bit of an embarrassment."

"Does this mean I don't have to study politics? I can take that dance scholarship, after all?"

"Can I work for the business too? I'm pretty good at marketing."

"And we need to reassess the staff pay and pensions," said Anika firmly, still holding on to Elisabeth's hand, but looking firmly at Ben. "They haven't had a pay rise since the early nineties I'm sure."

Somewhere, someone with a silver tray coughed. *"Late eighties."*

"Give it up, Uncle Kenneth," said Raj sadly. "All that hate you carry around inside you was never going to keep this family alive." He smiled at Ben and Elias. "But love will."

Ben nodded, glancing down and taking Elias's hand for everyone to see. Then he looked back up at the room. "Yes, it will," he agreed.

Kenneth puffed and looked around for support, but even

Barnaby seemed to have gone very quiet, inspecting his fingernails. So Kenneth turned to Noah, but it seemed Noah had some scruples after all.

"Did you really disown Thomas for being gay?" he asked bitterly, his jaw tight. "Because if so, you probably don't want me burdening you any longer."

Kenneth gritted his teeth and scowled at him. "No, I probably don't," he said loftily. Ben suspected Noah was hoping for one last speck of loyalty. His disappointment was clear on his face. "Very well, then," Kenneth continued. "If you're all going to behave like rats, I don't want to taint myself with you any further. I'll be at the Gloucestershire residence. You'll be hearing from my lawyers."

With that, he stuck his nose in the air, and marched from the ballroom to a sea of silent stares.

It took about thirty seconds for Ben to let go of the breath he'd been holding. Anika covered her mouth and looked at her grandmother. A small, high-pitched laugh escaped Raj's lips. "Is it over?" he asked.

"Maybe?" Anika replied.

Elizabeth stepped forward, offering her hands to Ben. "My darling," she said tearfully. "Can you ever forgive us?" She glanced at Barnaby, who also went storming out of the room. Ben watched him leave with a lump in his throat.

"Not them," he said angrily. "I don't think I'll ever forgive them. But it sounds like you supported my grandfather the best you could. The others didn't know."

"No, we didn't."

"But we do know now."

"And we support you, Ben," one of the men said, stepping forward. "I'm Tobias, by the way. We haven't formally met."

"I'm Charlotte."

"I'm Gregory."

Ben found himself shaking hand after hand as he was

drawn further into the ballroom. Some people – notably those of the older generation – defiantly moved to the edges of the room or skulked out altogether. Mildred went to stomp off, clearly in a huff, but she only got a few feet before she realized her husband wasn't following her.

"Harold?" she asked uncertainly.

He put his hands in his pockets and rocked on his feet. "I think perhaps we should hear more of what the young lad has to say, Mildred."

She spluttered. "But he's…well, he's…*gay.*"

Harold smiled and nodded. "Yes. There seems to be a lot of that going around these days." He stepped forward and shook Ben's hand as his wife's face went an ashen-white color. "Best of luck to you, chap. I'm here if you need anything." After that, he happily escorted his shocked-looking wife to sit down, handing her a large glass of brandy. Someone started the music playing again, and Ben felt like he could finally breath again.

More and more people kept coming to him, explaining who they were, how they were related, and what they were worried about or hoped for the family. And all the while, Elias stayed by Ben's side, with a hand on the small of his back, not interfering, but showing that he wasn't going anywhere either.

With every handshake, every smile, every 'it's a pleasure to meet you', Ben felt like he was accepting his place. He *did* belong with this family. They were his blood, and he would take care of them like he promised.

At some point, Ben glanced over to see Anika talking with Noah, which surprised him. Anika looked concerned, but Noah was shaking his head, his mouth in a hard line. He vanished from the room not long after that.

Ben could worry himself about that later. For now, he had plenty of family members to continue to assure. So far, it seemed like he was winning over those who had stayed in the room. It was a miraculous feeling.

But he couldn't have done any of it without Elias's belief in him.

When there was a moment of calm, Ben turned to his boyfriend and slipped his arms around him, resting his head on his chest.

"I'm *so* proud of you, sweetheart," Elias said, kissing the top of his head.

Ben smiled. "The feeling is mutual," he assured him.

They'd come so far on their journey together. But really, they were only just getting started.

24

ELIAS

"I can't believe this street," Ben said, holding Elias's hand and looking around in wonder. The reflection from all the colorful lights danced in his eyes, and his happy little laughs were coming out as smoky clouds in the evening air.

Elias knew Ben was being swept away by the magic of experiencing London in all its glory, decked out in the run-up to the festive season. It had been something that Elias had dreamed of seeing for years. But now, in that moment, he found it very difficult to take his eyes off Ben.

His beautiful, brave, Ben.

Seeing as they'd had to come into London to deal with various solicitors, Elias and Ben had jumped at the chance to see the capital city after all. Once their meetings were over and done with, they'd gone sightseeing, including visiting Tower Bridge like Kamran had suggested, taking selfies in front of everything.

As a couple.

They'd skipped any gory attractions, instead going Christmas shopping in the quirky Carnaby street. That had taken them to Soho, where they discovered China Town and

London's central gay scene. After eating themselves silly at an all-you-can-eat buffet, they were now bar-hopping down Old Compton Street

Elias had never felt so free and unbothered, holding hands with a man in public in his whole life. All the buildings had rainbow flags flying outside, with music pumping out into the street from the bars and pubs. A couple of places were hosting karaoke or drag shows. In the end, Elias and Ben settled on one of the bigger bars so they could have a table to sit at, watching the world go by from the window. It was a delight being surrounded by so many obviously queer people, and Elias loved how many men were holding hands and swapping sweet kisses with each other.

Which is exactly what Elias did with Ben.

Nobody looked at them sideways or commented on their age gap. In fact, he saw many other couples that had just as many years between them, if not more. He'd never felt so at home in a place he hadn't been before.

Well, aside from their cottage.

In the several days since their successful *coup d'etat*, many people in the family had encouraged Ben to come into the house and select a room to take as his own, as a lot of the family had done. It would be his whenever he came to visit, and not used by anyone else. However, Ben had asked if he – he *and* Elias – could keep the cottage as theirs instead. Some of his relatives had seemed a little perplexed by that, seeming to think it was below the family heir, but hadn't hesitated to agree.

The best thing was the lengths that Ben had gone to in order to impress on Elias that the cottage was *theirs*. Not his. "I know it's fast," he'd said a couple of days ago. "We haven't been together long. But this is where we fell in love. I want it to be both of ours, not mine where you visit."

Ben was so open and earnest, wearing his heart on his

sleeve. Elias couldn't quite believe how much he loved him. It almost felt like too much for one person to bear. But Ben was constantly challenging him. It was why their relationship was so strong already.

"What?" Ben asked with a laugh. Elias was holding his hand across the bar table, and he'd probably been mooning. He didn't care, though.

He shook his head. "Just...I love you, sweetheart. I'm glad I'm on my first trip to London after all these years, and I'm sharing it with you."

Ben blushed and grinned, making Elias's cock throb. There was no better aphrodisiac than seeing how much and how easily he affected Ben. "Love you, too, baby," he said, toying with his drink.

It had taken a few attempts, but he seemed to finally believe Elias now when he'd said that he wanted Ben to drink even when Elias chose not to. Because the truth was, Elias wasn't going to drink most of the time. But Ben clearly enjoyed it and Elias liked seeing Ben happy. He should get to revel in his wild twenties. Elias never wanted to hold him back from anything.

Plus, Elias *loved* the way Ben got a little silly and giggly after a few cocktails. And because they were in an LGBT-friendly environment, he also got pretty handsy. Like then, he moved his chair around their little table so he could place his hand under it onto Elias's knee.

It didn't take long for it to travel upward, stroking gently through Elias's pants against his increasingly excited cock.

Elias doubted he was going to make it back to Wiltshire.

"I have a crazy idea," he said with a grin between kisses. Ben's soft lips were sticky and sweet from the fruity concoctions he'd been drinking.

"Yes," he said with a twinkle in his eyes. The bar was pretty loud with all the people trying to make themselves heard over the music, but it was easy for Elias to feel like it was just him and Ben alone in their own little bubble.

Elias laughed. "You don't know what the idea is yet," he protested.

Ben shook his head tipsily, his lips only an inch from Elias's. "Don't care. If you want it, I'll do it."

Now that really *did* start to get Elias hard. "Let's find a hotel room and take the train back tomorrow. I need to get you into a bed *soon,* baby."

Ben blinked and opened his mouth, but then he paused for a second. "I was going to say that would be too extravagant. But, uh, we can afford that, can't we? That would be okay, as a fun one-off?"

Elias was very much enjoying watching the way Ben was maturing and growing into his new responsibilities. He'd never be frivolous with money, Elias was sure. But seeing him weighing up the options and making a responsible decision to have a moment of recklessness was particularly delightful.

"We can absolutely afford it," Elias murmured into his ear, nipping at his lobe. "Besides, we're on vacation. Let me treat you, okay?"

Ben blushed again. Elias wasn't sure who loved it more when Elias took charge of things. It wasn't all the time. But every now and again, Elias would get a little bossy, and Ben would melt for him. And sometimes Ben would make the decision, helping Elias relax.

It worked perfectly.

Which was how they ended up in a black cab on their way to a little boutique hotel Elias had found on a last-minute booking site. It was an old Victorian terraced building with narrow corridors and creaky stairs, but Elias found it far more charming than a fancy chain hotel. Besides, all he really cared about was the bed.

They had nothing with them, not even toothbrushes. The old Elias would have insisted they stop at a store for provisions. But the new Elias decided they could deal with all that in the morning. Tonight, he simply stripped his lover down, taking his time to kiss every inch of his beautiful body. Ben's hands felt so perfect trailing over his skin, their lips coming together again and again in the dark, their pants and grunts breaking up the quiet, the air thick with the scent of musky sweat, sweet cocktails, and spicy aftershave.

They traded blow jobs, doing their best not to be too noisy as the walls were pretty thin. That added to the excitement of it all, though. Elias loved watching Ben's face as he came. He couldn't believe this was his new normal now. They'd talked about it, but it was pretty clear that both of them wanted to keep dating when they returned to Pine Cove. For once, Elias wasn't dreading returning going back to work. Because now, he would have a life outside of it.

Although, the end of their trip was approaching, and he would be sad to leave Whittingar Abbey and everyone there. *Until next time,* he reminded himself firmly as he drifted off in the tangle of blankets, a naked Ben curled up beside him.

Before heading back to Wiltshire the next morning, they played tourist in the West End for a while, visiting souvenir shops and watching buskers sing in the bustling Leicester Square. It was everything Elias had hoped London would be, even better as he got to share the experience with Ben.

On the train from Paddington to Reading, where they would get a connecting service to the small town of Horncaster, Anika messaged the group chat they now had with her, Raj, and Antoni. She wanted to know when the 'dirty stop-outs' would be home, as they had a surprise for them. After a few messages back and forth, they established that they'd be waiting for Elias and Ben at the cottage, so they dashed into a drugstore at Reading station, then freshened up in the train bathroom en route.

Elias hadn't been this fun and spontaneous since his college days. "Thank you," he told Ben once they were clean and settled in their seats again.

Ben looked at him in confusion. "For what?"

Elias toyed with Ben's fingers, entwined in his own. "I promised myself that before I reached forty, I'd start living my life again." He kissed Ben's knuckles and looked into his hazel eyes. "Thanks to you, I've never felt more alive."

Ben looked almost teary at that. He snuggled against Elias's side. "I could thank you for a lot of things," he murmured. "But I just say thank you for being with me. Everything's better with you."

Elias couldn't agree more.

When they finally got back to Whittingar and walked down the dirt track to their cottage, they weren't surprised to see the lights on and smoke puffing gently from the chimney. But when they opened the front door, they *were* surprised to find a small party happening in their living room.

"You're here!" Anika cried, jumping up from one of the sofas. Raj and Antoni were curled up on the other one, but surprisingly Gazza and Mrs. Hollis were there too. They'd set up a lunch party with sandwiches, cakes, and tea. Treacle barked and barked at their return, both welcoming them and telling them off. But the most surprising of all was the presence of Luna in a basket by the crackling fireplace, her four babies clumsily walking all over her or curled up sleeping by her side.

"What's all this?" Elias asked in delight as he and Ben took their coats off.

"Well, the last couple of days are going to be hectic as we sort everything out," Anika explained, clasping her hands in front of her. "So we thought we'd have a going away party today!"

Ben laughed. "We *will* be back soon, though," he promised. "It's not forever."

Mrs. Hollis wagged her finger at him. "Never turn down an opportunity for my homemade Victoria sponge, young man," she said.

He grinned. "I can't believe it's better than mine...but it is."

"Let's call it a tie," Elias said diplomatically.

"Such a lawyer," Anika teased.

Elias and Ben settled themselves into the cozy scene. There wasn't enough sofa space, so they happily sat themselves on the floor by the cats, fussing them and Treacle. Mrs. Hollis plied them with tea, and wasn't satisfied until they'd had two platefuls of food each.

Raj cleared his throat. "So," he said, looking around the room. Everyone else was smiling, which made Elias think they were expecting whatever it was he was preparing to say. "We know you're going to travel back here often, but we were wondering if you wanted to take a little bit of Whittingar home with you to America?

Elias felt like this question was directed more at Ben, so he glanced at him to defer the answer.

Ben looked a little uncomfortable. "But...you've already given us so much?"

It was true. They'd been given all kinds of presents over the past week. From handmade sweaters (which the Brits called 'jumpers,' adorably) to British foods to take home with them to little family knick-knacks that some relatives wanted to pass on, like a watch or a pair of cufflinks.

The best gift they'd received was their acceptance, though. Some others, like Mildred, might be won over in time, but others might never accept Ben's place in this family.

That was their loss as far as Elias was concerned. He was thrilled to see the way Ben lit up as he slowly began to build relationships with his various relatives. He'd gone from it just being him and his mom and dad to dozens and dozens of family members.

Not to mention an adoring boyfriend.

Antoni shook his head, his arm around Raj's back. They were such a sweet couple. Elias was happy they'd been able to overcome the obstacles in their way to be together. Much like he and Ben. "This feels right. We all agreed."

Raj nodded. Then he extracted him from the sofa, crouching down by the cat basket, and gently removed the smallest silver kitten. The one Elias had saved. "They all need homes. I know it's a bit complicated to get pets through quarantine, but we all agreed that this little guy was already yours. If you want him, you can take him back to America."

Ben gasped and very carefully accepted the tiny fellow into his hands to cradle him to his chest. "Are you serious? Elias, what do you think?"

Elias swallowed the lump in his throat. Antoni probably knew that Elias had snuck out to the barn every single day since the birth to check on Luna and her babies. But especially the miracle kitten who was thriving more and more with each passing day.

He'd been dreading leaving the little guy behind.

"I'd be honored," he said thickly. He laughed as he sniffed and rubbed his eyes before carefully petting the tiny kitten's fur. The rest of the room laughed at him, too, but it was with affection.

"That's settled, then," Gazza announced.

"Wait, no," said Ben earnestly. "He needs a name! Hmm, how about…Romeo?" He raised his eyebrows at Elias. "You did kind of bring him back from the dead, and I always thought he deserved a happier ending than he got in the play," he explained.

"That fits very nicely with our love of English literature," he agreed fondly, hugging Ben to his side. "Romeo, it is."

It would take a while before Romeo was old enough to get his shots and make the trip over to the States, so they agreed that he would stay with his momma until Ben and Elias came back in the new year to travel home with him. Anika was also going to take the little orange kitten and call her Saffron. Mrs. Hollis and Gazza took very little bullying to take one each as well, meaning all four babies would have forever homes.

"But that means you don't have one," Ben said to Raj and Antoni. Elias loved how thoughtful he was.

But the couple grinned. "Luna always stops by the stable," Antoni assured him. "But it seems we have another pet that needs a home."

Treacle looked up as several people looked his way. "I'm sure he'd love to go to America with you, but Whittingar is his home," Mrs. Hollis said fondly. "Nancy would have wanted him to stay here, I think."

"Besides," said Raj with a raised eyebrow. "We couldn't possibly separate him from his best friend."

As if agreeing, Treacle grumbled and trotted over to drop his head over the edge of the cat basket. Luna made a half-hearted attempted to bat his nose but then gave up. Apparently, she'd accepted that Treacle was going to adore her, so she might as well get used to it.

The last couple of days were, as Anika had predicted, a bit of a blur. There was a lot that could be maintained for the estate and business over the phone and internet, but Ben wanted to make sure everything was set up and beginning to change before he left the country. Elias was proud to stand by his side as he and Anika drew up a new plan for Tipsy

Blossom, confident that the cider business could be saved. Work had already begun on the house as well. Now that Ben actually had access to his inheritance, he could start using funds appropriately, starting with basic repairs.

Their most surprising visitor during their final days was Noah, who appeared on the doorstep of the cottage one stormy evening looking very subdued.

"Oh, come in," said Elias in surprise. He couldn't say he felt warmly toward Kenneth's godson after the way he'd behaved, but the last they'd seen him had been at the ball and he'd looked positively miserable. Besides, it was too cold to hang around on the front step.

"Thanks," said Noah, wiping his feet on the mat and closing the door behind him. "I won't stay, though. I just wanted to apologize before I went back to London for good."

He shoved his hands into his coat pockets and looked sheepishly at the carpet for a moment. Ben came to stand beside Elias, who wrapped his arm around his back, presenting a united front.

Noah sighed. "I treated you both unfairly," he said, looking up to meet their gazes. "I was interested in you, Ben, but that was in no little part thanks to the massive inheritance you'd just received. Don't get me wrong. You seem nice, but the stability of your money seemed nicer. I was totally gold-digging." He huffed and scuffed his toe on the carpet. "Then I accused Elias of exactly the same thing. That was really shitty, and I'm sorry."

Elias glanced at Ben, who raised his eyebrows back at him.

"Thank you," said Ben. "I appreciate your honesty." He was getting so much better at speaking for himself now. It meant that Elias could step back and offer support rather than jumping in and taking over, the way he had in the start of their relationship.

"I'm sorry that Kenneth let you down," Elias said, guessing Noah was having to reevaluate a lot of things now. "Has he cut you off?"

Noah shrugged unhappily. "Not financially. I still have a reasonable amount in the bank for now. But he's not spoken a word to me since…well." He sighed heavily and rubbed his eyes. "I always knew he didn't like brashness. It made sense that he didn't like *that* kind of gay. But I always thought he knew about me. That he was fine with it." He chewed his lip, shaking his head. "Then finding out he lied for all these years about our grandfathers…I guess I don't really want to hear from him, at least not for now. I've got a lot to think about."

"What will you do in London?" Elias asked. He didn't really appreciate Noah's comment about 'that kind of gay,' but he didn't have the energy to argue about it when Noah would soon be out of their lives, possibly for good. They were never going to be friends, after all.

Noah gave a rueful laugh and shrugged. "Find a sugar daddy. Get a job. Who knows? I'm kind of sick of relying on other people for money. Being kept dangling is exhausting."

Elias felt his mouth twitch. "Getting a job sounds good, then."

Noah grinned back. "Sure. As soon as I find out if there's anything at all that I'm good at, I'll get right on that. Okay, well, that's all I came to say. I am sorry for being an arse. You two make an appallingly pretty couple. Don't fuck it up like I would have undoubtedly done."

Elias laughed and hugged Ben closer to him. "We won't," he promised, waving Noah back out into the night.

Elias treasured their evenings together, alone in their cottage once they'd bid farewell to any visitors. It was their own little heaven, with the log fire burning, Ben's baking, and endless old books from the big library for them both to snuggle up with on the sofa together. As the time drew near for them to pack up and return to Heathrow for their scheduled flight back to America, Elias could tell neither of them really wanted to leave.

But they would be back soon, as they assured the many, *many* people who came to see them off before Gazza drove them to the airport on their final morning. Mrs. Hollis gave them a whole picnic basket, despite them assuring her they'd be able to eat on the plane. Rochelle had quite warmed to 'The Yanks' as she called them, and insisted they take a bottle of Champagne for the drive so they could 'leave in style.'

Anika and Raj kept diving in for 'one last hug,' and Treacle barked most unhappily at them. "He's telling you not to be too long," Antoni said with a chuckle.

Elizabeth embraced both Ben and Elias warmly, hugging tightly for such a frail looking-woman. "Thomas would be *so proud* of you," she told Ben firmly, tears in her eyes as she clasped his shoulders. "He never felt he could come home. It broke my heart, as well as Nancy's. We want you to know you're *always* welcome."

Ben's lip wobbled as he glanced up at Elias. "Thank you." He wiped the tears from his cheeks with the sleeve of his coat and looked around at all the other relatives who'd come to say farewell. "We'd love to come back as often as possible, wouldn't we?"

Elias grinned. "Wild horses couldn't keep us away."

And he meant that. He and Ben had come to England looking for an adventure, but what they'd found was so much more than that.

Elias had spent so many years believing that somehow he had done something to deserve his HIV diagnosis. That he should hide himself away from the world for other people's sake. Words couldn't really describe how thankful he was that he'd decided to throw all that nonsense away at thirty-nine, determined to go into his fortieth birthday living life to the max.

But he never would have imagined happiness like this.

So he and Ben ended their England adventure, but it was just their first of what he hoped would be many. And it was definitely only the beginning of their adventure as boyfriends. Elias had begun to think that maybe he would never find love again.

How wrong he had been.

EPILOGUE

Two Years Later
Ben

"Treacle, where are you taking me?"

The Corgi just smiled up at Ben with his tongue lolling from his mouth as he trotted through the darkened halls of Whittingar Abbey. What a difference a couple of years had made. The carpets were no longer sad and tired looking. The banisters were polished to a shine, as were the painting frames, and the crystal chandeliers sparkled. New portraits had been commissioned of a number of the younger generations of the family, and not a single door creaked anymore.

Ben loved coming back here. It was incredible to him how easily he and Elias had been able to split their time between Pine Cove and Wiltshire so far. They'd made it four times in the first year when there had been more work to do, then only twice earlier this year, but they had been longer, more leisurely visits. Being there for Christmas made it their third stay of the year, which felt like a good average to aim

346

for going forward.

He wanted to keep his visits to Whittingar infrequent so they were special. It was still such a magical place to him, so different in every season. He didn't want to spoil it by coming back all the time.

This occasion was extra special, though, as made obvious by the insane amount of Christmas decorations Mrs. Hollis had organized to be put up. Ben marveled at all the wreaths, garlands, and mistletoe that was hanging everywhere he looked as he followed Treacle through the house.

The short dog had come bouncing into one of the sitting rooms where Ben had been spending the evening, drinking mulled wine and playing games with his guests. Treacle had barked and headbutted him, demanding to be followed, which Ben had eventually given in to.

He and Elias had decided to bring a party over from Pine Cove to show them where they kept disappearing off to 'live their other, magical life' as Emery had started calling it. Ben had thought he was going to burst from excitement, having never gone on a group trip before.

He was most eager for his folks to come and see where Grandpa Thomas had grown up. His dad was usually a quiet, reserved man, but he'd gotten a little teary on the first grand tour, and then again whenever he met a relative who'd known his dad. By the end of the first day, they were just as smitten with Whittingar as Ben was. Their approval of the place that had stolen Ben's heart was important to him.

The fact that they also adored the man who'd stolen his *heart* was even better. They thought Elias was completely wonderful, much to Ben's delight, always saying how polite and sweet he was every time they came to dinner, or spent a holiday together. Despite Elias's lingering fears, they didn't mind about their age difference at all.

Along with Ben's folks, Elias had invited a few of his

friends, like Darcy and her family whom Elias considered his own family, as well as Ben's friend Emery and his fiancé, Scout. Ben and Emery had gotten closer over the past couple of years, with Emery bringing Ben into his friendship group which mainly seemed to consist of the Coal family and a few others around their age. Seeing as Ben was closest with Emery, he'd just invited him and Scout this time. Maybe another time they could have a wilder party.

But Ben was almost afraid to share their sanctuary with the outside world. When his mom had met Mrs. Hollis, he'd been pretty overwhelmed with the sense of two universes colliding. However, nothing drastic had happened. The house hadn't fallen down, making Ben trust that he could share more of his Pine Cove life with his English fairy tale.

Treacle was wagging his tail like he was the king of the castle, leading Ben up some stairs. It was as if he'd purposely come to fetch him for something, although Ben couldn't possibly think for what. Maybe Treacle was just playing a game. He was very happily living with Antoni and Raj in their new house now, and Luna had even allowed them to take her in, now that she was getting a little older. They made a happy family.

Ben and Elias had almost considered bringing Romeo back for a visit, but flying would have been far too stressful for him. Instead, they video called him via the cat-sitter every day they were away, because apparently, they'd become those sorts of dorks. Ben didn't care, though. He loved his domestic life.

He'd moved in with Elias after they'd dated for six months. Elias had given Ben a key on his own fortieth birthday, saying living together was the only gift he wanted, naturally making Ben cry. But now he was a real grown-up with a house and a boyfriend and pets, not to mention being the technical heir to Whittingar Abbey and CEO of Tipsy

Blossom cider. He no longer felt like a boy pretending to be a man, and hadn't for quite some time now.

As for work back home, Ben had found the perfect solution to saving Rise and Shine, which was to buy the bakery himself. He'd never force Lars to retire, but now they'd hired a manager to run the day-to-day business, allowing Lars to come and bake at his leisure. Ben had taken some of Mrs. Hollis's recipes with him, trying them out on the patrons of Pine Cove who had loved them, much to Mrs. Hollis's delight. Ben didn't even have to work anymore, but he still kept regular part-time hours at the bakery for the love of it.

Everything was pretty much as perfect as life could be.

Or so he thought.

Treacle stopped in front of the closed library door and started barking. "What?" Ben asked in confusion. But Treacle just kept on yapping, dancing around. "Do you want to go in here? Okay, you crazy dog." Ben laughed and let himself into his and Elias's favorite room in the whole house. Ben still found sanctuary in the kitchen when the staff let him, but the library was a portal to another world that Ben and Elias shared together. They were always cuddled up in here with a good book, or taking volumes back to the cottage to enjoy.

And sure enough, Elias was already in here, waiting. He must have been hiding in here for a while, as Ben hadn't seen him in a couple of hours.

But then he realized why and what exactly he was looking at.

He sensed Mrs. Hollis's handiwork at play again. She liked to set up surprises for them whenever they visited, but so far, nothing had ever topped the fluffy handcuffs.

Until now.

This was...out of this world.

Ben felt like he'd wandered into Lothlorien, the elven

forest in Lord of the Rings. The chandeliers were switched off, and it was dark outside, leaving the library bathed in the glow from hundreds of fairy lights that had been draped over all the book cases. A flower arch had been constructed over the fireplace, and little artificial toadstools were standing on every surface. There was an honest-to-god old-fashioned lamppost next to the archway with fake snow on the floor, leading the way to Narnia, and someone had made a Platform Nine-and-Three-Quarters sign, like they were off to Hogwarts.

Ben realized he'd covered his mouth with his hands as he turned on the spot and saw tea pots labelled 'Drink Me!' and cupcakes with flags sticking out of them saying 'Eat Me!' There was a string attached to the mantelpiece with photos pegged to it like bunting. Under a plaque that read 'Ghost of Christmas Past' were childhood photos of both Ben and Elias. Under 'Ghost of Christmas Present' were several photos of them both, then the last 'Ghost of Christmas Future' just had a question mark underneath.

And there in the middle of the room was Elias, dressed in a gorgeous suit that Ben would put money on Anika picking out for him. Treacle had gone to sit at his feet, looking up at him patiently and, for once, quietly. Elias was holding open a large book with words artfully painted on the two pages that read: *You must allow me to tell you how ardently I admire and love you.*

Ben stared at the quote for several seconds before he dared to look up at Elias's hopeful face. Ben licked his lips, almost too afraid to speak. "You do know," he whispered, hugging himself, "that Lizzy rejected Darcy's proposal at that point in the book."

Elias swallowed and nodded. "I'm hoping I have better luck."

He closed the book and carefully placed it on the coffee table between teapots and toadstools.

Then he got down on one knee.

Ben's hands flew to his mouth as tears sprung in his eyes. Of course Elias was building up to a proposal, that had been obvious from the moment Ben had stepped into the library. But to see it actually happening made Ben's knees want to give completely out, like the romance heroine Elias was making him feel like he was.

"Ben, darling?" Elias asked as Ben stepped closer to him. He was opening a ring box that he'd pulled from his jacket pocket. "You're my happily ever after. Would you marry me?"

Elias was starting to cry. Ben was crying. Treacle was whimpering and hopping from paw to paw. They were all a mess, and Ben loved just how perfect it was.

"Yes," he managed to choke out. He dropped to his knees and flung his arms around Elias's neck. "Oh my god, yes! Elias, I love you so much!"

Elias hugged him back as Treacle started barking again. "I love you too, sweetheart," he managed to say between hiccups.

"He said yes!" a voice that could only be Anika's roared from the hallway.

Before Ben knew what was happening, their fairy grotto was being invaded by dozens of cheering, clapping, and whooping people, popping Champagne corks and confetti cannons all over the place. Ben and Elias were hoisted to their feet by Emery and Anika, with Raj and Darcy calling for Ben to put the ring on. People made sure Darcy could roll her chair through to see the moment Ben slipped the diamond band over his finger. Ben's parents were there among the raucous crowd, looking jubilant in their own, quiet way. Gazza was hugging Mrs. Hollis, who was crying as hard as she was laughing, and

Antoni was allowing Elizabeth to hold herself steady on his muscular arm while she bellowed *"Bravo!"* Since standing up to Kenneth, she'd really become quite rowdy. It was awesome.

Everyone was here. Ben thought he even saw Luna the cat winding between people's legs.

Ben and Elias hugged as someone started playing party music and the Champagne began to flow. Ben already knew that Elias would be fretting about getting the chaos away from the precious books, but they could savor the magical moment just a little longer.

All the people they loved most in the world were crammed into this unbelievable space that Elias had created just for Ben to show him how much he loved him. Elias had spent his whole life dreaming about England, losing himself in the books Ben would also grow up to read and treasure. And it was here, so far from home but so close to their hearts, they had found each other.

Now they were going to spend the rest of their lives together.

Elias had once told Ben that this wasn't a fantasy, it was their real lives. But in that moment, Ben had to disagree. This was a fairy tale.

And they would live happily ever after.

The End.

IF YOU WOULD LIKE to see what happened between Raj and Antoni, please visit http://www.hjwelch.com/freebie-shorts to download their FREE short story! You'll also find a sexy Halloween short of Robin and Dair from Pine Cove #1: Safe Harbor, as well as other stand-alone freebies.

For more information on living with HIV and to support

ongoing AIDS research, please consider supporting one of the following charities:

- **The National AIDS Trust** https://www.nat.org.uk/
- **Avert** https://www.avert.org/
- **I Want PrEP Now** https://www.iwantprepnow.co.uk/

Thank you for reading Bright Horizon. If you enjoyed Ben and Elias's story, I would very much appreciate it if you could share your experience with others online. Reviews, recommendations, fan works, and general love is the best way for me to reach new readers.

For giveaways, sneak peeks, ARC opportunities and general fun times, please join my Facebook group! Helen Juliet Books. We're very friendly!

Thank you to: my awesome beta readers, Amy and Mum; editor Tanja; cover artist AngstyG; cheerleaders, Ed, Amelia, and John; loving husband; fur babies Arya and Tyrion. Finally, thank you to Prachya and Ricky for their personal and cultural advice.

Helen xxx

Robin Coal wonders if asking his straight housemate Dair to be his fake boyfriend for his high school reunion will be the worst thing he's ever done…or the best. But there's no way he's going home to face his abusive ex alone, and former Marine Dair is just the protection he needs. So long as he doesn't find out about Robin's secret crush, everything will be fine.

Mechanic Dair Epping never expected to spend a week sharing a bed with his adorkable friend, however pretending to be bi is easier than he imagined. He knows he'll do anything to keep Robin safe from his ex-boyfriend, but as the chemistry between them grows, the line between fake and reality begins to blur.

Could Dair actually be bi? Even if he was, would an ex-Marine really be interested in a computer geek like Robin? When his ex's intentions turn dangerous, how far will Dair go to protect the man he's falling for?

Book One in Pine Cove. Safe Harbor is a steamy, standalone MM romance novel with a guaranteed HEA and absolutely no cliffhanger.

Click here to get the Safe Harbor eBook

Click here to get the Safe Harbor audio

Scout Duffy doesn't know what's worse. The fact that his scorching one-night-stand is his bratty new client, or the fact that he doesn't even remember Scout. But beneath all the bravado, Scout can see Emery is terrified, and he'll do anything to protect him from his attacker. If only he would lower his walls and let Scout into his heart as easily as he lets him dominate in the bedroom.

Being out and proud his whole life means Emery Klein has never been safe. But now his charity work and social media fame have put a target on his back from bigots, and his friends force him to hire a private bodyguard. Emery doesn't need to be judged by some straight former-boxer, but his attraction to the gorgeous hunk is insatiable. When Emery finally recognizes Scout, they can't keep their damn hands off one another, if only for as long as Scout's in town.

There's a reason Emery never looks too closely at the men he sleeps with, just like there's a reason Scout lives out of a suitcase in motel rooms. Will two men hiding from hurt realize the love that could heal them both is right in front of them? Or will Emery's attacker take everything before they have the chance?

Book Two in Pine Cove. Troubled Waters is a steamy, standalone MM romance novel with a guaranteed HEA and absolutely no cliffhanger.

Click here to get the Troubled Waters eBook

Click here to get the Troubled Waters audio

After Micha Perkins finds himself wrongly implicated in a crime, the last person he wants coming to his rescue is his secret crush Swift; his older brother's best friend. But when Micha returns to the town that never felt like home, he discovers Swift's young daughter is in trouble as well. If Micha can help them both in any way, he knows he will.

Self-defense coach Swift Coal never realized he was a father until he gets custody of five-year-old Imogen and her cranky cat. His neat and tidy life is about to come crashing down, but to his surprise, Micha Perkins is there to save the day. He's so damn good with kids, and just as cute as Swift remembers. When Micha moves in to help look after Imogen, Swift struggles to repress the feelings he's kept hidden.

Micha's always been a misfit and Swift's life was always orderly.

Micha may have taken the fall to protect those more vulnerable than him, but who will save him when his past comes back to haunt him? Was Swift a fool to risk the safety of his daughter around a bad element like Micha? When their chaotic worlds collide, perhaps love and family are the middle ground they both need to become stronger together.

Book Three in Pine Cove. Homeward Bound is a steamy, standalone MM romance novel with a guaranteed HEA and absolutely no cliffhanger.

Click here to get the Homeward Bound eBook

Click here to get the Homeward Bound audio

memory
LANE
PINE COVE BOOK 5
HJ WELCH

ABOUT THE AUTHOR

HJ Welch is a contemporary MM romance author living in London with her husband and two balls of fluff that occasionally pretend to be cats. She began writing at an early age, later honing her craft online in the world of fanfiction on sites like Wattpad. Fifteen years and over a million words later, she sought out original MM novels to read. By the end of 2016 she had written her first book of her own, and in 2017 she fulfilled her lifelong dream of becoming a fulltime author.

She also writes contemporary British MM romance as Helen Juliet.

You can contact HJ Welch via social media:
Newsletter (with FREE Homecoming Hearts material and original stories) – https://www. subscribepage.com/helenjuliet
Facebook Group – Helen Juliet Books
Facebook Page – @HJWelchAuthor
Email – helenjulietauthor@gmail.com
Instagram – @helenjwrites
Twitter – @helenjwrites